I0667394

A Crafted Beast

John E. Leffel

CONTENTS

"It's easier to fool people than to convince them that they have been fooled."

-Mark Twain

Chapter I

Dreadson and Grant

"Kitty? Kitty, are you there? Are you at your desk? God *damn* it! Where *are* you!" Shouted Dreadson, shifting from relatively calm to tense, burgeoningly irritable, following a silence on the phone of just under three seconds. He had just buzzed Kitty, his personal secretary, who's desk sat just outside of and adjacent to his six thousand square foot personal office. An office complete with private rooftop forest. A forest. *Not* a garden. A fucking forest. He liked to make that clear; and often in these precise words, to anyone who asked. When guests came to his office and complimented him on his garden, he would-as a matter of course- inform them that it wasn't, in fact, a garden, but that it was, in fact, a fucking forest with its own goddamned private landscaping crew complete with a full-time illegal Mexican leaf blower. Full time Mexican leaf blower -who did nothing but blow leaves- out there from 9am to 5pm every weekday recirculating landscape detritus. Him and the rest of the crew rarely seen and certainly unheard beyond the soundproof, floor to ceiling window panes. He was out there now in a lush woodland of impeccably and un-naturally contained nature. And what was that there leaf blower's name? Sanchez? Was it Sanchez?

Dreadson, quite slighted and pondersome in the same moment, began to foment on the state of his company. A company, as it were and upon further reflection, right verdant with sensitive Sallies and Nancy boys. He'd begrudgingly dealt with these types all his life. Women were naturally that way. Of course. He didn't fault them for what came by nature, he reckoned. But what he couldn't stand were these metrosexual Nancy boys all around his general orbit. Those dickless sacks of shit. Them hipster Nancy boys sporting their skintight jeans, flannels, and man buns. The only way you could even tell the guy from the girl in their seemingly ubiquitous pairings was by the pathetic boy band looking, impossibly short facial hair that, furthermore, looked penciled in half the goddamned time. And what were these girls thinking anyway? Being with boys that looked like that? Did they have an affinity for the bearded lady back when they went to the circus when they were five years old? Some perverted, unresolved sexual proclivity from their formative years? What in hell! God damn it all all anyhow. Dreadson's thoughts on the matter were presently cut short upon hearing Kitty, finally and most blessedly, getting back to him over the intercom. He was, to be sure, right pissed off now.

"Yes, Mr. Dreadson? I'm very sorry about that, sir! What can I do for you?" Kitty uttered in her shaky, near perpetually skittish voice. A little winded at present too, following her short sprint back from the water cooler to the phone. Kitty couldn't seem to evacuate her bowels calmly and contentedly at work, always in a rush to be seemingly constantly available. Poor girl. A basic human dignity. A trip to the John was, in and of itself, a paradoxically sphincter constricting affair. Oh, what Kitty wouldn't give for the guarantee of an uninterrupted, non-rushed, naturally progressing, late morning coffee-induced BM during her workweek. Meanwhile the paternal scolding unfolded much as it did upwards of a dozen times a day.

"Cutting it close, there Kitty. I don't like that one bit, missy. Alright? Now get on the ball now, sweetheart! Okay? Cupcake! Now get me Grant. Bring in that old chip off the block. God rest his father's poor, tormented soul. Gone too soon, he was, Kitty. I wish you'd had the pleasure to know him. Was a good man, he was. A fine man of a caliber rarely seen these days, Kitty. Believe you me when I tell you this, missy! Anyway, got some things to talk about with the *boy*! Some big things in the works for him. Big time stuff in the works, ma'am. Big time stuff! You hear what I'm saying? Now go fetch his ass on over here, honey baby."

"Yes, sir, Mr. Dreadson, anything else?" Kitty inquired as she fantasized beating Dreadson to death with various blunt objects. A fishwacker. A policeman's baton. An exceptionally large candy cane just for the irony of it.

"Yes, check on that fucking megalodon! Okay, baby cakes?"

"Yes sir, I'll call the taxidermy company directly after Grant."

"Good, good. Yes, that's good." Dreadson was growing appeased. "Thank you, Kitty, and, er, sorry I got a little loud there, for a bit. You know I don't like inefficiency in this esteemed place of business."

"No, sir. Of course not. Thank you." Kitty was googling *Jumbo Candy Canes*.

"Inefficiency is the hallmark of the free loader, sweet missy. And we won't be having it! No sir and no ma'am. Not while I'm captain of this proud vessel."

"Yes, captain. I mean, sir. Sorry, sir. We won't have it. I will contact Mr. Scott now."

"Bless your angel heart, sweetie muffin! And you can call me captain if you like. You know, come to think of it, lot of similarities. Alright, let's get on it. You're a sweetheart, Kitty."

"Thank you, sir. I'll contact him now." Hmm, a foot-long candy cane. Three inches in diameter. That just might do the trick. Would take quite a few whacks, though.

Kitty patched through to Grant and asked him to come promptly to Mr. Dreadson's office, which was just down and across the hallway- on a corner suite. Smack dab on the top floor of Dreadson and Scott Broadcasting Group. A towering glass leviathon standing proudly and conspicuously in downtown L.A. The Dreadson and Scott towers gleamed a vibrant aquamarine in the sun -tropical, calm, and inviting. Pleasing to the collective eye of passersby. It was a veritable L.A. establishment in conservative media. A force meant to be looked upon in awe and with much respect. It had been going strong for over fifty years now. Stronger than ever thanks to recent, what one could call, strategic analytics. Dreadson and Scott was certainly aided in its influence through ties to all the conservative media outlets (all those that mattered, anyway) with long beloved Marmot News its prodigal son and certainly most influential force.

"Mr. Grant Scott," Grant heard presently on line two of his office phone. Almost certainly, he well knew, this meant an imminent meeting with Dreadson. Grant picked up.

"Hello Kitty," said Grant in his honed and affected, direct and businesslike manner. Though Grant sounded the part, he was a bit socially awkward. A hopelessly left-brained egghead type who had few close friends in this place of business. Of course, he possessed neither the charm, nor wit, nor incessant desire to bullshit for hours on end that so many of his peers, including his boss, seemed to preternaturally possess. All of them qualities which seemed almost synonymous with success and climbing the ranks. He made up for it, though, with near uncanny efficiency and his ability to project a business, first and foremost, demeanor. This, if not enjoyed and warmly anticipated by peers, garnered at least a level of respect and accommodation.

"Hello, Mr. Scott. The president would like to see you," continued Kitty in her usual voice, which struck Grant as perpetually flustered and rushed, though maintaining a passable if superficial cheeriness. He felt for the poor woman.

"I will be there, momentarily. Thank you, Kitty."

Grant Joseph Scott (the Third) straightened his woven silk tie and got up from his chair briskly, though not rushed. Never appear rushed. It makes you seem unorganized and lacking in the realm of self-control. There was a distinction of paramount importance, he always felt, between a brisk demeanor and a rushed demeanor; a distinction requiring a sense of honed mastery in its execution in navigating toward the former. He slicked his chestnut-tinged blonde hair back and away from its left side part and stood up.

Grant stood just a smidge under six foot tall. Medium build with rather Aryan features. As he rose from his desk, he quickly brushed any discernable lint from off his three thousand-dollar, custom-fitted suit, and began to walk with purpose toward Dreadson's office. It was a short jaunt that he had made countless times before. He exited his much smaller, though still quite impressive (however minimalist in nature) private office. One small rubber tree, in basic clay pot, on the window ledge. One family portrait on his desk. Everyone smiling genuinely. A bright day on the beach. One coffee mug that said world's "okayest" husband and father. The coffee mug always emanated a faint whiff of watered-down excrement, for reasons that were ambiguous to all but Grant. One laptop computer. A necessity, of course. One abstract painting on the wall of who-in-blazes knew what, though which a local art gallery owner christened as "evocatively accessible." It was composed entirely of large circular shapes in primary colors of various hues. It looked as though the artist had thrown a few paint-dipped basketballs at a canvas. He figured one of his kids could make something just like it in ten minutes flat.

Grant began the hike up the Italian marble corridor- his right hand held steady across his upper abdomen. This was a personal habit. It was done to keep the tie straight and flush. As he liked it. He strode past Kitty's humble office and gave a quick nod toward the frizzy haired secretary who seemed to be just narrowly keeping herself together from day to day. He approached the familiar twelve-foot-high goliath. Dreadson's redwood cedar doors with rusted black colonial-style iron hand bars. It took a little heft to get them open, and he had to admit it was darkly comical watching Kitty throwing her full weight back anytime she was attempting to swing them open on business matters. Poor Kitty. And she always looked bound up. Or was it just him?

Grant perused his memory banks and could recall that Kitty was Dreadson's fourteenth secretary that he'd known in the nearly six years he'd been working at the company. A 22.35 week average stay at the company, per secretary. He could calculate these things in his head almost instantaneously. Kitty was at 21.93 weeks and he was hoping she might be an outlier, maybe have thirty to thirty-five weeks in her. Her distant predecessor, Joan, held the record at 48.62 weeks, which was legendary. Four years on, people were still talking about that one. Someday, someone might even make a year. It would be like when they broke the four minute mile.

As Grant hefted the doors, the familiar voice boomed on cue.

"Grant! My boy, my boy! Come on over."

The words emanated with a cavernous echo from forty yards off where Dreadson sat behind his ancient, meticulously hand carved oak desk of Spanish origin, dating back to the seventeenth century. It all sounded like hearing a voice from the other side of a vast canyon. In this case, a canyon consisting of finely polished mahogany floors, the largest Persian rug he had ever seen or could even conceive of (thirty by fifty foot, maybe?) and column after column of twenty-foot-high windows to his left. Windows with stained glass arches worn like crowns. In their forefront; vast hanging plants of various types on cast iron chains suspended fifteen feet above ground. A forty-yard-long chain of clay pots holding an alternating array of azizi and snake grass plants, spaced out at approximately three feet apart each. A random kumquat tree in an Italian ceramic pot from a trip to the Amalfi coast. Dreadson enjoyed kumquats. Said it was like eating a tangerine without all the bullshit.

Walking toward Mr. Dreadson, Scott glanced to the right side, which was wooden wall. Here, every fifteen feet or so he would pass by animal heads of different varieties and from locations throughout the world. Dozens of exotic heads embedded in wood paneling. Handcarved moldings that accentuated each head. Buffalo, rhinoceros, leopard, cheetah, caribou, moose, and some animals he couldn't readily identify. One was a water buffalo, maybe. Another (was that an emu?) he often wondered about as he strode past its large pink, peach fuzz neck. It looked like a giant penis with an awkwardly cocked, immense bird head atop, as opposed to your typical glans. This head was tilted as though confused, in real time, about just where it was located and why. "What am I doin' up in here and for the love of God, why? Answer me this, buddy. Did you at least have the courtesy to eat me?"

As Grant made his way closer to a beaming Dreadson, he saw, of course (how could anyone who had the faculty of even partial vision miss it) the familiar Kodiak bear, standing fully ten feet at its head, over twelve with the outstretched arms. It posed menacingly in the corner behind the desk, in front of a thirty-foot-high by fifty-foot-wide wall of books; first edition classics from as far back as the fifteenth century. The dawn of the printing press. As Scott reached his boss, he put his hand out toward Mr. Dreadson's awaiting mitt and shook it briskly. He uttered the same, brief and generic phrase as always, which was "Good to see you, sir."

Mr. Dreadson bade Grant with a quick and deliberate flourish of the hand to have a seat in one of two chairs directly in front of his desk. "Please do have a seat, Grant, mah boy," he said. Dreadson took care to add a verbal to the physical gesture, knowing that Grant was not always the greatest at picking up on social cues; sweet though often awkward young man that he was. The chair upon which Grant was now descending, Dreadson had numerous times claimed, was crafted by the same designer who had done custom chairs for Charles the Fourth, the late eighteenth-century king of Spain, along with his wife and queen, Maria Luisa of Parma. Mr. Dreadson had much in terms of Spanish antiquities,

13

as he claimed descent of Ferdinand the Sixth on his father's side, while his mother- bless her pea-pickin' soul and may she rest in peace, poor dearheart- was of humble Irish-Catholic origins. Mr. Dreadson, regarding his ancestry, would grow irate whenever anyone considered him to be of Latino origin. Didn't they know the Spanish were of quality *European* lineage, unlike those goddamned spicks from Ecuador, or Belize, or wherever butt fuck nowhere hole it was they crawled out of and seemed to continue to insist on crawling out of; much to his chagrin.

Grant sat in synched timing with Mr. Dreadson, as they both moved at roughly the same pace, which was something that Dreadson was acutely aware of and appreciated. One of the many elements that made him enjoy Grant's company despite his Poindexterish bearing. That, and the fact that he knew when to shut his goddamned yapper. An ever rarer quality these days in a world so chock full of bullshit spewing pieholes. In fact, ever since Grant was a young boy whom he would play with joyfully (to his pleasant surprise) on visits to the child's late father's home, Dreadson had developed a special affinity toward the neophyte, awkwardness and all. His father, the late Wallace Scott, was cofounder of Dreadson and Scott Broadcasting Group. His rock-solid partner for fifty years. The partnership going way the hell back to the mid-sixties. That was just before the goddamned hippies and LBJ started changing things for the worse with their social agendas. So many years back now. A simpler time it was, to be sure. A better time? In some ways…maybe. Though he was not one to fool himself with nostalgia and the mind's self-preserving tendency to hold onto the good times, while trying so desperately to dispose of, or put a sliver lining on, the unpleasant ones.

Mr. Dreadson sat beaming at the young man for a moment. He was livened of late by David P. Betty's growing appeal to the masses. This, along with steadily climbing ratings among his media outlets. He noticed Grant was a little distracted, which irked him. The reason for this was that, directly above and behind Dreadson, Grant's eyes were focused on his most prized animal head. Dreadson did not mind this for a brief period of time; proud as he was of this particular head.

Amongst those that appreciated mammalian craniums on walls this was the king severed mammalian cranium of, maybe, any wall, of any office, anywhere in the world. A ten by ten-foot section of Dreadson's beloved bookcase had to be torn out to accommodate it (Dreadson briefly wept when he looked on at the construction crew hacking away at centuries old, reclaimed wood). The one hundred square foot open space now held the fully reconstructed head of a mastodon; eleven-foot tusks looping toward each other and coming to their terminus just beyond the end of Dreadson's desk. The tusks adorned Dreadson on either side, just five or so feet above his own, firmly attached to its shoulders, head.

Dreadson had already told Scott the story of *this* head; and more than once. He'd acquired the specimen off the black market from his faithful Russian friend, Sergei, at a price that ran higher than the rest of his other various office adornments combined. Fuck it was expensive! Sometimes it made Dreadson shiver when he thought about the cost. Like briefly recalling a past near death experience. But it was worth it and that was for sure. You didn't find a goddamned, nearly complete mastodon skull for sale too often. And, if you had the money. Well, if you had the cheddar you best buy that mother fucker, son.

Mr. Dreadson would say, to those that asked, that the head was simply an expertly crafted reconstruction, though it was an actual skull and tusks, with hair and flesh reconstructed around this. He didn't want people yammering at him to donate it to a museum somewhere, lest they found out its authenticity. He couldn't imagine such an atrocity anyway. This grand specimen rotting in a museum somewhere to be periodically perused by the non-invested passing hordes of snotty nosed eight-year-olds on their piss-ant class field trips. Kids just waiting for the ice cream sandwiches at the cafeteria at lunch time afterwards as teacher promised them. They wouldn't appreciate something like this. No sir. No ma'am. Not like he did. One of the rare remains of the giants that once roamed the country and it was *his*. His and his alone. This specimen, he was told, was discovered on the island of Sakhalin in Russia, by a team of archeologists who it came to be suggested (probably at gun point) might consider a bribe of a few thousand rubles, along with a case of mediocre home-brewed vodka for their troubles. That it also might be in their best interests toward not making their findings known to, well, anybody.

"I see you're looking at the Mastodon," Dreadson said to Grant presently, smile etched on his face, nodding his head slowly up and down with outward pride at this vulgar display of wealth and the gratuitous and extravagant rewards it might afford. His eyes glowed like that of a candy-deprived child on Halloween night, pillow sack in hand, running out their parents' door. "Fine specimen indeed, my boy! You know what I'm working on next?" Without waiting for a reply, he continued. "My guy, David, you know, world-renowned taxidermist, is reconstructing a sixty-foot Carcharocles megalodon for me. Kitty's getting an update on it as we speak, come to think of it. The jaw contains two hundred and seventy-six actual megalodon teeth, including nearly all the largest known fossil specimens on the planet. Larger ones measure seven inches along the diagonal." Dreadson formed a triangle with the thumbs and index finger of both hands to mimic the size. "And those fuckin' teeth ain't cheap, by the way son. They go diving for 'em down in Florida, South Carolina. You know, some of those divers get eaten alive by gators while out looking for those things. Brutal way to go if you ask me. You know they actually spin you around underwater and fuck you all up that way before they eat you?" Dreadson made a downward spinning gesture with his right index finger. "That's a double whammy, son. Anyway, we're going to hang it, the megalodon that is, right there over the entryway facing guests as they come in to the office. How bout dat!"

"That's quite impressive, sir," Grant appeased Dreadson with just enough feigned excitement to seem believable.

"You bet your candy ass! It's the size of a school bus!" He jubilantly exclaimed, before taking on a more professorial tone.

"Now, when I say that I mean it quite *literally*, son, not as a manner of speech. When I *say* it is the size of a school bus, that is. It *is* actually the size of a goddamned school bus."

"Very impressive, sir," Grant replied as though on cue.

"You're God damned right!" The childlike exuberance resumed. "Son of a bitch could eat a full grown great white shark for lunch and have room for an orca at supper time. Could eat an orca eating a great white! Eat 'em both together like a God-damned seafood platter!"

"That is mind blowing, sir." Grant was trying, with gusto, to affect genuine interest and awe.

Professor Dreadson returned, didactically adding, "That orca eating a whale part might not have made sense to you, mah boy. Did you know that orcas can eat great white sharks? You see, how they do it is, they swim in real stealth-like and bump 'em with their nose. You see? *Bump* 'em. Okay? With the nose, that is." Dreadson tapped on his nose while he said this, as though it were unclear. "Then-after said nose bump- they hold the startled great white, the Carcharadon Carcharias, if you will, upside down until the beast then suffocates and subsequently dies. And that's when they go ahead and munch 'em down. You know, with minimal fussing and all now that they're recently deceased. Very smart animals. *Very* smart. You should see the things they do huntin' seals, too!"

"Amazing creatures, sir."

"Some people say they still exist, you know, the megalodon that is. Now, I'm getting back to the megalodon again, son. Not talking 'bout the orca anymore. Keep up with me."

"I'm not sure they're still around, sir. Some cryptozoologists might say so."

"Carcharocles Megalodon."

"Yes, sir." Best to just let the man talk. Scott knew better.

"Ancestor of Carcharadon Carcharias, some say. The great white shark."

"Mm hmm. Yes, sir."

"Who knows what's out there, Grant! Ya old chip off the old block." A pound on the desk and a jutted finger, as he continued using his outdoor voice indoors. "You know we've only explored less than five percent of the ocean. How bout that? Five percent, mah boy."

"I was aware that it was very small, proportionately, sir."

"Hell, they didn't know for sure that giant squid existed 'til a few decades back!"

"That is true, sir."

"The coelacanth."

"Yes, correct, sir."

"The Gott-damned megamouth shark."

"Yes, indeed, sir. The Gott-damned megamouth."

"That's a scary sumbitch, too. You ever see a picture?"

"Yes, sir. I have seen pictures."

"This megalodon's gonna look sweet. I'll tell you that much."

"Yes, sir."

"Enough dog dicking around, Grant!"

"Yes, sir. I'm sorry about that, sir. Won't happen again, sir."

"Let's get down to business!"

"Yes sir, Mr. Dreadson."

"Okay. All right now, here we go. Where were we at?"

Dreadson, sat back and put his hands up behind his head, interweaving his fingers. He looked up slightly. His eyes squinted in concentration as he thought about what he was going to say next.

Grant observed him. He was an aged man, in his late seventies he guessed, maybe early eighties, though he looked ten, fifteen years younger. This was partially a result of his working out daily in the rather impressive gym in the far corner of his office. A cubby hole, so to speak, that extended back behind the entryway door on the left toward the wall of windows. The gym came complete with a private bathroom, shower, jacuzzi and sauna with hot rocks. The man possessed a thin, salt and pepper mustache and balding, slicked back grey hair that showed parallel strands of follicles separated by liver spotted scalp along the top of his head. Very stately looking.

Dreadson, come to think of it, always reminded Grant of the man who played the boy's grandfather on the movie *Over the Top*- one of his childhood favorites. Grant restrained himself from humming the theme song on impulse- though he was already getting it stuck in his head like a phone number jingle from a shameless ambulance chaser's daytime commercial. Grant's thoughts had a tendency to race from time to time, in a semi-manic type fashion, from one topic to another, and he could perseverate now and then on his thoughts as they arrived. It was sometimes a problem, other times a catalyst for achieving a near absurd amount of work over the course of frequent ten to fifteen-hour workdays. Hypomanic tendencies, a mental health professional would likely call it. His mind continued to perseverate on the theme song from the movie. A corny 80s pop metal classic. *Winner take it all. Loser take a fall.*

"Grant?"

"Hmm?"

"Pay attention, son. This is important, ya awkward ass sumbitch!" Realizing he had grown irate, Dreadson paused, put his head down a little and shook it side to side. "I'm sorry, Grant. Shit, you know I'm just teasing, right? Besides, someone who can do math and all those algorithms in their head like you with lightning speed. Well, that is impressive son- even if you are a little awkward."

"Yes. Thank you, sir. That is much appreciated, hearing it from you." As relatively feeble a compliment as it was, Grant knew this was high praise coming from Dreadson.

Dreadson continued with the news of the day. "Did you hear about the ratings from last night's show? No, no, don't answer that. I'll tell you. Highest *ever*! That fat fucker is like buttah, as they say. Like *buttah*, Grant!"

"Yes, sir."

Striking a more thoughtful pose, Dreadson added, "he's eating plenty of that buttah, too, come to think of it. Probably eats it straight off the god damn butter dish when he gets hungry-which I'm sure is quite frequently. You know I once saw that fat motherfucker go through a whole double-decker tin of shortbread in one day around last Christmas. In *one* day, son. Who the shit else can even *do* something like that! Cool Hand Luke? With his fifty eggs? We've got to get him on a diet soon. I don't know if that fat fuck can survive another coronary. Shit, I don't know if his wife would even call the paramedics if it happened at home. You know, I get the feeling she hates his guts, Grant. I mean like, on a *visceral* level, son. It's in the eyes." Dreadson pointed at his own, wild and semi-psychopathic seeming eyes as he said this. "The eyes and the body language. She wants him dead. Not passively, but actively *wants* that man dead."

"I see."

"Grant, we need you to keep working on these algorithms, son," Dreadson continued, abruptly changing focus as he often did. "That's what I called you in for today. That's what we can use to keep boosting these here ratings, my boy. It's really working- ratings don't lie- and we appreciate it. Appreciate you, too. You really are like a son to me, Grant; always have been." Dreadson now reflected (he was getting a bit more nostalgic these days). "I was a little worried about you in your younger years. Used to think there was something, well, *off* about you. But hell, you had great people like your father around you all the way, and it paid off in spades. And well, look at you now, son. You're the greatest mathematician I've ever come across. I tell you what. How do you figure all those algorithms out, anyway? I'm always curious."

"It's relatively simple, sir. All it is, really, is a procedure for solving a problem. You want to attract as many individuals as you can to your radio and television shows, especially *True American Radio*. That's the goal, so you then have to figure out, mathematically, how to achieve it. All you have to do, really, is figure out patterns of interaction between Bud Harbaugh and his listeners. It all boils down to that. You start by analyzing past shows with higher ratings. More successful shows, if you will. You draw from those shows and look for consistent patterns among the higher rated shows. These patterns you then try to replicate. You can then improve upon them by expanding on the replicated baseline patterns of success to further the ratings. Some of these patterns will be beyond our control, of course. Social events, for example. Traumatic occurrences, such as terrorist attacks. They are harder to analyze, though the more frequently they occur, the more of a chance we have to come up with consistent analyzable patterns of discourse, content, tone, and inflections that- even in the context of relatively rare social occurrences- can affect ratings with significant magnitude."

"You're losing me, son." Dreadson chuckled and added, "funny how I always ask you to explain and it never fully makes sense to me, even then."

"Well, basically, Mr. Dreadson, I like to start by defining what it is that we are looking for. I mentioned patterns. So, a particular pattern that we correlate with success is Bud's *thoughtful pauses*, as we like to call them. The more he does this in a particular broadcast, the more it draws in listeners. Of course, you don't want *overkill*. We've calculated that roughly twenty, well placed, *thoughtful pauses*, correlate with higher ratings. We've also found that a certain volume of voice, certain tones-especially in conjunction with certain themes- all of these factors help to attract more fans based on these variables, as well as keeping current fans listening to him consistently. Bud really has these working parts down, by the way. He does his homework, Mr. Dreadson. He cares greatly about those ratings."

Dreadson laughed a laugh of self-assured knowledge in what followed. "I'll tell you what he cares about, sonny son. Getting the cash bonuses associated with higher ratings and using them to buy cheesecake and bourbon. And I'll tell you, the only thing he's thinking about, during those 'thoughtful pauses,' is getting a BJ from that feisty Latina wife of his. Assuming he can get it up at all anymore."

"Yes, well, whatever the case may be, sir. When we tell him the patterns associated with his consistently higher rated shows, he picks up on those factors and carries out our recommendations readily, and with, just, *uncanny* accuracy. Right now, we're starting to see a pattern involving use of words defining liberal mentality as emotionally weak, misguided, detrimentally open-minded, and feminizing, and seeing increased ratings along with increased volume of calls during said segments. The pattern is magnified when said elements follow periods of, what we call, 'reflective silence.' We're also seeing tentative correlations involved with harkening back to a past era in terms of subject matter. That is, reflecting on a safer time, nicer people, less crime, cheaper goods.

"You know," Grant added after a thoughtful pause, "Interestingly, inflation or wages congruent with price of products seems to matter not at all. For instance, hamburgers costing a dime does not seem to be considered in context of a person earning ninety cents an hour. Interludes in which a past time, namely the post WWII years up until, approximately, the mid-1960s is discussed or alluded to, have had much success on listeners and overall ratings. The more idealized the time period is portrayed as, the more successful the show becomes. Accuracy, in a strictly historical context, has little to do with it- as touched upon with the money aspects- which is helpful, for us, because it means Harbaugh doesn't really have to do any significant research on what he's talking about. It's more associated with creating an *idea*, per say. An image, if you will. He just has to contribute to that."

"Grant. Don't worry yourself about things like context and accuracy," Dreadson clarified. "This is entertainment, you got that. That's all it is. That's all it's been for some years, now. That's probably all it ever will be. Okay! We're just getting better at it, these days. Now, whether people *see* it all as such is really none of our business. However, *if* it affects people's actions in a way that suits our own interests? Well, what's wrong with that from where we stand, my boy."

Dreadson got out of his chair. Propping himself up with both hands on his desk, he leaned toward Grant authoritatively. In this moment, his presence loomed larger to Grant. It struck him that Dreadson, in this pose, would probably appear quite intimidating to someone who didn't know him. A tall man with an intense expression and a perfectly tailored suit- valued in the multiple thousands- framed on each side and above by an immense Mastodon head and tusks. Just to the man's left, an enormous Kodiak bear looking as though both its cubs were just kidnapped and it was gazing upon the doomed perpetrator.

The rustic framed picture of Dreadson kneeling down next to the deceased bear lay on his desk, directly facing the chairs of his visitors. Grant had noticed- after having looked at it hundreds of times over the years (though never sharing his discovery with Dreadson)- that he could see, in the distance between two fir trees, a barely perceptible section of fence. A tall fence-; barbed wire atop. He looked for it in the picture now. It was hard to find but it was most certainly there. His mind was drifting again, perseverating now on this new task at hand at the expense of lending Dreadson his full attention, as it often were.

"Grant!" Dreadson snapped his fingers directly in front of Grant's perusing face- the displaced air from the movement causing a wisp of wind to tunnel into his retina.

"Yes, sir! Sorry, Mr. Dreadson. I was just admiring that *wonderful* picture of you with that *massive* Kodiak. Very impressive, sir. *Very* impressive."

"Ah, er, oh, yes, son." The moment of tension eased as Dreadson started to reflect on the hunt. His chest began to puff out, subconsciously, as he recounted the details. "Yes, yes. Well, of course it *is* quite impressive, my boy. You certainly are right about that. A three-quarter ton, man-eating *beast,* he was! My buddy Dale, from Fairbanks, and I, see, we were hunting him down over four days along the deep Alaskan interior. Winding eastward along the banks of the mighty Yukon. Four days in the deep Alaskan brush. Pelted by the frigid wind and rain. The forest was so thick you couldn't traverse more than a couple miles a day. And when we finally stumbled upon him, that God-damned bastard was tearing apart the flesh of a young fawn as we heard the mother wailing helplessly in the distance. We both took aim as one and, well, let's just say it did not go down easy, I'll tell you that. But that's another story for another God damned day, Grant. *Focus*, my boy!" He snapped his fingers one again as he said the word.

"Yes, Mr. Dreadson."

"*Back* to the *point* at *hand*, son." Dreadson clapped his hands for each word he emphasized. To further emphasize the previously emphasized.

"Sorry, Mr. Dreadson."

Dreadson continued, easing off somewhat on the boy, though continuing to look quite intense; solely via his everyday, looming presence. Dreadson, in thought, seemed to briefly second guess himself, before thinking otherwise and continuing on to his next point.

"Grant, listen up. Let me tell you something now, regarding our audience. If these dear, sweet simpletons want to go around believing that these ramblings actually *have* any merit in a geopolitical context, go ahead and let them. Just go ahead and let them, okay? Don't worry too much about accuracy. It isn't *about* accuracy anyhow, my boy. These people want to believe in fantasy, alright? That the world was some magical place in the 'old days.' I say, let them believe it. People *like* fantasy, Grant. You know that? Hell, they *need* it, come to think of it. Want some evidence? Look how obsessed we are with entertainers. Can anyone even *name* a modern intellectual? Hmm? Modern poet? Modern philosopher? Hmm? Most people can't even name a modern author aside from one who writes romance novels. That, or the same style of murder mystery story, pumped out repeatedly by ghost writers. They can't do that name one, right? But they sure as hell can name a dozen new 'artists' singing rinky-dink pop songs with an auto tune making them sound like a damned robot half the time." Dreadson paused for a moment to let the point sink in, before carrying on.

"So, my boy, we're just giving them what they want and what they *need*. And at the end of day, what's wrong with that? You tell me, Grant. What's wrong with it? It's a business, ain't it? A business just like any other and we are making some damned fine money off a it, too. Shit, I remember you telling me recently that you just bought you a new four-thousand-foot ranch up in Burbank with that raise I gave you." Dreadson slapped his desk two times, hard. "Don't even think twice about it! The fruits of your labor, son. And you *earned* it, too. You'll be getting double that raise next year if we can keep up ratings like this. Treat yourself, my boy. Yolo! Isn't that what the millennials are saying these days? YOLO? YOLO and FOMO, son." Dreadson smacked Grant on his left shoulder, shifting his whole left side downward with the force.

"Umm, FOMO?" Grant questioned, rubbing his instantly pulsating shoulder muscles.

"Fear of missing out, son. FOMO! New millennial expression. Keep up with the times, mah boy. We're trying to get more of these kids in our audience. Heh! Even if they are a bunch of lazy, entitled sumbitches findin' the need to abbreviate everything. Can't even say the whole phrase. Too fuckin' lazy!

Sweet baby Jesus, don't get me started on the millennials!"
Dreadson swatted at the air with both hands, like an old Jewish
lady fed up with the current kvetching.

"I won't sir." Grant knew better.

"You better not! Sweet lord of mercy. LGBTQ! Now
there's another one. What the shit is that? Sounds like they just
threw a handful of random letters from the alphabet all together.
Mashed em' up and spewed 'em back out. And how many letters
can you throw in to an abbreviation? At least five, I guess."

"Yes, sir. By the way, I do appreciate the raise you
mentioned before. That and the generous salary and
accommodations. I'm committed to help boost your revenues, Mr.
Dreadson. I want you to know that, and, to be clear, I don't wish
to concern myself so much with the ideologies involved."

Grant eased himself back into his chair. After a brief pause
for reflection, he added, "you never did, Grant. And you know
what? You will never know just how much I appreciate that.
You're a good man. A damned *fine* young man! Shit, boy. You
are indeed a chip off the old block. Your old man was just like
you, you know. A go getter! Most reliable man I ever worked
with, too. A good, decent *family* man." Dreadson paused again for
a moment and started to rub his chin lightly with his thumb and
index finger. His face shape shifted to a more distantly thoughtful
expression.

"You know, he started going…soft, I'll say. In his later
years, that is. Yes, going soft, I'd call it. Started questioning if we
were doing the right thing. Started questioning the *rhetoric*.
Talked about how it was escalating. Talked about how dangerous
that might be. Said it was dividing people. Shit, boy. That's
probably why he died before his time. Massive stroke in his mid-
sixties. Old man *worried* too much!" Dreadson smacked his hand
loudly on his desk for the umpteenth time, startling Grant, who
had, unfortunately, started to drift off looking for the barbed wire
fence again.

"He should have *enjoyed* himself more, son!" Dreadson emphasized shrilly. "All that money. All that power and *influence*. He should be here today enjoying himself, matter of fact. Maybe thinking about retirement. Hell, maybe having been retired a couple years already. He started to get involved in all this existential quandary of the matter and that was his downfall. You mark my words, boy." The wagging index finger returned. "Don't follow that path. Keep it businesslike. This is a business and like any business we are looking to grow and looking to turn a profit… and looking to reap the benefits of that profit, naturally, of course."

"Yes, sir. Naturally, sir."

"Looking to keep thousands of the little people working here and earning a stable income at it, too. Feeding their families. Having some pride in being able to provide for their spouses. Their children. Goddamn it, Grant. I'm telling you now. Right here and now, and let it be a lesson to you, son. Don't go getting caught up in all the *politics* of this, you got it. Don't go down that path. It has no place in terms of the bottom line, alright! No place in terms of why we're here and what we're here *for*. You got it?"

"Yes, sir."

"This is a business. This is a business and that is all it is, all it's meant to be. Okay, sure, let me play Devil's advocate." Dreadson eased himself back in his chair and folded his hands squarely behind his head. "I can never help myself," he added. "Okay, so people may get some *extreme* views (Dreadson made a mocking gesture of quotation marks with the word *extreme*) from someone like Bud. A couple far right groups committing terrorist type events here and there. Militias surging. Hate groups surging. You know, we can't change any of that anyway. You know that, son, right? That's world politics to blame for that." Dreadson shoo-ed the matter of with his hand as though it were a pesky fly.

"I don't really pay much attention to those matters, sir."

"Good! Yes, that's good, boy. Doesn't really affect you anyway and you can't change any of it. No way, no how. Can't change it because it's about something else. It's not about *us*. You know that, right?"

Dreadson pushed himself farther back in his chair, reclining his back now. He folded one leg over the other, perpendicularly, most assuredly not the way women and sissies folded them- one leg hanging like a giant flaccid penis over the other one. Goddamn man bun wearing, skinny jeans having, iced chai Frappuccino drinkin' *Nancy* boys! Goddamn those Brits had the best slang words, he thought. Nancy boys! Twats! Fookin' cunts! *Hah*! His present ironic smile at the thought of it subdued itself gradually as he pressed the fingers of both hands together, putting the two index fingers up to his lower lip to gather himself and reflect. He looked downward in thought for a time before looking back at Grant with a more serious affectation.

"I'm just explaining to you the general idea that there are certain factors that exist outside of our control. Sure, these listeners are getting more upset these days. Sure, maybe some of them get out of control at times. Go on a shooting spree and what not. Make threats toward those liberal politicians that may or may not come true. They make threats toward us too, by the way! But yes, maybe they're going to get mad listening to Bud. Well look at their life, son! They lost their job to some Gook over there in one of them Asian jungle countries. Some jungle Gook whose daddy probably killed their grandpa over in Ding Dang Bang Dong. Gook can't even speak proper English. Hell yeah, they're upset. They got laid off from the factory because some damned machine can work with eight times the efficiency that they could on a conveyor built line…or some such shit. The factories that still have manual labor all gone over to China, or India. The God damned Philippines! That ain't *ever* going to change from here on out. Understand that right now, son. Hell, Betty says he's gonna bring jobs back and his own luxury clothing line is based out in Xinjiang province, China. Aint' that some shit! Half his constituency at least, doesn't even know that. And you know what? They don't even *want* to. It's not about telling them the *facts*. It's about telling them what they *want* to hear. We cater to what people show us that they want. Betty tells them he's going to

bring these jobs back here. Back to *Murica*. And they *believe*
him! They actually *believe* that horse shit. They believe it because
they're not informed of the realities of it, and they're not looking
to be. They just want to hear what they want to hear and they want
somebody to say that shit to them. What do you think about that?"

"Well, sir, I suppose it will only continue in that manner.
Lack of manual labor opportunity will grow exponentially as the
expanding technological base knowledge make further mechanical
advancements exponentially easier. For remaining labor work,
businesses will ship labor out to save on costs and avoid pollution
related restrictions."

"Sure!" Dreadson relaxed his posture somewhat more,
unfolding his legs and sprawling out on his oversized leather chair.
He would soon continue this mini tangent, as he was apt to do.
Few dared to check him on his tendencies toward this, as he was
the authority over everyone in the entirety of the eighty-floor
building.

"People are becoming obsolete, son. Get your rocks off
now while you can, I say. Machines are going to take over.
They're getting better by the day. Hell, they got a new cellphone
out every few months now. Can do twice what the model before
could! Got video games out there becoming like virtual reality.
Hell. *Will* all be virtual reality in a few more years. What do you
think's gonna happen then? Huh? It's all going in that direction.
Nobody will even want to live in the goddamn real world anymore.
So, what do you do? Distract them with something so's they don't
have to look at reality is what you do; just like they're being
distracted now with all these hollow promises. But shit, the
promises don't have to be real, do they? The people just have to
believe that they will be. Or that, if it doesn't happen this time,
with this one- this Betty guy- maybe it will at least happen with the
next one. Maybe this one at least put it all on the radar when all's
said and done. And, at the very least, we continue to learn what
works and what doesn't work from what Betty says and how he
campaigns himself."

Dreadson got back up and walked past Grant. He could never sit still for too long. A hypomanic type. He looked out through the glass door overlooking the rooftop forest. He briefly caught a glimpse of Sanchez chasing a Labrador retriever around with the leaf blower. What was a dog doing out there? And did he pay this man to engage in tomfoolery? Dreadson, thinking better than to pursue the thought, intertwined his hands loosely behind his back, choosing now to reflect on more pressing matters.

As Dreadson stood, he caught himself drifting off topic in his mind now, to the thought of technology. What would be the result of all this technological proliferation? What was all of it working toward? What was the eventual end game? He pictured a hypothetical, robotically dominated, future that yet included largely obsolete humans- humans existing for no reason other than to indulge their own base pleasures for the duration of their artificially expanded lifetimes. That, and to keep the tech machine running. He despised the idea of a disconnected, disjointed society that seemed almost inevitable. One where everybody would simply gravitate toward their own cocoon over time.

One day, that would be exactly what it was, he suspected. Everyone in so-called developed countries in a virtual cocoon of sorts. Their bodies to be slowly decaying vessels, stimulated artificially for as long as science could keep them going. A hundred and twenty years? Hundred and fifty? Fed through tubes. Urine and excrement coming out through other tubes and disposed of along the winding refuse shoots of dark high rises hundreds of stories tall. The entirety of their life lived through an avatar. The men six foot five with six pack abs, and a ten-inch-long, soda can dick. The women, looking like one of them six-foot-tall, blonde, Russian pro tennis players. Sporting improbable, gravity defying, size D natural tits; straight out of a comic book.

Relationships with other people would probably grow obsolete too, now that some fat kid who looked like the Elephant Man's ugly cousin could get it on somewhere. Living in a perpetual orange sherbet sunset on a virtual beach. Porking any actress or supermodel he wanted with multiple male orgasms sans refractory period. Could follow it up by diving down into the ocean to swim with the dolphins. Come out of the water and fly over it in a light, steady tropical breeze, no wings required. The power of imagination the only limit. Hell, imagination would become obsolete too. The machine would postulate something even better; analyzing and synthesizing the preferred fantasy based on neurological input and feedback loops. Dreadson shook the thought out of his head. Why bother with it? He would be gone in ten years' time, fifteen tops. He continued:

"You know what it is, Grant? You know what it's all about right now?"

"I could think of a number of factors that interplay, sir," Grant began to reply.

"*Fuck* that, son. It's easy," Dreadson cut him off. "Don't overthink it." He shook his finger at him. "You have a problem with that sometimes, you know. *This* is what it's all about. It's about people knowing that they're becoming obsolete. They used to subconsciously dread it, then, eventually, have a vague sense of it. But now, they flat out know it. That's where the anger comes from. This anger that people say they don't understand? This anger that people don't know how it's growing? Well, *that's* why it's growing. And what are we doing with that anger?" Dreadson waited briefly for a response from Scott, though not getting one in the short time he allowed, continued:

"We are *validating* the anger, my boy. We are validating it, and we are, in turn, making *them* feel validated by doing so. They think we're on *their* side. And they think that simply because we've tapped into the feeling. The *feeling*, my boy. That's all that matters, isn't it?" Dreadson, not interested in a response, continued. "The feeling is validated by us. You *should* be angry. You *should* be upset. If you're not angry there's something wrong with you. Then we take that anger and direct it toward the liberal agenda. And then, afterwards, we offer them a solution to their anger. This isn't the world you thought it should be, but...*but*...it once was. It *once* was. That's the key right there, son. Create that fantasy that will relieve all those uncomfortable emotions. It *once* was, and we are the ones that can, somehow, some way, bring it all back. It's a load of horse shit, of course, but at the end of the day that's what they want. That's what they've shown us they want. And they *desperately* want it."

Dreadson turned to face Grant. The sun was beginning to set and the orange and lavender backdrop framed Dreadson's taut figure, standing tall and black within the vibrant, multi-hued aura around him. His presence growing trippy.

"Shit, boy, I was born in 1936. Did you know that? Cheese 'n rice, I'm as old as dust, kid. I was already a young man by the mid-50s. And you know what? That time Betty says we need to get back to? Know what I remember? I remember men getting drunk all day long, chain smoking. I remember women on Prozac having little break downs every now and then because they wanted more in life than to stay at home and raise their shitty assed kids. But...*but*...feeling ashamed if they felt they somehow *should* want more than that; because that's what society told them they should want. Told them, over and over again, that's what should have made them content. And what else?" Dreadson paused to gather more thoughts on the times. He slowly paced a length of the panoramic view. He added:

"A war in Korea. *The Forgotten War,* they called it. That's because nobody wanted to talk about it. They mostly ignored it, really, because they were still dealing with their unrelenting shell shock from WWII. Those that didn't end up going straight *back* to war anyway. Drinking every Goddamn day. Start in the late morning, at work, before the coffee even wore off. Drinking to numb the pain. Angry drunks, too, shadowed by the skeletons of war. Husbands beating their wives behind closed doors and no one talking about it. And why not? Because no one wanted to *hear* about it. Racism right out in the open. *Right* out there, boy!" Dreadson walked in close, leaned on the arm of Scott's chair. "*Fuck* them niggers. *Fuck* them spicks. *Fuck* them kikes. And anybody else who wasn't white? Fuck 'em. This country ain't for you, buddy boy. Cold War with Russia with no end in sight. Developing ever stronger nuclear weapons and dropping them on tropical atolls. Ready to use them at any given time. What do they have to look forward to in life anyway?

Seven-month long winters and all the potatoes and cabbage you can eat? Kids in schools over here taught to hide under their desks in case of a nuclear attack, knowing full well it wouldn't help them one iota from being turned to dust on the spot." Dreadson snapped a finger next to Scott's head for emphasis. "Men piss drunk all day long, driving drunk. If you hit somebody? Hmmm? What do you think? If you hit somebody? Shit, act of God, that's all it was. The cops was in the same wars and they were drinking to numb the pain too. Didn't want to stop just cuz they were behind the wheel. *That's* what that time really was, son, and I saw it as a man. Not as a naïve, starry-eyed boy, like our late middle-aged base. As a man."

Scott shifted uncomfortably in his chair and replied "Well, I guess people want what they want, sir. Sometimes they get what they want and realize it wasn't what they thought it would be."

"Mighty perceptive of you, Grant. I think you've got it down, son."

Dreadson casually turned back around to admire the fading sunset casting the various shapes of the lush, tropical forest outside in black shadows. He looked out on it and thought, for a moment, on his younger days. Days when he used that forest for his sordid affairs. Scores of young women visiting his office on "business." They'd gotten down to business all right. He'd had some fun in his time, mercy *mercy* me. But he was getting too old for that malarkey these days. He was eighty. Time to take it a little more easy. Didn't want to go getting himself a coronary out there, though he had to admit, it wouldn't be such a bad way to go. On his back on the cool grass, one hand on each tit. His two kiwis kissed by the sun. Maybe he could get Sanchez, the leaf blower, to aim that thing on his ball sack during the act if he ever tried it again out there. Would be refreshing on a hot day.

Dreadson, recalling more serious matters needed attending, turned back to Grant with a new request. He noticed the young man lit up with color- cast from the stained-glass arches showing medieval scenes of Christian persecution. Grant glowed with purple, royal blue, rose, sea foam green and orange. Boy looked a little hippie dippy, Dreadson thought. Like he was wearing a tie dye suit with his face painted and about to go to an outdoor acid rock concert in some burn-out strewn meadow reeking of reefer. He concluded with business for the day:

"Grant, muh boy. In the spirit of expanding our influence, I want you to start looking into our affiliate, Marmot News. They've heard about all the work you've done for True American radio, and they've seen Bud's ratings rightly soar over the years. They're appreciative of the work, too. Make no mistake, my boy. Appreciative and proud to know you seemed to have an influence on that stubborn, fat S.O.B. They want your help with their news crew, looking at patterns and developing processes to utilize to help them boost their own ratings and expand to a larger audience."

Dreadson, seeming to offer brief concession to the novelty of the situation and the additional stress it would surely entail, added:

"Now, I know this will be a new process for you, as you will have the visual component to work with. You haven't done that before, have you?" Dreadson, as per usual, didn't wait now for a response, but continued, "No, I suppose you haven't. You'll receive a bonus as soon as you sign on with them. A tidy some too, my boy. One day a week is all, in a consulting role. You can take the time off from working with Bud's crew to go over there and work with them. He needs less and less of your help nowadays, anyway, as time goes on."

"I suppose I could do that, if you think it's prudent," said Grant, with minimal initial concern about the new role. He thought it would simply be utilizing the same knowledge in a somewhat different context. Easy enough to carry out, in theory. And he could use the bonus to put in that swim up bar that his wife always wanted to have. Maybe hire a part time barkeep to come on request, as needed. One that could make a variety of mojitos. His Ginny's favorite.

Dreadson turned back around to admire the fading sun. A brilliant lavender and blood red mixed in with the last remnants of bright orange. All of it pressing down under the enveloping soft, pinkish charcoal gray of the night. The night that was itself like a perpetual late dusk, with its ubiquitous, multi-hued city lights all a twinkle. He added:

"I do think it's prudent, my boy. I do. Very prudent. You see, the physical presentation that you see on the screen adds a whole new element. My theory is that if you can create a visual display that they had already hoped to convey through radio- Bud's domain- you can expand on the success of what it is you're espousing. See, I believe there is a physical presentation that we can convey through the news anchors that roughly matches the supposed presentation of Bud Harbaugh that they connect with so well. The idea is to mimic the image of Bud's emotions and presentation that Bud is leading his viewers to believe. Do you see? The presentation of being righteously pissed off. Having to sternly and exhaustedly deal with the liberal-minded guests. A breath of relief comradery around the similarly minded, by contrast. The physical image brings to life what is perceived through Bud's broadcasts. You see what I'm getting at, Grant? Do you understand, my boy? A visual representation of the aura that Bud creates. We're going to make it come more to *life*!" Dreadson raised both his hands from his sides into the air above, like he was willing Frankenstein's monster to rise.

"I understand, sir. It sounds like a natural choice to expand on Bud's broadcasts, as well as to expand on the demographic through offering a visual medium to relate to, in addition to the audiological medium."

"Correct, Grant." Dreadson chuckled briefly at the prized pupil type response (sometimes he thought about pinning gold stars onto the man's suit). "You get these complex things right away, son. You always do, and I can't tell you how much I appreciate it in this world chock full of mediocre minds. You really don't know how much of a day to day relief that is for me. How much time and effort it saves us." Dreadson went and tapped Scott a few times on the top of his head. "Being on the same level upstairs. I'd lost that, for a time, after your old man passed and before you had come up."

Dreadson paced back to the view the reflections of the setting sun off the cotton ball clouds. After a time, he turned his head to his left, just enough to be able to see Grant within his peripheral field of vision, and said, "You can go ahead and call it an evening, son. I'll fill you in with more details in the coming days." Dreadson now shooed him out.

"Thank you, sir, and I appreciate the opportunity," said Grant, composedly. He pressed his tie into his chest and held it firm, as he got up from his chair. With conviction, though not rushed, as always, he made his way down the long corridor thinking little of the new work. As he had already mentioned, it would be a logical extension of past and current duties. He did know, instinctively, it would add many more hours to his job than Dreadson let on (as there was no way he would be allowed to cut back on his time consulting with *True American Radio*). That was okay though, because it was temporary.

Scott's thoughts presently turned to calling his wife, Ginny, and coming up with a mutually agreeable spot for dinner to ring in the weekend. Hopefully it could be sushi, and preferably a rooftop deck reservation. Unagi, fat belly of blue fin, some purple seaweed salad, maybe a couple Lychee Martinis (his favorite). Some Taiwanese shaved ice with condensed milk and sweet red beans if he had room for dessert. He was hungry. And no kids tonight, either.

It had been an unusually long week among weeks that had already been unusually long. Grant made his way to the door, hefted it open with a hushed grunt, and exited Dreadson's office-smoothly and quietly as always. Make it look effortless, like all things work related. Kitty waved goodbye to him on his way out. She looked mildly relieved knowing that, usually, Grant's late afternoon briefings marked the end of her invariably shitty, overworked, and underappreciated days. He glimpsed her computer monitor and saw an image of an oversized candy cane on it.

Kitty breathed a long sigh and shut down her computer. She had resumes out at three different companies and prayed nightly for a response. She picked up the phone for one last call to Dreadson.

Dreadson heard the phone ring, presently. He smiled hopefully, knowing that it was probably Kitty and that she may, or may not, have some good news to share regarding the progress of the Megalodon. *Megalodon,* thought Dreadson. Carcharocles Megalodon. Ancestor of Carcharadon Carcharias. Eater of whales. Size of a damned school bus. You could bet your God damed ass, mister, nobody fucks with a megalodon.

Chapter II

Your Bud

"*True Murican Radio* here. Coming to you from the great
city of Los An-gel-ees. And we are *back*, folks. Back in action!
Back in bidness. This is Bud Harbaugh, '*Your Bud*' here,
welcoming all you *true* patriots back to these friendly airwaves
after that there short commercial break. With me as always are
good ol' Ted and Walt. Good friends. Good folks, the both of
'em. Okay, my friends…"

Bud Harbaugh shifted his zaftig frame from within his
ergonomically designed Office Master Corporate Executive model
chair (with built in massage function) in his sixty-four-degree,
climate-controlled radio broadcasting booth. It was, more so, an
opulent personal living space of sorts. An ornate enclosure
adorned in his preferred style- A Victorian era gentleman's den,
though with the oddly out of place, sporadically dispersed Mexican
flair; these mostly tchotchkes, compliments of his wife Esperanza,
from all-inclusive, celebrity accommodation trips to Cancun
(Sometimes Puerto Vallarta, but not lately. Place was going
straight down the shitter last few years.).

Within his burrough: A large, burgundy-hued Persian rug
of various accents and color patterns, handcrafted a couple hundred
years ago, at least, lay appreciating in value in front of a sleekly
polished, mahogany desk. The desk served as an ornate base for a
bottle of fine bourbon set atop a polished silver tray which
adorned, as well, a pristine crystalline tumbler which held his
favorite drink, straight bourbon, poured three fingers high. Always

twenty-three years aged, and that at the very least. Two thousand dollars per bottle the minimum he would oblige himself to pay for this; his fine libation of choice.

Bud liked to imbibe one third to one half bottle of good bourbon during his workday. He would polish off another one third to one half bottle after coming home. The habit had progressed slowly, starting many years back as a modest three fingers at work, then three at home, though increasing over time, like his girth and the accompanying stretch marks and lower extremity, diabetes related, sores.

Sometimes, it would be prudent to mention, Bud imbibed in whiskey- that is- when given him by a friend, or as a gift from his employer, Dreadson and Scott Broadcasting Group. He would oblige them, certainly. Stood to reason, this did. Don't never forget who butter yo bread, unless you a stupid sumbitch possessing not one *iota* of common sense. And there damned sure were more a few of them out there. More than a few. Though, if Bud were to be asked, he would say he preferred Bourbon to whiskey as he found it a more authentically American indulgence; like barbecue, baseball, and a slice of apple pie with cheese. As American as it gets. To hell with the rest of that nonsense. Goddamn it all to Hades and back!

Bud sat bloated and flimsily-formed. His clothes made him appear, at first glance, like a multi-hued sack of puddin'. Setting presently in his trademark Joey Bahama 4XL, button down Caribbean blue short-sleeve silk shirt and his size fifty-six waist, light khaki cargo shorts. Sweat soaking profusely through the hundred-dollar shirt around the neckline, in a blotchy rectangle down the center of his back, patches under both man boobs, and in the upper buttock area of his cargos. Pit stains around a foot in length each. A little more under his right arm, which he tended to use for gesturing more so than the left.

Bud sat flanked by various members of his radio team, some behind their own smaller, less opulent desks. Good 'ol Ted and Walt sat near to him as always, forming a blockish A shape with Bud at the top. Other personnel were nestled within glass sound booths around the three-man team; quietly conducting their various day-to-day, behind the scenes, production and administrative duties. These: a combination of trusted and reliable, aging cronies, mixed in with younger (late teens to early twenties) interns looking to make it in radio in some capacity of their own one day. These interns were, invariably, young, female and attractive.

Bud had a long history of picking out his interns by hand. His selections were based mainly (assuming they were attractive enough to bother with) on Bud's intuition that they might- just might, at some point- be willing to have sex with him in exchange for dinero (Bud made sure his selections had copious student loan debts to up the ante in his favor. Ah, sweet, *sweet* desperation.). Of course, he'd try to select those he felt could conduct these services with minimal risk of tattling to his superiors or, worse yet, the press. The God Damned, sumbitchin' press! Them self-righteous dotards had already found out about his so-called prescription pill "abuse," which was none of their concern no how, no way. But he had, unfortunately, once left a right mess of pills out (in a less than inconspicuous fashion) some years back. A photo, compliments of a disgruntled intern on the way out, got leaked and hell, you know the rest. Squeaky wheel gets the greasin' every time. Can't close Pandora's box once ya done popped open the sucker.

Getting back to those young interns. They was a shoe-in if they would also be willing to bang his old reliable buddies. His eskimo buddies; that is, "good ol' Ted and Walt." Bud didn't mind sharing, or even the occasional ménage trois, though he called it a threesome because he preferred not to speak French, for reasons he had never dedicated much time toward examining. He'd pay the girls a separate fee for the other two. He had money to burn and, if being entirely honest, it seemed to make them all the more loyal and dedicated to the day's work. So why not?

Ted and Walt. Hell, Ed McMahon to Johnny Carson had nothing on "good ol' Ted and Walt" (Phrase trademarked and adorned to various hats, T-shirts, jackets, coffee cups, beer can cozies, and so on- at a reasonable price- in *Marmot News* stores around the country). Every joke Bud told was greeted with hearty laughter, on both flanks, from whence his dos amigos sat. Every point meant to be taken as profound? These were greeted by drawn out validations and *mm-hmms* affected to convey thoughtfulness. "Yes," and "that is plain truth, Bud," and "you just can't argue with that." Bud hadn't been wrong in, hell, going on twenty-two years (at least that's what much of his audience seemed to believe) and that happened to suit Bud just fine, thank you very much, sirs and ma'ams.

Bobby Trenton "Bud" Harbaugh. *Your Bud.* The man stood five feet seven, tippin' the scales at well over three hundred pounds, nah. The man was perpetually sweaty browed and mildly winded. Struggle, he certainly did, with that adult onset diabetes (he done caught that sugar foot) and hw was gaining weight at approximately five and a half ounces per month for the past twenty years plus.

The man had dangerously high blood pressure, too. Matter of fact, he would've been dead by now if medical technology was even thirty years less developed than it were presently. In other words, if Bud were currently living in his preferred era, the 1950s and early 60s (the good old days before the Goddamned hippies took over), he'd have been pushing up daisies going on six years already. Maybe longer. As it was, three score decades on from those days, two massive coronaries had not dropped him yet, and he'd been preserved in his current, living form (a sack of puddin' and cottage cheese mixed together roughly fifty/fifty) to continue, for who knows how much longer, within his chosen profession; more or less unaffected, workwise, by the several pounds of cholesterol built up in his various arteries, veins and capillaries.

Bud viewed his coronaries as some sort of evil presence outside of himself. Viewed them as this, rather than the logical conclusion of his lifestyle choices, which included a laundry list of abused prescription drugs as part of a cocktail that had remained largely the same for the past eight years. A cocktail given him daily by his live-in personal physician, Big Dick. Nice to have that Big Dick around. Gave him just what he liked, whenever he needed it. Didn't give him any God damned shit, neither.

Bud Harbaugh. Your bud. The big straight shooter. The tongue of truth. The people's sounding board. Bud's "no bones radio show" was the most widely listened to broadcast in the nation at the present. Bud was, as well, the most famous and highest paid broadcaster in the country- second highest in the world (playing second fiddle only to some state-sponsored Ching Chang China Man over in Shanghai. But there were 1.4 billion of them to tune in anyways, so he didn't concern himself too much with it; unfair advantage as it were).

Bud was proud to say he kept between forty to sixty million listeners tuned in at any given time. His annual salary amounted to approximately a dollar and fourteen cents per every one of these listeners. Between this salary and his various endorsements, largely in hunting accessories, big trucks, and liquor, he was the eighth highest earning celebrity personality of the past year according to a recent *Cash Money "Show Me the Bling Bling" Magazine* article. His off-the-books earnings (the little under the table exchanges from special interests) gave him nearly as much per year in non-taxable income that those IRS bastards would never find out about and bleed him dry for. Mother fuckers. They made plenty from him to begin with, so why should they care what his friends in high places wanted to do with their spending cash? Thank you very much, but no sir, Mr. tax man. *The IRS* did not necessarily mean *theIRS* when it came to Bud's hard-earned wampum. And he made damned sure of that, too.

Today's broadcast, as the network would later confirm, would garner nearly sixty-five million listeners; damned close to his personal high to date. He would, upon reflection, consider today's show among his very best; particularly his closing statements. These, he would routinely offer at the end segment of each show. This was, in fact, his favorite part of the broadcast. Those hallowed last five to ten minutes where he could say what he wanted- unimpeded- sans the tedious daily framework given to him by his company president, Robert Scott Dreadson the Fourth, or, as Bud called him, "Bob." Unscripted, yes. Nothing previously prepared- that is- nothing more than Bud's own personal thoughts and reflections on a given subject matter and he would generally, "speak freely," as he liked to call it, with periods of dramatic silence for emphasis on what he perceived to be the particularly salient points. Or, on what he wanted to be sure his listeners would especially chew on.

Bud paused, in front of his array of microphones, for a moment. He sighed and ran his clammy tongue across perpetually sweat-glistened lips before continuing to the topic of the hour. He began, in his decades long rehearsed voice. This was a voice meticulously crafted over a lengthy career in radio to be smooth, feigned thoughtful, with an ambiguous southern accent of mixed state origins seeming to alternate with each other at random (though he had grown up in upstate New York to an upper-class family of fine repute in the area. This family who consistently seemed overtly disappointed in Bud throughout his youth and following on into his adulthood. The disappointment also manifested itself as a relative parental disinterest in investing sufficient time and attention to the boy in his youth. Some might say this had been character forming in various ways; leading to a personality seeking approval by any means necessary). He began. The subject: a protest turned violent, at presidential hopeful David P. Betty's political rally in Chicago, just the night prior.

"True Muricans. True *patriots* of deeze her troubled modern times wherein, uh, wherein the radicalized socialists are trying to take things over! 'Your Bud' is upset. 'Your Bud' is frustrated. 'Your bud' is just, just plain *stymied*! Confounded! And, er, and, and *flabbergasted*!

"Mm hmm, confounded," chimed in Ted.

"Flabbergasted, he is!" added Walt with much gusto.

"Nah, nah. Nah, I'd come up with some more descriptors, uh, mind you, but I don't want to waste your time on that there hogwash. See I'm not bout wastin' nobody's time here, as ya'all well know. That there socialist Nicaraguan, or wherever the hell he come from, that we got in office right now does plenty of that already for *all* of us."

"It damned sure ain't the U.S. where he come from!"

"Dat right! You got dat right, friend," said Bud with a self-assured smile at this little ad lib, compliments of Ted. "Now, now, I didn't want to say that, mind you, but since we're on the topic, heck, he probably grew up in a hut somewhere."

"In a damned hut!" Shouted Walt, several decibels louder than Ted's previous comment.

"Maybe? Right? I mean, who's to say? I'm not sayin' that fer sure. Don't get me wrong. Okay? Let's make that clear...but we don't know, do we? Hmm? You know what I mean? You believe that's a real birth certificate he showed us? Hmm? Think that's real? I'm just saying, nah. But let's not get off track here, folks. Now I'm fixing ta get right down to bidness and I am certainly not fixin' to pussy foot around like those liberal elitists be all apt ta do. Pussy footing around issues and not just coming out and telling it like it is. PC nonsense is what I call that! Don't say what's on their mind. That wastes your time, friends! Now how come, and uh, and...*why* come, anybody wanna go wastin' time like that."

"Wasting your time with *nonsense*!" shouted Ted.

"Wasting it with bull corn!" Added Walt.

"*Nonsense*! Dat right, Ted. *Bull corn*! Dat right, too, Walt. And I would add, most humbly to that, moo-larkey. Moo-larkey, too, fellas."

Ted and Walt nodded their heads in unison.

"Definitely some moo-larkey involved," confirmed Ted.

"Dat rot. Moo-larkey. Nah listen her, true patriots. Ya'all are *my* people and you are the *only* ones who understand what is *really* going on her. Okay? What's *really* going on...okay? Never forget that fact....okay?...understand that fact. M'kay? Cuz it's a *fact*, nah. Now, let's get right into it, nah. I want to conclude my final segment on this morning's broadcast with my thoughts on these her recent outbreaks that- shocker (Bud shook his head and rolled his eyes, expressing a comically exaggerated look of surprise from behind his booth)- turned violent *again* at presidential hopeful, David P. Betty's peacefully intentioned. Peacefully...*intentioned*...okay? ...political rally at the UIC pavilion in Chicago. Yes, I *know*! Believe me, I've seen it and I have heard it from *every* imaginable source. Believe me! I have done mah research, my *true* Muricans."

Bud had, indeed, watched a seven-minute segment on *Marmot News*, an ultra-conservative news network that marketed itself as "Plainly Spoken and Fair- Minded," on his 100-inch 4K UHDTV, in his fifteen thousand square foot compound, the night before. This comprised *sufficient* evidence, to the man, for his comments with regards to what had transpired.

"You know he has, *real* Muricans! This man her do his homework!" exclaimed Ted, who had just gotten a raise and now made over 2.5 million per year, for his work as a radio side kick. Ted's work consisted of picking and choosing from roughly three dozen various affirmations to utter- along with repetitions of certain key words deemed by Dreadson and Scott to be "of added long term value" on each broadcast. Ted was the level-headed sidekick. The rock of the group.

"Red-blooded, *True* Muricans!" added Walt, belligerently. Walt was the angry sidekick. The bad cop that Bud played off.

"You don't have to tell me what's what about this," Bud soldiered on. "Okay! Nah, uh, believe you me, I *know* what's what. I've been puttin' my mind to it, friends. Puttin' my best into making sense of it all. Nah, nah...nah, you might be thinking, Mr. Harbaugh -*Bud*- how could dis happen? Hmmm?...How could dis happen? Or, let's say, now conversely, umm, you might be thinking, uh, how could our just and *noble* compatriot. Hmm? Our voice and our sound piece, the good Mr. David P. Betty, hold a peacefully intentioned political meeting. A *peacefully* intentioned political meeting (Bud paused several seconds before adding) and encounter turmoil like this? Savagery! Unjusti*fi*able in its scope! Absolutely *intolerable*! You don't have to tell me, true Muricans. I saw the videos, okay. I saw these, so called 'inner city youth,' at least that what's those commie liberals like to call them, with their *thuggish* tactics. Hmm? With their *thuggery*,

45

trying to bully a *peaceful* and *civil- minded* political gathering. Let me repeat. A *peaceful*. Hmm? And a *civil-minded*...gathering, my friends. Thank God, okay. Thank the good Lord up in heaven above that our fair-handed Marmot News affiliates called them out for what they are. Thugs! Shameless and brutal. Okay? *Shameless*!...and, er, and *brutal*! You know what it's like in Chicago, too. A low down, dirty shame what's happening in Chicago. Makes ya think twice bout even stepping foot in that place."

Bud shifted slightly in his chair. "Shameful," added Walt in a hushed voice as he shook his head side to side. Walt was growing a bit distracted these last fifteen minutes. He was looking forward to some private time with Intern Jessica after the show. Bud had negotiated with her a few months back at five hundred bucks a round, sometimes with a tip if things got particularly nasty. It was cheap for a nine like her. She was paying her way through college quick, too. Good thing, Walt thought, cuz a degree in Communications didn't mean fuck all these days. Better to not have the debt on your back, at least.

Walt was a man who worked out daily and maintained a strict, mostly vegetarian diet, while steadily popping Viagra and snorting cocaine 'in moderation.' He fancied he had the sexual stamina of a nineteen-year-old and prided himself on that, because subconsciously he had come to feel he had peaked in life at about nineteen and because, at Walt's maturity level, nineteen was about where he wanted to maintain his actions and his mindset, indefinitely. If Walt were a woman, he would probably be one of those trash-talking, empathy lacking queen bees who dressed like their teenage daughters whilst in their late forties.

Bud recommenced. "So...what do we have? A crowd of protesters. *Lots* of Mexicans. La-*tee*-nos, as they like to say, up in dare. And why can't they just call themselves, Muricans I say. Hmm? Why can't day?"

"*Muricans*!" Walt obnoxiously piped, irritated, at present, by a half chub jutting into his pants zipper.

"Quite a few blacks, or whoops, sorry, sour-eee, my friends." Bud flailed his fat hands around in mockery. *"Af-ree-can Americans,'* too," added Bud, puh-shawing audibly for emphasis.

"Whatever happened to I'm *black* and I'm proud!" shouted Walt, a little too belligerently. He was getting more uncomfortable, thinking about Jessica with the tenacious hard-on. Should have timed that Viagra a little better. Kicking in too early.

"Now, now, Walt," Bud added, soothingly. "Let's calm down. Okay? Let's not rush to judgment. Hmm? We are not here to judge without looking at the *facts* first. Okay? The facts! Facts o' the matter, nah. Without spinning them all around with all a that pompous, over-educated, out of touch nonsense. Liberal malarkey.

"Moo-larkey!" Clarified Ted.

"Dat right! Moolarkey. Okay? Dat is some cotton-pickin' moo-larkey goin' on. And, uh, and, and, out of *touch*! And really, that's the key word, isn't it here, folks. Maybe well meaning, yes, maybe. But out...of...touch. Plain and simple." Bud waved a dismissive hand. "Plain and simple, folks! Don't overthink it now. It ain't complicated."

This back and forth banter was part of the show's ongoing format that had worked to a tee for the past couple decades now. Walt would get progressively louder and more obnoxious, which would necessitate Bud to take on a soothing, fatherly voice of reason to calm him down and -by proxy- project a fatherly aura of reason onto his audience as well. Ted would contribute to it all as his rock steady wingman. Adding crafted, subdued moments with Bud, to contrast with the angry projections of Walt. It was truly uncanny how well it worked. How well oiled, this machine had become.

The effect all of this had was, of course, Bud's main goal. He wanted to be seen as the fatherly voice of reason not only for his own ego (fragile and overcompensating with narcissistic traits) but also because he knew- knew on a visceral level- it was what so many of his audience members yearned for. Millions of good, hardworking (though often willfully simple-minded and scared adults) who felt vulnerable in their forever changing, increasingly competitive global society. Men and women who felt they were losing their place in this world. Men and women who were strong, but often unable to adjust to the pace at which this modern society was changing. The ever-growing pace, the diversifying culture, and the myriad fears and insecurities that arose with it all. This fatherly figure that Bud conjured cared about them and soothed them in the face of it. He surely did understand them and knew what they were going through. This man was there for them, always. Gave them the wisdom and guidance they sought, every weekday at 4PM sharp, Pacific time.

Bud continued with another, of many, feigned exhausted sighs. "Here is the hardest part to believe, people. I know I didn't believe it at first, but mind you, I've come to accept this fact in our troubled modern era. Okay? Wudint easy ta do, but I've accepted it. Now, here is the troubling fact of which I am speaking, my friends. Listen to dis. Quite a few *white* citizens protesting as well. Okay? Fellow white people protesting (a momentary pause for emphasis). Protestin' our *good* Mr. David P. Betty. Now, you know what dis is, friends. I'm sure it's already understood, but ima say it anyways. Deez are self-hating white people. Okay? Nah, I'll say it again now. *Self*-hating. Full of shame, they are, and, uh, and, full of guilt, too. Mr. Betty, her, is only trying to protect they own interests and give them pride to say and feel what they really want to say and feel. What they *really* want to say and feel. Not what the liberal media gonna tell dem they should say and feel. Hmm? Mixin' it all up with their PC nonsense about what you, supposedly, *can* and *can't* say. And we know damned well what we really want! To be truly, tuh, tuh to be *heard* in society again. To take the *reins* back and guide this society away from the forces that are leading it off the just and noble path that this great nation was meant to travel on. But them snowflakes. Them Betas. Them libtards. They don't get it."

"They don't get. They're lost," said Ted in a saddened, subdued tone.

"You know, they really is, ain't they?" added Bud. "That's what the problem is, nah. And, and, Mr. Betty now. Mr. David P. Betty, at this previously *peaceful* rally, was talking about the issues that are pertinent to *all* of them. Issues of immediate concern, nah. Nah, what issues you say? Okay (Bud began counting off on his fingers) he wants to keep out undocumented immigrants that are coming up in here to *exploit* this great nation of ours. Okay? To *exploit* it. To willfully *not* assimilate into it. Nah, how's he going to do this? Hmm? Well, he is going to do this through building a twenty-foot, interconnected series of electrical fences around our southern border." Bud paused for his "reflection" before adding, "Something we *should* have done a *long* time ago if you ask me. You know, come to think of it I brought that up over a decade back, now didn't I? Right here!" Bud jutted a finger into his desk. "Right here. Right on this show. Ya done heard it her, first. Maybe Mr. Betty heard me way back then too, huh?"

"Your bud already brought it up, folks," said Walt, in a more moderated tone after Bud's, "voice of reason," had brought him back down to earth.

"Okay, now, den, uh, on to the next subject. He talked about declaring *open war* on all those Muslims over there in, aw hell, I mean, does it really *matter*, folks? Over there in, friggin', Durka Burka Lurka Stan! How bout dat! Huh? How bout dat? Rightfully *declaring war* so we can *engage* by the *rules of war*. I will say that again. Okay? Rotfully. Okay? *Declaring war*...Mmkay?...So's that, uh, so's that we can *engage*...by the *rules*...of war. Okay? Cuz that's what we damn sure need to do, folks, and you know it all too well. And, and, nah, nah, and, war might get *ugly*. Okay?" Bud nodded his head toward Ted and Walt, looking for affirmation on the matter. Ted and Walt nodded their heads back, on cue. Bud continued:

"Ugly. Alright? War might cause a lot of civilian deaths. But you know what? These Muslims, all over there in Durka Burka Amma Dinanajad? They're causing problems not just over there, but throughout the world! I mean, why shouldn't we declare war on *all* those nations over there? They'd kill *any* of us at the drop of a hat. Any which one of us. Men, women, children…babies. *Your* little ones. Your precious little babies. Sweet, precious bundles of love. And you don't know 'bout them Muslims that are over here in our part uh the world, neether. Okay! So, uh, so let's not go discountin' *that!*"

Bud paused a moment, signifying to his audience that they should be letting that last point sink in.

"Okay now? And…and…and, uh, any of them. *Any*…of…them…could do something at any given time. Now you *know* that's true. Nah, don't be lost, folks…Okay?…Don't be lost. Don't you guys go getting *lost* like all those liberal elite sitting in their high towers! Grab yo self a compass or follow a riverbank er somethin' if'n ya don't have one. Look for the seagulls if'n you out at sea. Just don't get lost like they is be. So brainwashed by college professors that they ain't never gonna get they mind back right 'n proper. Okay? Lost in a book, tucked away at some fancy pants college with no idea what's going on outside in the *real* world. With us *true* patriots. Any of these Muslims could attack you and yours, at any time, in any location. That's the truth rot chair, friends. Hell, that's already a happenin'! Do you watch the news! Hmm? Have you watched the *real* news, Marmot News, lately?"

"It's all over the news!" Walt screamed, more obnoxiously again this time. His hard-on relentless.

"Marmot News!" Added Ted, jubilantly though rather gratuitously as it, was more or less, a given that this radio audience also watched, almost solely, Marmot News as opposed to any other news channel (Ted was, as well, under contract to utter the words *Marmot News* at least three times per broadcast. He tried his very best to say it in context when possible).

"Dat right! And, er, by and by, Walt, you need to, uh, you need to settle down, nah. Maybe drink you a little hot chamomile tea or something. Okay, where was we? Where was we be? Okay, rot, that brings me rot chair on to da next issue. And what that is, is, uh, is gun legislation, friends. Now, obviously you need to protect your family against these Muslims, right? Hmm? Gotta protect em, nah. Nah we can bomb the living crap out of 'em overseas anytime they step out of line, and believe me, Mr. David P. Betty is going to do just that, civilian casualties be damned! Heck, they're turning those kids into terrorists someday anyways! Am I rot or am I rot, rot chair? Hmm? Ya know ahm rot bout dat ovuh der rot chair. Already done planted those thoughts and their see-nister ideas to act out when them kids come of age. You want to call a future terrorist a civilian? You go right ahead but you gon' be dead wrong bout dat, friend."

"Dead rot bout dat, son!"

"Walt! Simma! Now then, once again I gotta axe myself what we was be talkin' bout. Uh, well, anyhows, the point is, best to take a proactive approach in general, in mah opinion. And just to round out dat der subject we on, let's not forget about them women. Okay? Them women likely to blow themselves up too. Mmm-hmmm, dat rot. Blow themselves up *real* good! So you go ahead and call them all civilians if'n you want, friend, but I'm not jumping on board that train. No sir."

Bud paused a minute before adding, "You know it's not just Muslim violence. Let's not put all the focus overseas, folks. Okay? Now follow me her, now. We gots problems in our own backyard and you *know* we do. See, you also got this thug culture mentality up in these black and Hispanic neighborhoods. And, and, uh, it done spilling over into the suburbs too, right? There's danger there too. These thugs come in guns a blazin'!" Bud started waving around make-believe guns at no one in particular. "Now don't be dense people. You know this thuggery isn't just in the inner city. It's spreading all over, and into society *as a whole.* Okay? Even affecting us *true* Muricans. Even, sadly, affecting how some of the so-called majority in this country act. Even some of our white kids chimpin' out when they get upset. Mimicking what they see these thugs doin' on the TV."

"True *Muricans*," added Ted, simply to repeat the mantra. Ted was under contract to offer up the words *True Muricans* at least six times per show. Eight to teen was deemed the sweet spot. He was currently at seven.

"*True* Muricans. Dat rot, Ted! And now, uh, and now we got these *thugs*…coming in from Mexico. These, uh, these drug dealin' thugs 'n all. Them, and also, along with these, the, uh, Af-ree-can American thugs. Mexicans coming in, come chopping people up with they machetes, nah. You her bout dis? Day come in tuh town hackin' people up with machetes! Den day bringing in drugs, too. Havin' teenage pregnancies to start the next generation. Afree-can-American thugs having babies with multiple partners and the father not even sticking around to raise them, half the time. Anyways, now we got this thug culture, coming in from different angles, den getting into the mainstream and *warping* the minds of the good folk of this her country. You got to keep the thugs from other countries out, first and foremost, then you got to work on the thugs from round her, too. You know what I say? Hmmm? To deal with all uh this nonsense? Stricter, longer prison sentences. That's what I say."

"And don't forget about capital punishment," Walt chimed in.

"Dat rot! You better recognize. Hmm? You want to run the streets, Mister Tyree DeBrackishash the Third? Hmm? You better be willing to pay the piper when you up and cause trouble, Mr. DeBrackishash the Third. So guess what? Betty say…uh, Mr. David P. Betty say…uh, he say, let's build us *more* prisons and have *stricter* prison sentences for drugs and violent crimes. *Dat* what he say. And you know what? Create more jobs doing it, too. How bout dat? Lot of good labor jobs involved in building prisons, ain't there guys?"

Bud looked toward Ted and Walt who both looked at each other, then nodded their agreement once again. Bud sipped libation and continued:

"We gon make sure these thugs have a home for them waiting when they want to steal, use violence, or incite riots. The communities don't hold 'em accountable. Hmm? The communities don't hold 'em accountable. They think that thug life be just fine. They must! Look at it runnin' rampant. They must! They got guns, people! They are violent because that is what their own culture taught 'em! And they got all the *guns*, too! What you think bout dat? They can come at you and yours wit dem, too! Everybody else afraid to say it. Not your bud! And by the way, Mr. Betty is advocating doubling to tripling the police force in these her violent communities. Because that is one of the few areas where we actually do need bigger government. To *protect* our people. To protect our *True Muricans*."

"Protect them from thuggery, they is," said Ted.

"They is! Dat rot! Okay, so that just goes right into the next point, nah. One naturally follows the other, you see. It all just fits in right together if you *think* about it, like a nice little puzzle (Bud enjoyed linking the act of thought with making gross generalizations, whenever the opportunity allowed). Keep up, okay. Okay now, so the next point is, uh, is this. Nah, how are you going to protect yourselves against all these threats? Hmm?"

Bud paused several seconds to let the point sink in. He slurped Bourbon. This ingestion of fine spirits was worth exactly $283.19, in U.S dollars. The pause ended.

"Okay?...How...are...*you?* How are *you*, my fine audience, gonna protect yourself? You need protection, nah! Okay! No ifs, ands, or buts. I mean, this schmo that we currently have serving as president. Prolly a Muslim, he is. And by and by, folks, there's evidence to support that theory, by the way. I ain't got time to get into right now with all the other tings weeze talkin' bout, but best believe me, it's out there. He's, uh, he's trying to turn us all into weak, socialist sheep. Yes he *is*! I'm sorry, I know a lot of you may not want to hear that, but he is. You know I've said it before. Now...and I'm not afraid to say it, folks...He wasn't even *born* in this country to begin with, and he's tryin' to get rid of our guns altogether. Wants to make you weak. Wants to take away your *protection*! Wants to make you think the government is going to somehow protect you and yours. Isn't that what they did in Socialist Russia? Hmmm? That what they did? *Protected* their citizens? Tarnation, folks, they did whatever in heck they wanted to as soon as the people let 'em all go Communist. Know what they up and done did? Shipped 'em all out to farms in Siberia is what they did! Shipped 'em all off to grow beets out in the Taiga is what they did. Under Stalin!...And, uh, and that's what they tryin' to do her, too!

"Growing a damned beet out int the woods! That what you wanna do?" Walt rightly screamed.

"Now Walt, okay. I understand your frustration, brother, I do, but we got to stay calm her. Calmer heads will prevail. Okay, old buddy? Can't go losin' our heads in times like deez. Okay, now, so what I is sayin' is, uh, is, they ain't gonna protect you and yours. That's the point. All they do is *take* from you and yours. They don't *make* for you and yours, okay? They *take* from you and yours. Raise your taxes. Hmm? Make you pay for so-called entitlements. Hmm? Ahm sorry, okay, but dat just is what is and it be's what it be's. Okay, so now, that's on to the next point again. The next point is, you need *protection* and what better way than to have access to guns without all this rigmarole they' trying to put you through now." Bud counted off to the next topic on another of his fingers:

"Gun laws, folks! The *good*...Mr. David...P...Betty, is trying to make it *easier* for you to obtain a firearm under your second amendment rights. *Not* harder! *Easier*! I mean, now think about it. *Think* about it, now! Just think about if your home is getting robbed (a pause for emphasis). Okay! Or, or, okay...or if you're getting carjacked by one these thugs with his pants hangin' on down his butt and a doo rag up on top uh his head. Even gettin' assaulted if you're at a peaceful event. A peaceful rally? Well, they ain't always peaceful are they!"

"Give us, us peace!" cried out Walt.

"Ooh, ooh, that's really clever there, Walt. Good on ya. Little play on words about that movie with the slave ship. I like that. Nah, nah where was I? Oh yeah, you and yours. You're out at what should be a peaceful, uh, dat peaceful, well-intentioned rally and then *bam*.

"*Bam*, son!" A la Walt.

"Bam!...son...Okay? *Bam*! One of them terrorizers come in shooting up the place with an automatic assault weapon. AK-47. What you gonna do without a gun, huh? What you gonna do? Throw a damned stick at 'em?

"Throw you a stick?" Queried Ted.

"I know. Folks, I know." Bud chuckled audibly over the airwaves. "It's just plum ridiculous, nah. Absolutely ree-dick-uh-liss tryin' to restrict gun laws when you got situations like dis dat you have to account fur in dis her modern age. So, Mr. Betty. Mr. David...P...Betty- God willing- our next president of the Ue-Nigh-Teed States. He is, uh, he is *proposing* an expedited process to acquire guns. An ex-pee-dighted process. Okay? Here's what you gonna do. Follow me on this one, nah. You gonna present a form of identification. Then they gonna run a quick online background check on you, through an approved website. Takes two minutes, tops, friends. Den, if'n you haven't been convicted of more than one violent crime in the past, then that gun is yours," Bud slapped his hand on his desk audibly over the radio waves for added emphasis. *Bam*! Rot den and dair mah friends!"

"Bam, son! *Bam*!" Added Walt, punching imaginary air targets.

"Bam, my friends! Bam boom *pow*! Bam!" Bud started shooting an imaginary rifle at imaginary targets while Walt continued punchin' at them. "Right den and dair! Don't nothing else matter. Okay? Don't nothin' else matter. Heck, nothing else should. That's *your* second amendment right we're talkin' bout, bout chair!"

Bud paused for a while again and took a more modest sip, around $242.16 U.S., or roughly 214.86 Euro at the current exchange rate, worth of Bourbon. One sip of fine libation, the cost of which ran, about, the weekly post-tax paycheck of his average listener. And, as for Bud's listeners, many were, at this very moment in time, now applauding on porches, in their cars or trucks, while out fishing, while at work in their offices, homes, or places of business. All over the country. Majority of them men, but a fairly high number of women too (nearly thirty percent).

Mostly white, but not as much as one might think (around seventy-five percent). Bud moved on to his next point:

"Okay, so now we got the next issue, and that is abortion. Abortion? What kind of bull corn word is that? Let's just call it what it is, huh. Killin' babies! You know some of these liberals. They don't think twice bout it, neither. These college floozies. They go down there to Panama City for spring break (Bud-as a matter of fact- for the past sixteen years, had timed his company "business trips" to Panama City to coincide with college spring break. He brought one hundred grand, cash money, in a small briefcase along on his private jet, each time, for various "requests." Esperanza was not invited). They get knocked up! *Knocked up!* Nah, of course, you see it coming, folks. They get knocked up, come back home. They come back home, nah, then go to one of these her clinics. One of these her clinics that *you* pay for…noble listener…with your hard-earned tax dollars. Then what? Hmm? Then what? Kill that baby like it's a Got-danged mosquito or somethin'. Then just go out and prolly do it again next spring. Or even sooner!"

"Even sooner," posited Ted.

"Definitely sooner," Walt added with a knowing look about about his lascivious smile.

"And we just up and let 'em do dat. What up with that? Dat dayer so *ridikulis*. Dat's the problem rot chair! Let 'em up and, uh, and do it like it ain't no thing. Hmm? With this liberal agenda we've got in place. You got conservatives of course trying to put more restrictions on it, so it ain't as easy as getting to second base on prom night."

"Bunch of liberal B.S!" Effers!" shouted Walt.

"Okay, now, Walt. I'm sorry, you gettin' a little too heated again tonight," said Bud in mock exasperation. "Nah, go on get up out da booth now and calm down. How bout you check out a little early tonight, friend."

Bud had "kicked out" Walt numerous times in the past. Upon his exit, Walt would usually grab one of the willing student interns for "supervision" before having paid sex with them in the women's single bathroom stall. Directly behind the radio sound room, separate from the main bathrooms in the hallway; for privacy. This time Walt quickly strode over to Jessica, who was flashing her new tongue ring at him from behind her sound booth. Jessica, that Bohemian trollop. That night she would earn enough for a month's rent at her Echo Park one-bedroom, sublet condo. Walt surely loved being "kicked off." As he led Jessica into the spacious, jasmine scented bathroom, complete with an enclave containing a large, padded bench, he thought being kicked off might just be his favorite part of the job.

Back in the main radio booth, Bud was contemplating over the airwaves. "Now, let me see. Once again, by the way, I'm sorry bout dat Walt, folks. I'll have a talkin' to him before next show. Don't you worry bout it. You know how he gets, and really…you know…we *all* get that way from time to time, don't we? Ah mean, we all got a little bitta Walt in us, don't we? Sometimes, uh, sometimes things just spills over a little. You know ah get it, too. He's a *passionate* man, folks. But know what? We needs summa that! Don't we, Ted?"

"Wouldn't trade him for the world, Bud."

"Dat rot, Ted. Good 'ol Ted there, folks. Okay now, folks, so now, uh, we've up'n talked about the terrorists, and, and, we've up'n talked about gun laws. Okay? And…uh…, and, ok, we've talked about thug culture and the need for more prisons and stronger prison sentences and den more cops *specifically* in these thug neighborhoods to fight it. Okay? *Specifically* to fight the growing menace of thuggery. Thuggishness, if you will. Okay, so we've talked about immigration, and now, oh yes, we're talking about abortion. So, as you know, the liberals have no problem at all with abortion. You know that, right? No problem with it at all, just go ahead and do it, hmm? Acting like that baby ain't got a soul or a right to life of his or her own. It's selfish! It's outright self-centered. It's immoral. Ahm sorry to say it, it's immoral. It's *wrong*! Folks, it goes against God almighty and I hate to say it, but if you're doing something so heinous in the eyes of God, well you must not really, I mean really *truly* not believe in him. Ain't that right, Ted?"

"You're probably right about that, Bud," confirmed Ted.

"Good 'ol Ted, folks. He knows what's what. I mean, when you see an action like that, so morally wrong, how could you not think this person must lack faith? This person is, prolly, uh, Godless. Prolly Godless, nah. Now, follow me her. You see how that makes perfect sense, people? You see how the action ties itself into the belief? Do you see? Mr. David P. Betty does not want abortion to happen, *period*. He wants to overturn Roe V Wade. Nobody else wants to come out and jess say it. He's going to *do* it! Okay! Back when I was a boy in the fifties, we didn't have that abortion nonsense (Bud's mother had a previous abortion, in college, conducted in secret -with only her mother knowing- that almost killed her via profuse internal bleeding. She and her mother came to an agreement that it was never to be talked about in the larger family). Okay? Didn't have that back in them days. Back then we simply had the child and we made it work. That's what we did back then. Okay? Yuh had the child. Okay? Yuh made it work. Made things work and now we're up 'n losing that ability. Didn't just sit back and whine about things we didn't like or didn't think we could handle like these kids do nowadays. So, uh, so David P. Betty will *overturn* Roe V Wade, and den, den, we will be better as a society for it. Hands down. End uh story!" Bud smacked his desk for emphasis.

Bud finished the last of his Bourbon with a mock cheers into the air, before downing what remained of his ultra-high-end drink of choice. He sat back in his chair and folded his arms in front of his formless, two sacks of drooping cottage cheese, chest, resting atop his bulbous abdomen that sank over into his crotch region as he flayed his legs to the side. He took a moment to reflect on this afternoon's broadcast and felt that it could truly go down as one of his greatest radio moments. He had spoken plainly about the issues. He had covered the bases, and he did not hold back.

The topics were always- more or less- the same and in line with his main week to week themes. Guns, religion, minorities and freeloaders (the latter two almost invariably went together, whether consciously or not), liberal mentality and its presumed ties to Stalinist Russia, women's issues, protecting the true and rightful American culture, and- in all areas- prescribing precisely how to both think and feel about it. He had touched on everything he wanted to touch on in less than ten minutes flat, by the conclusion of the day's show. Distilled to its essence with a honed craft. He reflected on the immense satisfaction it brought him, much as he would with the rarest and finest spirits that he had come across only at the most serendipitous moments in his life; never knowing exactly when that would be. Good fortune could be that way. Simultaneously unexpected and fleeting when it occurred.

As Bud reflected, he tended to lend little, if any, thought to the real-world consequences of what he did every day. Five days a week, his words and his rhetoric had, over forty plus years in radio, begun to devolve from a fringe-not particularly serious entertainment- to being used as political fact and fodder for discourse by his growing horde of listeners. Tens of millions of Thanksgivings, Christmases, Fourth of July barbecues, Easter brunches, progressively more often now involved tense and heated arguments where family members who had, historically, gotten along (or at least stayed relatively civil) would fall apart as his loyal listeners would fiercely regurgitate *their Bud's* political views and often come to see, with disdain, those who disagreed with them.

True American radio encouraged what they liked to call *heated discourse* for the sake of helping the lost liberals of society to understand supposed real issues. Like members of a cult or sect looking to increase their membership and hence their influence. Tens of thousands of family falling-out moments had occurred because of his encouraging freely going after those "pussy footing liberals." Brothers who would come to no longer talk to each other. Fathers and sons. Mothers and daughters. Previously lifelong friends. People who had been close for decades cutting off all ties over these communication disasters that Bud actively fueled and encouraged. A society both increasingly and more strongly divided as a result.

Bud almost never thought about such consequences. That is, not beyond a brief and fleeting feeling at rare times that it could; theoretically and on only a relatively small scale, cause some level of harm. The divide was constantly picking up steam as the vitriol escalated and his ratings went up, directly in conjunction. And the money. Oh, that money kept rolling in, baby doll. Growing exponentially from what once barely afforded him a cramped and dated one-bedroom apartment in Reseda. His personal rewards continued to amass in quantity, quality, and variety, to appease his ever more discerning tastes.

He began now with his wrap up. A self-satisfied and contented denouement. "Okay, my true patriots. We have covered the main areas of Mr. Betty's platform, but there is much, *much* more that we are going to get into come tomorrow's broadcast. Believe you me, my friends. Election time is only four months away, yuh her. Let's get behind our noble candidate, the good Mr. David…P…Betty, and, uh, and get out there and vote, nah. Also- and I don't want to get your hopes up too much, now- but there *is* a good chance we will have our candidate joining us over the airwaves at some point. You know, he said he would be a guest on the show next time he's in town. Mr. Betty, if you're listening right now, we're gonna hold you to that," Bud chuckled.

"Holding you to it, Mr. Betty. Come one over sometime," added Ted.

"You know, I believe he will, Ted. I do believe he will. Okay, my true Muricans. I am blessed to have you as my audience each and every day her on True Murican radio. Bless you all. Bless your angel hearts and your families. Bless your little babies in they cribs. Bless this great country of ours through all its recent trials and tribulations and all this liberal media bias and propaganda. We have a chance to take this country in the direction it needs, so desperately, to go in. To get back to where it once was and we will get there. We *will* get there, my friends. I bid you all a fine afternoon. Get home safe from your hard day's work.

Crack open a cold one on me. I'll say it again. May God bless this great country of ours. We will be seeing you all again tomorrow, same time. On behalf of myself, and good ol' Ted and Walt, good night everyone and God bless."

Bud took a moment to himself now, to bask in the essence of a broadcast masterfully executed from start to finish. An appeased nod and then, slowly, he began to detach himself from his chair. The sweat made his shirt stick to the back of it, which emanated a muffled peeling noise as he ascended. He lumbered over to Ted, slowly, and Ted always noted that even this short distance walk looked, for Bud, so disproportionately pained and strenuous.

"Great show, buddy, one of our best I think," said Bud, on his way over to say goodbye to Ted for the day.

"Was a real pleasure, old friend," said Ted as he stood up from his chair. "We'll see you tomorrow, Then drinks with me and the missus on Friday?"

"Wouldn't miss it, ol' buddy. I'll bring the bourbon, in exchange for one of those fine Cuban cigars you smuggled in from Vancouver."

Both parties chuckled heartily. Bud gave Ted, his decades long friend, a hearty bear hug and a pat on the back. Ted was his truest friend, no doubt. The only one in his life that just sat back and let him talk, no questions asked. On the set and off the set, too. No agendas. No bones to pick. No bullshit. He could be himself around Ted and Ted never judged him- just sat there silently for the most part, with a contented look and adding an occasional comment here and there (just like on the show)- sipping his drink and steady puffing his stogies out on the back deck overlooking the Hollywood hills. Ted was a good, simple man. The kind of man that you rarely found anymore with these passive aggressive, self-righteous, over-educated liberals.

Ted, for his part, did possess some, albeit, impalpable form of affection for Bud. He thought he was a blow hard, to be sure, but he came up with a good point every now and then, somewhere within the pith. He was, of course, the boss, and no getting around that. Ted had become obligated to spend time outside of work with him some years back, though, he had grown to tolerate it more so, over time, and even mildly enjoying it on the odd occasion.

Bud started his shuffle out the room, past his various team members. He gave a few nods and a quick salute to no one in particular, upon his exit. As he walked past the women's bathroom, near the private elevator down to the underground parking lot, he heard moaning and heavy grunting emanating from behind the locked door. Bud formed a portly fist and slammed it into the door a few times. Keep it down in there Walt! Your wife just got to the studio and she's out there a lookin' for ya!" Bud heard muffled cussing noises and zipping sounds now. He walked on to the awaiting open elevator doors and chuckled under his breath, "Shit, son. You simple sumbitch. We'll all be laughin' bout it come tomorrow."

Chapter III

Dr. John

"I know you don't believe me, Dr. John, but I saw what I saw, and I know she did it. It was my favorite hand knit turtleneck, Dr. John! She took it! She took it, and then she wore it all around town like a floozy, and she stretched it all out. She *ruined* it, Dr John! She ruined it because she's a big meatball and it doesn't fit her. You should see her. Oh Gawd, and she is brown like a meatball, too. To think about her wearing my best sweater? Oh, it makes me so upset. She looked like a meatball dipped in marinara with it on, I bet. I'd like to throw a meatball right at her." Mrs. Noretti made a hasty throwing gesture with her right arm. "*Plop!*" Now she tapped the bridge of her nose. "Right between her eyes, Dr. John!" She continued tapping for emphasis. "Right there above her jezebel nose."

Dr. John Edward Gavilan, Clinical Psychologist, was rubbing his eyebrows between his thumb and index finger as he listened, half-heartedly, to a variation on a story he'd heard from Mrs. Noretti at least a couple dozen times by now. He had started the day with a mild headache, though it had escalated to moderate, bordering on severe, despite two bottles of water within the last couple of hours, and an interlude in his car listening to blue grass music and nibbling a late lunch; some mini dark chocolate bars that he'd confiscated from the nurse's desk at Peach Grove Senior Living.

Dr. John exhaled, slowly and patiently, preparing himself to go over his part in this perpetual, absurd dialogue, yet again.

"Okay, now let me get this straight, Mrs. Noretti. Your twenty-something, overweight nurse's assistant broke into your closet- your closet that you secured with a steel cable and pad lock." Dr John pointed toward the security contraption he had just described. A steel cable wrapped sungly around and between the handles of Mrs. Noretti's folding closet door, with a hefty pad lock suspended in the middle around loops in the cable wire. "Then, after that, she stole your favorite homemade red knit turtleneck sweater. Then she wore it on a date or something of that nature. Then she returned it, stretched out and ruined, to your bedroom closet."

"Yes, Dr. John," replied Mrs. Noretti, cautiously relieved that he'd understood. "That is *exactly* what happened."

Mrs. Noretti was in her mid-eighties and if anyone looked like a meatball, it was her. A meatball with enough make up on at one time to last most women a week and a half. Perched on her faded, floral couch she was fanning herself with her right hand. She had grown heated. Presently, she gave a hesitant and half-hearted smile, hoping that Dr. John was understanding her and wouldn't give her any guff about it like those lazy, front office hoe bags who never believed her and never did a damned thing about this thievery. By Jonas, come to think of it, they never seemed to leave their enclaves; except to pay for their lunchtime pizza delivery, which they scarfed down like lumberjacks despite their sedentary state.

"Don't get me started on them," Mrs. Noretti thought to herself. Bunch of office butt having, fat hens. And that Puerto Rican? That booty-shaking floozy was going to get hers if she got Doctor John on her side. Which reminded Mrs. Noretti to add:

"She's Puerto Rican, too." She leaned in closer to Dr. John and whispered, "they steal, you know." She reclined back in her chair, waving a stern pointed finger waved around in front of her face, "steal *everything*. Just like the Gypsies did. I had to have my eye on them when I was a young girl in Tuscany, believe you me, Doctor. You know what they would do? If your family went on vacation, they'd set up in your front yard and you'd have a heck of a time getting them to leave. They might even put a curse on you if you gave them guff. And those curses are *real*, Dr. John! Why, my old friend, Francesca…"

"Okay, Mrs. Noretti," Dr John interrupted, having heard plenty for the time being. "I hear what you're saying. Here's the thing that I'm trying to understand. First of all, that CNA does not work in your room, or even your floor of the building. Second off, it's late July, and it's been over ninety degrees and humid for the last five days now. I'm wondering why she would choose to wear a thick, woven, wintertime turtleneck sweater in this heat. Third (Dr. John pointed to Mrs. Noretti's closet door now)- and once again, mind you- you have a plastic-coated, reinforced-steel cable wrapped around the handles of your bifold closet door; with an industrial strength padlock. In addition," Dr John pointed at Mrs. Noretti's neckline, "you wear the only key to it on your necklace. Always. Including when you shower and when you sleep." Dr. John throw both hands up in the air in confusion. "I'm wondering how she got in there in the first place. I'm wondering how she then *also* found a way to open the padlocked door, yet again- while the key remains on your neck, mind you- to return the sweater. Can you help me to make sense of this, Mrs. Noretti?"

"I don't know!" Exclaimed Mrs. Noretti, appearing slighted that Dr. John seemed to be, just possibly, doubting her on this one. "I thought *you* were the Doctor. Why don't *you* tell *me*?" Mrs. Noretti placed her hands firmly on her sides, tipped her head to one side and shot Dr. John a quizzical glance. "You know, maybe she's a gypsy herself. You ever think about that, Doctor?"

Dr. John began to rub his eyebrows again, along with most of his ocular cavity, from the two-chair dinette table on which he was seated across from Mrs. Noretti's couch; nestled within her small studio apartment with kitchenette. The headache was officially severe now, bordering on migraine status. He wondered if an afternoon iced coffee might help. He looked up toward her wall clock. Mercifully, his time with her was about up for the day. She was one of the clients he saved for last, because he knew he damned sure wouldn't have the will left in him to meet with anybody afterward. He began his wrap up.

"Mrs. Noretti, I'm sorry, but we're going to have to pick up on this next week. So, I'll tell you what I'm going to do." John pointed at himself. "*I'm* going to think about this. Okay?" John pointed toward Mrs. Noretti. "*You're* going to think about it. Okay? And we'll both just, kind of think about this together and we'll try to get to the bottom of it next time, alright. Just, let's try to be open minded and let's *consider*. Okay? I'm saying, let's just consider, that there can be various possibilities in a case like this. I'm going to repeat that, Mrs. Noretti. *Various* possibilities. Let's keep that in mind because I think that's important. I'll be back next week, and we can continue to process this, okay?"

"Okay, Dr John," replied Mrs. Noretti, "but if you see that no-good trollop, you tell her I know for darned sure that it was her and that I'm going to tell the administrator about what she did. Better yet, I'm going to call the police again. They better believe me this time. And she's still going to get up close and personal with a flying meatball next time they serve Italian food in the dining hall!" She added, "I'd throw a Swedish meatball at her too, if we have those. I'm not picky with what type of meatball. That reminds me, I'm going to look on the dinner schedule now, Dr. John." Mrs. Noretti shuffled through a stack of papers sitting next to her on the couch. "What day is Swedish meatball day? I know it's coming up. Oh yes, here's the weekly menu…"

"We'll talk about that next time," Dr John added as he began to walk toward her door, on the way out from his last client of this late Friday afternoon. "Wait until we can talk about it some more until you do anything, okay? I want to add that I don't recommend throwing meatballs. Just in general, in my professional opinion, that is, I don't feel it tends to accomplish anything productive." Dr. John waved pleasantly. "Have a wonderful night, Mrs. Noretti. Always nice to see you."

"Good to see you, Dr. John. Even though I'm a little worried you don't fully believe me, I'm glad there's someone here who actually listens to me."

Dr. John exited. He walked down the long, drab gray hallway- adorned with random paint smudges. These existed compliments of various electronic wheelchairs driven into them too hastily. He hung a quick right at the exit sign toward the staircase back entryway leading to his parked car, a Lincoln MKZ. His first higher-end vehicle that he was, just now in his late 30s, able to afford. His friends would poke fun of the car as a symbol of flaunting his money; a standard Midwestern no-no. They seemed to feel that he and his wife Nora had "made it," as they had more amenities than most their age. He felt compelled to remind them that he still parked that car on the street, still used quarters every time he did a load of laundry, and still had a crushing amount of student loan debt the equivalent of a second mortgage. If that was living the American dream, the dream was pretty compromised from how he'd envisioned it.

Dr. John fell into his low seat, push started the car, and drove home. Home, for him, was Evanston, Illinois. A generally well-off college town just north of Chicago. A blessed twenty miles and a lifetime away from Peach Grove and the dull, uniform 1950s ranch houses and apartment complexes of the west Chicago suburbs. Their faded, chocolate brown decks perennially stuffed with unused bikes and largely forgotten plastic children's toys. Mostly indistinguishable towns all, set up along both sides of traffic packed four-lane roads.

Peach Grove was one of eight facilities John went to weekly, as a private consultant for a small group practice that worked with the elderly. He also worked with the cognitively impaired (mentally retarded was no longer the appropriate term, though most people, ironically, still used its abbreviation MR, which no one seemed to mind). Once a week, he worked with students with learning disabilities from within the confines of a small office, complete with a window view of a red brick wall and a fake plant sprouting out from the bottom half of a plastic coconut. The fake plant was tinged brown, in various places, and sagged pathetically. He would, from time to time, observe this bleak plant, during breaks between sessions, and wonder, who in the name of sweet baby Jesus, would create a fake plant that looked as though it were dying? And who, then, decided to mass produce it, nestled as it were within a fake coconut, and sell it in stores? Why did this thing exist? How had it ended up on his desk? He could not say, but existential quandaries were frequently induced in conjunction with it all.

Dr. John was doing alright though, he had to admit, and lived comfortably. However, the starter castle, country club member image of a Doctor his clients seemed to have, his life was not. Northshore Chicago was ludicrously expensive. He had grown up in a small town and when his small-town friends asked him about real estate, he told them to look at any house in their neighborhood, estimate its price, then add a zero to that price tag to know what it would go for where he lived. Earlier that day he paid eight dollars and forty-three cents for a modestly sized lemon poppy seed muffin and large iced Americano coffee, at his local "artisan bakery." He was a sucker for that word, *artisan*. Artisan muffin. Artisan Mochaccino. Artisan hot dog. Artisan double ply toilet paper. It was a magical word that made the price of something double, sometimes triple (recent case-in-point- artisan Costa Rican street taco). And if you added the words *small batch*? Oh, then there was another price increase to go with that. He wondered presently if he could bill himself as an *Artisan* Psychologist- better yet- *Artisan Small Batch* Psychologist. Triple the price for a supposedly better service. Worth a try.

John unwound on the trek home as best he could, considering the hasty and illogical driving choices typically seen during metro Chicago rush hour. He drove with the window rolled down and the sunroof open- preferring this to AC- the disparity between that and atmospheric conditions this hot seemed to make him feel slightly nauseous; his body seeming to go into a sort of mini-shock every time he left said air-conditioned locale to enter the Louisiana swamp that Chicago could be in mid-summer.

Chicago, the city his masochistic self-loved with a passion ever since he moved down, for Grad school, from Michigan's remote Upper Peninsula thirteen years prior. The city where, considering wind chill and heat index, temperatures could vary by upwards of one hundred fifty degrees within a calendar year. Ditka. Bulls. Cubbies. Hawks. Never put mustard on a hot dog. No "dry" Italian beef. Summer festivals packing every weekend from Mid-May through late September. Asses and elbows and swamp ass but you went anyway because you could take it when you lived here. Not just take it, enjoy it and year after year come back for more after telling yourself *never again*. Outdoor patios open in the middle of winter. Just sit your ass next to a heat lamp and eat your Buffalo wings quick before the goddamned ranch sauce froze solid, like the parts of your fingers not suffering the alternative of being scalded by hot oil. Dr. John no longer had working nerve endings in the tips of his fingers, compliments of wintertime Buffalo wings. Cold fingers don't mind the burn; even welcome it.

Dr. John's mind grew paradoxically relaxed as he made his drive through the controlled chaos of mid rush hour on this late Friday afternoon. The crazy went up a notch on Fridays with people trying to catch the last fifteen minutes of happy hour, or to get in early to the hipster recommended restaurants before the seven o'clock crowds hit and kept them jam packed from then until the kitchen closed. The key was to simply accept it and not be too surprised or, worse yet, indignant. To view the snail's pace traffic backups as an opportunity to listen to music and settle in, rather than bitch and flap your arms around at people who forced you to slow down quicker than you would have preferred to. The average commute was well over an hour a day, so what other reasonable choice was there? To let it upset you was a near guaranteed recipe for developing a midlife heart condition, especially with a diet often laden with various ethnic sausages, craft beers, and deep-dish pizzas.

Dr. John found himself considering his work as a therapist this afternoon; how it had left him less fulfilled than the idealized notions he'd had of it as a grad student. He had pictured (as surely most of his peers did also) the private office overlooking Michigan Avenue or State Street, helping the working well- the elites of this great city- to become the idealized versions of themselves that only he in his wise, steady-handed patience and unwavering will, could help unveil through their work together. He thought of the portrayals of the therapists he'd seen in movies. Self-sacrificing and tired, though ever-present and somehow having an insight available always- something that could be a game changer- having the power to alter, for the better, no less than the remainder of a life's path.

The reality of the day to day grind was that no one could indefinitely function in that way. Much like the love interest in romantic comedies couldn't possibly be of perpetual intrigue and life-consuming desire. But, in the movies, they could end at a peak. A romantic pop song and credits. End it before a marriage eighteen years in with the burgeoning realization of sagging bodies, mediocre-fated children, and myriad unrealized life expectations. Twenty-something protagonists in the throes of a fresh love with endless potential was much preferred to most audiences over a love unfolding in time. One that included the inevitable, poorly anticipated life challenges that extended well past the honeymoon.

The reality of his work was- one might say- a full castor oil dose of reality. A steady office just one day a week- overlooking an El train to the west and a faded, red brick façade to the south. The other days Dr. John found himself working in floating private to semi-private spaces; whatever might be available at a particular day and time. Sometimes it was an empty conference room. Sometimes it was no more than a pair of chairs in a remote corner of a warehouse; where he counseled the mentally challenged at workshop programs. When he went to visit his geriatric clients at nursing homes or assisted living centers, it was usually on the end of a bed, or, if he was lucky, an old, worn in easy chair often accompanied by various sized, various hued stains of unknown origin. Hopefully, it wouldn't be damp and vaguely ureic smelling.

Dr. John had previously worked with children. He rarely did anymore after finding out that most of his child clients were simply acting out amidst incredibly dysfunctional families. Abusive parents, alcoholics, functioning drug addicts, distant and minimally caring parents, dropping off their child to meet with the Psychologist with a "fix my kid," mentality readily apparent in their words, their expressions, their expectations. Him being asked to convince the child of what *they* needed to change, with their parents minimally (or not at all) acknowledging how they contributed driving their child to the state they were in (let alone most of the parents then going on to do anything about it on their end). Precocious eight-year-olds who could already sense the burgeoning hypocrisy of being asked to change while their parents-who were, often, fucking up royally- accepted little to no responsibility for needing to change themselves.

John didn't last too long in that realm, though retained a penchant for helping teens and young adults. He saw a few in outpatient practice. At least, for them, the horizon held a potential break from the dysfunctional system they were in. If, that is, he could help them down the path toward self-sufficiency and being able to function in society. That was, really, in a nutshell, the general goal of mental health services. Just helping people function.

Dr. John found he much preferred working with the elderly over kids. He preferred it over working-well adults who came in with their layers of bullshit. Layers like a prized Vidalia onion at a Georgia state fair. An onion comprised of bullshit layers. A bullshit onion.

The elderly didn't tend to have as much time, or as much of a prerogative, to convince themselves of their own B.S. They simply didn't have the energy anymore. Much like working with teens, Dr. John appreciated the soothing freshness of simple, unadulterated honesty. It fueled him through days at nursing homes that could be challenging in ways he had never fully anticipated. Depressing atmospheres overrun with inflated and absurdly high-salaried, bean counting administrators. Forgotten places where he would walk the hallways and often smell the familiar combination of excrement and industrial cleaner. The latter mingling with the former, like somebody defecated in a bucket of watered-down bleach.

Making work more difficult, he couldn't find any competent or motivated interns to help him out as of yet- for more than a few weeks at a time anyway- in this consulting gig he had chosen. It was, for reasons he could readily understand, given what he'd experienced. The money was pretty good, though; aided by a steady caseload that were reliably *there,* if only by default. It helped him to feel as though someday he may actually get ahead on his student loans and build a financial safety net of sorts. Someday, he told himself, he would have the equivalent of just one, as opposed to two mortgages, once the two thousand plus per month (half of that interest) loan payments would finally piddle their way to a welcome end. Presidential hopefuls kept talking about how they would help people like him with this. John's financial advisor told him best not to bet on that.

Presently, Dr. John pulled up to his vintage condo, your typical urban, three-story brick number. He found street parking just outside the courtyard. His wife, Nora, was home, judging by the dining room lights being on (she liked to do her work notes at the dining table). It was a first- floor walkup, facing the street, and he could see the familiar mug of his dog- a cockapoo named Toby- looking down on him from his perch atop the living room couch.

Toby would bark unrelentingly when he heard John lock his car door with his remote key; familiar and attuned to this particular sound. He would bark the entirety of John's trek up the single set of stairs to open the back door adjoining the kitchen. Here, Toby would be waiting- his entire posterior wiggling side to side with the momentum of his rapidly wagging tail. Waiting to be picked up and held, ready to lick John for upwards of a minute straight. John would usually just let the dog do it, even if his breath reeked of something he would not want to guess. John was apt to just let people and animals go on with whatever it was they were doing-as absurd as it might seem- as long as it wasn't creepy or causing any harm. Sometimes, whatever works is what you need to do. After a particularly copious lick fest, he lowered Toby back to the floor and fed him an organic salmon doggy wafer; as he did nearly every day after work. He used to feed him one, just every now and then, but eventually Toby began to sit in a designated spot near the kitchen where John stored the treats, sporting a hopeful, pleading look, complete with holding one arm up and letting the paw dangle as though he were injured and helpless. John now fed him a treat every single day after work as his dog, he now realized, had successfully trained him to feed him treats everyday after work. Nora would kiss him once after Toby's excitement finally died down.

"How was work?" Asked Nora.

"Mrs. N was acting up again."

"Oh, sweet sassey molassey. The one who thinks she's having her plastic jewelry stolen.

"Yup."

"You should just mess with clients like that. I would. Tell her that there's a robber who comes over there specifically to take the plastic jewelry made at activity time, to sell on the black market for the big bucks."

"You have no idea how many times I have impulses like that. But, as long as I don't act on them, right. We looking at real estate tonight?" John asked with a tempered optimistic tone.

"Yes we are, honey buns. I found a couple nice places, but they're a little out of our price range. Maybe they'll come down a bit, though. The property taxes aren't too bad. Around 14k a year. That's doable, right?"

"I think so. It's tax deductible at least."

John and Nora went to sit down on their living room couch and, respective computers in hand, began searching the real estate offerings of Evanston. An average two thousand square foot home in a nicer area of the city cost about seven hundred thousand, with thirteen to sixteen thousand per year in property taxes alone. When John and Nora had seen one in their general price range recently they noticed it only tended to stay on the market for a day or two before somebody snatched it up, usually at full list price-sometimes higher due to bidding wars. The homes on the higher end of the market, one million plus, tended to go for about what they were worth, or somewhat lower. For couples like them who didn't have that kind of money, however, the competition was fierce. People in their price range often ended up paying more than the home was valued at, simply because they tended to have few other options to choose from when a home went for sale that they could afford in the first place.

This whole concept upset John tremendously, as it seemed tantamount to people being punished for not making more money than they did. Much like they were for credit cards and loans. Those with higher incomes were, in fact, rewarded with much nicer homes going for at, or below, their value on the market because they simply didn't have the level of competition for them. Those with a more down to earth income would fight for a much smaller home in a nicer area, or to live on the fringes, in "cozy" mid-century ranch homes near the freeway. Just to have the opportunity to go to the same schools and public parks.

John invariably felt pressured to earn ever more, work ever harder. Maybe then, he could get them a little above their range. This pressure was palpable throughout the area, leading to many of those homes seeming almost perpetually dark and unoccupied, as its owners worked absurdly long hours just to afford them. Even then, many had little money to do much besides stay at home, with sparse furniture and no budget to go out. "House poor," they called that, and it is was a dirty little secret around here that a lot of people were living that way solely to retain the image of being well off.

John wanted to get Nora and himself into a nicer home that was, proportionately, much more reasonably priced so that they wouldn't have to furnish it with milk crates and folding chairs. Maybe ten more billable hours a week could do it, along with some help from Nora's parents, who had graciously offered assistance with the down payment. Very few of their friends, or people their age in general, had that card to play.

"I'm going to try to work more, for now," said John. "I mean, I'm still pretty young."

"Thirty-eight is young?" Joked his thirty-three-year old wife.

"Thirty-eight is young?" John said in a shrill, mockingly irritated voice. "Yes it *is*!...smart ass. For the next few years I'm thinking maybe I'll put in some more hours while I can. Ten years from now I won't have as much energy to do it. But I do now. If I can put in more hours, we can afford a better home at a fairer price. Live in a nicer part of town, with better schools when we have our kids." John thought about kids now. They were planning a family, and just recently, Nora in her mid-thirties, and John in his late 30s, finally felt like they were in a position to get their feet under them, get a home, and be financially stable enough to make this kid thing work. Now it was also looking like they might have conception difficulties to look forward to thanks to a recent diagnosis of a chromosomal abnormality on John's side. Nora liked to kid that it explained a lot.

"That's great, boo. Can you fit it in?" asked Nora.

"I'm going to compress my schedule into longer days, I think, then try to add another day with my old Post-Doc supervisor, Dr. Tobin. She called the other day. She said she could use some help at her community outpatient practice, McCarver, down in Chicago Lawn where I worked back in grad school and Postdoc. She can pay me a flat salary of fifty bucks an hour for supervising some of her practicum students and taking on a couple outpatients. That's four hundred a week, about another twenty thousand over a year. I think I'm going to take her up on it."

Tobin was the closest thing to a mentor that Dr. John had ever had. A late middle-aged OG hippie, who'd never lost the idealism of her generation. Who never moved out to the suburbs, bought a starter castle, got a beamer and became jealous of what her neighbor had that she didn't. The Jones generation stereotype, she was not. Working for her, part time, had helped Dr. John to get by, during and directly after Grad School, and he never lost his appreciation to her for that. Taking him on and taking a chance on him as a comparatively undistinguished grad student among the hundreds to choose from in the area. The work helped him to pay for his own apartment. It also helped him get by without taking out too many graduate-plus loans with their higher interest rates that would have made his debt balloon even more. John shook his head slowly and thoughtfully, and added:

"I'd like to help her. Honestly, I'd like to work in the area again." These thoughts comingled and seemed to tell him this was the right choice.

Nora was proud of him for this, though worried about it as well. She remembered stories that he used to tell her. Stories about working with Dr. Tobin. He would tell her about travelling through the roughest neighborhoods of Chicago, where Tobin had connections with community outpatient practices. She remembered him telling her about having to take shelter in the inner hallways of his offices; when gunshots erupted directly outside. He told her about schools he was in having to go on lockdown because of an armed robber, or a gangbanger on the run after an area shooting. Cop cars cruising by, at forty miles, an hour through alleyways with their sirens blaring.

There were stories about shooting victims. Like one time where John's coworkers relayed to him there'd been a murder within a block of where he was working. Another time where a body of a murdered gang affiliate was collected around dusk; just an hour or two before John got to the office.

Stories of bullet holes in the windows and even inner walls of various schools he went to, to counsel children as young as six. How one of those children, DeMarcus, used to run his pinky finger around the concave circle of a bullet hole in John's makeshift office. Doing this when he was nervous, like a tic. It seemed to relax him. Nora remembered the boy's first name and had a visual image of the child. She pictured him as a sweet, quiet kid, beginning to understand the dangers of his world over which he had little control, though still trying to live as a boy would want; with a sense of wonder and an openness to his surroundings. She imagined the therapeutic focus of making a circle with his finger and wondering if he ever thought about what had made that hole and why. Maybe something as simple as a minor disagreement growing too heated. Rage from a less tangible element, much larger and more ethereal, taken out on the one presently at hand.

The one who was, simply, there in physical form at the time. There to have that rage taken out on them.

"I'm so proud of you for doing this, John," she said after a moment; a level of concern, though, in her expression. "Just be careful. Don't stay out late to do work at the office. Bring your paperwork home. Stay on the main roads. Stay in the office and make sure you have a parking spot reserved right next to the building." She thought about that for a moment and added, "you need to request that. She needs to do that for you. It's gotten worse down there, even just these last few years."

"I will," said John, grateful for his wife and for her understanding of the importance the situation held for him. It was an opportunity to provide. An opportunity to help a mentor- at least for a few hours a week- as he used to, in an area in which the word "underserved" had been attached for decades and would, surely, continue to be, for countless decades more.

These were areas of the city where he never felt he helped out very much in relation to the sheer magnitude of what those kids were up against. Despite that- during the times that he did feel he was able to make a difference- he was immensely humbled and appreciative to see that he had come up with ways, in conjunction with another human being, to override the hopelessness of their environment to eventually, maybe, even thrive using that strength to navigate most anything and everything else that life could throw at them from there on out. It was a difficult tipping point to make it to, but once it tipped. Well, at those times, it made for the most significant moments of reward he had ever experienced in his work.

John always felt that an individual who could come from such circumstances to a point of even relative success had discovered something so powerful that it seemed, almost, superhuman to him. Like something you could not even hope to comprehend because its origin was so elusive and its method so multifaceted in its execution. A balance between two worlds that seemed entirely at odds with each other somehow being achieved when a hopeless and traumatic upbringing could evolve into hope, fulfillment, even a level of peace, despite it all.

"I'll give her a call in the morning," said John presently. "Thanks for being supportive. It's going to be more fulfilling than a usual day I have right now, anyway. I think I'll be able to accomplish more. I'll be careful, of course, and I won't be beholden to it. If it's too dangerous, or if there's any trouble, I'll put in my notice. It's just a choice, after all. We don't need this money, but I think we both can agree it'll help."

"I love you, Gavvy," said Nora, and kissed his right cheek.

"I love you, lemon muffin bunny," said John (that was his preferred pet name for his wife. That, or LMB for short). He didn't know where the phrase came from originally, anymore. It made no sense whatsoever. But he started saying it a few years back and she didn't seem to mind, so it dug in for the long haul like so many dust bunnies under the kitchen fridge.

"You're okay with this, right?" Asked John.

"Your face is okay with this," replied Nora. A random *your face* or *your mom* joke was always close at hand with Nora. It didn't matter who you were or where you were. She would bust it out at random at people who were near strangers. John loved her for this and her many other quirks (One of his other favorites. She liked to randomly surprise him with a slap on his flat white ass. Being in public did not deter her in the least).

For now, he knew that she really was okay with it. He cracked his knuckles and got back to his computer to look at real estate, sitting adjacent to her on the couch. He came across a nice vintage brick home. Some ivy along the side and front. Nice little front porch with a hanging love seat, maybe big enough for two. This looks quaint, he thought. John scrolled down to look at the price tag for the eighteen hundred square foot home. Seven hundred and twenty-five thousand. Holy shitballs!

Chapter IV

Kenilworth

He stood on the corner of 59th and Lowe. Englewood neighborhood, Chicago. He wore his favorite shirt; a faded, pink polo with a patch that portrayed a man playing polo atop a horse. There were a couple of, just minimally visible (but only if you looked closely and squinted your eyes), oil stains on the top left corner of the front of the shirt, toward the left shoulder. This was the reason he had gotten the shirt so cheap. Just four dollars, at a local secondhand store, where he had been shopping for school clothes with his grandmother, Lorene. He had worn it so frequently that it began to show permanent, darker colorations under the arms; the result of pit stains over the last couple of years. Sweating occurred unceasingly this time of year. His grandmother's (he thought of her as grandmother, though she always insisted he called her grandma as it was less rigidly formal) house did not have air conditioning. There were just a couple of window fans meekly circulating the sweltering, midsummer air, of their 2nd floor walkup. Grandmother's electric bill for an AC unit could make her pass out much quicker than the heat, she would always say.

They lived in a duplex. Over the years, its crumbling foundation had shifted so that the floors leaned six inches lower on the south-facing side of the building. Outside, tall grass and untended, absurdly large weeds (some ambiguously resembling bizarre, little trees) had taken over the backyard, which was flanked on three sides by a jagged, rusted-out fence. Toward the back, cracked concrete chunks jutted out at various, craggy angles. Grandmother said these were once parking spaces for the unit owners' cars, though she hadn't known of any one in the unit owning a car in the forty-three years she had been a tenant. She had seen transients, who lived in their cars, parking there for a few days up to a few weeks, from time to time, but not of late. She'd seen countless young men, women, and families come and go from the units themselves. Had often smelled the familiar musky, skunklike scent of reefer, and- more so in the last couple decades- the acrid smell of crack pipes and heroin cooked in spoons; to be injected into the arms of those who'd given up caring for just about anything, foremost, their own lives. A last remnant of their caring having occurred before, and in conjunction with, the time in which they chose to use that Devil-made poison.

On the corner, the shirt he was wearing had started to pill somewhat, in parts. Though, like the oil stains and the armpit discoloration, you had to look closely to see it. The boy wore one hundred percent polyester pleated khakis. Wrinkle free, or so they liked to say. Five dollars, they were, also secondhand. This pair only had a missing button. Grandmother sewed one on, no problem, and the color matched it pretty well.

They took the El to Evanston or Wilmette from time to time. Rich white, East Indian and Asian people on the north shore donated all sorts of clothes to nearby secondhand stores for any minor flaw, often because they simply didn't want to bother fixing it. Or, maybe, it had grown out of current style in their minds. Grandmother would always say she hoped they didn't waste other things like they did clothes. How it was a damned, sinful shame when people couldn't learn how to fix things or would waste money that they didn't have to, because they were too lazy to put a little work into it. She talked about how privileged a person was who did this and how most didn't even realize this as such. A certain type of sin was inherent in it.

Grandmother was smart. So was mother, before her voices started. She still could be, from time to time, on the right day and at the right hour. Sometimes she was doing better, but it always seemed to digress, all-too-soon, to the cruel baseline. She was known, in the neighborhood, for things that he did not want to think about. Things that the desperate did to attain the fleeting comforts of their drug of choice. To have the comfort of temporary escape from their otherwise seemingly inescapable surroundings. The area itself. Cracked and broken, boarded up stores and apartment units, slowly going back to nature. Flanked by main roads with speeding cars. No pedestrian walkways or bike lanes. No grocery stores; a food desert. All of it conveyed the same, generalized, thought to those who lived within its confines. You do not matter and no one cares about you.

Then there were Kenilworth's shoes, well, the other kids called them his *old man* shoes. They were made for diabetics. High soles and soft leather. They came from a small company in Texas. A medium brown, non-descript in nearly every way (aside from adding an inch and a half to his height due to the thick, air-cushioned soles). The laces were red and didn't match the burnt umber of the leather. Its original laces were too worn to be of use. Kenilworth held a book that he had gotten as a gift for his seventeenth birthday last month. It was called *Between the World and I* and he had already read it six times over in the past two weeks. Reading was his main hobby, followed by sci-fi movies and comic book culture (he had been to C2E2 the last six years in a row). The book he was reading was about a black male experience that he could relate to in many ways. It helped him make sense of things a bit more. Just a bit. Some harkening to the difficulties he had, and these were many.

What he struggled with, moost pressingly and most dangerously, was in understanding people. He always had. They did so many things that didn't make sense. They talked in a way that didn't seem authentic to who they were inside; what they really might think, feel, or want. There was a book by Oliver Sacks that he enjoyed very much as well, as it helped to define the experience of being autistic (that was what they called him. High functioning autistic, or, alternately, Asperger's) in a way that no other publication seemed to manage. It made him feel connected and understood on some level, at least, by some people.

Most simply made fun of his quirks. Others threatened him more directly. On seemingly random occasions, some assaulted him physically. One seemed to enjoy the experience, as Kenilworth would never fight back. The perpetrator liked to smile beforehand and laugh afterwards. He liked to say something about how a "pussy just gotta get fucked now and then," before making the ironic, and seemingly ludicrous gesture of helping him back up, beaten and bruised, and giving a sympathetic pat on his back before walking away, strutting to a seemingly ridiculous extent, with his other friends laughing their way into the distance. Sometimes, he felt, he could see a look of conflict in certain friends' expressions if they looked back, though he was not sure. It just seemed to loosely mimic a type of face he would see on those emotions charts that his past counselors would show him.

It was 6:58 in the morning. Just prior to sunrise, and the sky cast a burgeoning orange and purple sheen that peaked out of a little enclave of open sky between the clouds on this mostly overcast day. It was peaceful and quiet, his favorite time of day for the temporary comforts this brought. A time in which navigating other people was at a minimum. The constant tension of not knowing what to expect from others did not have to be experienced as viscerally and immediately. The only people out at this hour were too tired to care about much of anything. They would be waiting for the bus; these people. Waiting to go to work at fast food restaurants, supermarkets, office buildings, clothing stores, coffee shops, or wherever else might accept a willing body with a high school degree, maybe some college.

Kenilworth, actual name Washington Carver Perriman, or Dub C as his only friend, Tarver, called him, observed his surroundings. He knew these were typically referred to as *urban blight*, but he found them, somehow, pleasing in a way he could not readily describe, though felt it may have something to do with being like nature in their way. This unlikely existence in the middle of a stretch of concrete metropolis that spread across three states. He always wanted to see real nature. He had never been further than the outskirts of Chicago, and only where a train or bus could take him, those rare times. This was the closest he usually managed to come. An empty concrete lot, with its scatterings of native weeds and plants. A small locust tree growing out of one of the larger cracks. A patch of purple coneflowers and a sprinkling of native perennial sunflower, among the less desirable weeds and shrubs. He hypothesized that this particular patch of busted up concrete may have, at one time, been a gas station. One of those older ones- he liked to picture- where you could see the gas levels through clear cylinders atop the pumps.

Presently, the 59th street bus came into view from under the rusting, abandoned train track where the street dipped low and often flooded on rainy days when the water pooled; nothing having been installed to create effective drainage. He had seen rats swimming on days like that, sometimes; scurrying up the hill to the side leading to the rusted-out, elevated train track above. Small trees now grew out of it. It was going back to nature, just like that city in the Ukraine, former U.S.S.R. Druggies and gangbangers would hide out and congregate there. He used to play there too, until grandmother told him to stop. She had told him boys had disappeared. Young girls, too. A body of a teenage boy that was in his class years back was discovered there three years prior. A patchwork of bullet holes in his fourteen-year-old frame. He had seen a picture that a young man had taken with his cell phone camera sometime between when the body was discovered, and the police showed up, several hours later, and in no apparent rush. Kenilworth remembered the expression on the boy. Anxious, scared, sad, confused, *all* seemed conveyed on his face, somehow, at the same time. All the various facial contortions he had seen in that picture, he had been taught to associate with a particular emotion. He thought that black people seemed to be able to convey multiple emotions like that, all at once, better than any other so-called racial demographic he had seen. He wondered at times how that came to be. He had seen the same faces on recent Black Lives Have Meaning (BLHM) protesters. Sadness, frustration, disbelief, resolve, hope, familiarity, all sometimes visible within one expression. The level of emotion astonished him, as he could only minimally comprehend the idea of multiple feelings at one time, aside from very rare circumstances that made him uncomfortable, such as confrontations, and times in which he did not know what to say to someone.

"Washington!"

He shook his head, on impulse, to clear away his thoughts and focus on what he heard. This was a familiar voice. Kenilworth looked up from the small locust tree he had been observing, though kept his eyes below the gaze attached to the words. He had a habit of looking off at various times and a habit of looking down when speaking. It made him feel comfortable-looking down; like he could focus and avoid the overwhelming stimuli of the world for a moment. He knew, for the most part, what to expect when he did this, though he wished people would not be upset by it. It offered temporary solace. It was as though he could hide, at least it felt like that. Hide away from people who mostly scared and/or confused him. People in his neighborhood seemed so unpredictable and so volatile for reasons that he had some grasp of, though, he still could not understand the relevance, or purpose, of the actions they'd often show. Kenilworth looked up, now, and replied to the voice:

"Yes sir, Mr. Landry, how are you this morning?" in his rather stiff, polite and prescribed manner.

"I'm good, Kenilworth. Hop on. Got a seat reserved for you right behind me today," Mr. Landry said, his tempered smile toward Kenilworth there to greet him as always.

"Thank you, Mr. Landry"

Kenilworth sat down with his arms folded politely in front of him. His, already, worn, and heavily annotated, copy of *Between the World and I* grasped tightly. There were only a handful of other passengers in their various spots on the bus, and they seemed half asleep. This made him comfortable. Tired people tended to leave him alone and he was grateful for it. Mr. Landry pulled the handle to his side, in its half circle motion, to close the bifold glass doors of the bus. He turned his head slightly to notice Kenilworth was holding a new book from the last.

"What are you reading now, Washington?"

"Between the World and I," sir.

"What's it about?"

"Well, yes, it's largely about the experience of being a black male in modern society, with focus on the emotions that go along with it, the factors that inform that experience, and how to navigate this in a more informed and realistic fashion with said knowledge. Fears of bodily abuse and violation, often at unpredictable times, are a major theme."

"Jesus, Washington, that sounds dark," Mr. Landry scoffed in reply, "but I commend whoever wrote that. You try to be safe, 'specially round here, but you can do everything right and still," he trailed off now; shook his head for moment, before adding:

"Shit *still* happens." Walter Landry looked down the road and reflected on that thought as he picked up speed. In the distance, in this grid system where one could often see up to several miles in a direction at any time, he saw the green trees and ivy of the campus of the University of Chicago. An oasis in the middle of this sad, blighted, and largely forgotten place. This place that only ever seemed to get noticed when there was a robbery, a shooting, or a carjacking. Attention for acts of good never made it to the headlines. That didn't pay the bills as well, and the media focus only on the negative could easily lead one to believe that the negative was all that ever occurred around here. Sadly, most people had no intention of coming to find out for themselves, so their information source was largely what the media put out.

Walter often thought about the kids like Washington that came from here. How much potential there was, though how, even if one made it through their teen years, the trauma of this upbringing could lead to a life never lived to what its potential should have been. Sad. It reminded him of a movie he had seen recently about a photographer who taught little children in India how to use a camera. Taught by this photographer how to take pictures and make it into an art form. Some of those kids, what they did with those skills. And they were just kids. Just a motley handful of kids, representing hundreds of millions like them, who you never heard from; their collective potential would never be known and never have much chance to be expressed.

In his own corner of the world, some of the worst elements of humanity had taken over the neighborhood, and many like it. Gangbangers who prayed on kids and who didn't much care if they lived or died, day to day; damned sure couldn't muster up much caring for anybody else. But among them- even within them- there was that type of potential that those kids in India had shown. Most of them would never have the chance to make it known. Beat down by the streets in a way that those who didn't live on them could never hope to understand yet would still, somehow harbor strong and authoritatively spoken opinions about. Opinions about these kids, these neighborhoods, and these streets that they would make known from on high, while hundreds, even thousands, of miles away. He turned back to Kenilworth, eager to put hihs focus on something more uplifting, for once.

"Washington, I heard from your grandmother the other day that you're heading to the *University* of Chicago this morning." He put special emphasis on the title of the university, drawing out the words and saying them with greater excitement than the rest of the sentence-conveying his pride to to say about one of the kids in this neighborhood.

"Yes sir," Kenilworth replied, a bit sheepishly. "I received a letter from the head of the biology department inviting me to meet with them. He was impressed with a recent essay I conducted in class. It was about the potential of stem cell research in relation to cancer treatment, while incorporating multiple treatment modalities in other areas of potential."

"Shit, Washington! The brain you got, kid," Walter chuckled, shaking his head in near disbelief at the words that came out of this seventeen-year-old. He took on a more serious tone:

"Just stay out of trouble, keep your mouth shut and keep your head low until you get there, okay. We need you to represent, got it! Don't have anywhere near enough of that around here. Seems like the best of us never live up to their potential or get shot up cuz someone was jealous of them. Jealous because they come

86

from the same place but they're not going anywhere. Best of us get killed sometimes, just for trying to do the right thing. Like that boy got his skull bashed in with a two by four, just for tryin' to break up a fight. That's what you get for doin' the right thing? Shit makes you wonder, sometimes, if you should even bother, with stakes like that in place. But, then, choosing not to bother ends up making it even worse, doesn't it?"

"Yes sir. I understand what you mean, though sometimes that behavior you speak of does not seem logical to me."

Walter chuckled. "Son, you are the most book smart kid I ever met in my whole damned *life*, but your street smarts are about on par with a white boy from a small farm in Iowa. Understand that street smarts are just as important to getting by in life, even more important, unless you're living in a bubble. Sometimes you have to abide by things that aren't logical in this life. Sometimes you just got to know what people are looking to hear and how to tell 'em that, so that you won't get hurt. You understand?"

"Not really, sir." Kenilworth looked down and away, painfully aware of how this was an area of personal difficulty. "I don't ever seem to know quite what to say, or how to anticipate my actions in relation to theirs."

Walter shook his head slowly, side to side. He had tried to make this point so many times before, but there was a block there. Still, he persisted. Resting at a red light, he turned toward him briefly. "Boy, you could start by not talking like a young physics professor all the damn time. Start right there. You part of a culture, you hear? People feel more relaxed and give you less shit when you're more like them. And that's not just true round here." He pointed at the boy for emphasis. "That's *anywhere* you go."

"I understand the concept, sir, but I just can't reconcile my differences with some of the behaviors, motivations, goals and vernacular of many of those around me here."

Mr. Landry pushawed, started to accelerate as the light changed. "Son, I'll just pray for you, cuz Lord help me, I think that's *all* I'm going to be able to do. If you don't get being street wise by now, I don't think it's going to happen for ya. I know you got that Asperger's thing going on. Your grandmother done told me that, and I know a thing or two about it myself, just from some of the passengers on this rig. I guess that plays its part, whether you want it to or not. Let me tell you this, though." Again, he turned toward Kenilworth as he came upon the next red light. "If you don't know what to say, or what to do. Just don't say anything. At least not while you're on these streets, okay? Just keep quiet, so you don't contribute to making a potential bad situation happen. Do you understand that? If you don't say nothin', then they can't hold nothin' you say against you. Like you're pleadin' the fifth. Got it?"

"Yes, sir."

Walter added with emphasis, "also, I better see you back on this bus at 9:45 sharp, once you done with your business over there. Don't you go getting lost on campus. You know this is the time of year when shit is at its worst. Gang initiation time right around now. Lotta young punks looking to make a name for themselves. Thankfully most of em aren't up till noon or later."

"Yes sir. I'll be careful, and I'll be back on the bus at that time." Kenilwoth meant this, sincerely.

"Good, don't do nothin' stupid. Sometimes, Kenilworth, I feel like you're the dumbest smart kid I know." Mr. Landry chuckled at this.

Mr. Landry, having said his piece in the spirit of making the young man's life a little easier, drove on in silence for the remainder of the trip. Kenilworth could hear him sipping, from time to time, on his red and black, plaid thermos. At intervals, the door would open with a slow squeak, followed by a "cuchunk" as it shut itself behind another weary passenger shuffling onboard, usually with a uniform or apron of some sort- the work-required garb of their, largely, service industry shifts. Kenilworth noticed sprawling Washington Park, just west of the University of Chicago, coming in to view. It was a rare oasis amidst the cracked concrete, ubiquitous litter, and random arguments of people on the streets.

This was where Kenilworth got out, thanked Mr. Landry and walked the trail that progressed, in a slowly arching loop, heading southeast along the tree-lined paths and interconnected ponds and streams within the park. After an all-too-brief period walking casually and enjoying the respite of it all, he exited onto the main campus, and the Department of Organismal Biology.

The sun was higher in the sky and days warmed up quickly. It was supposed to hit one hundred and two with the heat index by mid-afternoon. Even nights were relentless this time of year. A sticky, humid, high eighties in the charcoal pink urban night. Kenilworth was starting to sweat through his shirt around the neckline, which made him nervous and caused him to sweat even more in a hopeless paradox that repeated itself regularly. He hoped that Dr. Williams would not think he looked foolish. He was in a rush to make his 8AM appointment and did not want to be late; knowing Dr. Williams had come in early, just to see him and him alone. The appointment couldn't linger, either. His grandmother insisted he be back by 10AM sharp, no questions and no excuses.

Kenilworth came upon the gothic, faded gray brick façade of the building. Trees lined its south side so the structure was partially obscured, lending it, as well, an aesthetic of man's innovation blending seamlessly with the beauty of nature. He liked that. It made him feel he could relax and, like the building, be tucked away safe beyond the wall of trees. He walked up to the information desk and was led to Dr. Williams' office. He came upon a door slightly ajar and knocked lightly.

"Come in, Washington," he heard a calming, confident voice invite him.

Kenilworth walked in and was greeted, at once, with a hearty handshake by a large man with an impressively kept, short trimmed black beard. He was balding slightly on top. He appeared to be in his late thirties to early forties. A slightly pudgy man, though appearing physically healthy. He wore a short sleeve dress shirt and slightly wrinkled khakis. The man wore leather sandals with straps that were so numerous they practically covered the entirety of the foot. It made Kenilworth question why he would bother to wear sandals of this fashion unless it was simply *for* fashion. The latter part of that made little sense to him, either. He understood that people could do impractical things in the sense of fashion, such as wear six-inch heels, or, in his neighborhood, wear pants that sagged to the lower gluteus region and could only be held up through splaying the outer thighs at a certain distance from each other to keep the pants from slipping down all the way. He questioned if many of the people who "sagged" understood that sagging was initially started by prison inmates to convey that they were imminently available for anal intercourse. He noticed many of these people also tended to be openly homophobic. The infeasible irony. Or, the ignorance of the etiology of the custom? Or, maybe, it had a separate meaning to them that they distinguished from the emergence of the custom itself. He was starting to catch himself becoming lost in thought again. A common occurrence with the young man. Thoughts related to human endeavors that he simply could not understand were often the type that he would become lost in the longest and most hopelessly.

"Washington?"

"Hmm?"

He was looking downward again, and presently looked up, rather abruptly. Loudly and overexcitedly, he followed with, "Yes, *hello* Dr. Williams! Thank you for meeting with me!"

"Umm, it's my pleasure. I've been looking forward to this meeting, Washington." Dr. Williams was still smiling, still welcoming, though there was a hint of confusion in his expression. He seemed both intrigued with, and amused by, the prospective student in front of him.

"Thank you, sir," said Kenilworth, before adding, "that is much appreciated." He was remembering his grandmother's advice to add a separate form of polite reference to the "thank you" from time to time, so that it did not sound generic and repetitive, or half-hearted. His natural inclination in conversation always seemed to go back to the comfort zone of one to three-word responses to various utterances of others. He often could not readily see the need to elaborate beyond this.

Dr. Williams gestured Kenilworth to sit in one of two papasan chairs near his large, polished cherry wood desk; clearly seeming oversized for the room it was in. Much like the chairs which practically touched each other, and the book shelves that flanked the chairs on both sides. Kenilworth had to side step between the tow chairs to sit down. It struck Kenilworth that Dr. Williams would have an even more difficult time navigating the clutter, given his size. There were books everywhere. Stacked along both walls and two feet high in various places on the desk. His entire office, looking out from the papasan chair that Kenilworth now reclined in, looked as though a fort of books, with an opening in the central part of his desk from which the good Doctor poked his head through to converse with current and prospective students. He looked not too unlike a floating head framed by textbooks on three sides. Desktop below.

Kenilworth watched Dr Williams' visible head and shirt collar as he was perusing a file that had Kenilworth's name on it; his actual name. As he did this, Kenilworth observed other aspects of the room. Shelves along the entirety of the east and west flanks. Books from floor to ceiling. Six rows high, approximately ten feet long, on either side of a room he estimated to be an approximately ten by fifteen-foot rectangle. Kenilworth estimated the number of pages represented in the room in his head, including those on the desk. Eight by ten rows, times two. One hundred and sixty square feet of book pages, minus approximately nine percent to account for covers (largely hardcovers, which would be thicker than soft) open space above the books, as well as the wooden columns within the rows approximately every two feet. Average speed to read each book based on Dr. Williams likely Intellectual quotient, along with complexity of information and its effect on speed, along with genre and its related level of expertise based on its proportion within the context of the overall subject matter represented. Time taken to peruse foot notes, which he'd assumed Dr. Williams would have often done. All of this, along with other various intangibles, that he began to calculate as well.

"I estimate it took you seventeen point eight seven three years to read all of these books, Dr. Williams," Kenilworth blurted into the airspace of the former silence. He added, "this allows for a modest amount of time for leisurely reading, outside of your selected field of study, naturally."

Dr. Williams looked up from the file, surprised initially at the randomness of this comment, then, after, at how little time Kenilworth required to conjure up the estimate. What had it been? Roughly forty-five seconds of looking around at his books while he perused his paperwork. Could he possibly be in the ballpark?

"Well, let's see." Dr. Williams took a moment to compose himself in thought. Fingers emerged to rub the chin of the floating head. "This comprises just about every book in my general field of study, and in my specialized field of eco-physiology that I have read and accumulated since graduate school, and more than a few from undergraduate. I'm thirty-nine and seven months of age. I started graduate school at twenty-two years and three months of age. Take into account an additional, let's say, seven months to accommodate the amount of time taken to read the undergraduate books herein represented, and it has taken me seventeen years and eleven months to read all of these books. That would be seventeen point nine one seven years." Dr. Williams' features brightened in excitement. "That is *uncanny*, Washington! Absolutely amazing! I would love to pick your brain about the factors that went into that estimate sometime."

Dr. Williams set Kenilworth's folder on his desk. Kenilworth was slightly disappointed that his estimate was off by a few days and was hoping the disappointment was not showing on his face. He tended to frown somewhat in such situations. Squinch his facial muscles together in frustration. Dr. Williams continued now.

"I've read in your file that you wrote down your nickname is Kenilworth, and that you often go by that?"

"That is correct, sir. They've been calling me that around my neighborhood since the second grade. Though I initially disliked it's use, which I found misguided and out of context, I have grown accustomed to it over the years despite that. I am now familiar, and, I guess, therefore, comfortable with it."

Dr Williams sat back in his chair and crossed his right leg over his left in a smooth, easy motion. "Kenilworth as in the Northshore suburb, correct?"

"That is correct, sir, yes."

"By that notion, I'm guessing they are referring to the concept of the land of the multiple million-dollar homes where sixteen-year-olds drive around in Beamers they got from daddy as their first car. The land where kids are fast tracked from toddlerhood on up, wear polos, khakis and designer shoes by age three. That general type of idea?"

"Yes sir. I think they feel I am a snob who tries to be white. An uncle Tom, some of them say."

"Let me ask you this, Washington." The floating head levitated closer toward him through its frame of books. "Are you being who you think you really are as a person?"

Kenilworth had an urge to blurt out, "Mekka Lekka High, Mekka Hinee Ho!" As he perused the head; its features contorted in curiosity as to his answer, Kenilworth subdued the urge, shaking his head to get the thought out of it. Focus on the query. It was an abstract question in a sense. That accursed ilk. He preferred the more direct, logical and tangible variety of question whenever possible. He could see what Dr. Williams was getting at, however, and responded:

"Yes sir, I believe I dress, talk, and pursue hobbies and activities in congruence with what I feel is my natural sense of being."

"Then that's all you should need to worry yourself about, Washington." The head was appeased, and receded back behind its frame of books. Now, let's get down to business. You have had all As since first grade. You have a perfect score on your ACT." He paused for a moment as he continued shuffling through paperwork. "I see here, you claim to have read over five thousand books, including over one thousand in the field of biology alone. You have topped out on two separate intelligence tests… administered by a psychologist at your community outpatient facility, McCarver." He glanced back toward Kenilworth. "That means you're over one fifty?"

"Yes sir, probably well over that to be honest. Those tests were not particularly challenging, though I did find them relatively stimulating at times."

"Hmm, I'm curious, Washington. Given all this, how do you stay stimulated in the classroom? I've heard about the high school you go to. One that has a reputation of students, well, for the most part not caring at all, just being there because they must be. I don't want to offend you, it's just, well, I think I've seen your school on a recent documentary program about failed inner city education systems. What I saw were kids talking all day in class. Throwing things at each other. Threatening other students and their teachers. Teachers lecturing to a small handful toward the front that seemed to actually be interested, though distracted by a near constant need to try to discipline the rest of the class. Fights at lunch, seemingly every day. Gang members hanging around outside. Now, I don't mean to offend you with that, but, how do you learn in a situation like this? Even if you intend to?"

Kenilworth replied in a matter of fact tone. "I have found what you said to be, for the most part, the case. Many of the students are not interested in learning. Many of the teachers have, what I would guess to be burnout. Their voices are hoarse from yelling. They sound like the veteran basketball coaches that I see on TV. Other teachers are very young people from the suburbs who come in under a government program that helps pay off their student loans after a certain time commitment. Most of them don't seem to last, though. Most of them seem more interested in just biding their time until they can leave. Until their loans have been paid off. I should mention that it has gotten better, though. The worst students have dropped out by now. High school has actually been both easier and more productive than elementary and, especially, middle school."

Dr. Williams persisted. "But what do you do? All this time, how have you kept it together and achieved like this in that environment?"

Kenilworth continued: "I've largely been separated from my classes for years now. I simply go to the library and read books for the duration of the school day. When there are tests in class, sometimes I come in to take them, or, usually, they just give them to me in the library. They found the teasing to get in the way of things when I come back into class. Most of the other students see me as a sort of anomaly, you could say. Aside from the ones that have talked to me when they see me in the library. I have had many interesting conversations with my friend, Tarver. He comes to the library sometimes too, though mainly only before and after school. He doesn't seem to want people to know he is there, which I used to find strange. I think I understand it more, now."

"How do they give you tests when you are just reading books outside of class?"

"I start by reading the text books for the different academic subjects first. I read them both during and after school and on the weekends; one chapter per text book alternating by subject, for the first several weeks of school. By the time we have our first tests, I have usually read over half the material for the year. After a month, I have read it all. I can then retrieve the information from my mind to answer the questions, as they all, of course, originate from the textbooks. After those first few weeks, I'm free to read whatever I want. My goal now is to complete the entirety of our library. I'm roughly sixty eight percent finished at this point, though seeing as I only have one year left, I estimate I'll be at about ninety one percent by the end of this year. I would say that I would come back in the summer after the school year, though I plan to leave my neighborhood as soon as feasible. It is too dangerous to stay in longer than is absolutely necessary."

"I'm sorry, Washington," Dr. Williams sighed as he closed his file. "One thing I can tell you is that, now I can't say this *officially*." Air quotations emerged next to the framed head. "But we are looking forward to seeing you next fall. Between your standardized test scores, your school credentials, and what we're hearing from the teachers and administrators at your school, you are more than ready. I hope to see more of you when you get here. What do you hope to work on once you're with us, as far as major, and other areas of study? Clearly biology seems to be an early preference."

"I would like to study aspects of biology related to stem cell utilization in the field of medical research. Of course, there are other areas of study in which I would be interested in. I feel that research in a laboratory setting within a growing field of potential future breakthrough in healthcare technology would be quite intellectually stimulating, as well as, personally rewarding."

Kenilworth had some awareness that his voice was becoming monotone and didactic sounding and felt a sudden and intense tinge of nervousness as related. The nervousness was not because he felt it was wrong, but because he'd been told- many times over- that this was something that put people off, meaning, he supposed, it must by annoying to others. Kenilworth quickly added:

"I'm sorry if I'm sounding professorial. My grandmother says I tend to come off that way, particularly in areas of great personal interest."

"You might be just that, someday, Washington," Dr. Williams responded, amused. "A professor. Therefore, I don't see too much harm in you sounding like one. Let's show you around a little bit first. I've got the next forty-five minutes blocked off before my office hours begin. I'll show you a little of the campus, some of the buildings you'll be getting acquainted with soon. Oh, and we'll hopefully be able to introduce you to a few of my colleagues."

With that, Dr. Williams gestured Kenilworth out the door and took him on a short tour. They walked across the sprawling campus. To the west, spanning the entire south to north of campus lay the sprawling, and, he felt invitingly named, Washington Park. Dr. Williams lead Kenilworth through the heart of the university, past the ornate reflective dome of the Mansueto Library and

Botany Pond, which was blanketed in lily pads and surrounded by beds of multi-hued, regional flowers. They walked through the massive central campus quad full of old growth trees, grad students, and young professors. Students playing Frisbee golf or, wisely, getting a head start on their reading for the fall. Many of them eating breakfast sandwiches, bagels, or muffins. Drinking coffee. So many coffee cups (it appeared twenty-ouncers were the minimum required size). Students of all ethnicities, including so called African-Americans such as his himself, though Kenilworth had long since traced his lineage to the Caribbean. Kenilworth walked up to one of the young black students drinking coffee and studying U.S. Lit.

"Hello, young man. Yes, my name is Kenilworth. How are you today?" May I ask you a question?" Forgetting to wait briefly for a reply, Kenilworth, looming rigidly, continued, "How would you define your experience at this institution thus far?"

The young man looked up from his book, squinting a bit in the morning sun that framed the comparatively dark shadow of Kenilworth. Kenilworth usually expected at least a short initial period of insults at this point, maybe of being mocked in the form of an exaggerated, robotic-like taunt of his mannerisms. He would soon find that such would not be the case here. The young man simply smiled, amused, and replied:

"I love it here, bro. It's no joke, though. You'll be studying your *ass* off come September."

"Thank you for that assessment," Kenilworth responded, pleasantly surprised. "I am sorry to have interrupted your breakfast."

The young man chuckled briefly and shook his head, before adding, "by the way, my name is DeShawn, man. Who are you?"

Kenilworth thought for a moment. His impulse around his peers had become, over time, to simply introduce himself as Kenilworth, though he seized on an opportunity to avoid that title now. "Washington. Yes, my name is Washington. I'm sorry I didn't ask you your name."

"It's alright man, I'll see you around." DeShawn took an impressive gulp of coffee and went back to reading.

Kenilworth nodded slightly, in a rather quick, almost twitch-like fashion, before walking back toward Dr. Williams, who pleasantly commented on his making friends already, before leading him around the quad to meet a couple more of his colleagues. Eventually, they started to head back to Dr. Williams' own building. As they walked together, in between conversations about biology, mathematics, world history, and notable aspects of the campus he hoped to be a part of soon, Kenilworth reflected on the demeanors of the students he passed. They appeared comfortable, relaxed, more-or-less devoid of fear, aside from a controlled level of understandable, and functional, anxiety related to their studies.

Washington felt that he had never seen a young black man growing up in his neighborhood not being afraid in some way or another. Defensive toward anyone else they didn't know. Nobody ever really seemed to be at ease. Not like this, anyway. Who could even just hang out, like DeShawn? Alone and without a crew for protection? Out in the open with no fear of gangbangers or potential robbers? He thought about the irony of how, just a few blocks away, this demeanor, this presentation he had seen among the students, it wouldn't be possible, without at least a hypothetical repercussion of being harmed in some imminent way. He knew this personally.

After Dr. Williams had shown Kenilworth around some more of the campus on their return walk and had him shake hands with colleagues, who also expressed how impressed they were with his intellectual functioning and obvious interest and competence for working within their general fields of study, Kenilworth saw the same demeanor in these men that he saw with the students on the quad. He wanted this, too. To lose the hypervigilance, if possible. To do this even while being a young black man on the south side? This was revelatory to him. He found himself obsessing, at some point, on getting into this campus as soon as he possibly could. Obsessing about finding his part in *this* world. He felt he would never go back to his old one -ten blocks away- once he had come here. Then he wondered. Should he feel bad about that? It was abandonment of his neighborhood, but wasn't it justified? He hypothesized now that he could do work study during the summer, perhaps arranging a deal to keep a dorm year-round by doing research for Dr. Williams, or other professors he would meet. It was all he could think about as Dr. Williams now lead him back to the front of the ivy covered building of sun washed granite. It was here where they shook hands and agreed to meet again in the late fall when Kenilworth would be sending his official application, as a formality, prior to his acceptance at the university.

Kenilworth checked his watch. It showed the time as 9:02AM. He had about forty-five minutes before he was required back at the bus stop, and a roughly twenty-minute walk to get there. He made his way back slowly ("moseying" as grandmother liked to say). He felt an opportunity to do one of his favorite things in life, which was, very simply, to walk for a level of time, ideally, with a minimum of fear. He wished to make the most of this chance. He began to walk south through the western end of campus, along South Ellis Avenue to Midway Plaisance Park where, turning right, he walked along the north edge. It was an overwide boulevard, running east-west, lined on both sides by verdant trees. There were the outlines of two soccer fields where Kenilworth observed more students and faculty coming out of the woodwork now, playing Frisbee, hacky sack, tossing footballs, even a couple small groups playing corn hole on university labeled boards. Kenilworth noted the bizarre irony again; of parks not too dissimilar to this one in his neighborhood where you could go, he supposed, though almost nobody did. He was told from a young age that these were the places you would be most likely victimized by the gangs, by drug addicts, or anyone else who knew their crimes would be less likely brought to justice under the cover of trees, distance from witnesses, and, especially, the cover of night without ample street lighting. Here, this appeared to be the place on campus comprising the least amount of fear and the most readily apparent signs of joy. Kenilworth sat on a park bench and observed it for a short period of time and read more from his book,

Between the World and I. Of course, he became absorbed as he always did.

Kenilworth checked his watch after, what seemed, a brief moment. It read 9:36AM. He'd done it again. He tucked his book by his side waist and began to run awkwardly toward his destination; his feet shuffling and chafing the pavement, as he ran. He almost tripped several times as he shuffled/ran awkwardly along the rest of the Plaisance, before heading northwest along the winding trail south of Bynum Island. As he came upon the stop, he noticed the bus. It was 9:50AM. Fortuitously, it had been late. Kenilworth stumbled onto its front steps. He briefly looked up to see the frustrated expression on Mr. Landry's face before taking his seat directly behind him; sweat soaked clear through his pilled, pink polo.

"Okay, ladies and gents. Looks like that engine problem went away for us," Mr. Landry huffed (looking sternly at Kenilworth as he said this) before turning the ignition key to start the bus up once again. He turned around and looked at Kenilworth. He added, in a hushed voice, "Don't expect something like that to happen again, Washington. You understand?" Kenilworth nodded in response. He was pretty sure he understood, now, what had happened.

The bus drove due west, and Kenilworth observed how quickly, almost instantly, the environment changed. As the green of the pristine park he had just run through faded into the distance, he saw the litter begin to accumulate along the sidewalk and sides of the streets. Styrofoam cups with plastic straws, broken, discount-priced forty-ouncers, errant, crumpled up, oil- stained bags that once held cheap, greasy fast food. The sidewalks, block by block, became progressively more cracked, weeds sprouting up through the cracks. The resident faces went from exuberant and hopeful, to tired and world-wearied, all within two or three blocks.

Kenilworth, still catching his breath, glanced out the window at a red light. His eyes fixated on a cash store, where he could see a young woman walking out in high heeled shoes that seemed they would be quite difficult to move on. Three boys, about Washington's age, came up to her at once. Two pushed her in unison, to throw her off balance, while the third grasped her purse in the disarray and ran off- the other two falling in step close behind. The woman, pushed hastily to the ground, screamed and cried from the pavement. He again saw the face, just as the bus lurched forward on its route. *Her* face now. The face of the black person encompassing that multitude of simultaneous emotions. She looked toward the boys as she cried, wearily propping herself back up to stand- and hopelessly watch- as they began to slow their pace. She faded into the distance and the boys came back into view for a spell. Less than a block away from her, they ceased running now, and morphed back into a strutting walk which seemed to be, almost, taunting. They looked back as if to assess whether or not she would give them chase, but she stood outside the store with a look of hopelessness and familiarity as her fading form looked on at those who assaulted her.

Now, less than forty yards away, walking with the purse as though nothing had happened. One looked back at her. His look, briefly, seemed maybe sorry for her, though at the same time, resigned. Resigned to the fact that this was simply how it went around here. Maybe he was sorry. But it wouldn't change anything. A situation presented itself. She was outnumbered. They were stronger. Kenilworth thought about how cruel it was that she could simply do nothing now but look on; less than one block away from them. He could still hear her distant shrill and the pleading screams. Her purse and the money inside was gone. Money that she needed to pay her rent. Money that she needed, maybe, even to feed young children who might be down to peanut butter and stale bread by now, just before the paycheck came. A humble paycheck made even smaller by the fees the cash store took out. And these were the only banks around here.

Kenilworth, in a state of ever dwindling shock the more he saw things like this, took note that he was now only a couple of blocks from grandmother's. A few moments later, Mr. Landry told him to take care of himself, once again (though with a hint of his initial glare resurfacing, as a warning, it seemed) and that he would be talking with his grandmother soon to check in on her. He told

Kenilworth to never forget that he had a community. Told him that people were starting to forget that, or not believe it, sometimes. To never forget that he had support, even if it seemed lost in the tide of constant fear of victimization and being brutalized. Kenilworth exited the bus. For what seemed just a moment, he again found himself observing the weeds growing from the immense cracks of the ghost of a former gas station. There were patches of Joe Pye weed, and several stalks of giant hogweed over ten feet tall. They looked like the bizarre vegetation of a different era in time, perhaps. A time when leviathans roamed the still budding earth.

Kenilworth checked himself, knowing that getting lost in thought had gotten him into trouble before (and certainly more than once). Still, it was hard to keep it from happening. The mind attends to what it wants. He began to walk back to his grandmother's, though almost as soon as he did, he saw three familiar faces approaching. Instantly familiar. The boys who had robbed the woman of her purse. Kenilworth looked slightly downward and tried to turn the corner to grandmother's, hopefully unnoticed, but was stopped abruptly by a hand jutting into his chest. The force nearly caused him to lose his balance and fall. He looked up and could tell, from the face that greeted him, that these boys could do him harm. Though the facial expressions he saw were difficult to identify, he knew the best term to use as a descriptor would be *emboldened*. One of the two pushers was the first to talk. His features contorted and turned to ugly face as he spoke.

"I heard some *nigga* from around her snitched on my man JaQuan. Now, who the fuck round her foolish enough to fuck wit *mah* crew! Huh? My homey bout to get five to ten for assault and robbery. Said he saw *you"* The boy poked his finger into Kenilworth's chest, "on the corner when he got into it with some punk old man who didn't understand the game round her and tried to fight him off. Shit didn't end too well for his ol' dusty ass. You know what I'm sayin!"

Kenilworth knew that there was nothing now that could keep him from eminent harm. He had seen boys like this before.

They had familiar look of sagging pants, wife beaters, do rags and knock-off jewelry. Eyes that conveyed little to no emotion. Eyes that seemed dead, like on the mugshots of those famous gangsters from the 1920s. These boys seemed already fully grown and heavily muscled- prematurely- from working on building a level of intimidation toward others, early in life. Intimidation was survival itself to them. Kenilworth positioned so that, if he were knocked down, his head would most likely land on a relatively soft patch of weeds he had just been observing. Knowing that he would be hurt now, no matter what, he decided that his best odds would be to convey sympathy for the accuser. He knew that to identify himself as the accuser would likely get him killed. He also knew that denying sympathies for the old man would be even more likely to get him killed as they would not believe him. A moderated approach was his best chance. Kenilworth looked up and said:

"Yes, though I do not know who reported your friend, I was there, and I think that crimes should be reported in general. So, I would say, whoever reported it sounds like they did the right thing."

The boy, taken aback by this response and not quite sure what to do with it, paused for a moment. He began to laugh at what he saw as the irony of the words. What kind of bitch ass nigga would say something like this? He glanced back at his two friends. Both were crossing their arms, smugly, and seemed to be waiting for their leader to do something. One lobbed the purse they had recently snatched over a fence past the small wooded area beyond the concrete. Apparently, they had gotten what they wanted from it by now. A car rolled up slowly, and Kenilworth hoped the occupants might help, but as soon as he felt help might be coming, he saw the passenger shout out the window:

"Get his ass, T-Drizzle! Get his *ass!*"

There was Chicago drill music emanating loudly from the car. Its doors shook rhythmically to the apocalyptic sounds with their indecipherable lyrics.

"Foe-tee thah, tuh hunnah thah. Hunnah thah notha hunnah thah. Ther hunnah thah, fah-hunnah thaw. Mill yaw, less havva munnah shah.

"This goofy mother fucker," T-Drizzle said, laughing. "What's your name anyway? You bitch ass *nigga*! Kenilworth? Ain't that what they call you? Ya'all a bitch ass motha fuckin' nigga." The young man pushed his finger aggressively into Kenilworth, to the tune of every word in this last sentence.

"Yes, that is what they call me," Kenilworth said.

Kenilworth tried to affect a stunned and sheepish look, while still maintaining an expression to convey a sense of stubborn pride despite it all. This, he had come to find through experience, was his most logical facial expression to utilize in a situation like this. He was emulating a scene from a well-known actor in an early nineties hood movie, when there was a shotgun pointed at him from the back seat of a car while he was standing outside his house. This was the look he had shown. Acknowledging what was happening, that he was afraid, but that he would also stand his ground, albeit in the impudent way available to him.

"Kenilworth." The boy/young man put his hand on Kenilworth's shoulder, gently, as though about to give him a bit of fatherly advice. "Let me teach you something today, *patnah*." He put his head so close to Kenilworth's that he could feel the air coming out of this mouth. "You know what the name of the lesson is, *bitch!* Youse a *bitch* you know." He jutted his finger within an inch of Kenilworth's left eye. "Youse a snitching ass *bitch*."

"What's the lesson?" Kenilworth asked now, rushing this to conclude, before the anger could brew any further. Inside grew the familiar sensation. Like something vast was wiggling. His head was getting dizzy at the same moment. Unable to think, though knowing the paralyzing sensation would come.

"Snitches get *stitches*! Bitch!"

Kenilworth briefly peeked the blurred image of a fist inflicting a blow to his left ocular socket. He fell back and his vision blurred before going black. His last sensation, before losing consciousness, was the soft yet firmly supporting giant hogweed on the back of his head, and a fading voice spouting, "*Oh*! He got his ass. Shit, son, he got his *ass*!"

Chapter V

Thugs!

"*Thugs!*....Alright? Let's call it like we see it! Okay? See, the liberal media, nah, as it were, is portraying another circus of lies, recently, with this her Michael Red story." Bud Harbaugh sighed audibly over his microphone. "Now, here's what *they* say. The liberal blowhards, that is. Spinnin' it all around until you're dizzy in the head."

"Dizzy upside yo head!" Shouted Walt. He had come into the radio booth this morning with a sloppy, white powder goatee of sorts. It was already shaping up like old Walt would be getting kicked out by halftime on this day's broadcast.

"That's right, friend! Dizzy upside yo head. Dizzy upside *yo* head, and that's, uh, dat cause you be getting *spun*, you see. You see what I mean, friends?" Bud made a spinning motion with his upwardly pointed index finger.

"Spun like cotton candy on a stick," added Ted.

"Dat rot, Ted! Dat rot. You be fixin' tuh get spun all around, dis way and dat. Spinning around until you find yo self landin' in the destination that *they* want you to reach, not, uh, not the destination you're *naturally* supposed to reach. Huh? How bout dat? I'll say it again, friends. The destination *they* want you to reach and *not*...okay?...*not* the one you s'posed to. Heh? 'What dat,' you say as they putting a blindfold on you and spinning you off course. And looka her, now you all dizzy like and what have you, goin' 'who dat?' Nah, that ain't no good, nah. You see what

I'm sayin'? Then they gon' go sending you out into the woods, getting you all lost…cuz you'se all spun around. Dis way 'n dat? Hmm? Now, by and by, you know what I mean by *they*. Don't make me go and have to repeat mah self." A sardonic chuckle followed.

"Don't get yourselves lost, true Muricans," came an assist from Ted.

"Murica*s*! Muricans! *Muricans*!"

"Now Walt, settle yo self down. You gettin' a little loud, nah. And, uh, and, little redundant too, if'n I can speak plainly. Now Ima warn you early on, don't start, nah." Bud waved a warning finger at Walt, as though he were a dog trying to inch toward his treat when commanded to stay. "We got a story to tell, nah. Okay? Alright, where was we? Ok, hee we go. Squeaky wheel gonna get that greasin'. You know what I mean? Nah, here's what *actually* happened. Okay? As I sees it, and, and, uh, I'll add, as the cameras *showed* it to be." Bud paused for dramatic effect. The timing and the duration of the pause honed masterfully, as always.

"Michael Red! Hmm? Eighteen-years-old. A man. A *man*! *Not* a boy. First and foremost, let's get us that straight, my friends.

"Get that crystal clear," said Ted.

"Dat rot, Ted. Dat *rot*! Nah, her's what we know. Shot and killed by one of our boys in blue.

"Support our boys in blue!" added Ted, more animated than usual.

"Dat rot! You better choose a side, friends! Who dat gonna be? Our boys in blue, fightin' the good fight, or deez her thugs? Hmm? You decide, friends. Nah, where was I? What was I sayin'?"

"Murica!"

"Heh? Walt! That don't make no sense. I mean, well, it do in a way. But we got to get a little more *specific* than that. Now don't you start. Nah, uh, oh yeah…Okay, so our boy in blue, who we can only *assume* was just out trying to do his job. Mmkay? Nah, and listen here. Okay? We *know* he roughed up the cop in some way. We have pictures. Okay? So we knows that. The officer had bruises and cuts on his face. All around it, nah, folks."

"All over his face," clarified Ted.

"That's right! Hmm? Dat rot. All…over…his….*face*! *His* face. Okay? *Not* the boy's face, mind you. *All* over! Now, now, uh, clearly...*clearly*, he was roughed up. Okay? So now, the officer…in this, uh, this moment of being roughed up…mind you…*pull*s out his gun, fahrs it at the young man. *Fahrs* it! Nuh he dun fardit. Den what happen? Hmm? Well, ain't no surprise after that. Reckon' he done kild 'em. *Fahrs* it, and then…well, what…*often* times…gonna happen in dat case? Well, he kild 'em. Now, mind you. And, nah, don't forget, he's just been roughed up. Okay? *Don't* forget about that. *Very* important! Ver-eeeee…important. And why?"

Bud eased himself back in his chair and folded his hands over his hefty girth (an oft preferred pose whilst about to make a point).

"Why? Well, uh, let's take a shot at dat. No pun intended, folks. Walt!...Walt! Stop laughin' back dere." A Gavil pounding sound on the desk. "We serious nah! Walt, dammit, you workin' my last nerve. Nah, uh, okay, the point I'm making is, okay, it dis. It's pretty damned hard to think clearly when you've been roughed up nah, ain't it! So, let's *not* go acting like makin' a decision is *easy* in a situation like that. See, they want you to believe it's easy. The liberal media elite, dat is. Dat's part of the prollum! Nothin' these boys in blue do is easy. Our good boys in blue. Let me tell you that much. It ain't *never* easy! Dat why nobody wants to do the damned job! Would *you* want to? Hmm? Would ye?"

Placated by the thought that he had made his initial point, Bud paused, again shook his head and exhaled audibly and deliberately, to portray a sense of tension that would have to, of course, be based on actually caring in the first place. Another pause to let that succinct noise, and its associated connotations of concern, sink in.

"Now, true Muricans, I *do* regret that this young man, this, here, umm, this (papers shuffling) Michael. Michael? Michael Red, that's it…uh, that he dun dod. He dun uppin' dod, folks. He done up'n dod own dat not nah he dade, nah. But hey, folks. Nah let's face it, nah. He made some poor decisions leading up to all a dat. Okay? Ahm uh rot? Roughed up an officer. Hmm? *Roughed* him up! They say he tried to run away and got shot, but reports ahm seeing from my *un-biased* sources. Hmm? Reports ahm seeing…from my *un*-biased…*sources*…dere are that he charged the officer, and that's when he was keeled."

"Keeled him!" Added Ted.

"Kilt him, now he pushin' up daisies!" Contributed Walt.

"Now Walt, calm down. Calm down, buddy. And, nah, fur God's sake, would you show some compassion, friend? You workin' my last nerve, ol boy. Nah, I dun told you, don't start. Okay? Where was I, folks? Walt, I see you chuckling unduh yo breath, nah. Nah simmer down, nah. Okay, so now, folks…now you got the BLHM protesters up in arms saying this man was straight up *murdered*."

Bud threw both hands up in the air in exasperation from behind his desk, paused for a half finger sip of bourbon, and continued.

"Ah ain't lyin', folks, nah dat what they said! Trying to make him out ta be a victim. Oh yes they is." Bud pounded his desk three times, one per word, as he repeated, "Yes…dey…is! You got them posting pictures of this young man in a grad-jee-aye-tion cap. Posting pictures of him in a three-piece suit at prom. Well you know what? Hmm? You know what? I've also seen pictures, true Muricans!"

"Seen him some pictures," confirmed Ted.

"Seen 'em! I done *seen* em. You know what I saw? Hmm? Know what I saw? Know what your Bud saw? What I done up'n saw?"

"Dun uppinsaw!" Said Walt.

"What I uppinsaw is, uh, what I uppsinsaw, is, uh…

"What you uppsinaw?" Asked Ted.

"What I uppinsaw is, uh, it was a picture I done seen. I done seen me a picture of this young man smoking a big, fat *doobie*. How bout dat? A big, chubby *doobie* full a that tea."

"*Full* a that tea!" Added Walt for emphasis

Bud paused momentarily. "Hmmm? Nah, you ol' timers know what I mean by *tea*, don't ya? You young 'ins might call it the Mary Jane. But, uh, point is, that what we got her…nah, what we got her is a doobie smokin' young thug. And guess what else?

"What else, Bud? What else?" Walt queried with gusto.

"Well, I'll tell you, friend. Hold your horses, nah." Bud gestured with his hand for Walt to calm down. "Ima tell ya. I'll tell you what *I* saw. Alright? What *ah* saw. And what did ah see, folks? Well, I saw him throwing up what *appeared to me*…to be a gang sign, too. I'm looking at that picture right now, too! Got it raht her in fronta me….and, you know what. I mean, I can't say this *o*fficially, but I think that looks like a gang sign to me. Hmm? What you boys think?" Bud flashed a piece of paper with a veiny cock and balls on it, at Ted and Walt.

"That's a gang sign," stated Ted, with authority.

"MS-13! MS-13!" Walt screamed, shrilly.

"Definitely a gang sign, den," added Bud. "Maybe MS-13. You might well be rot, Walt. Well, hell, folks, I'm just gonna say it, flat out. Gonna put it rot out dere, and you heard it her first. That's a gang sign. I don't rightly recognize *which* gang. Okay? But that's a gang sign of some sort, to be sure. Yup. Yup, folks, no doubt about it. No…doubt…about it…folks. Don't let them tell you no different, nah!" Bud then paused, again, to create the impression he was perusing evidence as opposed to giving a pre-rehearsed response.

"He got a fifth of something next to him, too. Getting drunk *and* high. Drunk and high, folks!" Getting drunk and high! Take a look again, boys. What that look like to you?" Bud flashed Ted and Walt the same picture, except with a crudely drawn female hand now cupping the nutsack and another stroking the shaft.

"Drunk and high! Hoo weeee!!" belted Walt. "Ah see it there. No doubt about it, sirs! No doubt about it, ma'ams!"

"Simmer down, Walt! Now you simma down, ya her!" Bud pounded his desk again, several times, like an irate judge with a gavil. "What you think bout dat, Ted?"

"Definitely drunk and high," Ted agreed.

Bud crumpled up the piece of paper and threw it at Walt hastily, to Ted's faintly audible laughter. Walt swatted at it, frantically, as though touching the penis drawing might turn him gay. Bud chuckled under his breath, took a long draw of bourbon, popped three prescription pain pills, and continued:

"Bet he was drunk *and* hah when he was roughing up that cop, too! Hmm? Think about it, nah." Bud tapped on his noggin. "Not too far of a stretch is it? Drunk and hah. What you liable ta do in dat dere state a bein' drunk 'n hah? *They* might. That is, uh, that is, the liberal *elite* media mot call what ah jess said. They might call that speck-uh-laytin'. They mot call it speck-uh-lay-shin. Hmm? Well, know what *I* call it? I call it damned good 'ol common sense. A young man, drunk 'n hah, acting stoo-pid. Acting a damned fool."

"Acting a fool!" Walt parroted as he gingerly flicked the crumpled dick pic off his desk.

Bud paused again to let the point sink in, before segueing onto the next point of discussion.

"Saw some video of him, too."

"Saw him some video," said Ted.

"Dat rot, old friend. Good ol' Ted over there, folks." Bud pointed a thumb to the side over toward Ted's desk. "True Murican, he is."

"*Murican*! Woooo!!! Murican!" Audible, simultaneous, chimp-like thumping of a desk heard, distinctly, in the background.

"Ow! Dammit! Now, Walt, that was straight up *ear* piercin', mah friend! Ouch! Mah *ears*! I'm gonna have that tinnitus, nah. Got damn it all! On account uh yer nonsense. Settle down, now. You listen up good. Ya her? You listen up, nah. You need ta take a time out. Count to ten, okay? Okay, uh, so like I was saying. Where was I? Mah ears is ringin'! Okay, like I was saying. I saw the video. Saw me the video with mah *own* two eyes, mind you. Saw this man, not fifteen minutes before this event went down. You can see the video too, by the way. Won't see it on too many liberal elite news networks (it had, in fact, been shown dozens of times on any number of them) but it's around. Shows this Michael Red stealing a box of cigars at a gas station."

"Stealing! Stealing to make doobie blunts!" exclaimed Ted.

"Rot chew ahr! Stealin'. Steals him some cigars for, uh, prolly to roll doobie blunts full a that tea. Then what happen is, uh, then the elderly clerk, he come up to try to take 'em back. Make sense, rot? He don' want to stand for no stealin' going down right in front uh his eyes. And then, guess what? This Michael Red. This her BLHM darling. Hmm? This poster child for their movement. Hmm? This three hunnerd pound, six-foot five druggie...Alky.

"Alky!"

"Walt, dammit! And, uh...and, likely gang member, too."

"Alky, druggie, thug, gangbanger."

"Dat rot, Ted. Dat rot. Know what he do?"

Bud paused. A lengthier than typical pause. The last finger in the current glass of bourbon down the hatch. Another three hastily poured.

"What's he gonna do?" Asked Ted.

"What he gon do? Hmm? Know what he do? Ah tell you what he do. *Ah* tell ya. Pushes this elderly clerk. Pakistani, I think. Pakistani? Let's go ahead and say Pakistani, folks. Any hoo, pushes him rot into an aisle of candy bars and what not, knocks the whole damn aisle down. Whole damn aisle go tumblin' down like a losin' hand on Jenga. He has now *assaulted* this man. *Assaulted* him! Then, after all that, takes the cigar box and walks on out, just to put the icing on the cake."

"Stealing *and* assaulting. Double whammy." added Ted.

"Dat rot, old friend. A double whammy, right then and there. Stealing *and* assaulting within the span of seconds. Seconds! And smokin the doobies."

"Smokin' the doobies!" Walt confirmed, redundantly.

"Dat right! Nah, *think* bout dat, nah, folks. Let's get them noggins going on dis."

Bud tapped his desk audibly with his right index finger as a gesture of thoughtful authority, then paused and sipped another half finger. He tended to drink a little more on occasions like this when he was getting fired up. Sometimes his voice would slur a bit toward the end of broadcasts, though his feigned country drawl masked the effects quite well. It was part of the reason his voice had sounded progressively more down-home country as the years progressed. A cover for drunkenness, as long-time alcoholics tended to discover, and become progressively more skilled at over time.

"Okay? Now, not fifteen minutes later. Not *even* fifteen minutes later. Hmm? He's reported walking down the middle of the street. What dat mean, you ask? Ah tell you. *Jaywalking* he was!

"Doing the stealing, the assaulting, *and* the jaywalking," said Ted, counting off the offenses, one by one, on his nicotine-scented fingers.

"Dat's right! Dat rot! *And* doing the jaywalking, too. How many crimes we got her already now? I see you countin' em off, Ted. I see you over there, friend. I'm counting 'em off on my fingers too and heck, might need to switch over to the other hand soon enough. Right? Ah mean, seriously. Okay, so now you might be sayin', 'Bud, what is all this got to do with what happened between dis *obvious* thug. I think we can say *obvious* at this point, folks…and, uh, and with what then went down with one uh our fine, *upstanding*, officers uh the law? Hmm? One of our boys in blue. Our nation's *finest*.'

"You lookin' out for our *finest*, or for our thugs?" Asked Ted.

"Damn, Ted. Dat a mighty fine question tuh be axin. And we all should be axin' it, shouldn't we."

"Muricans!"

"Walt! Damn it! Well, that's a good question Ted posed, folks, and uh, somethin' to stew on. Now Imma get back to the question of how all this relates to the eventual, deadly altercation, like I done said I would. I'll tell you the answer tuh dat, right her and now."

Bud placed both elbows atop his mahogany desk and leaned in toward the microphone to further magnify his voice.

"See, when you have a crime occurring, you are obligated to assess the *character* of those involved. The *character*, you see. You see what I'm sayin', folks? What kind of character does a person have when they have committed three…count 'em now… *three*…known crimes *just* prior to a forceful encounter with a law officer. What kind of *character* do you think that person has, who committed those crimes? Now, we're talking about character here, folks. This person who has committed multiple crimes in a matter of minutes beforehand. What makes you think that person can't then go ahead and commit a serious crime against a law officer afterwards? Hmmm?"

Bud sat back in his chair, for a moment, to let the point sink in. He farted into the padding of the chair, which, itself, smelled like a perpetual fart. The cleaning lady, Camila, knew this well. Bud wafted the scent of a butter fart toward Walt and continued:

"Answer me that, folks. Any of you bleedin' heart liberals want to give that one a try? Well, just you dial up and we'll have a nice, lengthy talk about that. You know I'm starting a new segment where you'll have just that opportunity. More to follow on that, but for rot nah, back to assessin' the character. Okay? Most important thing! Always is, nah. But tell all these things to the BLHM movement and they'll just show you the picture they got of him in a graduation robe. Just ignore the other pictures altogether. Ignore the crimes caught on video. *Ignore* it! And on top of that, ask for this officer's head on a stick!"

"Want it on a stick like a damn corn dog!" shouted Walt, between a round of coughs.

"That's right, Walt! Now simma down. Okay?" Bud and ted both could barely suppress their chuckles, as Walt struggled, coughing and flailing his arms within the stagnant cloud of butter fart. "But dat rot, though. Like a damn corn dog. Okay? Over dere at the state fair. Hmm, a corn dog over dere at the state fair. Yeah, you know, come to think of it, I'm going to get me one of those next time around."

"They are delicious," nodded Ted.

"Yes sir. Dip 'em in a little barbecue sauce."

"I like to dip my hot dog in a lot of things," Walt chimed in.

"Walt! Aw, nah, nah...*damn* it! You workin' my last nerve nah! And I already done told you that! Watch yo self! Don't you go think' you slick! Okay? You ain't gonna get that little innuendo past me, friend. Ah wasn't born no yesterday. Now, by and by, uh, and hey, when's the next state fair, guys? Do you know? Anybody up in the booth there? Le Tuna, you know anything about that? You guys? No? Gonna get me a deep-fried Twinkie, too, come to think of it. You know, nah, at the risk of digressing just a tid, one time I was at one a them, uh, them yuppie *gastro pubs,* ah guess you could call it. You know, overrun with hipsters. One a those ones."

"I've regrettably had to frequent those, from time to time," said Ted, in knowing comradery.

"You know what they like den, rot Ted?"

"Yes, sir."

"Alrot, den. So, I'm surrounded by man buns and flannels over dere, in this hipster gastro pub, of sorts, by and by. And, uh, ah had just finished a delicious, but rather bougie, cheeseburger with, uh, with the caramelized onions, blue cheese, and sautéed mushrooms and all that bougie crap (these were common toppings on burgers that Bud's private chef often made him). They come up, and they gave me a deep-fried Twinkie for free. How bout dat? I was plum impressed with the gesture, until, that it is, I noticed a prollum with it."

"What was that?" Asked Ted.

"Well sir, only prollom was, it, uh, it was pointed vertically on the plate, the twinkie, that is. Pointed vertically on the plate with, uh, two scoops of ice cream directly underneath it and, uh, and chocolate swirled in little circles above the Twinkie. Now, it don't take too much imagination tuh know what dat looked lock, ah tell ya. Looked lock a damned cock and balls with pubes is what it looked like. Frickin' whiny, skinny jean wearing, PC talkin' libtards! Ah know that was on purpose. You bess buh-leev I done knows it. But…uh, know what?

"What's that, Bud?"

"Well, Ted, I won't be made a monkey's uncle for nobody! I ates it anyhows. Was none too bad, neither. You guys should get you one. But, okay, I done digressed. I'm sorry, True Muricans. You know, I speak my mind. Okay? Speak my thoughts. The good, the bad, and the ugly…so to speak, friends. That's how it sposed ta be, nah. How it used ta be, too. Used ta be that way, and we gonna git it that way again, yes sir…but, uh, let's get back to the point at hand. Let's get on back now, hey. Let's get back."

"Back in black! I hit the sack!" sang Walt in a high, shrill voice.

"What the *F*, Walt! What? Nah, nah let me say somethin'. Let me tell ya, somethin'. That's not even here nor there, friend. What are you talkin' about, son? You ain't makin' no sense. Let's get on the ball, now. What was *I* talking about? Getting distracted over her again, by tomfoolery. Now, by the way, I don't know what's going on with Walt today, folks. Got a bug up his keister, maybe. You know how he is, but God bless him anyway. Alright now. We was talkin' bout character. Character and *portrayal*. Call a spade a spade if you will, no pun intended."

Bud paused and chuckled under his breathe at the self-perceived witty comment.

"But, let's face it. This is just a young thug that got what was coming to him. Let's call it what it is. Why does BLHM stand up for young thugs like this? Hmm? Of all the black folks they could stand up for? Hmm? Of all the black folks they could stand up for, how come and, uh, and *why* come they gotta stand up for the ones like this? They wanna act like anytime a young black man gets shot and killed by police, it can't be for no valid reason. Can *never* be for a valid reason, can it? Hmm? They always have to be the *victim* each and every time. And why is that? Cuz they harbor that victim mentality in their culture."

Bud paused to let this point marinate. He sat back in his chair and crossed his hands behind his neck and looked upward toward the ceiling. He belched bourbon fire. Gathering his thoughts, he added:

"Rick Ganner."

"Rick Ganner. What a joke," said Ted, setting the mood.

"It *was* a joke. *Suffocated*, they called it. All they did was hold him down. Man was morbidly obese. Okay? Prolly had him some serious health problems. Probably one foot in the grave already. Hmm? Okay? Prolly one foot in the grave and, uh, and the other on a damned banana peel. Smoking *and* eating way the heck too much. Already middle-aged too, and black people don't live as long. Now don't make too much of that, now. Just don't take care of themselves too well, that's why. That's why and that's all. And why did they even have to pin him down in that chokehold anyway? Hmm? Why? Because he was *antagonizing* the police. *Antagonizing* them. Nah, nah, all you got ta do. All you got ta do is, uh, is just be respectful to the officers and do as they ask. That's it! Simple. Nah, come on, folks. What's so hard about that? But again, you got BLHM all over it, laying no part of the blame- not one single *iota,* mind you- of the blame…on this man. This, here, Rick Ganner. Irresponsible with his business, his health, *and* his time. Sound like a damned born loser to me, but he can't be blamed for anything uh tal…according to the liberal media."

"Liberal media elite. Agenda pushing, fact spinning, liberal fascist, fact denying, discord sowers," ranted Ted.

"Wow, Ted. That really sums it up!" Beamed Walt, genuinely impressed. "Good job, old buddy. God dang, if I had a gold sticker somewhere around here. Anybody up in the booth, der, got them a gold sticker? Where'd Le Tuna go? Anybody else up there might have you a gold sticker? No? Cuz if you did, I'd say give it to Ted, right now. Good 'ol Ted, folks. Okay, so that's Rick Ganner. Let's throw out another name, too. Tavin Matten. Tavin Matten! What kind of name is that anyway? Sounds like someone just made it up, on the spot, without thinking about it. His name sounds like Martin, but in a thick Boston Accent. "*Mah*-tin.""

"Mah name's *Mah*-tin," joked Ted.

"I live ova by the *Hah*-bah. I pahk the cah in the yahd, by the hah bah," added Bud, chuckling again, at this self-amusing anecdote. One of many he felt right proud of on this afternoon's broadcast.

"Okay, so, any hooter, Tavin Mah-tin gets himself killed by a watchman who happened to be volunteering. Protecting his community. *Protecting*…his…community. Fo *free*! He doin' it fo *free*, folks. Anyway, this her, watchman. No, let's not call him that. Let's call him a *protector*…says that he saw Tavin walking around the neighborhood. Didn't recognize him. Thought he looked suspicious. Well that's reasonable enough, isn't it?" Bud looked side to side toward Ted and Walt, for confirmation.

"Sounds reasonable." Ted affirmed on cue.

"Right!" Bud gave Ted a nod and a pleased, knowing wink. "And, by and by, that is, uh, that is what you on the lookout for in that position, by and by, that is. *Protector* says he went to talk to Tavin and it escalated into a confrontation. The *protector*…say dis…volunteer."

"Workin' for free!" Added Ted.

"Dat rot! Working fo free. Fo *free*, people! Name of George Mason, by the way. This man…a man of color himself, for those of you like to use that term 'people of color.' A biracial man, he is. He says Tavin threatened him during said confrontation, and reached for his gun, so, well, uh, unfortunately…really, unfortunately…George Mason had to shoot him. *Had* to! This Tavin, by the way, also had a documented history of problems at school. Disrespect toward teachers. Drug use. History of making graffiti on walls. Had items in his backpack that clearly didn't belong in the backpack of a teenage boy. Jewelry…*women's* jewelry. What that doin' in der?

"What it doin' up in there!" said Ted.

"Dat right. What it doin'? So now, uh, the question of *integrity* come back up again. And the question of *character*. Gettin' back to that character thing. Remember how important that is in cases like this, my friends."

Bud took another, uncharacteristically long pause now, to let the information sink in for his listeners. He was implementing somewhat longer pauses, at the request of Grant Scott and his research team. Experimenting to see how these may tie into his ratings. Scott, that friggin' poindexter trying to tell him how to do his show. Shit, he did make a couple of good points, though. Like amount of repetitions, volume, tone of voice, key words; all being experimented on and scrutinized ever more thoroughly and accurately as to their effects. Bud was looking to time the pause, at this moment, to within a split second of the theoretical ideal-basing length of pauses to the topic at hand's recommended pause length a la poindexter's recommendations. He checked on a stopwatch periodically. Bud had a cheat sheet, based on topic theme, in laminate coating on the center of his desk. This particular topic: Quality of character. This one demanded, first, multiple repetitions on the importance of the quality, followed by a longer pause than typically. More time to let his audience ruminate on how perceived poor character traits could instill doubt as related to the actions of those that Bud and his network wanted doubt instilled. More time, after this, for his listeners to think and reflect; hopefully navigating their minds to the quality of character that Bud crafted for them. Thoughts and reflections both based almost entirely on what they had just heard from "Their Bud," as-in many cases- he and Marmot News were- it was well established-the only news sources for much of the audience.

Bud took another half finger of his exorbitantly priced, and oft-consumed, hooch. He lifted the glass high and admired the quality of the meticulously etched crystalline patterns reflecting light spectrums before taking up the mic once more.

"What it doin' in there? Hmm? The women's jewelry, dat is. Simple question, right? What kind of behaviors was this young man engaged in? BLHM wants to call him a *boy* and that's fine. But seventeen. Damn close to being a man, good folks. And look like a man, too. Believe you me, my friends."

"Youse a man, baby! Woo!" screamed Walt, getting more out of hand. His sloppy, powder white goatee was expanding under his nose and spilling onto the top of his desk, impelling Bud to place his hand over his microphone and to admonish Walt in a loud, hissing whisper, "Gott damn you! Ease up on that shit, son! Who do you think you is? Heh? Scarface, about to take out his little friend?"

Bud removed his hand from the microphone. Quickly recomposing himself, he added:

"You know, you could argue that, couldn't you. You really could. So again, who do you trust? Dat da question at hand... okay? We got George Mason, dere, on da one hand. Clean record, he has. Hmm? Clean record. How bout dat? Steady work, and *volunteering*, even, on top of that. As a watchman. As a protector, people! A *protector*! And! And? Workin' fo free. A volunteer. Now what kind of character do you expect to see in a man who volunteers for his community? Hmm? You gonna believe a thing or two about what George Mason has to say about the matter? Or!....or...are you going to trust how BLHM spins it. Calling Tavin a victim. Let me tell you something, True Muricans."

"*Muricans!*" said Ted, quite redundantly, but he was currently in the position of not quite having met his quota for *Murican/Muricans* today.

"*True* Muricans. Lot of people call themselves Muricans, by and by. But, uh, but we here...we here only interested in the *True* Muricans, as you well know. Now, my *true*...uh, Muricans, are you going to have yo self believin' that this young man was a victim? Hmm? A victim of racism? *Or!*....or...uh, do you see this like I done did see it. Which is, a question of a young man involved in thuggery. Okay? *Thuggery*...who made a stupid and, uh, and a unfortunate decision...in part cuz he was probably drunk *and* high at the time. So he, uh, made the *unfortunate* decision in that state to then mess with a larger man who happened to have a gun. A young man who, because of this stupid...stupid and, uh...*senseless* decision...simply got what was coming to him. Alright? Nah, it sounds harsh, I know. I *know*, my friends! It sounds harsh. But that's what I see as having happened. That is, uh, given what we know. And that's the prollum in a nutshell. You got BLHM taking things like this. Okay? Then spinning 'em! You know they do some spinnin' to try to justify their own interests. Spin it into this young man being a victim. And then, uh, then they go out and protest. Throwing rocks at police. Breakin' windows. Settin' their own communities on fire. And they want to call themselves a socially *just* group. Working toward progress? If you're a black person and you believe that BLHM bunk, you know what I'd call you?"

"A tar baby!" screamed Walt, pounding his fist on his radio announcer booth.

"Aw *dammit*, Walt! What in hale! Ya up and dun did it again! Now you go on, get yo ass up on outta here! I mean it now. We aren't racists up in her. You hear me? I will not have that nonsense. We tryin' to *help* the black folks. Help 'em see things the *right* way. Now get up on outta here."

Walt hustled out of the room in mock, silly jog. He crop dusted Ted and Bud, and gave a hasty, two fingered salute, on his way out the booth. Bud noticed that Walt and partially unzipped his pants and unfurled one nut, which hung down in front of his pants. Bud cursed him under his breath but couldn't help BUT suppress a giggle or two. Good form, my friend.

"You take the rest of the week off and then you apologize when you come back!" Bud shouted, as the door was closing shut behind his sidekick. He turned this attention back to his audience over the airwaves:

"Ladies and gentlemen, I am *so* sorry about that. Please don't make too much uh that little verbal miscue. You know Walt ain't a racist, nah. Heck, I believe it was just last week I saw him cuddling up with one our young interns." Bud turned to look into the glass booth holding the interns, various sound techs and administrators. He could see Walt was back there now, presenting with both hands, his exposed left testicle to a new buxom blonde technician. He seemed to be trying to gauge if this aroused something akin to sexual interest in her. Bud, after having peeked this, then tried, unsuccessfully, to shake the image from his head.

"Uh, yes, one of our lovely interns. A beautiful young Nubian princess, she was, uh, she is. Nubian? That's another word for it, right? Nubian?" Bud looked around at Ted and toward the booth for confirmation. The blonde was aggressively trying to push Walt away from her now, which seemed to surprise and disappoint him. "Anybody? Well, anyhows, oh hey there, hello." Bud caught a glimpse of the only black female in his general vicinity. "I see that same princess shakin' her head over there from behind the glass booth, folks. I'm sorry about that…uh… LeTina…Hmm?...LaTesha? ....Tesh? Like, as in Jon Tesh? Piano player. Big guy, plays the piano? No? Tash? Tosh? Spelled with an A, though? What are you sayin'? Latasha? Okay, got it, sorry about that, too. We're so sorry about that, honey baby. Walt's gonna get a talkin' too, believe you me. Isn't he your boyfriend, though? Huh? He ain't? I thought I saw you two together recently. Right? Wasn't that? Aw, folks, she's got her hands on her head, shaking her head. I'm *so* sorry, La Tina. Right? La Tina? Like, *The* Tina, en Español? What are you saying? La? Ok. Tash? Ok? Put 'em together? I got ya. You're saying put 'em both together, with your hands? LaTasha? LaTasha! That's right, I'm sorry. I'm so sorry, my soul sister." Bud gave himself two chest pumps as he said this. "Hey, wait a minute, now. Heh? Aw, come on! You ain't need to go running off now! What are you doin'? Le Tuna! Aw, come back, nah! Oh, she's upset, folks. She up'n ran clear off outta the booth. Le Tuna done up and ran away, nah."

Bud leaned back in his desk. It was Tuesday and the broadcast was coming to an end. Bud always seemed more exuberant on Tuesdays. He took a sip of bourbon. This particular sip was valued at $183.14. He reflected on this day's broadcast and was feeling proud, small hiccup with Walt aside, of course. And he would be sure to send that De La Tuna girl a fruit basket or something next show. Maybe a bottle of that cognac them black folk seemed to like so much. What was that one called? Himiny? BLHM would probably make light of the matter. BLHM, that obnoxious and unwelcome thorn in his fuckin' keister. Calling his broadcasts hateful, ignorant, uninformed and agenda pushing. He showed them *good* today. Punks and thugs posing as a somehow justified movement was all they was. Calling *him* agenda pushing? What was *their* agenda? Wanting all black people to be able to dress and act like thugs without any consequence? Not on his watch. No sir! Bud had one last golden nugget for this broadcast. A top ten all time, he felt. He was in the zone today. No doubt about that. He continued:

"True Muricans, on to something nah, that, uh, that I am *incredibly* proud to share. As you know, I will be broadcasting out of Chicago next month for mister David Peeee Betty's rally over at the UIC pavilion."

"Meester David Peeeeee Betty," Ted repeated.

"Dat rot, Ted. Dat rot! I am, uh, and I am *proud* to report that I'm going to be there in town, standing beside our noble candidate. A candidate of the people, nah. And I will be joined up in dere by a special panel that will be in town and doing play by play all the while. But that isn't all, folks…that isn't all, cuz very soon in the coming weeks…I can't tell you exactly when, cuz we're negotiating a time in his schedule right now. But rest assured, *very* soon folks, our good David Peeeee Betty."

"David Peeeeeeeeeeeeeeeee Betty!"

"Dat rot!" Bud clapped his hands one time. "The *man* himself…will be talking with me for *True* American Radio. How bout dat? Hmm? How bow dat, folks? And you can bet I'll be bringing up many of the key points that we've been talking bout on my show over these past few months, as well as those core, down home values that just never go out of style. Remember those old-time values, folks?"

"I sure do," replied Ted. "Wish we could get back there again."

"Me too, friend. Bring it back!"

"Bring it back, friend."

"Dem good 'ol days. Back den, uh, member those days when a man could be a man, and a woman could be a woman?

When people worked hard and held themselves accountable for their actions? We'll bring them back this election, folks. David Betty and Bud Harbaugh are working on it, you can bet. And, uh, and good 'ol Ted workin' on it, too. And even Walt, with his unhinged behind. So, dere it is, folks. Until next time, true Muricans. This is *Your Bud* signing off.

Bud Harbaugh pushed the swing mic away and propped himself up off his desk chair. He reached across the top for his bourbon. He drained the remaining two fingers like a roofer downing the first swig of iced tea while taking a break on a sweltering summer afternoon. He gave a quick, half drunken salute to Ted and headed for the door. He lumbered his twenty-two-stone ass noticeably quicker than usual, though this was not to presume his movements were still not *very* much strained from aching limbs and joints. Limbs and joints ravaged by gravity and time as the years passed and his weight climbed steadily higher. His liver grown steadily fattier. He didn't seem to mind the pained shuffle on this particular day. It was Tuesday, after all. Ted watched him from behind and noticed, as he always did, how Bud always had an extra spring in his step on Tuesdays.

Bud came upon the private elevator to his broadcasting station and was carried forty-three floors down to his underground parking spot. His four point eight million-dollar, custom silver Bugatti Veyron sport car awaited in the closest available parking spot. Right smack dab next to the elevator door. Custom, in his case, meant an extra wide driver's seat, at the expense of the passenger's side (Esperanza was petite anyhow, and two thirds of a seat seemed to be plenty enough for the old girl). Ample padding, of course. Soft leather. Even softer than the calf leather comprising his size seven and a half diabetic shoes. Supple skin of baby cow to caress his back most supplely. His back sores that came and went barely felt the friction as the seat seemed to fold around him like a soft, fluffy bovine pillow, the gentle give seeming infinitely accommodating to the increasing heft of its occupant. This comfort to mitigate the seriousness of his worsening physical issues kept him from actively addressing them. Put them, to a large extent, out of his mind.

The pleasing, light ding, and the elevator doors opened up to the cavernous lower level parking structure. Bud tottered to his car like a freakish, fat, giant baby, and gave a quick nod, along with a hundred-dollar bill to Victor; the guard who kept watch over his car while he gave his daily broadcasts.

Bud plopped to the sound of air hissing from the pores in his leather seat, hit the gas with a start, and sped off toward the electronic exit door and the glamorous bustling streets of downtown L.A. that opened with it. As the door ascended from the oil-stained concrete, the ample southern California sun hit his pasty face, though his eyes were protected by sunglasses he always kept hanging from the top button of his shirts. These were handmade by an Italian master who worked only for A and B list celebrities. The occasional has been, maybe, if he were a fan of them prior. They were studded, around the frame, with two carat diamonds. The Burgues Script initials "BH" were etched in aquamarine, his birthstone, on both sides. The cost was four hundred thousand per pair, cash, to be paid directly to the man in Euros, which Bud did on his trips to Tuscany biannually. He had similar design back up pairs, utilizing precious stones of various types. Rubies. Fire Opal. Alexandrite. The value of his total belongings just on his person (including a two million dollar-plus Swiss watch, handcrafted over eight months and made exclusively for him on a recent trip to the Alps) and including the car, exceeded eight million dollars.

Bud observed, briefly now, as the door raised skyward, legions of fans lined up on the sidewalk outside by the street-flanking the underground parking exit. The fans. Bless them all and praise Christ Jesus, (Bud fancied himself a good Christian) knew within minutes when he would be leaving each day.

Bud put in his signature routine. This was to slow his auto to a low idle to wave and shout out the question they all cherished, "Who's your bud?" before kicking it in, blazing off on all eight cylinders toward his secluded compound in the Hollywood hills. A fading chant of *"You're our Bud…you're our Bud…you're our Bud,"* in his wake. He was happy with this always well received, though possibly somewhat ostentatious, flourish. Image, after all, had its place. He well knew this fact.

Bud's car had showy flourishes of its own that abound. The shift handle made of polished amber with inlaid aquamarine stones forming his initials. The petals on the stick shift car were of solid platinum, with inlaid diamond stones reading "Who's" then "Your," then "Bud," going from left to right- clutch to brake to gas. With Bud's neuropathy, his semi-numbed legs sometimes struggled to find their proper rhythm with them. There had been times (more so recently) in which he had attempted his typical macho send off to his fans, only to find his car stalling out and rolling, pathetically, a few yards, before he'd start it up again and say, "mercy me, must have been a libtard mechanic," to a round of hearty laughter, and hopefully a successful speeding off on the next try.

Bud's routine went off without a hitch this time. He cruised down Avenue of the Stars with the fading chants in his dust. He waved, at times, to small groups, scattered across upwards of several blocks past the broadcasting tower, as they often were. "Bud's buddies," they were. They held their assorted signs and banners advertising his most popular quotes and sayings from the show. He gave a smile and thumbs up as he passed what looked like an aging Midwestern couple. Their sign read, "Your bud knows best," which the wife waved side to side, standing just off the entrance to Santa Monica Boulevard. He thought to himself the influence he must have had to bring couples like this, prolly from butt fuck nowhere, all the way here to downtown L.A. Making a trip halfway across the country, just for a chance to see him briefly speeding by. He bet that thumbs up just made their trip, and the half chub raised a little more in his pants at the thought. "Estoy listo, Esperanza!" He exclaimed aloud, his head falling back on the neck rest as he hit the gas hard and the car surged on its mission.

Bud pulled up to his home T-minus twenty minutes later. The residence was gated off. A cobblestone path wound its way through a massive tropical display of native trees and flowers that extended a football field's length before opening up to his equally vast back lawn. The home was visible past another hundred or so yards of pristinely kept grass. The domicile a hulking compound of three levels, each containing several thousand feet of living space. The walls were of massive stones, in varying hues, from wide-ranging pockets of the globe. Precious stones dotted the mortar between them. Large, heavily tinted rectangular windows jutted high up the sides: Thick, bullet proof windows that did not open. Bud preferred easier to control AC over windows letting in natural winds, which never seemed to cool him down enough anyway.

The terrace atop the structure came into view with the rest of the home. It was visible to cars pulling up to park around the brick cul de sac in front of, and adjacent to, his thirty-car garage (more of a warehouse, really) that was jam packed. The value within exceeded seventy-five million dollars. A giant cluster of grapevines extended in a large swath along the wooden top beams of a massive rooftop deck. Rare, finely polished Koa wood, his favorite, shipped in from Hawaii illegally and against environmental regulations, composed the whole of the deck and terrace. Palm trees, roots tucked into giant, custom Mexican ceramic clay pots, reached toward the sky. They soared over the terrace every few yards of its length.

Bud parked his car hastily and threw the keys to, fuck, what was his name, Eduardo? Sanchez? No, it was Pablo. Was it? He'd have to ask Esperanza later. He made his way through the entryway. A waterfall cascaded directly in front of and along both sides of a giant fifteenth century Spanish wooden door from a castle somewhere in Ibiza. The waterfall itself was flanked on both sides by the initials "BH" formed entirely in aquamarine stones, ten feet high, in Burgues Script once again. The door was a gift from Dreadson after a classic broadcast about "how to talk to a liberal if you just sumbitchin' can't get out of it." The wooden door was not visible from the outside as it appeared part of the waterfall that fed a moat, of sorts, around the compound. The center of the waterfall was holographic and one could walk right through it. Bud never tired of the looks on the faces of new guests when they saw that little feature. Kept the potential burglars at bay too, he figured. They wouldn't have the slightest inclination where to find the God damned door that it mostly obscured. Bud used the eye scanning software located on a tiki torch- indistinguishable at first glance to dozens of others that lined the entrance to his home.

Esperanza's sleek form came into view, across the expanse of the family room. She was sprawled out on a deck chair by the infinity pool that ran half the length of the compound, fed by a waterfall extending all the way from a languidly winding, natural stone waterslide meandering its way from the rooftop terrace. The first floor was open and vast; the opposite end from the door nothing but a massive, polarized window, that changed its tint based on the intensity of the sun- interrupted occasionally by weight-bearing, roman style pillars atop Italian marble floors which were in place to help support the second and third stories. Bud shuffled in a strained, though doggedly determined fashion, to the pool area to take a seat next to the missus.

A customary post broadcast, chilled bourbon milk punch awaited him on the arm of his deck chair. Bud took a long sip, slurping audibly and smacking his lips in a sketchily merited display of triumph as he savored the aftertaste. His personal mixologist, Paulo, had, prior, hocked a loogie into it after indulging in pasta aglio e olio. Bud felt he could discern just a faint hint of garlic in the beverage. He would have to remind Paulo to wash his hands more thoroughly when making his drink next time. Those damned Italians always reeked of garlic, wine, cheap mistress perfume, and shittily-scented cigarillos.

Esperanza had been observing Bud this entire time as he savored his drink, and was enjoying what she saw, as she had, as a matter of fact, convinced Paulo (noticing he seemed congested) that he should probably just go ahead and hock a loogie in it. She was pleased at the ping pong ball size of what came out of his mouth. Presently, she was glaring fiercely at Bud from behind her dark sunglasses and oversized straw hat, while her lips pursed into a faint smile that coincided with Bud's glugs. She almost always wore sunglasses these days, so she could glare at Bud, unbeknownst to him, all fucking day long. Glare all fucking day at that fat fucking God-damned asshole. Bud could not see this look, but he often didn't look at her face anyway, preferring instead to look at her body, especially her tits. He still had a half chub and his little head was starting to take over the task of thinking for his big, three chinned, head.

Esperanza was, Bud had always felt, the most beautiful Latina he had ever seen. A true ten in his book, in a world he rarely felt he ever even saw a nine. Those perky, gravity defying size C tits. All natural too. Just, fucking *impossible* tits. Tits that you usually only found on a comic book heroine. The type often drawn by fat conspiracy theorists who lived in their moms' basements into their thirties. Rotund, socially embittered poindexters who had never touched a boob that they hadn't paid to. His mind turned to the thought about whether a titty fuck might be in order. A good old-fashioned titty fuck, old boy? Bud liked a good old-fashioned titty fuck from time to time. But no, not now. Not today. Today was for the old Tuesday special. He now admired her hourglass figure and her silky dark hair that always seemed to frame her bosom on both sides when she was reclining like in this moment. Her light brown skin (she was light skinned for a Latina, he always felt). A little more conquistador in the gene pool than squat native. She could pass for Italian or Greek. That helped the relationship as she was close enough to being White for his mostly white friends not to be too uncomfortable around her. A subconscious, primitive and tribal notion that if other white people where part of her gene pool, she couldn't be too *other*, and therefore harmful in some ambiguous way. Anything darker than Burnt Sienna often seemed to arouse an edginess shown in nonverbal gestures of various sorts- the cheerful service staff excluded, of course. Those people tended toward browner. Bud's moment of physical admiration was interrupted as he heard her speak.

"I heard your broadcast." She laid her book down to half face him-her head cocked in his general direction. "You're really sinking to new lows. All black people are thugs? All Mexicans have to, quote, 'swim back across the river' unless they're legal, fluent in English, and have no criminal record, including misdemeanors! Culo gordo, I'm Mexican! And I had misdemeanor drug charges in my early twenties in college! You know what for, pendejo? For splitting a pinche joint with my friend Jasmin."

"I'd keep you around," said Bud, cheerfully, waving his hand at the absurd thought that a woman as hot as her would get anything more than a slap on the wrist for such a thing. Didn't she know how the world worked? A different set of rules for the ultra-wealthy male and ultra-hot female.

Esperanza continued. She had been silently surging about this broadcast for the last hour plus, thinking it one of the more depraved that he had ever managed to offer up like a shit sandwich with pepper jack cheese and browning lettuce. And they had certainly been growing increasingly depraved in the past several months, come to figure. David Betty's competitive poll numbers seeming to be tied into this in some way. He had some nut job supporters spouting the same type of gibberish as Bud and being enabled, all the way, by Bud's digressing rhetoric. Included: Bud alluding to the possibility of a white ethno-state. Alluding to diversity as having been a failed system. Alluding to a lot of things more openly now than ever before, and all of these snowballing, picking up dogshit buried in the snow along the way.

"Pendejo, I ain't kidding, you're going overboard!" Her volume rose steadily. "People listening to this shit. This pinche mierda! They think you really *mean* all this. That David Betty. I think he's taking a page from your book on the campaign trail and his constituents are eating it up, too. Dios mio! It ain't even funny. It's fucking *scary* is what it is." She picked her book back up momentarily, before slamming it down, the weight of things still unsaid eating away at her to the point she couldn't read it now, anyhow. "You're supporting the worst in people. No. That's not even it. It's worse yet! You're encouraging them to bring it out. Now they got that McCannon guy sounding like even more of a nutbag than you!"

"Don't worry about it, chica," said Bud, unphased as he took another long draw on the bourbon milk punch. He rubbed his tongue across his upper lip. Fucking garlic was definitely coming through now. He should ask Paulo for a new one he thought, but he was already halfway through it. Ah, fuck it. He took a long drawl and drained what was left. God damn milk was thicker than usual. Bud began to caress his wife's lower body, letting his pinky finger run along the crease between her upper thigh and her bikini bottom. Esperanza scowled from behind her glasses-wrinkles emerging on her forehead with it. God damnn it all to hell, he was prematurely aging her in this and myriad other ways. Bud's half chub was up to about a fifty eight percent chub now. Getting it much harder than that was always the trick, though. It was as though the penis itself sensed that, were it to become, and stay fully aroused, it might put the whole system at risk. A stroke or heart attack eminent. As it were, Bud frequently struggled through sweaty, huffing intercourse with Esperanza. Thrusting into her with a Johnson that would push into itself like an accordion. It certainly didn't help when Esperanza would tell him to stop playing polka music with his dick and fuck her already. She would such phrases would be emasculating enough to get him to stop, but this rarely worked. From Bud's perspective, as opposed to his obesity due to physically torporiss lifestyle, it was simply sumbitchin' age. What can you do? Gets harder to get the little man to stand at attention, even with a smoking hot Senorita bonita like this.

"By the way, I never said *all* black people are thugs." Bud suddenly felt the need to clarify. Esperanza's earlier remark had made him feel uncomfortable, in its presumed undertones, that he might be racist.

"But you don't talk about any that *aren't* thugs, do you? Ever! The thugs are the only ones you *ever* bring up. How do you think that makes people think about black people? I shouldn't even ask, you know damned well how it makes them think. You're getting worse, Bud. You have to stop this. Tell them it's for show. You don't really believe all this stuff. Poor people are all entitled and lazy. Liberals are all brainwashed by college professors. You're going to make people not even want to go to college with that shit. Maybe that's what you want. Talking about them as all too timid and P.C. to speak their minds and say what they really think and feel. Immigrants are destroying this country and using up all its resources, taking away *our* culture. What do you even mean by *our* culture. White culture? You live in what *used* to be Mexico. You have a fucking Mexican wife. You eat God damn Mexican food all the time and are surrounded by your help, Mexicans, all motherfucking day! You take most of your vacations to Mexico. You're more of a beaner than I am. What is all this shit? I can't believe the man I married is talking like this. You aren't even like this at home, but your ultra-conservative, money bags friends come around and all of a sudden you're another man entirely. Your liberal friends, which are a *lot* of your friends, come around and you can talk with them. Find common ground. But would you ever mention that on your show? *Ever*? No, you don't. It's all a lie!"

"Don't worry about it," repeated Bud, gesturing with his hand for his wife to calm down (which he should have learned by now, never worked, though he never paid much heed to how this and other things he did affected her). And don't go getting all hysterical. "You're doing fine, aren't you? Hmm? All this stuff?"

Bud gestured at the patio, infinity pool, and surrounding expanse of tropical yard with his upturned hand. He added:

"Your daily cocktails made from scratch. Your lazing around the pool reading those shitty romance novels. Devon Chadwick slid his ample, pulsing bratwurst into Buffy Whitney's quivering love hole! Real fine literature, there, missy. Well done. And shopping wherever you want. Whenever you want. As *long* as you want. As *pricey* as you want." Bud huffed. "You never complain about any of *that*. We don't even have any kids you have to tend to, cuz you're apparently the only the Mexican woman around these parts who can't get pregnant five to fourteen times over."

Bud chuckled, impressed with how this monologue had been going. He thought for a moment on the whole kids thing that tended to be a sensitive subject with the woman, so decided to elaborate.

"I don't mind that, by the way. Us not having kids. But if we *did* have kids, you'd have a fleet of nannies at your disposal. A fucking fleet. You wouldn't have to do anything at any time that you didn't want to do right then and there. You get to do nothing all day in the lap of luxury. All day, every day. Nothing. You know how many people out there would kill to do nothing all day? Everyone! Don't let them fool you. Everyone, deep down, wants to do *nothing* all day. You think you'd be able to do all that *whole lotta nothing* if I was doing some run of the mill political broadcast on the radio? Some every day nonsense. Some meek, objective, forget it an hour later radio program. Ain't nobody wants that these days. I figured that out a long time ago and you should count your lucky stars that I did, missy, for both our sakes. I'm telling people what they *want* to hear and that's damn sure where the money follows. People only tune in to what they want to hear anyway nowadays, with all the options at their disposal." Bud shook his head and gestured Paulo with his empty glass for another drink. Esperanza's forehead grew a new wrinkle almost instantaneously. The phenomonen went unnoticed, as Bud continued his shpiel.

"So why not do it, huh? It's the information age, chica! They can find exactly what they're looking to hear somewhere. The information is out there. Might not be fully *accurate,* but who gives a shit. You can find thousands of articles online about people telling you everyone in power is really a shape shifting lizard from another planet. And millions of people believe it. Millions! You think what I do is any worse than spreading ridiculous conspiracy theories. The British royals are living so long because they eat babies? Drink the blood of virgins? Come on, I could be saying a lot worse than I do, and people would believe that too. Anyway, the point is, if someone's going to tell them what they want to hear, it might as well be me, mi mujer. And I *entertain* them while I'm doing it, too. That's the difference between me and most of the other guys. That's where the big bucks come pouring in. Shit! Doesn't really change anything anyway. Anybody with half a brain can see the program for what it is."

"Anybody without half a brain will be misguided and bigoted by it," gasped Esperanza, glaring still, behind her oversized sunglasses.

"Anybody without half a brain don't mean a Goddamn to no one anyway, chica. Never did, either, and never will. They just simpletons looking to be appeased. Looking to not have to take on the burden of thought if they can at all help it. Worked a long day at some department store, or factory, or machine shop, or out in the fields in fuckin' South Dakota or some shit. They got enough on their minds. Why complicate life any more? Just make it simple. That's what the fuck I do. Give them the 'straight dope,' (Bud smiled superficially and made air quotes) quick and easy, and spoken plainly. That's all they want, and if it wasn't me, it would damned sure be somebody else. Hell, Marmot news has a whole fleet of 'em like me. Took after me cuz they know no one does it better, babycakes. But none are on my level, ma'am. *That's* the difference. I make all these listeners feel like somebody understands and is looking out for them when nobody aside from their mommy dearest really gives half a shit. I understand them well. Ain't too hard. If you wrote a book on these simple sumbitches, wouldn't be but a few pages. Shorter than a list of famous Jewish athletes."

Bud got a kick out this last comment and snorted as he laughed, shooting some of his bourbon milk punch straight out of his right nostril and onto Esperanza's left tit.

"Sorry about that, chica bonita" he said. He noticed the sight of it- garlicky mucus milk on a boob- for some ambiguous reason made him a little hornier. "Hmm," he thought, "best not to examine that one too deeply." He looked at the mostly empty glass and noticed a clump of something toward the bottom and thought it must be clotted cream. Paulo came back with another libation and Bud gave him a contented nod.

Esperanza sighed and shook her head. She took her book up and pretended to read it, but her thoughts were elsewhere. She reflected on the fact that she had never loved this man. She had never, really, even liked him. But she could, at least, tolerate him at one time. For the majority of her marriage to him, she could do at least that. It had never been a true love type of marriage. She was not idealistic enough to have expected that, given the circumstances of her youth. It was an arrangement. Beauty and sex for money and power. They both knew what it was. It was fully two thirds of all marriages she knew, among her friends in the Hollywood Hills. Older men with much younger women; often younger than their grown daughters. The men always going on long business trips and cheating on their wives. But the women would cheat on the men, too. This was often with the help. Young, virile men whom they would not be seen about town with and would not even have to leave their expansive homes to find, half the time. Men whom they could be with discreetly, which was the name of the game. Men who could maintain an erection and with whom having sex seemed natural, as opposed to a desperate overcompensation for age and the growing and undeniable evidence of the bodily decay of these older men. Always older men, she thought. Older men of dyed hair and obsessive exercise routines trying to ward off the ravages of time spent partying like a young man. Bleached teeth and plastic surgery to ward off age. To ward off wear and the non-fully alterable signs of it. None of this hid the liver spots on hands, the stale breath of a rotting, twenty ounces of prime rib in the gut, cigar smoke in the mouth and esophagus, of these men. The audible cracking of joints sitting down or getting out of chairs. Old timers who wanted to believe they would never die and never be held accountable for what they had done in the present, past, or future, as related to the hereafter. And that was if they believed in one (not believing was certainly easier and less guilt-inducing for the lifestyle). Old men who wanted to believe that these women thirty, forty, fifty years younger, truly loved them and were attracted to them beyond all others. It was an illusion that so many fought to keep constantly, against all mounting evidence to the contrary.

Esperanza had come to believe that narcissism was the only defense for all of this. Narcissism that generated mental gymnastics in these old, sad men committed to an illusion life. Narcissistic thoughts aimed to convince the brain, somehow, that they really were what they so desperately wanted to be. And what was this? Forever young, virile and attractive. Loved, somehow for inner beauty and personality (one or both of which were often non-existent). Loved, certainly not for their wealth. Sure, the wealth helped, but it was a ways down the list of things. Right?

Bud had digressed, Esperanza felt, as the years went on and it made the illusion more difficult to maintain for her. Then again, Esperanza's investment in the illusion was not what it once was, anyhow. She had gone from amazed by, to excited by, to moderately affected by, to neutral to, to finally apathetic toward, the luxuries of her life, over time. They were, now, simply a part of the background; like cream colored bathroom wallpaper adorned with turquoise sea shells. The obscene wealth no longer elicited the joy it once did, or a source of pride even, as it became clearer what she had to put up with to maintain it as well as how goddamned wasteful it all was anyway when you gave thought to what this kind of money could do for others, and ended up asking yourself the question, "how much could you possibly need?" Worse yet, she realized the ultimate. All of this. All of this. It *wasn't* the answer. Yet she couldn't imagine herself outside of this bubble. She had heard the phrase "golden handcuffs" from a friend recently, who had recently contracted HIV from her husband; after he returned from a long business trip to the Phillipines. She could not leave him. Esperanza knew the feeling. The fear of a life without these creature comforts, no matter how exciting or freeing it might be. A different life than this would be more difficult and require more effort. She was chained to her comforts.

And this fat fucking asshole, cocksucker, mother fucking son of a bitch, ass clown. She had felt, as the years went on, that Bud had only become more emboldened by this character he'd created for the radio. A freestyling southern charmer. A good 'ol boy. A character that was also becoming more a part of himself outside of work. A character that she, by proxy, had to deal with. A persona that was spreading like a fungus, spewing ignorance. Among the traits of this character: offending minorities at parties (the few that were there, who often acted whiter than their counterparts both to be accepted by them and to deal with their own insecurities), and for that matter offending half of the white people as well, with his racist and xenophobic comments. His "off the cuff," style of speaking that his supporters ate up. All the ones with big money, anyway, and those were the only ones Bud really cared to schmooze. Ironically, he was a thoughtful man at home; more or less, anyway. His voice had just a hint of a southern accent, compliments of spending part of his early broadcasting years in southern Georgia. He had used his intellectual and verbal skills to craft his radio persona, over time, of, "*Your Bud.*"

Bud, for his part, was under no delusions about his wife and their situation. Certainly it was beauty and sex for money. He knew it. He also knew that she damn well knew it, too. And it was a fair deal in his mind. A mutually agreed upon and fair dinkum contract. So many of his friends could not accept that simple fact and actually had to construe their own world- deluded and narcissistic- because of it. David Betty was among the many. His impossibly- not of this world gorgeous- Ukrainian born model wife, late twenties he supposed, though probably in actuality at least thirty-five. He knew David to be a prime example of one who would rather fool himself that this was something real. That this woman truly loved him. That this woman looked forward to fucking him three to four times a week. That this woman desired no other man but him. The problem with that line of thought was that one had to construe a whole false narrative to go along with it; one that, at face value, would seem quite absurd. If these men were that amazing, then all the sycophants at company meetings really did think all their mediocre jokes were minute-long, guffaw worthy, flowing tears of joy-inducing, events. That they really were right about everything because none of their many dependents had the cojones to call them out on anything. That they really were the best racket player at the club because none of their subordinates ever seemed to be able to beat them. Not even once! Bud knew this crowd well. The crowd he mingled with. The crowd that accepted him based on the fact that he, clearly, was one of their tools to keep the plebeians in check, in this case by focusing their anger on the "snowflakes" versus the growing income inequality that clearl, almost entirely, benefitted the one percenters he hung out with. Bud knew he wasn't accepted based on his looks, his intellect, his worldliness, and certainly not for his shitty, marshmallow body (all of which, for the record, he couldn't give two shits about). The point was, he still got what he wanted anyway, didn't he? But Bud was pretty sure of one thing. Esperanza was probably fucking the pool boy. He didn't really give a shit about that either. He already had HPV anyway. Bud did give a shit about one thing, at present, of course. The half chub in his shorts. He leered in the direction of his wife.

"Chica bonita?"

"Yes, Bud," Esperanza sighed knowingly, after a short pause.

"It's Tuesday, mi chica bonita."

"I know. Your favorite day." Esperanza sighed, again, more audibly so that Bud could clearly hear her disapproval. Like the honey badger, however, Bud didn't give a shit.

Esperanza looked vacantly at the pool for a moment, then turned her head slowly to look over at Bud. The image that greeted her was of Bud now wearing nothing but his majority sweat stained Joey Bahama shirt, sandals, and a floppy, semi-erection which was jutting up slightly below the waist. His khaki shorts and underwear were on the ground below his dangling feet. She would not wish this sight on anyone who had not committed an unforgivable crime.

"My uh shorts uh far off!" Bud exclaimed, incredulously, in a ridiculous Asian stereotype impression. "Whah uh happen uh down derrr?" Bud, with squinting eyes and his two front teeth sticking out, continued, "I don't ah no know wha happen! You uh know a wha happen? I was uh eating da poke flied lice and a dah egg lole and den my pants a just faw off! I say, Oh no! Why ah dis always happen to Mista Lee like ah deese? Oh no fo po Mista Lee!"

Esperanza threw her book with a smack on the ceramic tiling surrounding the pool, though knowing Bud didn't really give a rat's ass about her signs of disapproval anyway. Bud mistook this gesture for her being excited and wanting to get down to business. Now his shitty impression of a Chinese man he called Mister Lee, or "Mista Lee," harkening back to the Asian stereotypes of cheesy nineteen fifties comedies of his boyhood, grew increasingly obnoxious.

"Oh lady! Whah happen? Whah you gonna do to haylp out uh po Mista Lee?" Whah Mista Lee gonna do when he got a no pants on? And den, arso, he gotta to go keetchen and make uh mo poke flied lice!"

Esperanza, going away in her mind, already, felt she might as well get started on what she knew he wanted. If nothing else, just to shut him up. She made her way sluggishly off of her deck chair, biding her remaining moments of relative peace, and eased toward Bud's half chub. He was still looking at her, head cocked to the side, with his two front teeth still poking out. His eyes still squinted.

"Oh, whah happen, lady? Oooh, I see whah you gonna do fo Mista Lee. Oh, Meesta Lee gonna enjoy a deese!" He folded his hands behind his head.

"Just shut the fuck up," she thought as she grabbed the penis with her thumb and two forefingers and put it in her mouth. She did as she had promised, when they were married fifteen years ago. She was nineteen and had met Bud while working as his maid at a vacation rental outside Playa Del Carmen. Her parents had pushed her into the marriage, telling her she must marry a man with money before her beauty faded. She had to be married by twenty, at the absolute latest, and hold out for the wealthiest man she could find. Those at the resorts had a pretty clear understanding of who these men were. Her mother and father knew she was destined for wealth, and they had arranged for her to learn English at a young age and to use that skill, along with her God given beauty, to work at the poshest resort areas in Quintana Roo, so as to be in close proximity to the elites. It would only be a matter of time before she would make the family proud. Everyone always said she was the most beautiful girl of the Mayan Riviera.

Her sex life in those early days, for a short time, was at least tolerable. She felt cheated, though, of the young men with sculpted bodies who could- from boyhood onward- sail, fish, build, and do things with their hands like she felt real men should. The men and boys of humble origins who had tried to court her since she was thirteen years old. Many had very little, sure, but it still would have been a good life. A humbler, yet, maybe, more fulfilling one. Somehow it was all out of reach now, and to think about it arose a deep, inconsolable sadness.

Bud was a man not unlike many others who frequented the posh resorts. Aging quickly from partying like a much younger man. Soft, entitled, and lazy. A walking, talking sack of marshmallow fluff. Unskilled in any tangible way, beyond having a certain panache with words. Bud mentioned, early on after meeting her at a resort welcoming party, that he was always afraid, once he got married, that he would no longer receive blowjobs after the first few years. He mentioned this as though it were a deep-seeded fear. As though the lack of this were an atrocity on par with a great famine, or nuclear fallout. A fear that had kept him from getting married until he was nearly fifty years old and suffering a mid-life, or what he called his mid-life (it would be a miracle at this point if he made seventy) crisis. Esperanza had promised him, in her youthful naivete, one blowjob a week, guaranteed, for the rest of his life. She had been true to her word for the last fifteen years.

Presently Esperanza found herself looking for the moment at Bud's sad member. The process could take upwards of an hour these days before he finally finished; sweat drenching his hundred-dollar shirt just from the effort of receiving oral sex lying down. She hoped that, one day soon, it would push him over the edge. If he had a coronary during the act, she had already decided she would wave away the staff and watch him die. She knew they wouldn't care, and they wouldn't say anything to anyone about it. The thought of it was a pleasurable distraction during these times. She imagined the scene as she sucked on the half flaccid penis. Her fantasy this day included her masturbating vigorously while watching him die, seeing the life fade from his eyes, and it was all leading to one of the most satisfying BJs that Bud, aka, Mista Lee, had had in months.

Chapter VI

The Agenda

Grant sat, ill at ease, in the dining nook of his home. He sipped on his chilled Arnold Palmer. Now he observed the ambiguous multicolored reflections in the condensation circle the glass had left on his polished cherry wood desk nestled within the north facing side of his open kitchen/TV room/dining nook area. The reflections emanated from decorative Mexican plates that his wife, Patty, had nailed toward the top of the wall encircling the bay windows in a 3/8ths octagonal arrangement surrounding the nook. These overlooked La Tuna Canyon Park. Grant often stared out at the park, in moments such as these, in which his thoughts began to drift. They tended to drift as such after long, semi manic periods of working from home, and he found himself having difficulty maintaining focus on any one thought, in particular, for any significant period of time. Perhaps, the mind's self-preserving tendency to mitigate itself from the prolonged rigors of deep, critical thought.

Presently, in his state of thoughts drifing toward the docile, this particular thought arrived: Why did they call it La Tuna? Oceanlike it was not, in any capacity whatsoever, in fact. It was arid, semi-desert even. Fish of no ilk had any business here. It consisted of the type of rugged terrain you would expect to see in Spaghetti westerns of the 1960s. The only "la tuna" that ever saw its way here was bathed in mayonnaise, with relish and a squirt of lemon juice; a bit of finely chopped red onion. All of it sandwiched between two slices of bread with lettuce and fresh tomato; stuffed in a handheld wicker basket. La tuna on wheat.

Sweet tea and lemon indulgence in tow, he reflected during this perusal, as he considered in admiration his daily beverage. Ginny, his wife, made the best Arnold Palmers; he would say to anyone who asked (or didn't). She insisted on making them a particular way. Simple syrup so as not to give a sugary graininess- one of the textures that Grant despised due to certain tactile issues (He couldn't even eat hot dogs that had raw flour on the buns, as the grainy feel on his digits was intolerable. Peach skins were another, absolutely unacceptable sensation. What business did hairlike fluff have on edibles?). The simple syrup was cooled before being blended in with a three-quarters, fresh squeezed lemon, and one quarter, fresh squeezed lime combo. To this was added a filtered, alkaline water to just below halfway. The rest, cold brewed homemade organic iced tea. It was all organic, really. That's all his wife bought; thinking it made much of a difference. Grant wasn't too sure.

There was always a pitcher of Arnold Palmer in the fridge at any given time. Grant enjoyed one at around the same time every day, approximately 3:30PM, when the sun seemed its most intense. Though, Ginny liked to call them half and halves. He always thought that was strange, wasn't that colloquially known to be milk and cream? Who else called them half and halves? His thoughts meandered now to the theoretical issues associated with the application of this terminology. How many pimple-faced teens around the country would be stymied at any given time- he wondered- if a customer asked for a glass of half and half with their burger and fries? Had any gone into the back cooler and poured half and half into a glass only to be greeted with a confused half cock of the head at what they'd done, after doing exactly what they thought they were supposed to? Or, wait, why would they go and pour the half and half anyway? They couldn't just do that. It wouldn't be an option on one of those little push button cash registers they had. And what did those little push buttons actually show? Little diagrams of a burger with cheese? Fries and chicken sandwiches, too? If somebody wanted a chicken sandwich without mayo, would there be a red circle with a slash through a jar of mayo next to a picture of a chicken sandwich? If all the keys were pictures, could you be completely illiterate and work a full career there? No one any the wiser? These thoughts necessitated further research when Grant's time might allow.

Grant shook his head vigorously and slapped the right side near this temple. Focus, Grant! Obstructive, obsessive, perseverating, semi-manic thoughts again! And he hadn't even solved the original question posited. Now, if they did actually pour the half and half? No, they couldn't do that without a button to push- for that specific item. They would have to, first, ask the manager to clarify what to do in such situations. Let's say his name was Gary. Gary the manager. Gary, the fifty-something, balding man, with just a slight hint of girth protruding from under his overstretched, blue polyester polo. The girth would most likely be overhang- hanging over the waistline dropping below the belt a solid three inches- hairs under the belly button poking out. Dark, curly, and ambiguously pubic. He was getting off topic. So, yes, Gary the manager would have to ask the customer if what they in fact meant by half and half was probably not the milk and cream version. Gary- the manager- would know damn well that this was not a dairy based beverage request. This wasn't some fancy shmancy new yuppie coffee shop like that one across the boulevard serving hazelnut breves and the like. And at six bucks a cup? No, sir! God damned yuppie nonsense! This customer should know that, would think Gary. This is a burger and fries joint, damn it! Gary's subsequent action would, of course, give the customer the benefit of the doubt that they were not referring to a cold breve type beverage at a place like this. Could this man want two separate fountain items, perhaps, blended together? That would likely be Gary's next thought. Perhaps Gary had heard this term before, some years ago, and could vaguely recall the customer actually meant... Dammit, Grant! Stop it! This is counterproductive to the assigned task.

Ginny was reclining on the other end of the vast, three open room space. Atop her Northwest Elm, oatmeal-toned, canvas couch which formed an L shape next to the flat screen TV. She noticed Grant presently and knew that this was around the time he would become burnt out, most weekends. Burnt out from his obsessive tendencies related to his take home work. He wanted things done well. Unrealistically well, God bless him. Ginny looked at him with an understanding demeanor. She was a striking woman, Ginny.

Grant's lovely wife conjured the image of a classy blonde rock star girlfriend from the sixties who, maybe, had a penchant for lead guitarists. A look that belonged in the sixties and hinted at its sexual awakenings and an open mind to all that life could offer. A Helen of Troy face to whom time-tested songs might be written for. These sung and sung along to, decades later, by their weathered writers and continuing generations of fans. Guests to the home would frequently stow glances her way, knowing that Grant, with his relatively poor eye contact and awkward demeanor probably wouldn't (A) notice, or (B) say anything about it anyway, the poor, meek S.O.B. Dreadson was fond of casting inordinately creepy glances toward Ginny and had once told Grant that the best way he could think of to describe her was, quite simply, as, "boner inducing." Grant had shot back an awkward and briefly combative expression, before it eased, just as quickly to a sheepish, one quarter smile, before looking down and away. Dreadson grabbed him briskly by the shoulder, brought him in for a hug/vigorous shake, and played it off, explaining how he was just fucking with the young man.

"You know I kid, mah boy. You know that, right? Just jerkin' yer gherkin there, fella!"

Ginny, concerned for her husband's current mental wellbeing, decided to intervene. She put down the shitty women's magazine she was reading (The main article this week was *15 Tricks to Surprise Your Man in Bed That Will Blow His Mind*. It was shitty advice written by a twenty-something millennial with a B.A. in English Lit, and fleeting dreams of writing a YA novel centered around high school dating escapades and lessons learned. Years later, the author would indeed publish a book of lowered personal expectations- a book largely composed of embellished or entirely made up, mortifying sexual melees supposedly occurring throughout her late teens and early twenties. The endeavor would become moderately successful and spawn a couple of watered-down follow ups that still managed to be nearly as financially lucrative). Ginny cast a familiar half-amused, half concerned glance Grant's way; similar to one given him around this time of day for the last several years running. She stated the routine, concerned but casual.

"Grant, it's time for your afternoon walk, hon."

Grant heard this, spied his watch briefly and observed it was ten minutes prior to his typical, designated walking time. This was deemed close enough for him. Within the realm of acceptable deviation. Grant trudged over to Ginny and gave her a quick peck on the cheek. He might see if she were interested in a quickie later, he thought, if there was time, of course. Time was in such short supply these days. He caught a glimpse of the magazine and the main article headline. He thought to himself, "if she does anything different in bed tonight, Grant, be sure to act surprised and as though your mind has, indeed, been blown." Grant wondered briefly what a blown mind expression might look like. He felt the need to know, since so many online articles he saw talked about the things that could supposedly blow your mind. Just the other day he'd perused one of her magazines and come across a picture of what looked like a bowl of rice noodles that had various vegetables and a few chunks of, what looked like, butternut squash on top. The article read *"Five Variations on Pad Thai That Will Make You Reimagine Everything You Thought You Once Knew and Blow Your Fucking Mind Stupid, You Big Silly!"*

Grant exited the back of the home, whose yard connected to a neighborhood path leading into the canyon, and eventually linking up with one of its main trails. He began his long, winding ascent into the rolling hills. He often went with one or both the kids, but on this occasion, he had glimpsed, from the top of the basement stairs on the way out, that they were enraptured in some sci-fi movie that had just been made available to stream. His kids, Jackson, age eleven, and Lily, age nine, were at a wonderful age. The least difficult part of childhood, he imagined. Self-sufficient, more or less, around the home, and without all the pubescent nonsense that could hopefully be staved off for at least a couple years more. Grant didn't mind going alone, though, as he enjoyed both quiet times to himself as well as time spent with others in conversation and activity. His psychologist noted this as characteristic of mental health and a correlate to adult contentment. Grant appreciated that, as he felt like he was just starting to gain some control of this adult thing.

Grant observed the sun baked hills. He admired the high grass flanking the sides of his preferred trail. The valley oak trees provided the occasional shade from a midday sun and its accompanying ninety-degree heat. The ubiquitous chilopsis shrubs of all sorts and size. Wispy, delicate Populus Fremontii trees swaying lazily in the gentle, gusting wind. Grant felt the air was a bit cleaner here, both above (due to elevation) and just outside of (due to location) the ever-present L.A. smog. Grant began his deep breathing exercises. Breathe in the air for five seconds. Hold for five seconds. Release the air, over another five seconds. Fifteen second total process. Repeat a dozen or so times, until a feeling of increased ease and reduced tension becomes palpable.

It had been a stressful last couple weeks, to be sure. Grant had started advising staff and various TV personalities at Marmot News. It was something of a difficult transition as they seemed to find him a bit awkward, and lacking "leadership qualities," which apparently initially justified their minimally engaged and, he felt, rather overtly disrespectful conversations with him. Grant heard them referring to him by his most common nickname several times, The Egghead, when they thought he was out of earshot, which, of course, he sometimes was not. Thankfully Dreadson, early on, caught word of this through one of his various eyes on the scene and decided to pay individual visits to each of the offending parties. Whatever was said, the following day he was no longer known as Grant, or any of his other various mildly to moderately insulting nicknames, but simply henceforth as "sir." One young weatherman had gone so far as to refer to him as, "sir, Mr. Scott, sir," without a hint of irony in his tone. Perhaps his former military service had been conjured by the interaction with Dreadson.

Conversations at Marmot were, of course, focused on ways to bolster ratings in various regards. Bud Harbaugh's tremendous success and the innovations behind it were often utilized as a framework. This framework was one which could theoretically be expanded on (much more so than an audiological element alone) through the additional visual component that cable news provided. Grant had started out with the recommendation that every TV show should both fade in and fade out with accompanying older (pre-1990s, before they started getting all pop sounding) country music songs, and/or classic rock with a country twinge. Bonus if the songs additionally possessed a "folksy" quality.

Grant, by now, had presented lists of several hundred approved songs that his research crew had correlated with theoretically bolstered ratings. Songs that could be put on loops that cycled through about once every three months; a time interval deemed undiscernible by the vast majority of listeners as what practically amounted to a never-ending loop.

Grant had also implemented what he called "facial and presentation elements of consideration." In one of his early meetings, he encouraged the women to wear copious make up. He presented a hired model donning this amount to the ladies of the station. It was an amount of makeup whose consensus view was that of bordering on the absurd. One female lead anchor referred to it as "corpse makeup," and this was because she felt the only other bodies that hosted this level of facial cover were on the freshly embalmed, dearly departed, at open casket funerals. Grant, however, had convinced the women to wear the surplus facial cover to reflect and compliment personality demographics of their viewership. In relation to this, he presented the various anchor leads with information showing personality elements of much of the female viewership indicating above average levels of insecurity. In fact, such above average levels of insecurity were also found among much of the male audience and correlated with the preference among both sexes to view the "cut and dry" Marmot News channel over other news channels as it presented information in a manner that seemed clear, concise, and certain. This format of news both comforted the audience as well as catered to and legitimized their insecurities. Grant had correlated female insecurity, in particular, with the use of heavier amounts of makeup. Grant then correlated more copious amounts of makeup wearing with increased audience feelings of comfort in viewing other females also having rather copious amounts of makeup. It lent to the feeling that they connected in some way- were on the same page in some way- and thus the female audience would become more open to listening to and trusting these purveyors of information as a natural, albeit almost always subconscious, result. Indeed, whether this preferred viewing was conscious choice or not, Grant argued, was irrelevant. It was strictly a numbers game, as always. A game based on years of conducting surveys, gathering statistics, and developing algorithms to bolster ratings and, hence, bolster revenue.

Grant also gave out recommendations for the appropriate amount of cleavage to be shown. Enough to assert what the network liked to call, "comfortable femininity." Grant often repeated this phrase at meetings with female staff. "Comfortable femininity," sometimes with the aid of finger quotation marks. It was defined as accentuating the female form to a clear extent, but not enough to be labeled a jezebel, floozy, or even, God Forbid, a hoe bag. There was, of course, a line to tow here. The statistically confirmed ideal amount of cleavage to be shown as approximately (within a sixteenth of an inch or so) two and three eighths inches, top to bottom, and measurements were being taken to create an entirely new female wardrobe to incorporate this measurement as often as feasible. However, cleavage was deemed to be appropriate only when shown moderately- certainly not on every broadcast- thus every second to third broadcast would provide audiences with cleavage from at least one of the head female newscasters. The others? No cleavage of any sort, to assert a level of decency and discretion in dress, though of course, not doing so fully. These women weren't prudes either. Grant noted he was still working toward a more certain formula for this and was considering what level, and frequency, of leaning forward were most conducive to higher ratings. Measures were currently in progress to pinpoint this.

Next on the long docket were facial expressions. This was about equally relevant for male and female anchors. The statistically deemed "preferred look," was one of consternation amid initial presentation and discussion of current issues (the issues focused on being selectively handpicked to be consternation inducing, along the lines of "This country's going straight down the shitter!"). This consternation in relation to social issues was to be followed up with expressions of steely resolve; to combat what was to be seen as consternating- so to speak- in the world. The inducement of consternation, of course, was most frequently attributed to liberal ideals. Expressions and verbalizations conveying knowledgeable resolve and didacticism in presenting the "correct" way to perceive the information were then needed. Grant noted that this confirmed the thoughts of the viewership. The viewers were consternated with what they felt was a society becoming more liberal at its own peril. Issues being presented always in liberal terms every which way they looked. Terms that were getting too loose, free flowing, and relative. Taking them out of their comfort zones.

The anchors had a duty to first be consternated by the presupposed liberal "spin" on any number of stimuli presented to their viewers, which they would verbalize upon discussing the issue. They would convey the supposed mainstream liberal spin in a type of "Oh, come on!" eye rolling consternation, before they would then move toward a teacher-like, didactic presentation to deal with the skewed and misguided visions of those who were leading society down the tubes. The *libtards*. Such presentation was ideal in talking with guests and commentators who leaned left, as it confirmed initially (via the consternation) that the leftist views were the equivalent of a steaming turd on a platter. Red cabbage, whipped potatoes, and a pickle on the side. This would placate the viewers and their belief that the liberal commentators were overthinking things and forgetting about that good ol' down home common sense, which they were led to believe had no place in much of liberal thought.

Next the anchor would lead the conversation with the liberal and do so didactically, so as not to blatantly disrespect the views of the left leaners, but rather to teach them- as though a naïve and unknowing child- how they should be viewing any number of geopolitical issues. This would confirm the want of the viewers to be able to see their own evolving views (evolving directly with what was portrayed by Marmot News) with relative certainty, much like the wise teacher from the news program that they were viewing was showing them.

Grant worked on other ways to bolster not only the ratings, but also the credibility of Marmot News, which was growing ever more popular. He discussed marketing strategies. The propagation of Marmot News stores to sell shirts, coffee mugs, calendars, bumper stickers, and posters. All of them devices to display Marmot News approved views and Marmot News personalities (i.e. "I'm Not Letting no Kenyan President Hijack My Country," as the most popular current bumper sticker being sold. This was followed closely by, "Whatever Happened to Good Old-Fashioned Values?"). Stores were being opened, by the dozens, largely in rural and southern areas of the country. The logos incorporated the proud rodent with its hands on its sides and its head held high atop an elevated hill. The rodent donning an American flag T-shirt, army green cargo pants, and a trucker hat with the phrase, "Bring America Back" on it.

Grant discussed ways to reduce the argument that the news program was biased to the right by providing increased verbal output from the, rather paltry, cast of liberal anchors of various programs. One method in which he did so was by having them do introductions for guests as well as introducing topics on various segments. In addition, they were given near exclusive time to verbalize issues in relation to aspects that were deemed apolitical. This would then cause a numbers inflation when examining liberal versus conservative anchor communication time on various shows that could then be used to make the argument that the two different views (if one were to simply research *time* allowed to the more liberal commentators without assessing actual *content*) had a fair balance. These statistics could then be utilized whenever the network was accused of bias. Sure, they may have more conservative minded anchors and hosts, but the liberal minded among them were getting nearly as much speaking time. Compare the talking times. It's right there on paper. Just take a little looksey poo, Mr. Joe Q. Doubtsalot.

Grant also talked, specifically, with the handful of liberal commentators about preferred personality characteristics for them to convey in order to bolster their ratings for the news station, and thus, ensure their ongoing job security. Conveying these accurately in the minds of Grant and his researchers would be directly correlated with hefty cash bonuses. The preferred presentation of the few liberal commentators was to be presented as wishy-washy, over-intellectualized, and book smart. The latter presented as inevitably going hand in hand, for reasons unexplained, with an unacceptable expense of being lacking in street smarts. They were to be portrayed in positive ways, too. As kind hearted, well-meaning, teddy bear-like. However, near hopelessly naïve and idealistic in the face of an increasingly harsh and dangerous world that had fallen from grace in the years since its silently agreed upon 1950s ideal.

Grant had hired actors. Actors to model the sought-after traits. Actors who were involved in regular training sessions with the liberal anchors. Voices were to be inflected in higher tones than their conservative counterparts, among the mostly male liberal news anchor staff, as this subtly conveyed a reduced level of masculinity as compared to their right-wing counterparts. The voices conveyed by the actors who demonstrated this were initially seen to be near comical to those at the meeting. The ideal tone and inflections seeming to mimic an insecure thirteen-year-old boy whose high voice had a tendency to crack pathetically and at random. You expected the person modeling it to look down his pants and exclaim, "Oh criminy, I see hairs sprouting up down there. What's going on with my body!" There was disapproval, but not at the level one might expect given what was being observed. The cash bonus certainly could be said to play a hand. Grant was also, of course, aware that this exercise of tipping the scales in favor of the opposition was not something they were necessarily unused to. A game they already knew was being played and one they accepted. Grant had made it known that

Dreadson was considering an additional one and a half million dollar per year salary raise, on top of the initial bonus, to each of his liberal commentators this year. The board of directors was in agreance that this was fair, in order to account for the extra burden of presenting liberal views on a network that the higher ups had conceded, maybe leaned a little toward the conservative side of things. One of the liberal men was heard muttering, in earshot of one of the voice actors, "What, do you think? That we're at this network for our pride?"

Grant, in the present moment, was about two miles from his home now. He had reached the top of the ridge overlooking the San Fernando valley and was taking a moment to be at peace with the panoramic view of it. He had put his mind much more so at ease with the help of his long, brisk walk of routine. He was further comforted with the thought that he performed what he'd wanted to, indeed, exactly what he'd been asked to do, by Dreadson. His mind turned to upcoming business with a fresh young male anchor who was showing much promise on the network. His name was McCannon. The man represented the ever more difficult to find confident, articulate, old-school value retaining, young, conservative male. A blowhard to those who disagreed with him, maybe, but a savior to those who didn't. McCannon had already written a small handful of books and was just in his mid-thirties. His most recent book, specifically about a more youthful liberal element, and entitled *Pot Smoking Socialist Whiners,* was about how the millennial left was actively willing the country toward socialist policies. Socialist policies which McCannon equated, for his readers, as being roughly the equivalent of Stalinist Russian fascism, or, at the very least, spearheading a path toward this. The risk of a Stalinesque Russian fascist state developing at the behest of drugged up, androgynous and sexually confused, late twenty-something millennials living in mommy and daddy's basement. Little fairy boys who couldn't even bench press the bar if they went to a gym. These, and also, modern "fag hag" young women primordially threatened by traditional masculinity. McCannon had just gotten his own show and seemed to, already, instinctively incorporate many of the elements Grant had been working on with Marmot News commentators. By all accounts, the young man was a "natural." Some did think he went a little too far. Of course, this wasn't for Grant to judge.

Grant found himself observing, for a spell, the Burbank skyline. It stood in clear view from the westward side of the sloping hill on the outer banks of the park. His home was distantly visible from this spot. He could imagine right now that Ginny was busy in the kitchen; their two children helping her. She would be making one of her famous, made-from-scratch, chicken pot pies. Grant's favorite food, since his earliest memories, was chicken pot pie. His mother was fond of telling friends that this was one of only three things he would eat between ages four and seven (The other two? Twinkies and String Cheese). He'd taken quite a step up from the preservative- laden, frozen pot pies of his youth, with Ginny, though. Her pot pies possessed, hands down, *the* best crust he had ever tasted. With fresh, free range chicken that she roasted herself. Just like in the old days, she used the fresh gravy for the pies. The vegetables for the pie were handpicked from their greenhouse garden out back. His son, Jackson, would probably glimpse him, upon his return, through the dining nook window and wave with an ear to ear grin. This was his favorite meal, too. Like father, like son. He was a good boy, with a bright future very much ensured both genetically (as he'd inherited the looks of his mother and the brains of his dad) and environmentally (his trust fund was approaching seven figures already). Grant smiled with his thoughts and began his descent down the final hill back home.

Chapter VII

A Trip Back to the U.P.

John Gavilan pushed the button to roll down the driver's side window and took in a deep breath. His senses were greeted with the smell of pine and fresh cut logs, burning in wood stoves, pumping out cedar, birch, maple, and oak from within the cabins that speckled the coast of northern Lake Michigan's west shore. He was just past Menominee, traversing through the southernmost tip of the U.P. Nora was rousing from her nap, with the sound of the wind tunneling through the front car window. His cockapoo, Toby, was sniffing frantically now from the backseat, poking his apricot hued, fluffy head out of the car from his back-window perch. A city dog rarely encountered such a cornucopia of nature's scents. John felt the dog knew that these smells signified a trip to grandma and grandpa's house, a backyard, and miles of lake front park to walk, run, chase sticks and tennis balls through. Going to the beach to plop in silty pools in the sand, getting his belly wet on the shores of the calm and mild summer waters of Little Bay de Noc.

John and Nora frequently visited their parents in Michigan. Hers lived in the Detroit metro area, while his lived in the U.P. Michigan's upper peninsula to those who didn't know the abbreviation. God's country to the people who lived there. The fact that he came from the U.P. made John a Yooper (derivation of U.P.er). His wife he would sometimes jokingly refer to as a "troll," while among fellow yoopers. "Troll" was what yoopers called those from downstate who lived south of the Mackinaw

Bridge. As they lived "under the bridge" so to speak, they were known as trolls. Nora disliked this nickname and would often lightly punch John whenever he called her this, being sure to remind him that they were both from Michigan which- in case he didn't know- was the same fucking state.

This moment of the drive always was John's favorite part of trips back home. Taking in the refreshingly temperate, clean, and forest fragrant air- something that simply did not exist quite like this around Chicago. The air was almost always cool at night, even in mid to late summer never seeming to get above the low seventies once the sun set. Now, it was probably in the low sixties and the air had a slight chill to it- which started to come in at night in this part of the country around, even a little before, Labor Day. As John took in the air, Nora looked to her right and observed Washington Island, which she knew signaled they were getting close to Escanaba, where his parents still lived in their home that they had owned since the early seventies. She enjoyed visiting. The home was located right by a park- Ludington Park- and its adjoining harbor off Little Bay de Noc, which jutted north off the top of Lake Michigan. A home this close to the lake, complete with a three-season sun room surrounded with windows on all sides taking in the lake breeze; was simply unattainable where they lived. His parents, retired teachers, lived in this area much like millionaires would on the opposite end of the same lake. Nora sometimes joked about how she would like to have the house lifted via Boeing Chinook helicopter, to be planted on a strip of land in Chicago's north shore for them all to live in. Also, how this would, of course, instantly add a zero to the home's value.

The road they were on now was lined with forest trees, a mix of pine and deciduous. A goodly amount of old growth maples which produced the top of the line maple syrup that they would take back regularly, sometimes accompanied by a cooler full of pasties in the winter months (which numbered a full five of the year around here and pushed in on the other seasons). They knew they were in the U.P. and no longer in Wisconsin when the landscape changed. From the city sprawl of the Chicago-Milwaukee metro area that spread across three states, to the vast

Wisconsin pastures that smelled like cow shit and lead to the occasional, disgusted remark from Nora that John must have passed gas.

Finally- four hours into the drive- they would reach the forests of the U.P. The U.P. was basically one massive forest- a part of the vast, transcontinental Taiga and flanked on the north and south by a great lake. To the east by the Soo Locks. This forest stowed the occasional small to medium sized town tucked away within. It was one of the most ruggedly beautiful, as well as one of the most willfully isolated places in the country, with all the good and the bad that went along with that type of isolation. The town they were soon to enter, at just over twelve thousand people, and a quickly aging population at that, was the third largest city on a peninsula nearly twice the size of the state of New Jersey. The largest town, Marquette, where they would make a ninety-minute drive from Escanaba on an occasional day trip, had a permanent population of just over twenty thousand.

When they reached the town of Escanaba, John made the final turn down Lakeshore Drive, to his parents. Toby was starting to yip and pace back and forth around the back seat. He was smelling parts of his territory he'd marked during walks from past visits. John pulled the car up to the modest, colonial style home, just as Toby's barking hit its nadir and Toby jumped out as soon as the door was partially opened, doing a beeline to his parents, Larry and Joann, who were coming out the back door as they heard the car pull in. Hugs abounded for this first visit since Memorial Day weekend, and the reunited extended family retreated to the den to talk about the Tigers, what to cook for the long weekend, and maybe getting the damned boat out for a good, brisk sail, finally. Then on to less palatable topics too, like Larry and Joann's growing health problems in their late seventies, and the growing drug problems around town. Recently research came out that over one in a quarter of all infants born in the county had been exposed to some type of narcotic in-utero. An unfortunate nickname of Methcanaba had recently sprung up.

As everyone settled in to the family room, Toby crawled onto John's mom, Joann's, loveseat, cuddled up beside her and went fast to sleep after a long and stressful car ride. The dog had been picked up from his breeder in a car at eight weeks old and driven hours away to his new home, whining until he wore himself out and fell asleep. He had a fear of long car trips ever since, and maybe some deep internal intuition that they might lead to something traumatic. John and Ana soon enough took him and themselves upstairs to sleep in his older brother's childhood room, still lost in the eighties, complete with a Judas Priest banner hanging over the bed and a poster of the band Heart on the north wall. A collection of beer cans from the seventies and eighties hung on the south wall. His brother, Guy's, sculptures and art work from high school adorned the room in various areas.

John woke around ten-ish the next day and spent some time talking with Larry over oatmeal scones and coffee inside the canvas top, mesh sided, veranda set up in the backyard terrace. The scones were hearty and warm. The coffee was strong. The weather remained just slightly cool, not yet fully warmed by the sun, with the remnants of dew on the grass. Jeans and long sleeve T-shirt weather, as was much of the summer around here. A view of the harbor through the side yard lined with small locust trees, one planted by him for a fourth-grade project over twenty-five years prior. It was over twenty feet tall now.

The conversation centered around his trials and tribulations in the real estate market this morning. His agent who, out of laziness, was showing very few properties to himself and Nora and who- out of an empathy lacking self-interest- was laying guilt trips on them for their want to look at properties before they were in a position to buy outright, or to look at more properties than the piddling amount she was showing. It was the type of conversation that John enjoyed talking with his father over as it felt comfortable to both. It allowed Larry to continue to instill advice and wisdom regarding an area that his son had not fully experienced, and these areas were ever dwindling with his youngest son now well into his adult years.

This backyard area, that once was simply an outdoor table and chairs atop a mossy brick terrace, now included a veranda so that his parents could stay outside in the summer for hours on end in rainy or windy weather, or on the days when the weather was too hot, which were few here, even in the heart of summer. They often stayed out there half the day or more. To the right of the veranda was a humble herb garden and a small, tiered koi pond with trickling waterfall and lily pads. A toad had made its home in there and would pop it's head out of the murky water from time to time. A couple Adirondack chairs stood facing the garden. A small, glazed-tile book stand in between them. Across the walkway and in the side yard, by the back door, stood the remnants of an aluminum swing set and the stump of a large maple tree that once held aloft a treehouse Larry had built for John and his brother, Joel. It was long since weather beaten and eventually torn down with an axe and crowbar by the brothers when they were, years later, in their teens and no longer interested. One of John's errant swings of the axe came within inches of his brother's head; a memory that made John flinch from time to time when he thought back on it.

John and Larry had had many conversations here since his childhood, becoming more focused and long term in nature as John grew up. Conversations in high school about basketball (which started John's sophomore year when he made the JV team, and which heated up by the time he had become starting center on varsity). Would he want to play college ball? How far would he eventually want to go with it? This conversation fizzled out, abruptly, his freshman year in college when, in a scrimmage match, he tore his ACL tendon from trying to pivot too fast. A few weeks later he really sealed the deal by re-aggravating it twice when he tried to come back prematurely. It was his first adolescent experience of his body not being able to do- more or less- whatever he wanted it to. The start, also, of various realities that one began to contend with in adulthood that made it ever clearer to a person what their limitations were, and both the immediate and longer-term consequences of their actions.

They had talked about practical matters. Larry was an old school German descendant, and ever practical. Where John should go to college, what he should study, how he should consider the job market in relation to what a degree would provide in terms of real-world options. They talked about grad school and, eventually, his various jobs afterward. Scraping together clients, whatever issues, whatever location within reason, wherever he could find them. That is simply how a person did things starting out in the workforce. After that, how to best move from one position to another until he had finally gotten to a place in which he felt a semblance of control and respect from his coworkers. Building a position that could potentially be longer term and more sustaining.

They had talked over the years about his various girlfriends, then his fiancée and eventual wife, Nora. They talked about his two brothers and their non-traditional paths through life which they were both continuing to slowly understand and come to terms with- even gradually respect. Things turned out as they did. You adjusted to that easily, or more slowly, over time.

Politics. Politics always got into the mix and took up a greater amount of conversation these days, as his father had become more staunchly and outspokenly anti-rightwing as the years went on. He viewed the entire GOP constituency as living in a fantasy world in which outdated lifestyles and values that conflicted with modern realities kept people from adapting as they should be. John felt he also saw their more traditional religious beliefs as a strong part of this fantasy. A belief in a God who was simply an entity that substituted for their daddies who no longer held them and read them lullabies. An actual father who, maybe, was no longer on this earth with them. Larry had lost a couple friends, as agnostic liberals were rather few and far between in this town (or, at least, those who made those views known). The more economically depressed it became, the more people seemed to reinforce what he considered to be their delusions. Delusions that seemed to help people through hard times, though which also conveyed weakness and kept them from dealing with their problems in a more practical manner that might change their situation. Delusions that amounted to childlike fantasies living on in scared adults. Delusions that, at their worst, facilitated *not* changing, when change was, in fact, a necessity.

John picked himself up around noon, slowly. Slow paces were fine as the pace was much more relaxed in these parts. Part of it was that people here weren't, so much, *striving* all the time, as Joann had noted about Chicago area urbanites. "The Strivers," she called them. There was a tangible will toward this, John had to agree. It was hard for a person to distinguish oneself in the big city (whereas here you could probably get your name in the paper just for moving into town). You could either resign to that fact or fight against it, often in visibly pathetic and image-driven ways. Around here, people could be distinguished in some way or another much more easily. They were known by their deeds and their personalities much more readily. And they could go about their days contented amid those facts; be less concerned about the existential aspect of always feeling the need to show a unique identity relative to the people they lived amongst. They were not so burdened by the false notion that the busier a person was, the more important they must be, which was part of the fuel that fed the fire in so many people living in the City by the Lake.

Presently, John was getting himself up to go out to the Farmer's market to pick up some kale, blueberries and whitefish fillets-caught fresh out of the bay- for dinner. He took the car over to the stands a few blocks away, picked up the ingredients and brought them back home. The whole process took ten, maybe fifteen minutes. You could do a whole lot of things in these parts in ten, maybe fifteen minutes. Folks could get anywhere in this town in about five minutes, or less, by car and there weren't that many places to go, anyway, in which to expand on even *that* miniscule amount of time. Subsequently, one had to find ways to fill up their day here. Larry was known to make trips to the grocery store for things as trivial as a can of refried beans. Fill up the day; that's what you did around here. In this spirit, John decided to drive around until he found something that seemed suitable to occupy himself with for a spell.

He drove out to Ludington Street- the town's main street section- and took it toward 41; the main north/south highway through town. He drove past the stores on Ludington. About every fourth or fifth store seemed vacant, though it was a slight improvement over years prior; this related to a recent downtown renovation project. He recognized several of the store fronts from his childhood. There was Gusty's, the little convenience store with the late nineteen-forties era neon sign. This was where he used to buy candy bars with his allowance, or with money he collected from returning cans and bottles. There was Sayklly's, the chocolate shop that also featured Yooper tchotchkes, and crystal ornaments, often in the shape of animals; squirrels, turtles, pandas, dolphins jumping from a wavy base. He drove past the red hots stand run by a guy he graduated with, from the same public high school (the *only* high school). He ran it, along with his brother. They were good guys from what he remembered of them. Probably, they were more than capable of making it happen in a larger urban area for the bigger bucks. They chose to stay and just maybe found a way to be happier.

He drove past the bars. So many bars. There had, always, been so many bars here. Largely, they were the same ones that he'd gone bar hopping to during and just after his college years, when all his friends would reconvene over Christmas, spring break, and the summertime. A time just before they had dispersed, ever more so, around the country, the last fifteen years thereabouts. The bars weren't smoke pits anymore, like they used to be; poorly ventilated, as they were. He remembered how the stink of stale cigarettes and cheap cigarillos worked their way into the fibers of his clothes, which mingled with the comparatively pleasant smoke of bonfires out in the country. He thought about how younger generations would, thankfully, not have to deal with cigarette stench like that anymore. Fill their own lungs with toxins spewed out of the lungs of others.

He thought about the number of bars, too. How many there were for a town this small. How many hard drinkers there were here and how many of them he had once gone to school with; seen around town from time to time. People who would drink specifically to get drunk and to get drunk each and every time. People who drank to escape their lives. So many of them, he felt, never found a way to reconcile getting older; never, truly, saw a life they could invest in beyond that of their high school glory years. Beyond, he figured this meant, their childhood. Nowadays, when he would see these people, he could already see the effects of

162

the lifestyle they'd chosen. The drink that had made their features weathered and prematurely aged. Bloated faces with tired eyes.

John found himself driving down 41 and taking it north along the bridge overpass hovering over the Escanaba River where the odd fishermen in bass boats, or on the river's bank, cast for walleye (though would also accept yellow perch, humbly, if that's all that might be in store for them). He drove past the old log cabin restaurant, Delilah's, where he used to get breakfast, hungover (or sometimes stoned after a wake n' bake with his friends in his college days when he delved in and out of pothead status). A "garbage omelet" and wheat toast, and lots of watered down, shitty coffee. Of course, he didn't think of the coffee as shitty back then. He didn't think about it much at all back then, among other things that he now saw through the lens of unfolding life experience.

He drove to the next town north. This was the town of Gladstone. Driving around this small enclave of five thousand or so people, he found himself parking his car at Van Cleve park, to walk around and look out onto the bay at the handful of sailors enjoying the brisk, early afternoon breeze. The small skyline of Escanaba was visible, enveloped by a light haze off the bay. In the distance, its tallest building was most clearly seen. This was a senior living home built for an aging population and it was eighteen stories tall; quite an anomaly in a town this size. It was the town's only building over five stories. He looked back to the boats navigating the bay, keels leaning nicely with waves splashing over the bow and onto the people sitting up front. More fishing boats here, too. Boats that were tricked out with all the latest, fish-finding sonar equipment, forty HP outboard motors, and state of the art deep-sea fishing rods. These boats cost more than most people's cars around here- even more than some people's homes- and you could often see them displayed proudly in open garages across clear cut yards. The ones who brought in the big hauls, of course had bragging rights, but the ones with the nicest boats –if they could bullshit- could weasel in on the glory of it all even if they weren't usually bringing in enough catch to provide a family meal.

John parked his car and walked along the lakefront park for a spell, looking across the bay at the rolling whitecaps, glancing over from time to time at the limestone cliffs of Stonington peninsula trailing off into the distance; a brilliant, illuminated cream compliments of a near cloudless sky. John people watched as he walked- one of his favorite past times- on par with sleeping in late without an alarm clock or having a non-rushed bowel movement while reading a good book. Nora joked that he was a premature old man and that she could already envision what he would be like in his seventies. He was starting to grouse more about things that upset him these days, too, which didn't help with the *young old man* jokes. But now he was quite enjoying his old man hobby. He enjoyed this past time particularly when coming back home, as he found so many differences of note here, that only came out more so with time away from his hometown.

There was so much here that made it seem a world away. The dialect and accents. The bawdier talk. The sassier women. The simpler dress not looking to impress anybody much. The people were so in contrast with Chicago's north shore, which was yuppie saturated. Yuppies were, for the most part, all you saw. Even in the service industry jobs; yuppy college students, or the teen sons and daughters of yuppy families. Self-satisfied yuppies in beamers. All very similar to one another at first glance. Sure, there were the variety of teens walking the streets in the garb that highlighted their various phases. Goths, jocks, cool nerds, uncool nerds, artsy kids, insecure and reclusive kids. By adulthood, though, most of them looked like either a standard college-educated (usually with an advanced degree), corporate, businesslike, office all-star, or professorial seeming, adult. Book smart, they were, mostly liberal-minded; comfortable in their presentation and general life choices thus far. Everyone talked easily and eloquently. Looked pretty well put together. Took themselves a little more seriously with it all.

At times, and juxtaposed with their general casual presentation, these midwestern yuppies could become upset. Irritated if they felt they weren't being acknowledged fully for how special they thought they were. Some had reconciled the fact that they weren't particularly special once seen in context of their equally, or more successful, neighbors; but some never seemed to get over the insecurities of not standing out amongst their counterparts. Most had accepted that they weren't quite the special flower that Momma always told them they were. The ones who couldn't handle this simple conclusion, John figured, probably found it a path toward becoming one of the assholes of the world. Assholes driving forty-five miles an hour down neighborhood streets, cutting people off on the highways in their luxury cars, sighing loudly and audibly when having to stand in lines beyond three patrons deep for their morning lattes and their French-inspired pastry of the day. Other people could be such an inconvenience. There were the trophy wives too, of course. As money congregated here, so followed the trophy wives. A prerequisite often seemed to be that they had to have half a brain and thought-provoking things to say at least some of the time. A level of intellectualism was required of the residents here, at least those in any close proximity to the lake and Northwestern University. Many of the trophy wives here, therefore, had gone to college to earn their M.R.S. degree.

People in the U.P. They were of a different ilk. There had always been a humility about them. This endeared them to others throughout the northern Midwest. The hard workers among them-the *strivers*- almost invariably did well wherever they went, though most never left the vicinity of the great lakes area. Their humility and their accent (which sounded Canadian to most) made them approachable, presumed friendly, and easy to get along with. This, combined with their work ethic, gave them an excellent reputation in their general part of the country.

They had some stereotypes too. They were considered hard drinkers to most (relative light weights to their neighbors in Wisconsin). They had old world, Finnish tempers that could flare up at random times. Sometimes a disproportionate anger could come from a distant place; maybe the insecurity of feeling they were always, somehow, thought of as naïve country bumpkins at heart- never to feel as though fully belonging, or fully accepted into the cities that they moved to in search of work. The anger had a level of truth to it. Naivete was often presupposed by those outside of here. Naivete and a feeling that these people, this rare tribe of roughly three hundred thousand, lived in a world apart. A world where there were twice as many deer as humans living in the same land area. A world of log cabins and outhouses, where hunting and foraging where not only a way of life, but a necessity for many. People who lived in nineteen seventies era trailer homes and drove rusty cars from the late eighties and early nineties; even now. People who built their own humble dwelling places with their hands and made their livings with those same hands through odd jobs, supplemented by their skills in the north woods. The ability to distinguish edible from poisonous mushrooms; to know when and where various wild fruits grew. To know how to spear fish and evade the DNR. To hunt all types of wild game and, at times, to make meals out of animals that some would scarcely consider eating. A world where trucks and boats were almost necessities and devoted much of a humbly earned income. The home was not the priority or where one got their bragging rights from. A home was utilitarian. *Things* were not important. *Uses* were, and a thing without a clear *use* was of little to no value.

John had noticed something in recent years, though. Something different beginning to emerge in some of these people. A people whom he still considered his own, as a Yooper always left a part of themselves with their roots. They always returned, throughout their lives, and often came back in the end for the peace of it. This connection to the people he saw made it more difficult for him to accept the changes he saw in recent years; recent months, even.

Walking along now, he looked at the men who passed him on the humble dirt trails. He saw chests puffed out, arms held outward to the sides. He saw glances toward him and toward others, as though questioning their motives; as though questioning what others' intentions were or what they might do to them, or maybe, assess what, somehow, they were about. Whatever that meant. Looks that, even behind wraparound sunglasses, were seeming to convey a certain us-versus-them impression. A sternness of the look that seemed to pose the question, "are you one of us?" Where was this coming from? He couldn't help but wonder that.

The women seemed a bit different, too. He always knew the women here to be bawdy. The type of women that would freely go toe to toe with the men when it came to drinking, cursing, and telling dirty jokes. Women that you did not want to mess with, but, almost invariably, loving women when it came to their men and children. Women who, underneath it all, cared deeply for those around them. Who cared enough about those around them to keep them honest and on their toes; knowing this as a way to bring out the best in them.

He saw, now, women that appeared different than he remembered. Walking by, he saw more tattoos on them, and a similar edginess he had seen in many of the men. A little less of the easygoing and the (most of the time, though not always) platonically inviting smiles that he used to see. He thought he saw more of a weariness, among many. He saw more premature aging. Drugs? A harder life or harder living? The tow often went hand in hand. He saw an anger, too. A palpable anger with a coexisting weariness. He saw more overweight women (the men were bigger, too, come to think of it). He wondered if more of them were stress eating. Not caring about eating unhealthy foods? He wondered if, for many, overeating or eating junk food was just another form of trying to find comfort in the world they existed within. A world that, ironically for many around here, did not truly exist outside of several neighboring counties. Because of this it only provided, by proxy, through goods and media brought or projected into this small, largely isolated area.

Something else that John noticed was the he was seeing more of the elderly and less children. Ever fewer children and young adults. He knew that the town was aging. The surrounding area was, too. Almost all the towns around here were shrinking in size. Homes were on the market for dirt cheap. Family homes could go on the market for the price of a luxury car, a used one, even. The kids who went to college rarely moved back, and it was known, was almost a given, that they probably couldn't if they tried. With an aging population, and less kids, many of the schools were closing down, so there were less jobs for any incoming teachers, principals or administrators. This had been a town known for quality teachers, too. For the laborers, the local paper mill was perpetually downsizing. The papermill was the top employer during John's childhood. And the town was already well saturated with various professionals such as lawyers and doctors, bullheadedly trying to make it work in their hometowns. The former getting much of their work from drug prosecutions and the latter getting much of their business from accidents involving alcohol or drugs, or from the physical ailments that went along with aging populations and their increasingly overweight clientele. People making poor life choices due to not being particularly invested in their lives, it seemed.

John hooked a left toward the end of the dirt trail and walked away from the beach and toward the middle of town. Approaching the neighborhood homes, he noticed similar looking men in groups, with cutoff shirts and toting beers on front lawns. He saw the looks again from errant glances. Are you one of us? He continued his jaunt and noticed that more than a few of the people he was walking past, on their porches or in their yards, had their radios turned on. Then, he heard a voice; faintly familiar that brought with it a visceral, nausea-like feeling of sorts. A voice that he knew belonged to a conservative radio personality. A modern-day muckraker pushing his agenda through the airwaves. He listened more keenly and soon recognized the hallmark traits of Bud Harbaugh. The periods of silence. The clearly conveyed implication that only certain Americans were *true* Americans and many others weren't. The loud, brash voice completely certain of what it was saying. Much more dangerous than that, a voice *also* believed to be certain by those who tuned in.

John's attention diverted to the form of a woman ahead. She sat, shaded and alone, on her porch in front of a humble house that was unkempt and in rough shape. Her features became more evident. She appeared in her early to mid-fifties, maybe. The porch was weathered to the point of being precarious. It sank downward at maybe a ten-degree slant from back to front. Weeds poked out of the crawl space and up through gaps between the wooden slats of the porch. Sliver inducing wood fragments jutted out at various angles from the tow by fours. The faded white paint of the home peeled copiously, with dull gray wood showing in numerous patches; the bleached, bare wood nearly as represented as the stubborn areas where the chipped paint yet held. There were assorted plastic toys spottily adorning the backyard, beyond a low, rusted-out, chainlink fence. A small, inflatable children's pool, maybe half full of swampy looking water, sat mid-yard.

There were children in the backyard, too. They looked to be in late elementary school by the looks. A boy was in a hyper back and forth run with, his friend, maybe. This was a girl just a little younger, trying her damnedest, it seemed, to be accepted. He heard them shouting and playing and heard them swearing freely in a way that seemed comically exaggerated and over the most minor of things, while their mother (maybe their grandmother?) sat on the front porch with her radio on.

She sat there, haggard. She was smoking a cheap, amaretto scented cigarillo. John saw the same look he was thinking of and seeing. This time it was on her. Are you one of us? John, a careful and calculated man- qualities honed by years of discussing the most delicate of matters with his clients- decided, in a rare moment of impulsiveness, to talk with this woman. He felt compelled to get a sense of her. He was not exactly sure why. He usually kept to himself and was just fine with it.

As John approached the home, he heard a raspy and harsh voice question, "What are you doing? Do I know you?" It made John feel like he was, somehow, up to no good just for approaching. He answered:

"I don't think you do, but I grew up not far from here, down the bay in Esky (Esky was the local colloquial for Escanaba)." He felt this should put her more at ease.

The woman lifted her left eyebrow slightly at his remark, then exhaled a long stream of smoke. She ashed her cigarillo in the open air, toward no place in particular. "Well, whoop dee do. Does that make us friends? Hey, you want to come in and I'll bake you a Goddamned apple streudel?" She got up off the chair briefly, making as though about to go to the kitchen, for emphasis.

John could already tell that this wasn't going to go very well. Still trying to make nice, he searched for something to talk about that might brighten things. He looked at her shirt; a black cutoff to go along with ripped jeans. The shirt's logo and illustrations were for a metal band that he was a fan of- Iron Mistress.

"Up the Irons!" John exclaimed, pointing at her shirt. This was fan vernacular, and a sure way to show the other you knew the band, beyond just the name.

"Oh, you're an Iron Mistresss, fan, huh?"

"Yes, ma'am."

"Well forget about the streudel, then. You get a four-course meal and a hand job! Let me go back to the kitchen and make sure I can find the hand lotion, too. Hold your horses, it's in their somewhere." She got up again and comically tried to wave John in. "It ain't like this is the first and only break I get all day from them little shits back there," she grunted, pointed with her cigarillo, behind her toward the backyard. "Hey!" She got up and walked over to the end of the porch, turned her head abruptly toward the rusty fence. "Stop cussing back there, youse two! Eh? Ya here me! Alright now, where were we? Oh, yeah, just what the *shit* are you doing here, son? By the looks of you, I figure you may have been from here once, but I can tell you ain't lived around here for a long time. What with that Swiss watch, Italian sunglasses, yuppie looking leather sandals. You're probably a FIB (Fucking Illinois Bastard) by now, I'm guessing. Climbing the corporate ladder, are you? Eh? Burnin' it to earn it, are you? Hmmm? Well, good for you, snowflake." She plopped back down in her rocker with an exhale of cheap smoke.

"Okay, sure, I live in Illinois," John conceded. "But I lived here for twenty years, too. I think that counts for something." John decided not to offer to many personal details, and especially not to mention he was a Psychologist. He knew there was still quite a bit of mental health stigma around here.

"Well, you done converted. You maybe were a Yooper once, now you're just a yuppie. A Yooper yuppie. A yoopie? I think I just made up a new word. Hah! You're a fuckin' yoopie, son." The woman slapped her knee and started to cackle, which lead to a round of fitful coughing, capped off by the hocking of an off-colored, brown loogie. The loogie landed on the edge of the porch floor and hung there, half on the wooden slat, half hovering down the side, and stubbornly held to keep from tumbling downwrad toward the overgrown, bedraggled grass.

"That's very funny." John, uttered, with a subdued look of disgust, as he watched the phlegm wad inch toward the tall grass like a drunken slug. He was filling a brief void in conversation, having a hard time taking his eyes off the sickening spectacle. Forcing his thoughts elsewhere with some effort, he thought about her frequent use of the word *son*. It put the speaker instantly into a power position. Put them into a more experienced and knowing role; presumably dealing with the naïve. It reminded him of when older queen bees called young women *honey* or *sweetheart* when addressing them. It put them on a lower peg in the eyes of the speaker, and also, in the eyes of the listener; that is, if they accepted the position thrust onto them. That of one who needed to be taught, or, at the very least, spoken gently to, or placated, in some way. Like an igorant but well-meaning child, maybe. John's thoughts were interrupted with a start.

"Now, pardon me, son, but why are you still here?" The woman questioned. Her tone having grown progressively curter and more perturbed.

John pointed to her radio, which sat near her feet, facing her. "I wanted to ask you some questions about that radio show you're listening to. That's all."

"Now if you're talking about *My Bud*, tread lightly, kid. This is one of the only men out there anymore who tells it like it Goddamn well is." She pointed her cigarillo at him. "You ain't some PC libtard lookin' to start something are you?"

"I don't know what you mean. Are you saying that being PC is wrong and on par with mental retardation? Also, probably best not to use 'tard' just in general."

A sarcastic "pfft!" noise followed. The woman threw up her hands. "Oh Gawd, here we go. Lucky for you, Bud just had a radio show dedicated to how to talk to you people last week."

"What do you mean *you people*? We're half the country. More than half. And anyone's political opinions are only a part of what makes them a person. Yeah, I'm a mild to moderately leaning liberal, depending on the current agenda of the party. I'm also a lot of other things."

"Yeah, like a walking talking sack of cat shit, it would appear to me."

"You can call me John."

"Lindsay." Another deep exhale of shittily-scented tobacco smoke blew, this time toward John's face. John was trying not to get flustered and it was growing more difficult.

"…And even the major differences between your views and mine probably fit on one hand," He continued. "Look, I just want to know one thing." John again pointed toward the radio with the blaring speakers. "That's why I walked over here, just to talk for a minute. I'm hearing this guy, Bud, on radios all over the place around here. I just want to know. What do you get from listening to this? It seems to me all this guy is doing is dividing the people. And he's blaming all the issues his listeners are struggling with on the liberals. Then he defines what a liberal is- in ridiculous terms- for his listeners, and people just seem to go along with it. Then, once they go along with it, they go on to blame all of their own, as well as their country's problems, on this made up caricature of what a liberal is, without looking at what *they* need to do, personally, to change their *own* situation. It's weakly researched and warped, and it keeps you from trying to improve yourself in a way that would make your life easier for both you and the people around you in the *right* kind of way. Not just giving you fodder to direct your complaints, and your problems, onto some, largely made up, *other*."

"What do you know about it, eh?" Lindsey retorted venomously. "You walk up here. You don't even know me… don't know anything about me and you want to tell me what I should *think*? Who I should *listen* to? How I should spend my time or change my predicament. You don't even know anything about me, son." Another, larger exhale of smoke, more willfully directed to land on John's face.

"I know that, I'm just saying." John waved the smoke away to keep from coughing. "All I'm trying to say is, shouldn't you be thinking about what this stuff does? It's toxic. It just makes you angry and accusatory. Everything is the fault of other people who you're made to feel are sabotaging your life and your country. What good does that do you? If you're angry and unhappy, why don't you think about what you can do to change your own situation?"

"What do you know about it!" Lindsay hollered back, pointing aggressively with the nub of her cigarillo at John. She lit up another from the burning embers of the one she was finishing and then flicked the old one inches from John's side. Another deep draw and an exhale. She pointed the cigarillo at John aggressively, again, as she made her next points.

"I'm working two jobs right now. Alright? Part time, both of 'em. No benefits! At neither one of 'em." She pointed down the road in front of her, diagonal toward main street. "One is over at the local video store, renting people VHS tapes and DVDs. Only reason they're still in business is cuz so many people around these parts can't afford no cable. But they're *barely* staying in business. Paying me minimum wage. They could go under any time now and probably will. Other job?" She pointed her smoke behind her, toward the commercial strip off the highway. "Working as a cashier over at Mickey D's. Not exactly dream jobs, kiddo, but I gotta do something to support my family." Another long draw on the cigarillo. She pursed her lips to blow it out to her side, at least. Her story continued:

"Boyfriend ran out on me when I got pregnant with the second one. How bout that? He didn't want to support two kids with his drinking problem. Beer came first. So here I am, doing what I need to do to get by. And yeah, I've tried to get better jobs. Okay?" She leaned forward in her rocking chair, continuing to jut the cigarillo toward John as she made her points.

"I've been trying to work at the paper mill for years, but nobody gives up their jobs over there. Once they're in, they stick to that place like flies on a sloppy turd, and why wouldn't they. Huh? What else are they gonna get around here that's any better? There ain't no other jobs if you don't have a college degree. Libtards made it so you can't do anything these days without a God-damned degree anyways."

"That's not true." John replied, knowing any rebuttals probably wouldn't be well received, but giving it a try anyways. "Bay college, a few miles away, has a bunch of skilled labor programs and apprenticeships. How about one of those?" John pulled out his left hand and counted off quickly on his fingers. "You could make more money as a carpenter, or electrician, or plumber, or even a city worker than you could with a lot of those college degree jobs you're talking about. Yeah, manufacturing and factory jobs are fewer and farther between, but that's not the fault of some liberal agenda. It's the fault of companies that would rather sell out American workers by shipping overseas to save a few bucks and avoid a few restrictions; restrictions that are well-needed, by the way, for things like keeping our air breathable."

Lindsey had collapsed back into her rocking chair and was now sporting a non-commital, mocking gesture on her face. It certainly wasn't going over all too well, but John persisted.

"Those same people are also contributing to this crumbling infa-structure through taking advantage of and creating tax loopholes and hiding their money in offshore accounts. But beyond that, machines are starting to do a lot of the work that people used to. That means people have to start looking in areas they didn't before. They have to adapt. Like I did. Not just say, 'hey, my family's always done such and such, and now that we

174

can't, we're just gonna find a way to go on disability or work service industry jobs indefinitely' which is bullshit. It's just an excuse to lazily disengage from addressing the real problems. You shouldn't do that if you can adapt. You can find other things to do because you *have* other options that you just choose not to pursue. Maybe you think they're too far out of your comfort zone, or you convince yourself you can't do them. Look, we're from the same exact place, you and I, and I did it. If I can do it, so can you. That's the way all of us who moved away feel. We know we're no better and we don't say we are. But you tell us we are and you shun us. Why? Seems to me it's because you don't want to shine the light on yourself."

Lindsay looked at John with a blank stare for a moment, then slowly rocked forward and leaned in toward him. She began to shake her head slowly, openly glaring at him before taking a long, slow draw on her cigarillo and again blowing the smoke directly into John's face. This time it made him cough.

"You don't know what you're talking about, yoopie," she said, with a dismissive toss of the hand. "You're not from around here anymore so you don't know about us or what we're going through. But...but (shaking the cigarillo at John) you talk like you do because you got educated, or should I say *brainwashed*, at some liberal university. Now you think you can speak for everyone because of it. And you sure sound like you enjoy doing just that. Maybe you mean well, but you're misguided. You live in some yuppie Disneyland over in the big city. I live here in the real world, with real people, who do real work and have real problems. What kind of problems do you have? They ran out of prime rib at your favorite restaurant and you had to settle for New York strip?" She sat back, folded her arms, and waited for his reply.

"I got problems, and I try to do something about them when I can. But what do you do about them, your problems, besides blame someone or something else? How about you actually tell me what I supposedly don't get. Tell me anything. *Anything* about what I just said that was wrong. Please! What in the hell is it that I don't get? Or is that just something you like to say. That I don't get it. Telling me that as your go to phrase so that you don't have

175

to actually talk with me and hear what I have to say? Then you won't have to be informed about my views, right? Then you'll be even more susceptible to what *Your Bud* tells you to think."

Lindsay, having had quite enough already, reached behind her chair and pulled out what looked like to be a toy rifle. She pointed it toward John and continued:

"Conversation over, Mr. Yoopie. I told you *not* to go there about *My Bud*. Now, this here is a B.B. gun, son." She petted the barrel, lovingly, as she looked down at it. "I'm going to give you five seconds before I shoot you a new petite asshole with this mother fucker. Okay? Here we go, now. five…four…three…" Lindsay worked the pump handle as she counted down.

John, seeing that this conversation was now *definitively* over, walked backwards at first, before turning on his heel and pacing rapidly back to his car. He looked toward Lindsay, from over his shoulder, as he walked, in case she really did start shooting, in which case he would have to break into a full run. He traversed by a group of men who were lounging in a nearby front yard. The group of men in sleeveless shirts and trucker hats. He noticed one smirking at him. John guessed that he had overheard the conversation and was proud of how Lindsay had told him off. He probably considered the train wreck that had just occurred as some sort of victory for people like her and him, even though it was a victory of nothing more than bad-tempered retorts, closed-off thinking, and, ultimately, threats of violence. John now heard the sound of the gun being stowed back onto the porch and the still very much audible raspy voice behind him say:

"Hey Tripper, you want to come hit this here peace pipe with me? Yeah? Oh, you hear me now, huh? But you didn't hear me last night when I asked if yuh had an extra beer in that cooler of yours. You got some real good hearing when it comes to free shit, don't yuh. Well get yer ass over here, then."

John found his way back to the car and fiddled with his keys; trying to get the right one in the ignition as his hands shook. He was upset and starting to fantasize about getting aggressive with those people. It was a bad habit and something he needed to stop. It jacked him up over something that was not even real; just a hypothetical fantasy about giving someone a proper ass whooping. He never would or should do that. He knew this. Yet, his body grew tense and his right temple pulsated with the thought of it. Despite himself, he resented the fact that there still existed people like these today. This resentment that might one day turn to bitterness if he didn't watch it. About men whose only claim to power existed through bullying and intimidating others with a slack jaw and an alcohol and drug addled brain. Men who possessed an ability to lack empathy for others they considered outsiders through being dumb enough to convince themselves that they were inherently different from that outsider. Gaining leverage through physical intimidation and often causing physical pain. Women who did the same, though on the much more powerful and destructive, emotional and relational side of things.

John took deep breaths on the short drive home. Long breath in, hold, slowly exhale and repeat. Same thing you recommend to your clients. Progressive relaxation. Tense your muscles, then relax them. Tense and relax. Feel how much better the relaxing part feels. Feel how much your body wants that. He rolled down the window and felt the cool marine air. He thought about what he had seen this afternoon. These were not quite the people he remembered. He did not remember this type of anger or a person being so quick to react. He also did not remember this kind of flexing, or this kind of xenophobia toward other people, who so many seemed to be sizing up if they didn't outwardly recognize.

He wondered if he had just been unlucky. Had he just come across some of his people (and they remained his people) who were simply having a bad time recently? Maybe the paper mill had downsized again? Maybe they had siblings, cousins, or children who had recently lost a job? He looked at his hand and noticed that it was, at least, shaking slightly less now. The breathing exercises and the thoughts, trying to relate, seemed to help. Despite these thoughts, however, John knew that he had already seen too much and too strong of a pattern to explain away what he had seen with something like local job losses, or the odd rough days.

John drove back to his parents' home. As he pulled into the driveway, he saw that Nora was now up after a long night's sleep. She never slept enough during the week, and she could sleep upwards of eleven, twelve, thirteen hours straight on the weekends to make up for it. She was reading with his parents in the gazebo and drinking coffee. She always seemed so comfortable with his parents at their home. John was not a particularly spiritual man, though he always did feel blessed that their respective parents seemed to like who their child had married. He thought of how much easier this would inevitably make their lives over the coming years. He knew that this was just one of many good fortunes that either they had both been born into or earned on their own.

John also knew that these good things in life were both made and maintained actively, not passively. Not only during his life, but during his parents' lives, well prior to when he was born, and throughout the years following. These positive relationships needed constant pruning to remain so. His nice job required steady ongoing effort. The good things, in order to be maintained, were an active process. They did not simply *exist,* like he felt many who had less of these things seemed to feel, when they saw people who had more. Still, he sometimes felt guilty knowing that he had been given so much in his life; health, a mind that seemed to be able to do nearly whatever was asked of it, moderate attractiveness, and a steady and able support system on both sides of the family. He knew, as well, that many of these blessings came through meticulous planning, along with hard past, ongoing, and future work in any number of areas to put himself in a place where good things were more likely to happen both to and for him. It kept the guilt of having these things from impairing him to also find ways to simply sit back and enjoy life as it came; not to obsess too much about what he had, versus what others did not, so as not to feel selfish about enjoying his life. What good was constant guilt to anyone?

John walked up to his family and quietly picked up the paper to read for a while. The thin, local, conspicuously right-leaning paper, with its typos and all. His father let everyone know that, hough today was a little too windy, tomorrow would probably make for a good sailing day. John told Larry that he was looking forward to this, and he was. He knew of no greater peace in life than to get out into the open water, whether sailing, fishing, powerboating, or swimming. He also knew that any sail could end up being the last for the family, as his father, for several years now, was pushing the realms of being able to keep up the large, wooden boat. He thought about this and appreciated each outing more for it. After a spell he asked Nora if she wanted to walk over to Aronson island- about a half mile from the home- to go for a swim. She said, "why not."

After a quick change of clothes, they strolled toward the beach. He told her about the confrontation he had had with the woman on the porch. She listened to him and shook her head in a simultaneously frustrated and thoughtful gesture. She noted how sad it was. She also told him to be careful with things like that. Not to waste his time and put himself in harm's way over discussing politics with someone who simply was not going to concede any points with him. What was the purpose in that? Nora reminded him that he was letting it encroach on a much-needed break. This break would be over, all too soon, and they would be on the way back to the hectic, sometimes crazy making pace of city life. John agreed, wholeheartedly, though continued to struggle to find peace in the moment.

They made their way over the short bridge onto Aronson island and did a bee line to the beach- walking through the sand trail flanked by golden reeds and down the stretch of shore looking southward to Little Bay De Noc. They walked silently along the sand for a stretch, enjoying the growing orange glow of the late afternoon sun blending into the surrounding limestone cliffs. The same orange glow was made brighter by the white limestone, capped with the deep, verdant green hue of the pines adorning it. They started into the cool water. Water that took several minutes to get used to before you could really start to enjoy being in it.

Water that might make men say things such as, "sweet sassy molassey!" when it hit the crotch region. He thought about dinner later, and he knew they would come back to grill the whitefish and to help his mother with making the wild blueberry pie. Made with berries they had picked twenty miles from the home, in Hiawatha State Park, the summer before. They would pick a new batch, together, tomorrow.

Nora ran cavalier into the waves before remembering just how cold it was and deciding to ease her pace, to get used to it, before plunging in. John's mind was growing a bit calmer as he waded in, the waves crashing into his shorts and stomach in the choppy northern wind. Sweet, sassy molassey, there it was. He looked down the bay toward the horizon. Nothing but deep blue, with the shimmering reflections from the setting sun.

His earliest memories took place here from when he was a toddler. Memories mostly of sensations and the white light dancing on the cold, navy blue water. He remembered the feeling of rubbing the gritty mud on his body, while still in diapers. He remembered keeping his eyes closed and looking up to see the pinkish glow from the sun through his eyelids. He remembered always being drawn to the reflected light of the water. White light that danced and glowed vibrantly like the crystals that hung above the table where he ate. His parents always liked to tell stories of how he would run toward the water as a toddler. They had to watch him, because he would have gone in up to, and over, his head without a moment's hesitation. His parents still liked to tell stories about a two-year-old John escaping from his baby sitter's house down the block and running clumsily across the park toward the harbor. The babysitter, Mrs. Cheves, spotting him from out her bay window and frantically giving chase.

Present day John swam and laughed as Nora splashed him. They were the only two people on the beach right now; all the other swimmers having gone in for the day as the air began to cool. Nora jumped onto John, kissed him, and gave a suggestion they might get frisky. John tried to indulge this, but soon realized that in this cold water there was no way that little John downstairs would be open for business. After a time having fun in other ways, they walked back, admiring the sun casting its glow over the harbor and on his parents' home looking out over the attached Ludington Park.

John felt a semblance of contentment at this moment, for the first time since the morning. When they got back, the family enjoyed a meal of grilled whitefish and sweet corn, with kale salad and a made-from-scratch wild blueberry pie. Everyone had pitched in with the cooking. He stayed up late watching streaming TV with Nora and Joann, after Larry turned in early, around ten o'clock these days. He'd be hunched over and worn from stubbornly doing, during the day, more than his aged body could reasonably handle. Eventually everyone said good night and John and Nora went up to his older brother's childhood room and the makeshift air mattress they had set up there. John felt it was a good day in the end, although he would have trouble sleeping tonight.

Into the wee hours, he wouldn't' be able to stop his mind from drifting back to his talk with Lindsay and trying to make sense of the changes he had seen in some of the people on his walk; people talking and acting differently from what he remembered as a child and then a young man growing up here. A semblance of this feeling of frustrated *wanting* to know something, but not being fully able to understand it, remained. This feeling of a growing disconnect with his hometown that he had never felt before. He would think about these things from time to time and when he did, it would come to disturb him to the core.

Chapter VIII

A Curious Young Fellow

Dr. John was nearing the end of his first day back at Ada McCarver. It was a return of mixed feelings, mostly pleasant. Feelings that largely validated the choice he'd made to come back. He remembered much of it as it was, five years ago in his former role supervising four entitled practicum students and one, woefully underprepared, intern. It had been his first supervisory role and left something of a bitter taste in his mouth, even years later.

John found his past students to be largely passive in relation to their fledgling real-world working experience; that being, offering counseling or psychological testing services to inner city youth. Their level of work, for the most part, was tailored toward accomplishing the minimum of client contact hours or completed psychological evaluations (whichever was their practicum requirement). This often accompanied by complaints that they weren't garnering more from the experience. John heard much about how difficult it was for them to engage clients, though very little about what they would do on their end to get clients, in near hopeless environments, to want to engage in something like therapy from week to week. The answer was usually on par with needing to put in more effort to make connections but not being particularly willing to do so. Of course, it was always easier to focus on others as opposed to self.

John sadly encountered various millennial stereotypes firsthand. Most clearly, a sense of personal expectations to be catered to. Wanting more time from those around them, though seeming to give only a modest investment of their own. An overall goal simply to accomplish the bare minimum toward what would be required to move on to their next phase in the education process. A quickness to complain about how the experience was not meeting their rather lofty expectations, though no concerted effort to make it more fulfilling.

Toward the end of his last yearlong service here, the head supervisor became upset when one of the students dictated when she would be leaving her work duties without notifying anyone as to this self-made decision (and, not surprisingly, the student left significantly earlier than the others). When this didn't go over well, the student reacted strongly toward the supervisors. The resultant poo-pooing emboldened the remaining students, who stayed weeks after said student's rather early departure, to do some poo-pooing of their own. A group poo-pooing most foul resulted. And this happening, of course, with minimal self-awareness and reflection on the part of the students. Complaining about the site and the supervisor's various failings. Neglecting any mention of their own obvious lack of effort, yet still expecting a glowing review on the resume, all said and done.

John had seen, firsthand, the personal traits of laziness, entitlement, narcissistic slight, and expectant praise for lackluster performance as evident nearly across the board. It made John nervous and saddened for the future of his profession and world. It had temporarily made him a prematurely grizzled and cynical old man, after just one year with these young, almost entirely attractive, white, upper middle-class suburban women. Clearly, they expected the world to offer them much, and even prior to a degree or certification of any sort.

His experiences prior to that train wreck were what got him coming back and he tried, always, to keep this forefront in mind. He worked here as a consultant some eleven years prior. Early in his doctoral education. He initially consulted area Head Start programs, before moving into psychological evaluations. He was paid generously for a student. Thirty-five dollars an hour, up to forty after an eventual raise. His job, though, was neither an easy or safe one. It was in the ever unsexy and unpopular community outpatient realm; this also in communities that most outside observers would actively try to avoid; dismiss it all as failed. He would come to work in a multitude of them. Englewood. Chicago Lawn. Back of the Yards. Austin. Fuller Park. He went to some of the most dangerous areas of the city, to schools, daycare programs, and homes; often to the dismissive expressions of teachers, workers, administrators, and parents. Their expressions usually seemed the verbatim, nonverbal equivalent to the phrase, "God damn it all. Here we go again. Another upper middle class, suburban white boy trying to make a difference and having no idea, at all, about what he's getting his lilly ass into."

John's formative years did actually match those of his clients in many ways they did not know of and might never fathom to guess. He grew up in a largely disadvantaged area himself, worked throughout college and grad school to help make ends meet, and had no financial help from his parents, post college. His appearance, though, brought with it assumptions about his upbringing. Assumptions about his intentions and method, too. What was he there for? Was it just because he *had* to be? Couldn't he get placed in some posh office on Michigan Avenue if he was any good at what he did? Was he trying to aggressively pay off student loans through a federal low-income service deal? Only to split after putting in the hours? John understood this. Most of his cohort ended up being, often in more than one way, what the stereotypical perception of them was. A safe upbringing with financial security. Everyone of driving age in the family with a nice car. Regular trips both domestic and abroad. Their experiences growing up congruent with their thoughts of what life *should* be. Enjoyable, secure, and (often more than) fair. Sad, though, that initial presuppositions directed how people chose to interact with one another; at least for a good long while. Provided an often defensive and negative framework for working relationships, based, deceptively, on so many false perceptions.

Dr. John, in his years doing this type of work, had seen much of what could only be described as horror. Horror that many only saw on movie screens or read about in newspapers. He had walked by patches of sidewalks cordoned off by police tape, blood still on concrete or splashed as though from a bucket of paint onto faded brick walls; the aftermath of a recent shooting, or aggressive stabbing. He had walked into apartment complexes harboring gang members who hovered around the entryways, so that he could meet families living in one-bedroom apartments with no furniture save a couch, a mattress or two on the floor, and a small dining table with rickety folding chairs. Roaches were often in plain view. Roaches accustomed to not being afraid of, or bothered by, people. So comfortable you might not be surprised to see them riding around on little dune buggies. They were almost expected as part of the home. Much like the generic beige walls that hadn't been repainted in decades.

John had worked in schools with bullet holes in the windows. He regularly saw what people described as "ghetto face," on teachers and staff. This was a permanent scowl with its rage worn on surface level and looking, hungrily, to project itself onto any students or workers foolish enough to dole out any bullshit. He had brought children into hallways, scuttling them by hand to squat down on marble floors of old, tri-story schoolhouses in ill repair; to seek safehaven after hearing gunshots outside forcing them into the interior. Cupping both ears to muffle the firecracker pop sound and the, nearly as loud, shouting of profanities and gang loyalties. He would look at the children's faces sometimes, during these moments, and see not so much fear, but sadness. A hopeless type of sadness that was accompanied by a learned resignation, mostly. Just another moment of the many they would encounter where the world they lived in seemed to tell them, "just give up. The problems here are too entrenched and don't change. They don't change because nobody cares. Accept that. Learn to live with it, as best you can. Try to survive and don't presume to do much beyond that. Because survival alone is success around here."

John met people here who inspired him, despite it all. His former boss, and now colleague, Dr Tobin, was one. She had put in work, quietly and methodically, for over forty years in these communities. She sent out upwards of a dozen students at a time to offer psychological services on the cheap. These services were desperately needed and, as a matter of course, underprovided (if at all provided). It wasn't uncommon to have a learning disability go unnoticed and unconfirmed until junior high; even something as blatantly obvious as dyslexia. Push them through to the next grade with barely passing marks year to year. Who cares if they can barely spell their name.

People like Dr. Tobin just seemed to get lost in the mix. Few people knew of her existence despite how much her services helped these kids. Validation, though, was rarely achieved in these places. John knew this well. A person learned to accept this fact. A validated person beamed. A validated person had boundless energy and enthusiasm. What he saw here looked far different. What he saw here were tired looking, mostly African-American and Hispanic women, in these community centers (though more than a few men, too). Women with master's degrees who were getting by on a little over thirty thou a year in a colossal, and often unsympathetic, metropolitan area. Women who, some for decades now, would see clients regularly and know that, maybe one in ten or fifteen with whom they worked, they had made some tangible difference for. Women who lived in these same neighborhoods and worked hard all their lives, often raising children, often without the help of the men who had left them out of shame, fear, economic despair, laziness, or some combination thereof. Women who quietly did their work in the same places that few from the surrounding, more affluent, areas seemed to give a rat's behind about, that is, beyond the occasional "those poor people on the south side." This was a phrase that was almost always followed by inaction and continued going about of daily activities. Workers here would watch interns, practicum students, and Postdocs come into their world, for a time, gain experience, and go on to their eventual private offices on Michigan Avenue, State Street, or the North Shore burbs. All the while *they* stayed. While the gangs proliferated and while the violence worsened; their city becoming a political poster child for failed policing, failed community, failed gun control, and failed culture. Those looking to dismiss these cultures grew emboldened with each passing year, even though they did little to nothing to change the systems these people were enmeshed in, which were put in place a long time ago.

John recognized these faces and said hi to those he recognized. The ones that were still there after the five-year gap since he'd last been around (staying five years was quite an accomplishment here, after all). They remembered him in ways almost like a family member would. What he liked to eat. His favorite music. His old penchant, when he was fresh out of grad school, for busting out late eighties hip hop songs, word for word, two percent vanilla latte in hand and diesel engine Jetta parked outside. A white guy stereotype, he was. They remembered how he liked to cook and would ask him about new recipes. They remembered that he spoke mediocre Spanish and ate too many sweets. Hide the cookies and birthday cakes, or at least get your share before Dr. John sees them.

At McCarver, when he was frustrated, he could say what was on his mind. Here, when he was goofy, it was okay. There wasn't pretense. What working in a place like this afforded was the option to be more fully who you were, so long as you took care of your shit on the job. That was the payoff. That and the relationships that seemed somehow more real than at other work places. It was one of the things that people who weren't there didn't know. It was something that many might never find at a more common type of workplace; instead just the typical office politics, tense demeanors, petty competition and passive aggressive remarks aimed at climbing up the pecking order.

This place was, thankfully, largely free of all that nonsense, though the environment, the frustration, the hopelessness of it, hung like a pall that you simply tried your best to ignore. The pall, however, was relentless. A dense fog that never seemed to clear. This ghetto mindset, with its hopelessness and indifference that mimicked the way the rest of the world saw it would, inevitably, get the best of most people who passed through. They would leave abruptly, one day, often with short notice; usually as soon as another option became available. Then? Then, gone, in every sense of what the word entailed.

John had shared some memories early in the morning with Dr Tobin, as he made his way back into old routines; their respective, oversized, coffee thermoses in hand. She was the only mentor from his grad school days that he had kept in touch with. She liked him, but she was also real with him. She helped him to look at all aspects of himself and his practice as a therapist and appreciated him for his willingness to do so honestly; a quality John sensed that she found to be dwindling with her younger students. Even constructive criticism had become a no-no, she lamented. It could, and often *would* be used as an opportunity for a student to define her, the supervisor, as biased against them in some abstruse way. This as opposed to her, actually, being *fair* in her assessing of their abilities and needs for growth. Any words deemed mildly unfair, biased, judgmental- often by self-perception alone- to be used as leverage by the student to get her, the supervisor, to ease up on them and make the experience easier to just glide on through. She noted feeling this same type of trick was happening on college campuses. Students bullying and intimidating professors they found threatening to their views, beliefs, and unrealistically positive self-perceptions. The same subconscious goal of having things made easier for them on their path to get a degree they considered a requirement, worse yet, an entitlement, these days. As entitled to as home, food, and clothes on their back.

John and Dr. Tobin waxed psychological about such modern world social realities as the fragility of the young ego in the face of the ever-higher levels of qualification required for any number of positions in various fields. A level of education considered overblown and gratuitous, for most of these fields, just a generation ago, was now simply par for the course. The ramifications of the reduced value of the degree tying into the reduced value of the person holding it. The insecurity that went with that.

Dr. Tobin had already compiled a caseload for John upon his arrival. John had stipulated that he would only be working in the office (he was no longer desperate enough to risk his safety going out into the community, as he had years before). Mostly testing cases were assigned. These had high "show rates." Despite parents or caretakers usually not having a car, or the convenience of getting off work easily, they generally found a way to get to the office for psychological evaluations for their kids as these often had direct impacts on school and classroom placement. John was also given referrals for some afternoon therapy clients between three to five PM; kids and teens coming over from nearby schools.

John found himself getting back into his old routine with relative ease; meeting with kids in the small conference room in the interior section of the one-story, 1960s era building (that looked like a shrunken version of a basic elementary school of the era). The only patch of windows were caked with dust; a couple partially cracked, facing a residential home's unkempt backyard by the alley. He met with two different kids. Both in-utero drug exposed, and both taken care of by their grandmothers. The birth mothers were on the street (the most common general scenario amongst his testing clients). Assessments were aimed at finding out whether they were cognitively delayed, developmentally delayed, and/or learning disordered. Short periods of testing, ten or fifteen minutes (as they often had poor attention spans and low frustration tolerance) followed by breaks in which they would play, and he would observe them. He would record all the relevant observations in his report.

John's day had been going smoothly, for the most part. Clients were often challenging, but in a way in which he was experienced and comfortable navigating. After an initial evaluation and therapy session with a teenage girl having academic and home issues, he found himself almost caught up on paperwork and taking a moment to himself to reflect on being back. After a short spell, Bryant, the security guard/front office worker, came to his office and let him know that his last client of the day had arrived a little early. A young man named Washington. John let Bryant know Washington was welcome to come in.

Moments later, Dr. John was observing a young man, posed awkwardly, in his office doorway. He wore an aquamarine polo shirt with white, pleated khakis and nineties era, Doc Mason, boots. His clothes were noticeably worn and a little frumpy; secondhand, though still presentable. Like a grunge-era preppie in *very* minor rebellion, he thought. The young man's left eye and the surrounding cheekbone were discolored, John noticed at once.

He sported a small bandage on the left eye brow, just above the puffy orbit. The young man looked around the room, scanning it, before extending his right hand, rigidly, breaking the short silence to say:

"I'm Washington, but everyone calls me Kenilworth. May I sit in this empty chair?" He gestured with a stiff, gentlemantly wave of the hand, which seemed from another era. The voice was unusual, too. Uncommonly formal and somewhat monotone.

"My empty chair is your empty chair. Until you sit in it. Then it won't be empty," said John, trying to sound easygoing and welcoming, but coming of as somewhat awkward as well. He was a little off guard trying to make sense of this unusual fellow and feeling slightly unsure of himself in trying to make things out. Figure out what this guy's "deal" was, so to speak.

Kenilworth sat, briskly, shot a few short glances at various areas of the office, and began to make statements about its details.

"You have a pension for travel, and apparently for reclaimed wood frames to host its pictures. I see that you have been to Oahu, assuming that is Diamond Head, as well as to Iceland based on the volcanic formations and Scandinavian minimalist design, as well as, I will say that is Ireland, based on the color of the grass behind you. Also, hmm, yes, I see that you went to graduate school in the area. At an institution that markets itself on diversity and community practice."

"Impressive," replied John after a brief and baffled silence in which he was truly awed by the quickness and accuracy of the assessment. Washington had made it within about ten seconds of taking his seat. John pointed to the pictures in succession as he confirmed Kenilworth's guessing. "That is Diamond Head, from our trip to Oahu in 2011, Iceland from the spring of this year, and that last picture is indeed Ireland. Clonmel, near where they make Bulmer hard cider. They call it Magner Cider here. Bulmer over there, though. Oh yes, and the frames are from a frame shop in Wicker Park where I used to live. Reclaimed local wood, mostly from older buildings that had been demolished. How did you know all this?"

Kenilworth cocked his head as though he found the question a bit odd. As though what he had done was self-explanatory. "I've seen pictures of all these areas before and recalled the scenery," he replied. "I've been told I have an eidetic memory." Kenilworth seemed to show no particular emotion regarding having this rare ability- more commonly known as photographic memory. "I've seen Diamond head," He continued. "I've seen those same latitudinal grooves and charcoal color poking through the green moss in pictures of I've seen of Icelandic terrain." He waved a finger as though proud of not being fooled by something. "I *did* think there was a small chance it was the Shetland islands, based on recent increased tourism to the area, however, felt odds were in favor of Iceland based on its more navigable infrastructure. And then, finally, I've seen pictures of that, rather particular, hue of grass in Ireland, due to the unique rain and cloud conditions native to the island."

"I'm impressed, Washington. Let me ask you. Have you ever had any IQ tests done? There is a memory index that, at the very least, I'm sure you would score off the chart on."

"I've had that done before," replied Kenilworth, nonchalantly; seeming somewhat distracted and distant as he continued to scan other areas of the room. He jerked his head back toward John, to elaborate. "They said one fifty, though that it was probably higher. The school psychologist said one fifty was as high a measure as she could attain on the test she had. It was facile, as I recall. Some of the words in the Vocabulary test were rather obscure and took a moment to conjure a response for. Words that one doesn't hear often, so as to be, as well, words that one has a reduced context for, in terms of interpreting and defining, at least." Kenilworth changed course, seeming eager to get to the point immediately. "I'm here to process with you, Dr. John. I feel that making small talk is helpful to what other therapists have told me is the *rapport building* process, though I felt I should let you know why I am here. Grandmother thought it would be helpful, particularly with regards to my interpersonal functioning. My peer related issues of main concern."

"Yes, okay. Speaking of peer related issues, then. Did a peer give you that shiner?" Dr. John pointed toward the underside of the small eggplant framing Kenilworth's left eye.

"Yes," Kenilworth gently rubbed at the area, "ten days ago a local gangbanger who thought I might have ratted on him and his friends, for robbery and simple assault, punched me in the eye. Thus proving the point that, at the very least, that they were well capable of simple assault. I did contact the police, that is, after I gained consciousness and returned home. I was knocked out. I did reduce the damage, somewhat, by breaking my fall via landing in a patch of large, treelike weeds."

"I'm sorry this happened to you. Has it happened before?"

"Yes, on more than one occasion, but this one was a little different than the others." Kenilworth continued unhindered, with unexpectedly little emotional involvement in even this; this, trauma. "Grandmother was worried that this one may have caused a level of brain damage. There was, what was considered a mild concussion, though no permanent, internal damage, of any sort. The level of severity scared grandmother, though. She wants me to talk with somebody about how this makes me feel, as well as about how to make choices that will help to keep me safe before I start at the University of Chicago."

"You're going to the University of Chicago? Congratulations!" Dr. John was a little more exuberant than typical in saying this, both for the fact that he rarely heard such good news, as well as for the fact that he was trying to see if he could get a little emotion out of this young man.

"Thank you." Kenilworth replied rather flatly.

"Mission failed," thought Dr. John, before asking, out loud, "How has this, all of this, made you feel? College? The assault? That must have been a traumatic experience and I can only imagine the damage ten days ago."

Kenilworth paused and appeared thoughtful for a moment before responding, "I suppose it was, and I feel saddened and angry that I cannot simply go about my life without being physically harmed and harassed in myriad ways, day to day." He sighed, before continuing, "I am told that my experience might be different in the future and others are trying to safeguard me, though moments like this continue to happen and I seem to be at the mercy of, what would you call it? Thuggery, I suppose."

"Can you tell me more about what's going on, Washington? How about you help me to get to know you." John felt a little more hopeful that the young man was at least a verbal person regarding his experiences, if not particularly emotionally-invested. High functioning autism spectrum was clearly a working hypothesis for one of his diagnoses.

Kenilworth seemed somewhat confused by Dr. John's question, however. The question itself, "Can you tell me more?" It was uncomfortably abstract and requiring of elaboration in ways that he was not entirely sure of. More *what*? In what area, this, more? He preferred concrete lines of questioning. The neophyte stared blankly at the floor for a spell, before asking, "What, in particular, would you like to know more about? I find the need to pinpoint an area more so in this case."

"Sure, let's start with what your main issues, or problems are right now. How about telling me about those."

Kenilworth nodded slightly, pursing his lips and squinting his eyebrows in thought. It seemed an exaggerated expression of thought. An affectation poorly mimicking what the expression looked like in most other people. At the moment, at least, he seemed satisfied with the specificity of this particular line of questioning.

"I'm in fear of my safety," he began, "and I don't know how to relate to many of the people in my neighborhood. I often both don't understand them and fear them. I've been assaulted on more than one occasion and I live in fear. I live in a state of what you would call it…jitteriness? Do you know the feeling, Dr., that you get when you are in a situation that you cannot control, and in which situation you might be harmed at any moment? Do you know this feeling?"

"Yes, I do," John confirmed. "A very visceral experience, to be sure. For me, I feel light headed, hyperaware, my body preparing itself to fight or flee. My stomach seeming to drop down, very low. Then, my body also becoming uncontrollably shaky, unable to contain its nervous energy. Something like that."

"Yes," stated Kenilworth, slightly nodding again, seeming relieved at the accuracy of the depiction and how well he could relate. It comforted him to feel his experiences recognized similarly within another, even if, in all likelihood, having been experienced to nowhere near the same extent or frequency. He continued:

"That…array of feelings, is, more or less, exactly how I experience my daily life anytime I am outside of grandmother's. Sometimes, even while I am inside, I hear violence around me. At any given moment in time, this violence can happen. Randomly, it happens. Random gun shots. Fights breaking out. They can be related to something as minor as one person saying, "were you looking at me, nigga? What're you looking at? Fuckin' punk bitch. What, nigga? What? (Kenilworth's voice inflection changed noticeably upon saying this. Clearly trying to describe the sounds as accurately as he remembered them being uttered before by others. It was probably, very nearly verbatim, given the young man's memory)." Kenilworth again seemed to change topic rather abruptly; promptly following this up by posing a question:

"Doctor, did you know that, statistically, you are more likely to be physically harmed or murdered here than in many designated war zones?"

"Yes, I've heard that, and I'd imagine you're going through posttraumatic stress just living here." John elaborated on this point. "If you were to look up the symptoms of PTSD, as well as the typical causes. I'm sure you'd find both would match your experience and that of many people around here. But the thing about that is, it also helps you to understand how people act, and how people react given what goes along with that diagnosis. When a person has PTSD, they are hyperaware, and they are afraid that they might be victimized, because they have seen it, and see it continuing to happen to others around them, and it's probably happened to them. More than once. This can also lead people to respond violently to others. If they fear that they might be harmed, even over something minor or trivial, doesn't it also make sense that they might react strongly- even violently- toward others, in order to protect themselves?"

Kenilworth's expression seemed a bit distant, in relation to this line of thought. Dr. John, spotting this, tried another way of shedding light on his point.

"What I mean is, if they are the ones initiating a hostile situation, maybe the person they thought might harm them would back down, if they see that the other person is ready to get violent. Maybe also, if they harm someone they feel they can harm without significant consequence, especially in front of others, it will show those around them, who they feel are a threat, that they can fight too. Then, maybe those ones they view as a threat will back off of them. Just let them be."

Kenilworth continued to look back at Dr. John with an expression he could not quite pinpoint; putting him a little on edge. It seemed he was attentive, though with no particular reaction to what he was saying. Did he agree? Disagree? Did he care? Dr. John continued, despite his reservations.

"Well, whatever the reaction and however it is handled, it's all a form of self-protection is what I'm trying to say. It's just with varying degrees of harm to self and others. I'm not justifying the violence in any way, please don't misunderstand me…but when you look at it like this, it helps to at least educate yourseld on some of the ways people react, even as outlandish as those reactions might seem. Understanding something, even if it doesn't change it, *even* if it doesn't make it better, well at least you'll feel more in control because you have a better idea of what it is. At least you'll be a little less confused; able to start to empathize when you see the point of view of others. I hope I'm able to help you in this regard, Washington. Helping you to elucidate a few things a bit more."

Kenilworth, after an uncomfortable period of silence, began to seem a little more placated and nodded. He sat back in his chair, his posture relaxing, somewhat, though continuing to seem largely stiff and rigid. Seeing this, Dr. John initially felt it to be a sign of anxiety or defensiveness. In time, he would come to see it as the young man's general presentation in any variety of situations.

Kenilworth resumed looking around the room, scanning it anew. He was trying, it appeared, to commit it to memory. Dr. John found himself looking at Kenilworth as the young man was distracting himself, looking around the office. Several quick gunshots sounded in the distance. "Pa-pop..pa pop…pop…pa pop!" Dr. John quickly assessed they were at least a couple of blocks away, so need, this time, to take shelter. He did notice Kenilworth wincing as he heard the distant sounds, as if he had just been poked in the arm with a needle for a blood draw. He scowled for a moment when they ceased. A moment of tired anger, it looked like, over having to deal with this so regularly. It wasn't hard to empathize. Nearly every fucking day; being so sick of this. Dr. John reflected, for a moment, on the effects that must have on a person over a lifetime. Premature aging, stomach aches, ulcers, restlessness, from staying inside most of the day. Along with this; high blood pressure, permanent scowl, heart issues. Then, finally, the logical result of it all; a premature death. But a premature death, sadly, considered a *mature* death, given the surroundings. Dr. John knew, if you were a man who even hit your sixties around here, you were already considered ancient and it was no surprise if you went to the grave soon after.

Dr. John observed this…*curious* individual. He was, clearly, highly knowledgeable- yet lacking many of the basic social skills and street smarts that seemed tantamount to survival around these parts. Silence ensued, alongside his thoughts, though Dr. John was quite comfortable with this. He had learned, from years of experience in his position, that some of the meatiest parts of therapy followed periods of silence just like this. Thoughts gathered, and reflected on, which lead to some of the most significant of insights, on root psychological issues. Most of his clients tended to be bothered to some extent by it, being unused to it. To them, it portended there was an issue hanging around in the air. An unwelcome haze about them that they wanted cleared. Like somebody else's stale, silent bomb fart, lingering unnaturally in a tiny car.

To John, this haze was the breeding ground for the moments of reflection and subsequent discourse that paved the way to lasting change. For moments say, in which a couple might come to mutually realize that their relationship was functionally over- had been for some time prior- to when they finally sought out therapy. That now it was just a matter of making it official and trying to be amicable. Or, for moments in which a person might realize they had animosity toward a parent that projected itself onto their other relationships, causing them to fizzle and die over time in the form of a rancor that didn't, in the end, have much to do with the other person at all. A hostility that stemmed from daddy never being at high school sporting events. Mommy never showing the type of physical affection that other kids' mommies seemed to show. As John reflected on this, Kenilworth continued to seem lost in silent thought. John, at length, decided to break the silence.

"What are you here for, Washington?" Dr. John asked, templing his hands, resting his two index fingers on his chin. "I know that your grandmother has her reasons for bringing you here. But what do *you* want? What do you want to get out of our meetings? Which I hope we can continue to have weekly."

Kenilworth looked at Dr. John for a time. He seemed to struggle with a response, perhaps due, again, to the abstractness of the question. Clearly, this was a young man who preferred concrete communication. Communication, as such, that was specific, direct, and based on clear facts and figures; that mimicked mathematics and offered certainty of a specific answer following a specific set of thoughts and actions preceding it. How unhinged it must have made this young man to live a life where this was so often not the case- was *usually* not the case. Dr. John had worked with several children and teens with autism spectrum in his capacity, and had noticed, on many of them, a sort of permanent irritated look. Not anger, no, not that...but some milder and ever-present, close cousin to it. Like constantly being irked by an itch that wouldn't go away. It was a look that was the result of their experience, repeatedly, not matching the way their mind operated. Every day, this disparity. They couldn't make sense of it. Hell, social scientists couldn't fully make sense of the world around them, and far from it. Dr. John found himself drifting in his own mind, reflecting on this concept, when Kenilworth broke the current silence.

"I think I do know what I want, Dr. John," he stated. "How can you help me to succeed without hating where I come from, myself, and the people around me? How can you help me to feel proud of myself and my experience? How can you help me to accept myself? I know I'm…not like others." Kenilworth looked sheepish for a moment, in acknowledging this, yet another disadvantage to add to the list. "I know what it's called, and it fits me. I'm autistic. That's okay. It's just a word to form a paradigm around a general set of observable behaviors. I want to be comfortable with myself, though." Kenilworth's tone became more confident, upon identifying this. "I want to be comfortable with all people, including people who look like me. I feel disconnected from my own culture. Do you know how that feels?"

Dr. John nodded his head. "I do. Where I live and work now seems worlds away from where I grew up, sometimes."

Kenilworth, appeased, continued and elaborated. "I feel disconnected as well, from other cultures, because they act *differently*. I feel very…solitary. You could described it as, like a room in a house attached to everything else, but not of any use to it. Connected, yet still not a part. Not in a way that seems to really matter, anyway."

Dr. John found he was again taken aback by this young man. He was certainly perceptive, seeming to realize more than he let on and able to convey a more abstract understanding; though it didn't seem to come naturally for him. He needed time to reflect, to sort of train his cerebrum to think outside of its default settings. He had the capacity for cognitive flexibility, and this was a starting point for productive therapy. This was good. Dr. John reflected for a moment on the depth of the questions asked and tried to formulate a response that matched their level, so the young man could relate.

"Washington. I think this is a great starting point for our sessions. As we get to know each other, I think I'll be able to help you more. For now, I can start by saying this. I can see that you are a highly intelligent individual." Dr. John put his hand up in a gesture of, both, further thought and warning, to make sure Kenilworth would follow his train of thought in context of the caveat to come. "I don't usually *like* saying that to people, by the way. I think that people thinking they're highly intelligent is practically the norm these days and therefore pretty incongruent with reality. In some cases, though, its undeniable, and I can see that with you. Before you get too big-headed about that, I'll say that intelligence is very much a multi-faceted thing. If you wanted to look at your intelligence, realistically, across various domains, I think you would find your results would look something like a heart murmur." Dr. John began to mimick the form of a heart murmur by making jagged waves with his hand, before continuing:

"For instance, you would be off the charts in areas such as logic, reasoning, vocabulary, and I'm guessing memory as well." He placed his hand flat, high above his head, to mimic the high scores. " But," and John lowered his flat hand toward the floor, "if you were to look at other areas, such as social intelligence, physical/athletic intelligence, maybe abstract intelligence, you would not be as strong and your measure on a chart would be far below your areas of strength." John folded his hands back in front of his stomach. "The reason I'm letting you know this is because I want you to be able to reconcile the fact that, even though you are highly intelligent overall, there appear to be gaps in that intelligence. Those are the areas you will struggle in, despite being an, overall, highly intelligent person. That is the insight I think you need, because if you look at the gaps, then you'll understand why you're experiencing frustration. If you were to see yourself simply as a highly intelligent individual, overall, you would be much more frustrated about why some aspects of your life are so difficult for you. How could this be, if I'm so intelligent? You know what I mean?"

Kenilworth nodded, and mumbled, "mm hmm."

"Great. I want to work on those gaps. Makes sense, then, yes?"

"Yes, it does," Kenilworth replied, seeming affirmed, which presumed he felt understood. "And you are correct, I do become frustrated when people describe me as intelligent. As though that is an all-encompassing word. Like an expert in certain areas assumed to be an expert in all. Like a celebrity actor, who has honed their craft masterfully, over many years, then being expected to know, and inform others, about political solutions and real-world issues they are not particularly knowledgeable in. I know I have deficits, yes, and that's fine that you say that.

"Good."

"It doesn't upset me in the least, because I have known it exists. Some things do not come naturally to me, especially things that I perceive to be illogical." Kenilworth winced upon the last word, as though the illogical caused him physical pain.

"Good. Okay, I'm glad it does make sense," replied Dr. John, relieved that a lengthy, at times complex, explanation of the issue was so readily understood. "And yes, a lot of what you see around you does probably seem illogical in many circumstances. But I would say that there *is* logic to a lot of it. This environment that you are in, for example. Part of how you might try to view it is, well, as being *reactionary*. You are in a reactionary environment. Yes, there is a lot of violence here. Yes, there is a lot of hostility and the tension that inevitably goes along with it. Yes, there is also a lot of hopelessness, which leads many people, even capable people like yourself, to sort of give up over time in a, sort of, long term attrition process…I guess you could call it."

Dr. John reflected, in burgeoning sadness, for a moment, on what he had said; thinking, now, about his time with Lindsay in the U.P. and how she had seemed to have given up, before continuing:

"And people do have the ability stop trying. Hell, people even like to make excuses to stop trying. Shooting themselves in the foot, maybe, but still, it's understandable how it happens. If you can understand what you are seeing around you a little more in depth, a little more thoroughly, you can also start to reconcile some of the elements that upset you or don't make sense. Then, if you can reconcile this, however long it takes, however difficult it may be, this will help you."

"Can you give me an example," said Kenilworth, hurriedly. He was looking down and giving a start of *come here* gesture with his right hand, as though wanting to coax more information out of Dr. John. "But, please, something more tangible as related to what you call reactionary, and to the reactions themselves."

"Sure." John was growing more confident, though cautiously so, in his ability to relate to Kenilworth. "By the way, by reactionary, I mean that much of what you see is a reaction to the circumstances that people are in. The circumstances that people are in are related to the environment and the culture around them. Culture affects so much. Let's give an example of the, well, typical upper middle-class culture of a white person from the suburbs. Someone who looks like me." Dr. John pointed to himself and gave a goofy smile to ease the tension that always seemed to arise with talking about race and demographics in a general sense. "I find it's always easiest to start with what you know, in trying to explain something. Of course, that also means you have to try to do justice to your experience. Try not to be too biased about it or see it as the norm or ideal. Rather, to see it as a dynamic, kind of amorphous thing, simply evolving from a set of circumstances and guiding experiences and behaviors."

Dr. John noticed that he, unfortunately, seemed to have lost Kenilworth, again. He now looked as though confusedly trying to piece together this information he was being fed; biting his lower lip and squinting his brow. This would be an advantage, Dr. John thought. This fact that Kenilworth wore his emotions on his face. It would serve to guide John's advice. How interesting to see this kind of authenticity in expression, also. So little of the guardedness and the mental gymnastics so many clients fell back on, to lazily work around the perimeter of issues rather than delving into them, directly. Therapy was often like peeling the layers off an onion, he felt. Layers of bullshit peeled from an onion whose only authentic part was its inner core. The problem was, as the therapist you, early on, pretty much knew what the center would look like. You just couldn't get to it without all the peeling first. Done over months, even years. Peeling the bullshit off the onion. The bullshit onion. They should make a diagram with the onion, naming each of the layers of bullshit with what the particular bullshittery was; denial, repression, minimization, ego-preservation at the expense of others, etc.

"I'm sorry," Dr. John continued, though his mind still wandered for a moment, picturing as it was, a multi-colored onion with its named bullshit layers. "I'll try to get more concrete now." He thought for a moment about how to frame what he would say next before continuing:

"Okay, so the example. White, upper middle-class and suburban. This tends to carry with it a set of circumstances that affect worldview, how one relates to others, thoughts about how to help and how to relate to people. These thoughts have to do with growing up safe, acknowledged and validated by society, with not only your basic, but also many higher-level needs met. It comes with hope for your future given that everything has turned out, more or less, okay- in both past and present. So, of course, most likely it will work out in the future as well. Wouldn't you think? Now, if this your background, you might also relate to others as though they should have *hope* just like you do. As though they should feel like *if* they work hard, things will automatically work out. Also, to feel like they have inherent value as a person. Like you would. The problem is if another person's background is different. If they have little hope for the future because nobody around them seems to thrive. If they feel they live in an area and community nobody cares about, with *people* nobody cares about. If they feel like life is unsteady and unsafe. Well, then they are going to take the thoughts of that other person with a big grain of salt, or worse, simply feel that the other person doesn't really understand them or know what they're talking about as related to the situation they are now in. They will feel they are talking with somebody who doesn't *share* their background, therefore doesn't *understand* it. Following so far?"

"Yes, it's a little clearer," replied Kenilworth, though Dr. John still had concerns about how well Kenilworth was staying with him, giving his obvious penchant for concrete over abstract thought. John felt the common therapist's insecurity over whether he was making his point in a helpful way. Psychological methods never were an exact science, as much as they so often tried to be. Dr. John marched on in the hopes of making an insight. Insight. That elusive golden nugget that you hoped to find, though could go weeks at time without being able to.

"Good, okay. So, given a certain set of values such as the upper middle-class white person likely has, they may be frustrated when the other person doesn't understand and then responds in the way that would be hoped for- the way that correlates with their own experience and set of beliefs. This can then lead to frustration, burn out, not wanting to work with someone from a different set of circumstances. And why? Well, very simply because it's too hard. They have to *change* their mindset. That's not easy. They have to understand that their own views are limited and based on a set of particular circumstances. They also need to try to learn the other person's viewpoints and accept that they might be more difficult to work with as that set of values won't lend itself as easily to the idea of simply working, with minimal difficulty along the way, toward a common goal. If your experience is that you don't succeed in many cases even if you *do* work hard, why would you necessarily even try? And why would you automatically believe that a person from a different background altogether, whose life has been *much* easier compared to yours, by design, would be correct in telling you that you can succeed simply by working hard?"

Dr. John continued, "so, that leads to a reactionary response. The reaction is in relation to what the person experiences. The upper middle-class white person reacts with frustration because their experience with the working-poor African-American person clashes with what they thought it should be. The working-poor African-American person reacts with frustration, as well, toward the upper middle-class white person because they don't feel the other person understands them. Worse yet, is trying to teach them something *without* understanding. It happens in a place like this all the time, because that's the most common circumstance between therapist and client."

Dr. John paused for a moment while considering other points. Kenilworth's expression was silent and ambiguous; his features giving away little at this point. Dr. John moved on, trying to get into more specific details. Things more concrete.

"And other elements to consider. The upper middle-class white person may feel that talking with others very *nicely*, portraying themselves as a very *nice* person is the way to associate with other people. It has positive connotations. For the young person he/she is working with, however, this presentation may represent naivety. How can you survive in an environment like this if you act cheerful and nice all the time? You can't get by around here being that way. Probably that makes you a mark. Maybe the person the counselor is working with tries to take advantage of that niceness because that's what they see happening to people who try to be cheerful and nice around these parts. In these parts they can get taken advantage of for that, much more so. That's *not* the way it should be, of course, and they know that, but that's the way it *is*. And you have to acknowledge and work with what *is*. If said upper middle-class white person doesn't understand this, they could start to resent doing the work they're doing. They need to have some knowledge of how they're coming across. They also need to try and understand how the other person is seeing them and be open about the situation. You can shed light on the views of niceness in this situation, how to react to it, how environment effects it. But you also have to see how that quality can mean different things in different areas, and different contexts. That's what keeps you from just getting upset and frustrated when someone doesn't understand things the same way you do. So, the reactionary element depends on how you view what's going on around you and how you understand that. The reaction is based on the culture and how that influences thoughts, and it's vastly different within the two cultures mentioned, on the whole, and both of these cultures are part of a larger culture as well. A macro-culture, you could say, whereas these specific examples are more a micro-culture. You can imagine how many more dynamics there are to consider in the wider culture."

Dr. John was finished now with this line of thought. He feared- as he sometimes did- that he was becoming didactic. He was often put in a leadership position and asked for advice by those around him. He tried to follow suit, but the pitfall of it was always this felt hypersensitivity as to whether or not he was doing so in a way that respected the other person's knowledge and didn't come across as too teacherlike or paternalistic. He was an intelligent man but burdened by the fact that it was so elusive to pinpoint the specific things that seemed to come easier for him than to others. Often, he would be stymied by what other people knew or didn't know. Things that seemed obvious to him not so obvious to another. Things understood at various times by others, that he did not understand readily himself. What did he know that others didn't? What did they know that he didn't? Everybody is trapped in their own head, in the end. And the worst part of all was the subtle animosity that could project from others toward him at times. Animosity over the fact that they were coming to another person for advice on matters they couldn't figure out sufficiently on their own; much as they wanted to. The animosity of being dependent, in some way, even as a capable adult. Navigating this was not easy, or even accepting its existence to begin with.

Kenilworth remained silent for a tangible amount of time as Dr. John became lost in his own thoughts. Both had an unfortunate habit of that, and both seemed painfully aware of it. And this Kenilworth guy, he was a curious young fellow indeed. He reminded Dr. John of an overzealous, grad student professor's assistants in one of the hard sciences. He found himself following suit with the young man's professor-like presentation, despite himself. Maybe it was because he thought at times about becoming a professor, though anytime he thought about it more extensively he eventually dismissed the idea; knowing from experience the politics involved. The focus on kissing the right asses and always, *always*, trying to preserve often already narcissistically inflated egos. He had taught for a brief period as an adjunct professor and felt now, his professorial voice coming out, as well as his own inner conflicts regarding his want to teach others and how to go about it in ways that didn't downplay their own intelligence.

Therapy itself was a form of teaching, of course, but left one somewhat unsatisfied as to what was taught. Any good therapist knew the therapy was directed by what the client wanted to hear and was ready to hear, thus taking a large element of control of the discourse out of the hands of the therapist. A good therapist needed to possess the almost impossible combination of extreme confidence without going overboard into narcissism while also being uncommonly humble, to allow therapy to be directed by what helped the client. To be fluid and base method on what worked for *them*. Then, knowing when and how to make points and guide the conversation in a subtle way in which the client would still feel in control of the vernacular. That was the art that the years of experience after grad school taught a person, and what made them able to actually do work like this under the auspices of delving into the human mind. Being put in the position of going in there, messing with and rearranging the parts, and trying to help them function more effectively without causing lasting harm. It was no less than neurological reconstruction through words.

Doing therapy was difficult as hell, and some people on the outside seemed to think all this shit was easy. Seemed to think they could do it on their own with no training whatsoever but just good ol' common sense and some basic life credence. That, and maybe having been told by a few people, here and there, that they gave good advice. MDs didn't have to deal with this kind of encroachment on their knowledge and advice; at least not anwhere near the same scale. He envied that, though not most other aspects of their jobs. He looked again at Kenilworth, who remained in ambiguous thought, and felt the need to clarify and get back to his main points.

"What I'm trying to say," he continued with an exhale, "in a nutshell, and this time I really will put it in a nutshell. What I'm saying is that there is a rhyme and reason to how people act. This includes how people around you are acting, and part of it is that they are reacting to and trying their best to adapt, in whatever way they've learned, to the circumstances they are in. The violence and anger and presentation you see on the people around you may not be who they are deep down; however, it is a mask they wear to navigate the environment they are in. A lot of people wear masks, Washington. Masks that change depending on the people and the situations they are involved with. People often feel they *have* to wear it. I think you have a hard time doing this. It seems to me that you simply are who you are. You say what you feel. You act just how you feel. However, in order to help yourself survive, you have to learn to have some more discretion with that, and to learn to navigate others. To navigate others, you have to try to understand them and try to be a little more flexible on how you come across, as well as flexible on how you see them."

Dr. John sat back in his chair and to a look at Kenilworth, still hoping to assess how he had affected him, and still not really knowing. He continued:

"I want you to see the logic, however catastrophic and despairing it is, in your environment here because, if you understand that, you can empathize with others here and hate it a little less. When you understand someone or something as it is, as well as understand how it *became* that way, it is much harder to hate that thing, that person, that circumstance. If you don't hate your circumstances and your environment because you understand and empathize with these things, you also will be less likely to hate yourself, by that same understanding. You can succeed despite your circumstances, but you must be willing to to put in the work to understand them so that you will be less likely to be torn down by them for reasons that you, maybe, didn't even know. You can survive and even thrive, but you must be willing to accept the factors that surround you and, at times, be flexible regarding how you present and what you say and do based on the circumstance. In the end, that is just a more long-winded way of saying 'adapt.' I'm going to try to help you adapt, Washington. Let's call that the nutshell. Is that a good start?"

"Adapt or die," said Kenilworth, interestedly. "Isn't that what they say?

"For our purposes let's say adapt or have unsuccessful therapy with continued insufficient insight into past and ongoing life difficulties."

Kenilworth laughed at this. It was a loud laugh, disproportionate to the joke, and rather monotone and high pitched. It struck Dr. John as another affectation. Something along the lines of, this was what you did when you sensed that another person was trying to be funny. Another idiosyncrasy in his presentation, though the components of said presentation did seem to fit together into an interesting, though rather bizarre whole for the young man. Appeased, for now, John decided he should get back to the more standard first interview format with the time remaining.

"Okay, Washington. I need to ask you a few questions now. Just standard first session stuff, really. A few questions to get to know you a little better." Dr John shuffled through his files a moment and pulled a questionnaire out.

"Okay. That's fine."

"Okay, good. Good, good. Well, let's start with this standard question." John looked down at his clinical interview questionnaire. "Do you ever struggle with anxiety?"

Kenilworth looked at Dr. John as though he had just pulled out a crack pipe, taken a puff, and passed it over to him like a peace pipe. It was, by far, the most expressive he had been all session.

"Why yes, Dr. John. I do," he replied.

Chapter IX

Betty

Grant stood just outside the familiar, oversized, and centuries old doors- which looked as though yanked off the hinges and then shipped across a vast expanse of ocean. Far from their origins as adornment for a medieval castle on the Iberian coast (and he didn't put it past Dreadson that this type of event may well have preceded their showing up here). Now they were here, to serve the purpose of marking the entryway of a bullshitting fossil. The doors were scented just faintly of Valencia oranges and winter spices from the Middle East. "Nice," thought Grant, as he took a whiff.

Grant was a bit winded from his brisk walk down the hallway, following a routine request to meet with Dreadson. He was taking a moment at the doorway, to compose. His presentation had grown ever paler from spending the duration of his daylight hours indoors the past several weeks; working with the now familiar, and now also begrudgingly accepting, personnel of Marmot News. His constitution was weary and weak from the combined stress of meeting his goals with the network as well as trying to be liked by staff. Or, if not liked, at least something more than offered an obviously begrudging, painfully forced and dully superficial, form of respect. These stressors were having a cumulative effect that was beginning to show.

It was now early October. The election drew near. Exactly one month away at this point. Dreadson had Grant working eighty-five to ninety-hour weeks, utilizing everything at the network's disposal to promote David P. Betty, a career business man and B list reality TV star, down the path to becoming the next POTUS. Grant remained another spell outside the doorway to adjust his tie and run his hands down the front of his suit, pressing it lightly to his body. He took several deep breaths to calm himself, cracked the knuckles on both hands finger by finger, and, finally, thrust open the hulking door.

"Oh fuck *me*! Goddamn shit! *Fuckballs!*" Grant cursed as he found himself wrapped in a fetal position, covering his head with both hands. His infintile digression happened so quickly it seemed instantaneous. Some moments later, he would wonder how the exact word *fuckballs* came so readily to mind. Above Grant's quivering body, twenty feet in front of him and hovering ten feet off the ground, hung a massive prehistoric shark as big as a school bus; its gaping, open jaws sporting hundreds of teeth the size of pie servers. Its impossibly monstrous jaws that, open as they were now, were tall enough to swallow an NBA center. Standing fully upright. Wearing a top hat, even.

"I ain't about to fuck you, son," a mocking voice came to Grant in reply (and for a brief moment, Grant cocked his head, in a daze, thinking it might be the shark). "You better go see one of them tranvestites down on the strip! I don't do none of that queer shit," continued the booming, now familiar echo of Dreadson from across the expansive room. "Get on over here, sonny boy. We got work. Come one, now!" Dreadson clapped his hands a couple times, briskly, as though calling a labrador-retriever inside after a successful potty break in the backyard. "Squeeky wheel gets the greasin'. Come on, nah."

"I'm sorry, Mr. Dreadson," Scott gasped feebly as he found himself working to regain his already unsteady composure, as well as checking to make sure that he hadn't pissed or soiled himself. He had not. Okay, maybe just a little spot of piss slightly left of his front zipper. He buttoned up the front of his suit to hide it and walked toward Dreadson. He looked at the open mouth and eyes of the beast in the same fashion he would look at a fatal car wreck being cleaned off the autobahn. He noticed its eyes first. A glassy, deep, obsidian black faintly reflecting the various hues of the stained-glass arches, giving them the look of multicolored irises set amid shiny, tinted darkness. Teeth an array of weathered and mottled colors. Colors that had no seeming relation to each other. Colors blended together in a random array of pale silver, copper, plate steel, jet black, matte cream, all adorning a meat tunnel entryway to a black abyss. Raw, blood red splotches atop pink flesh- several feet in length- on both sides of the teeth. Grayish white scars were strewn about, in various sizes and angles, along the face and gumsl; additional assorted scars along various other motley patches of its body. Its face reminded him of pictures he'd seen, online, of the moment a Great White leapt out of the water to catch an ill-fated albatross or juvenile grey seal.

Grant walked past the skin of the beast. The skin was a lighter shade of gray, atop a cream white underbelly. He walked past a pectoral fin that jutted out above his head. It was ten feet in length, or more. Then a tail two stories high, its lower caudal just above his head. Grant found his way to the familiar chair and sat down, being sure to look straight ahead, the opposite direction of that sixty-foot-long, forty-foot girth monstrosity. His body was inadvertently shaking to a noticeable degree.

"You okay, son?" Queried Dreadson as his head followed Grant's body while taking its seat. "Betty got you a little flustered? That it? That's Betty, by the way." Dreadson pointed back at the creature. Grant kept his face fixed forward. "Yup, Betty. Named after our soon-to-be POTUS, Miss-ter. David Peeeee Betty. Hot dog!" Dreadson slapped the desk in front of Grant, which added a sudden nausea to his symptoms. "They just hung her up over the weekend, too. She's a beaut, ain't she?" Dreadson shuffled and bobbed his fists in a little dance.

"(Hurf) yes, sir."

"Simma down, now, son."

"Yes (hurf). Yes, sir."

Dreadson stopped with his makeshift dance and looked toward the creature with a glowing pride and satisfaction that emanated from the very core of his being. Like a brand-new father cradling his newborn baby girl for the first time.

"I'm...huh....uh (hurf). Hoo!" Scott wiped his clammy brow with his sleeve. "Sorry, sir. Just...that's...isn't that...that...*thing*...hanging just a little low and, uh, and...just a little *close* to your doorway?"

"Ya think so?" Dreadson queried with the invested concern of an artist receiving constructive feedback on his magnum opus. He folded his arms and perused the beast. He made a rubbing, pinching gesture, on his upper lip. "Should I move it up a few feet, then? You know I was recently struggling with that very notion myself. After much deliberation, with myself, that is, I came to figure this; I don't want it too high because I want people to be able to admire the details, you see." Dreadson gestured toward the monstrosity. "See, I spent a lot of time on the details, son. Such as the scarring, for instance." Dreadson made tapping gestures with his finger toward the myriad scars of this thing that looked a little like Freddie Krueger might, if he were turned into a giant ass fish. "The amount, and location of, scars meant to correlate with the age of a full grown megalodon, and the battle wounds it would have, most likely, sustained over the forty or so years it would take to reach maturity. And let me tell you, son, in that day and age, there were some God-damned motherfuckers in that ocean to contend with."

Dreadson looked back at Grant with continued, authentic concern. "By and by son, you sure you're okay right now? You ain't got some sort of undisclosed heart condition, do you son? Might want to stay off any big rollercoasters and what not, just in case. Why, you look as pasty as a white crayon come out a bucket of bleach. Do I need to have a defibrillator handy?" Dreadson reached over the desk and smacked Grant's chest with both hands, to mimic a defibrillator, which caused Grant to cough, sputter, and hurf- holding back a sudden urge to wretch. "Hah! Okay, sorry bout that, son. You're looking a right mess. Breathin' a little funny, too. Is that a green tint I'm starting to see in your complexion, Kermit?"

"Sir, I'm…I'm fine," Grant gasped. "Could I? Could I have a sip of some of that, uh….*hoo*!…some of that whiskey on your desk, please."

"Mi whiskey es tu whiskey, my boy. Help yourself. De nada, amigo. You should imbibe more often. Calm you nerves, for Chrissake. You need a hankie to wipe your sweat, son? Sweet Jesus on his throne."

"No…sir," replied Grant, pulling out a handkerchief of his own to wipe his drizzling forehead.

Dreadson, clearly itching to elaborate on his prized possession, continued, "Anyway, as I was saying, Ms. Betty over here came in over the weekend and, you know, I've got to say, they did a marvelous job, don't you think? I mean truly *exceptional* craftsmanship." Dreadson gestured toward the creature. "You notice the teeth when you came in?"

"Yes, sir," I certainly noticed them. Grant took a slug of whiskey. It was significantly moore than he was accustomed to, and this begat a rather lengthy coughing fit and a few droplets, worth several dollars each, to dribble out onto Dreadson's favorite Persian Rug.

"Oh, good Christ! Get it together, son. You're going to be seeing a lot of Betty from now on. You better get used to it quick. Now, as I was saying (cough!). All of those different colors (spew…wheeze!). Goddamn it, Grant! (hurf). You done?...You done?...Let's just give you a few moments….ok…..alright, okay? (sputter…wheeze) Alright? Yuh okay? Now…as I was saying, the teeth. Glorious teeth! A vast array, m'boy." Dreadson looked toward the creature, folding his arms and nodding his head once, self-satisfied. He observed the beast like it were a beloved son who'd just scored the game winning touchdown at State finals following an eighty-five-yard run with half a dozen broken tackles.

"Yes, sir (wheeze). Ahem! Yes, I noticed. A vast array."

"Come with me, boy," and with that, Dreadson lead Grant back across the room to gaze upon the gaped jaws of what had caused the young man to, very nearly, shit his pants, and to, in actuality, pee them a little bit. Dreadson ran his arm in a sweeping gesture in front of it, as they came upon the ichthyo giganticus. "A vast sea of teeth, if you will. A *sea*...of teeth. Those colors you're eyeballing on those teeth, son? All those colors are dependent on where the teeth were harvested, mah boy. Observe those matte white teeth." Dreadson pointed to the random assortment of chalky white choppers intermingled amongst the various colors. "Those pale, bleached ones, with the chalk white enamel? You see?"

"Yes, sir, Mr. Dreadson. I definitely see," Scott winced.

"Those are from the Bone Valley region of central Florida. A lot of the smaller ones toward the back rows come from that area. Those tended to be smaller, because that was thought to be a juvenile breeding ground during the time. The larger ones are quite rare, and believe me, when you come across one of those, you pay a hefty fee. Hoo-wee, son! That big one right up front and center?" Dreadson gestured toward a particularly gaudy specimen the size of a quarter of a pie. "Seven plus inches, in measurement along the diagonal. That would've been from the momma. Several thousand for that one tooth, alone. You see that powder white color? That is a result of the phosphate in the water, a result of the mining that used to be done in that region, back in the old days."

"Very interesting, sir," was all that Grant could, or wanted to, muster.

"The other colors?" Dreadson continued excitedly and without regard as to whether Scott wanted to continue conversing in the area (which it would seem clear, to most, that he did not). "I'm sure you saw there are quite a few. Jet black teeth from the Savannah, Georgia region. Copper enamel teeth from the St. Mary's river along the Florida, Georgia border. And, of course, your standard steel gray, bluish gray teeth, greenish grey, among others. You see the teeth take on the sediments, over time, from the waters from which they were harvested." Dreadson tapped with randomly alternating fingers of his right hand onto various spots on the back of his left hand, to imitate the sediments going into the tooth. "A multitude of colors is the result, my boy. A vast array!" Dreadson threw out his arms to mimic a rainbow.

"Yes, sir. A vast array."

"A rainbow of colors."

"Yes, sir. Rainbow of colors."

"But not like, one of them *queer* rainbows or anything."

"No, sir, certainly not one of them queer ones."

"The skin of the shark, that's called 'faded charcoal grey.' Dreadson was growing more animated by the minute. "The underbelly, why, that color is called biscuit, son."

"Biscuit? Huh."

Dreadson leaned in close. "Biscuit, Scott...*biscuit*. The eyes. Those eyes, up there? Those black, reflective eyes? Why, they're made of hand polished obsidian, from Iceland."

"Iceland, very nice."

"Hrafntinnuhryggur."

"Hraffa what?"

"Say it with me, Grant. Roffen."

"Roffen."

"Tinna."

"Tinna."

"Rye gur."

"Rye gur."

"Put it together now, son. Hrafntinnuhryggur."

"Hrafntinnuhrygaggur," Scott struggled to blurt out, and began a renewed coughing fit from the whiskey residue in his upper respiratory tract.

"Oh, Got damn, boy! Come with me." Dreadson guided Scott by the arm across the vast room and back to his desk. "Have some good, cool, clear water, now. Here you go." Dreadson snatched a water bottle from a mini fridge built in the inner side of his desk and gave it to Grant. He took a moment, as the young man sipped, before continuing, sitting now on top of his desk and facing Grant:

"And that's the right pronunciation by the way. You got it, son. Hrafntinnuhryggur. Otherwise known as Obsidian Ridge. Northern Volcanic Zone. Not too far from a nice hot spring area east of Akureyri. Real nice, stable water temperature. Not too touristy. You should go, sometime."

"Yes, sir. Very nice."

"Biscuit."

"Umm…biscuit. Yes, sir."

"Hah! Who comes up with these names for the different paint colors?" Dreadson wondered aloud, rubbing his chin and giving the topic much thought. "Was that guy just hungry? Thinking bout biscuits, but had a job to do, at the time, as well. Had to name a goddamned can o' paint? Boss come up, says, 'well, what do we call that one?' Guy can't think of anything but the breakfast he skipped, says, fuck it, let's call it biscuit. Boss says, 'okay, biscuit it is, bub. You can go on break now, and go get you one, too. Get you a biscuit and bring me one too, while you're up. Fuckin' biscuit. What the fuck?

"Crazy, sir."

"Grant?"

"Yes, sir."

"We're getting off topic again."

"Yes, sir."

"Now, you know how I feel about that."

"Yes sir, I'm sorry."

"Back to the topic at hand, son." Dreadson subdued his moment of irritability, composed himself and recommenced. "Now, I came in to talk with you about our new guy over there at Marmot News. Fella goes by the name McCannon. What a fucking name by the way, huh? Would you want to mess with a fella named McCannon?"

"Well…"

"*Fuck* no, you wouldn't son!" Dreadson answered for him without a moment's hesitation.

"Yes, sir. Fuck no!" Scott shouted back, trying, awkwardly, to match Dreadson's exaggerated energy level and expression.

"*Fuck* no! That's God damn right!" Alternating staccato slaps of the table. He waved a finger of warning in front of Scott's dreary mug. "Liable to knock your ass out in front your grandma right there at the dinner table. Hooo! For not passing that butter tray quick enough! Bitch! Take that!"

"Yes, sir. Dinner table. Grandma. Pass that butter…uh… bitch"

"At Thanksgiving dinner! First one with the whole family there in the past thirteen years. A no fuckin' around mother*fucker*, my boy."

"Yes sir, no fucking around, fucker, mother fucking…a mother fucker who is fucking not fucking around, that is."

"You got it, son! Damn right!" Dreadson reeled his right arm and slapped Scott square on the back, sending him into an unfortunately familiar forward lurch and another brief coughing spasm.

"Aw, shit, son. Better watch yourself, now."

Dreadson, recommencing his typical pacing, perused Grant for a while. He felt, for a moment, the familiar fatherly instinct for this young man. So much talent. But talent was only a starting point and just one part- albeit a significant part- of what must comprise an overall successful equation. Raw talent had to be in combination with work ethic, proper guidance, and, especially, circumstance (Dreadson wasn't one to deny that), to really take off. To really find its mark in the world. This, Dreadson knew well from the ones who came and went, like a revolving door, over his nearly sixty years in the biz.

Dreadson had found Grant's talent fit a rare dynamic. It was talent that was actively utilized and not squandered. Talent that- better still- could be harvested and directed to serve a particular purpose. To guide others down a particular path that, in this case, Dreadson felt would keep the American people in a place where they needed to be. Where was best for them (whether or not they knew it). Grant's skill set, Dreadson knew, would guide others to seeing the viewpoints of those in charge like himself. Protection of their own interests, to be sure. But also, men like him justified, keeping the people on the right path. A path away from what was, by contrast, clearly the wrong one. One of pussy footing liberal agendas and their moral relativism that simply left one without any solid ground to stand on. A swampy muck of liberal relativism where you couldn't even get your footing. That relativism was the cause of the crippling fears, anxieties and inactions of so many, Dreadson feared. And it was dangerous for that. Make no bones about it. So many people who thought they could function within this mantra of general relativism, though finding, as time went on, their lack of grounding principals left them lost and drifting. Without the solid base that they needed to function day to day. And that, Dreadson and Associates could damn well give to them. Traditional values. Hard work, without thinking too hard about bigger picture business that, let's face it, they had no mind for no how. Unexamined pride and patriotism. God and country. And enough of this damned white guilt nonsense already, for fuck sake! He was getting sick of that shit. And real quick, too.

Dreadson wished to convey these things to Grant, whom he could see now was tired and struggling under the weight of his load. But that was okay. It was only temporary. The young man would be handsomely rewarded and on a long, well-earned vacation in a month's time. Dreadson continued to pace, and came upon the familiar, forest facing windows. He liked to pace. He was, of course, a notorious pacer. He stopped for a moment to continue his conversation.

"Grant, before we get to McCannon, I want to tell you something. Do you know why I admire that creature up there?" With reverence, he turned and gestured to Betty. "Do you know why?" He repeated. "Why I spent nearly eight million dollars to put that thing up there? That thing, that cost the GDP of a small third world nation, hanging from the ceiling on specially reinforced steel beams and chains?"

"No, sir," replied Scott, simply wanting, at this point, to be off the topic altogether.

"No, I thought not," Dreadson replied in a tone that conveyed understanding. "But, I'll tell you why, my boy." Dreadson paced himself back to the whiskey set on his desk, grabbed the chalase, then slowly poured himself a finger. Its value was on par with liquid gold. He held it up to the light filtering through the windows and observed its color and clarity approvingly; tilted the vessel toward, then back away from him as he finished. He observed the sluggishly cascading droplets along the inner side, gave a satisfied mumble of sorts, then sipped again. He moseyed away from his desk area and to the glass door overlooking the forest surrounding his office on all sides. With his back to Dreadson, he sipped on his drink again and admired the foliage of this forest, as he often did; especially towards unset when its beauty was at peak. He continued with his back toward Grant, though voice still projecting boomingly; as it always did.

"That beast up there is the greatest power that ever roamed this earth." The volume of his voice had ascended a notch or two, somehow, even with the distance between them and his back turned. He rubbed his chin and thought for a moment, thinking of an aside. "Well, maybe a leviathan whale, a *livyatan melvillei* might be able to put up a fight…maybe the toothed sperm whale, the *brygmophyseter*, might stand a snowball's chance in hell. But, *but*, nothing, really, my boy, would be able to stop a fully grown, sixty-foot megalodon in its prime. If you were to encounter one, you would know at that instant. That instant. And with *absolute* certainty, son, that your fate was at its whim. What it represents is absolute power and absolute control. Understand?" He cocked his head to the side, for a moment.

"Yes, sir," Grant replied. God, he just wanted to go to bed, but he sensed that what was unfolding was something that he should be taking heed of; was expected to, at least.

Dreadson turned slowly back, to face Scott, and took a few steps toward him. "I'm trying to explain to you, son, that power must be conveyed absolutely. *Absolutely.* In order to command the respect of others. But that this power, also, can be utilized, or *not* utilized as seen fit. That beast up there. Say it had just eaten a giant prehistoric sea turtle, cracking its foot-thick shell, as easily as you could a peanut, ten minutes before it saw you personally. You out there flopping around in the water, shitting your pants at the sight of it. It would do nothing to you at that moment, of course. Absolutely nothing." A slurp of beverage and a satisfied smack. Hr began to pace the area around his desk, circling Grant like the alpha of a pack of wolves around a wounded doe. "Wouldn't have to. Fully belly and all," he clarified. "But that *power*. That opportunity to either assert or not assert it would rest not with you. Rest *not* with you, young man." Dreadson pointed at the creature. It would rest with the beast. With Ms. Betty. You see?"

"Yes sir." And Grant did see.

"The beast asserts its will, boy. That's scary, I know. Scary stuff, but if the *will* is for our *good*. Stay with me now, son. If the *will* of the beast is toward a purpose that is only natural and that was meant to be, what is inherently wrong with that will being asserted? And what…what is wrong with that level of power? Hmm? That creature was put here for a reason, by the creator, after all. Wasn't it? That immense level of power? It shouldn't exist? But it did. Existed in nature itself! Do you see what I'm saying? Let me elaborate on that for you, son."

Dreadson got back to his pacing, then reached across his desk and poured another glass of whiskey. He stopped, took a slow draw, and collected his thoughts to continue his point. A point that was growing moderately inebriated in its disclosure to the young squire. His right finger unfurled from the whiskey glass and pointed aggressively at the creature again, spilling a few, several dollar drops, of whiskey onto the dark marble floor. A few, also, onto Scott's pleated, polyester khaki pants (wrinkle-free, supposedly, but that was bullshit. None of them were ever wrinkle- free).

"That beast existed because it was made by our creator." The volume had gone up to eleven, at the moment, and Scott grimaced as it pained his ears. Dreadson continued, unabated and unaware.

"The same creator that made us, mind you. That beast was given great power for a *reason*. And that reason? It ain't too hard to guess what it was. It was to keep the populace in check. To keep *other* creatures of the sea on their toes and in *their* proper place. And they damn well, knew it! They were damn well aware of the actual reality out there. Damn well aware that they were not only weak, but also expendable." Dreadson paused for a moment before continuing, voice just as loud, his facial features also becoming more animated.

"Because they *were*! When they saw *that!*" His finger again jutting. Whiskey again spilling (on desk, floor, bullshit wrinkle-free, polyester khakis). "They knew their *place*. And because that *thing* existed, and they could see it with their own two eyes and they knew. They *knew* that there was something out there greater than them, that they needed to bow down to. That they needed to respect. Because it existed in their midst and it deserved respect. What we are doing here, Grant is creating the beast. A beast for our current age. A beast for our current purposes. A beast to rival that thing up there, and we're damned sure doing just *that*!"

Dreadson, properly jacked up now, and looking manic, continued glugging bourbon, though more aggressively, and began to walk with a commanding strut along the rows of windows, walking first to the back of the creature, then around its right side and then toward its front. He stopped for a time to observe the teeth again with pride, then walked slowly back toward Grant, along the left flank of the beast, casually and contentedly observing it. Running his raised, free hand along its underbelly. He took his position back behind his desk and observed Grant with a patient smile, leaning back now with his hands locked together, and his right leg folded atop his left at a perpendicular angle (not hanging over like women and sissies do).

Dreadson took a spell to observe the boy. He noticed now that Scott looked a bit sheepish and confused. It struck Dreadson that this young man, more capable than he, even after eight decades on this planet, was still lacking in his sense of able-ness and self-worth. And he wondered for a moment how much of one's confidence came simply from the ability to adeptly navigate the people that came into their various days; one day to the next. Grant clearly struggled with this. Struggled to find a way to work with others with the confidence he should have, deserved to have. Because he was *special*. Few could do the things he did. The boy struggled to place himself in the position of the expert. Which he was. He just didn't seem to know how to *own* that position. The boy needed to be the authority that Dreadson was, but he didn't feel comfortable letting others know they were below him. Didn't feel comfortable conveying that knowledge with his choice of words, his demeanor, his general presence. If only these things were easier to teach. These, so-called, intangibles; soft skills. There was nothing "soft" he knew, about either cultivating or conveying that you were a person not to be fucked with. Ah, poor marshmallowy Scott. His life would be so much easier if he knew and had the will to become a boss. A fucking *boss*. Step up and take your rightful place, son, why don't you. Why can't you and why shouldn't you?

Dreadson continued, intensely resolved now, wishing to instill a more visceral and tangible image of power, which was, of course, why he had a creature the size of a two-small bedroom, one-and-a-half-bathroom, bungalow hanging from his wall to begin with.

"Grant. I'll put this in a nutshell for you. The new beast is the assertion of our will through our media. This is (and Dreadson now raised his hands to make air quotation marks with his fingers) *The New Beast*, my boy. Say it with me!" New Beast!

"New beast, sir."

"Louder m'boy!" Dreadson yelled, rapping a fist on his desk.

"The New Beast, sir. The *New Beast*!" He shouted back, obnoxiously loud, his voice cracking midway through. Grant looked sheepishly back at Dreadson after the last utterance, feeling that he had gone too far. He just wanted to be done for the day. He wished, mightily, to simply be on a couch, alone, nursing an Arnold Palmer. But here Dreadson was, forcing his presence and demanding attention. Worse yet, the topic, deep and disturbing, was only halfway being received by Scott, in his work-addled torpor. Maybe that was why Dreadson felt comfortable enough to get into it. Like free associating to your pet dog out on the porch on an oppressively hot, August Sunday in low country.

"All right, son!" Dreadson was, actually, most pleased at Scott's last proclamation. Finding it not frustratingly and placatingly loud, but rather, appropriately enthusiastic and powerful. He had put a rare amount of oomph into his words. It occurred to Dreadson that Scott might, indeed, simply be trying to placate him, but that was okay. Because he sold it. Good on him. Maybe there was hope to cultivate a bad ass boss out of the boy, yet. Grant began to pace the area of the room behind his desk. Even in his advanced years, he never seemed to sit still for very long. The man needed to be in motion. He stopped to pat the side of his massive Kodiak bear, with its look of perpetual menace (though in reality, Dreadson had shot the bear whilst it was peacefully lapping water from a stream inside a fenced-in nature preserve. Shot him from behind a tree. He pumped his fist several times after the bear died and screamed a primal whooping sound, vindicated after eighteen minutes of stalking it ("hell yeah, motherfucker! That's how we does it!" is what he said). Dreadson now sidled up to the cotton-stuffed mammal, leaning into it with his arms crossed and his head held proud- and a little cocky- next to the monstrosity.

"M' boy, m' boy. Do you know that the viewers of Marmot News have different personality characteristics than the viewers of selected other news networks? That the loyal listeners of True American Radio largely possess these similar personality characteristics that differ from the norm in ways that can be, let's say, capitalized on?"

"Yes, sir. We have assessed that."

"Tell me the differences, son."

Grant took a moment to gather the facts in his mind. God damn it, he was so tired. Also, he was feeling a bit uneasy around Dreadson now. He couldn't readily identify why, but his body felt slightly colder around the man. He had before had this feeling, this visceral feeling, in his life, though it was only a small handful of times and with a small handful of people. The feeling of his insides becoming colder around a certain person, and he did not know why this happened. Those who elicited this feeling within him tended to be corporate higher-ups; usually ones who had ascended rapidly. Mostly male. Sometimes, female. He didn't make too much of it in this situation. Maybe it simply had to do with his recently weakened constitution and nothing more. He consoled himself in this moment, with that assessment. After a reflective period that took longer than it should have, due to this distraction of thought, though unnoticed by Dreadson, Grant noted the differences in a rather rote fashion. Exhausted as he was.

"Our viewers are more paranoid, less trusting of the government, more readily angered and/or frustrated, more fearful, more insecure, and less willing to process ambiguity than the typical sample subject who watches other mainstream news channels."

"That's correct, Grant. They are. Maybe always were…to an extent, but we suck them in and make them even *more* so. And do you know why?"

"Because of what information we present and the manner in which we present it."

"That's correct, son. Good on ya, once again!" Dreadson made a boxing gesture, punching rapidly into the air with both hands. "And that's exactly what you're doing for us. Helping us *choose* how to present information, my boy. It's all in the presentation, and there is so much *more* to that presentation than others even know or are willing to look at. So many details to be explored. So many elements to be brought out. Right down to how much makeup our female anchors wear. Hell, right down to how much titty they show. Who'd a thunk it, my boy? Who'd a thunk?"

"Yes, sir. Who'd a thunk?" Scott sighed. His sigh went unnoticed.

"We are consciously selecting not only *what* to present, but *how* to present it so that we can harbor these characteristics. *That* is creating the beast. When we condition people to feel paranoia, fear, and frustration, what do we get? Generally speaking of course." Dreadson looked toward Grant for a moment before, unsatisfied with the lack of a quick response and, in an effort to aid him further, gestured a large rectangular picture frame with his hands. "As related to the *big* picture, son. Think about it now."

"I've not thought about that particularly, sir."

"Of course not, we're talking about the larger picture now, my boy. Stay with me now." Dreadson's pacing picked up speed. "When we *feed* these characteristics." Dreadson stopped briefly and counted off on his fingers. "The paranoia, the fear, the frustration." Pacing recommencing. "When we do this, we inevitably either create or exacerbate a pre-existing distrust, and with that, a lot of negative feelings that nobody likes to have. Nobody wants to be all fearful, all paranoid, all upset all the time. Makes you all wiggly jiggly inside. Like somebody shaking a jello mold on a plate. That's no good, right? Esto no es muy bueno, senior! Aye chihuaha!"

"No sir. No good, sir. No bueno."

"And?"

"And what, sir?"

"And *aye chihuahua*!" Dreadson shouted in a shrill, high-pitched caricature of a Spanish speaking voice.

"Yes, sir. *Aye chihuaha*!"

"No bueno, my boy. Dios mio! No es bueno como los tacos y los burritos. So, then, what logically follows?"

"A need for resolution of said fostered negative feelings?"

"Smart boy. Yes, indeed. A need for resolution, which is a need *we* have created. So what do we do? We groom that need for resolution, my boy, then we give it to 'em." Dreadson started to vigorously hump the air, now. "Yeah! Oh yeah! Give you that resolution? Oh, I'm gonna give it you. Give it to you, good! Oh, you're dirty aren't you. What's that? What did you say you wanted?

"Sir?"

"Huh?" Dreadson replied, making no attempt to curtail offering sweet nothing's to the make-believe Marmot News viewer. He humped the air in front of him with what appeared to be an emerging erection. "Damn, those blue pills are something else!" He added, looking downward at his bulge.

"Could you please not, sir?"

"What? Am I coming on a little strong for your delicate proclivities, gentle flower?"

"Umm, can I say, yes?"

"Indeed, you can, m' boy!" Dreadson smacked his desk hard, sending Scott reeling and the nerve endings firing throughout his exhausted body.

"Good on ya for saying what's on your mind, boy! Now, where was I? Oh, yes…"

Dreadson sat down again, this time in the leather chair to the immediate right of Scott. He adjusted his pants (that had indeed grown tighter) and leaned in to continue.

"Son. Now, during this last part. Ok? We groom them toward a certain, let's say, conclusion. We groom the traits needed to resolve the negative feelings that we helped to *put* there in the first place." Dreadson had reached over to poke Scott in the chest as he said this. "We groom them to feel anger (poke). We groom them to feel frustration (poke). We groom them to be paranoid and distrustful (poke, poke). It's not that hard to do when you have people who seem to be struggling more so, year after year. And then, the logical conclusion is to give the people an answer for all these traits that we help to feed them. What is the answer? They need to know now! Good God, man *what* is the answer? The answer is the resolution. The resolution is the answer. What's the answer? Well, less government. Lower taxes. Bring business back to our country." Dreadson made air quotation marks, "Traditional moral values. More importantly, stop all these libtards from trying to give all our money away in taxes that goes to all the illegal aliens, instead of your own children. Stop them from killing babies! They out there killin' babies! Not abortion, son. Not pro-choice. Say it with me, now. Killing babies!"

"Killing babies."

"Killin' *babies*, son! With emphasis, now!"

"Killin' *babies*!

"Killin' em good, nah! Killin' em *real* good!"

"Killin' em good. Killing them! Killing all the babies! Killin' em nice n' good, nah!" Scott was clearly getting obnoxiously loud, trying to reach a decibel level that would finally appease Dreadson and not knowing if he ever, physically, could get there. But this time he had.

"Hoo wee, ease up, now, son! You're getting a little heated." Dreadson started fanning Scott with his two hands. "Do I need Kitty to come bring you a mug of nice herbal tea? Hmm? A little ginger lemon for ya? Some honey to soothe that raw throat?"

"No, sir. I just wanted to do it right, so we could move on. Can we please move on?" Grant asked, his voice starting to become a bit shaky in his desperate pleading. Dreadson was always pushing him out of himself. Trying to get to him to be more animated, fired up. He did not like this. It felt neither necessary nor natural to him. Why couldn't this fucking manic geezer with an articially induced erection understand that?

Dreadson continued and decided to take a bit of edge off his presentation. "Pay attention to the vernacular is what I'm saying. Always. It is *all* important. Control the vernacular and you can control the people. What do we say about differing views on religion? Well, that we need to stop their non-Christian attitudes and morals, of course. *They're* the beast! The beast that will destroy the nation. The beast that will eat you, shit you out, and go about its business like nothing happened. We make *them* the beast, my friend. To our viewers, the liberals are the beast that needs to be destroyed and we reinforce that notion minute after minute, hour after hour, day after day, year after year. *Not* differing attitudes. *Not* diversity. Don't use words like that. Say the libtards and the damned foreigners are taking over the country. That's what it is. That hits you right square in the gut! And it's so easy to say it like that. It's so damned easy. It takes all the effort out of it. All the damned thinking. Who wants to do all that thinking about complex issues like politics and different cultures and ways of life, hmm? Especially after a long day of back-breaking work. People just want answers, m' boy. So, we damn well give it to 'em. Give it to em, good. You like that?" Dreadson stood up, abruptly, and recommenced his air humping. The erection was growing, steadily.

"Oh God, sir, please."

"Okay, sorry. Got a little over-excited." Dreadson made a calming gesture toward Scott with his hand. He took out a handkerchief and dabbed some sweat off his forehead. "Alright, that's my bad. Now, where was I?

"Umm, libtards and foreigners?"

"Yes, okay, let's go with foreign peoples. From different nations around the world. And hell, let's throw in other nations around the world that we need to fear. Eminently fear, m' boy. We *create* that which is to be feared, and then we push it. The beast we have created, and we push it. Real good! Over and over again, we push it. Real good!

"Yes. Push it real, real good, sir."

"Yes, m' boy. Once we've created that beast to be feared, it's easy to control the populace. Keep us from this beast! Please, Marmot News! Please, Bud Harbaugh! Please Dreadson and Associates! Keep us from being swallowed whole and alive by this fearsome beast. This beast of different views and different peoples of different colors. This beast of changing times and culture. This beast of scary liberal thought that isn't necessarily cut and dry, or easy to swallow, like it damn sure oughtta be. This beast of acknowledging things we don't want to acknowledge. Please! Don't let it all swallow us whole!"

"Swallowed whole. Yes sir, nobody likes that," Scott confirmed, gratuitously.

"Damn straight! You wanna be swallowed whole my boy? I damned sure wouldn't!" Dreadson jutted a finger toward Betty. "Shitting them britches looking at that sumbitch coming to chew you up? No sir!"

"No, sir. I don't want any sumbitch coming to chew me up while I'm shitting them britches!"

"Well, just to be clear. You wouldn't *initially* be shitting them britches. You'd be shitting them britches once you saw the beast!"

"Ok, got it."

"Get it?"

"Got it."

"Get it, got it, good! Okay, mah boy, now, let me explain the nuances, to help you wrap your mind around this all."

Dreadson continued, putting up two fingers like a peace sign, then rotating his hand like the Queen's wave. "The beast is twofold and powerful. More powerful than you think *precisely* because you don't know it exists. Just like we don't know, for sure, that there sumbitch, hanging up there, ain't still lurking around in the depths, eatin' a fucking giant squid for a light lunch. You turn the liberal agenda into a beast to be feared. You then take that fear which *we* have, and will continue to condition, and you give an *answer* to that fear. Because now they're just begging for that answer, of course. And that answer is our main agenda, my boy. And that agenda becomes another beast in and of itself. A leviathan. Why? Because they need an answer to their fears. They need resolution, my boy. Remember that. Resolution. I can't say it enough. So we present ourselves as the answer to their fears. And *because* they fear, because we've stoked that fear even further, now they need resolution, our agenda becomes another beast, just as powerful as the beast we've created, which they fear. Follow me?

"Yes, sir." Scott sadly did and was sensing a more sinister ongoing element than he wanted to process unfolding at this moment in time.

"There's more to it, of course. There's more to our agenda, but that's neither here nor there and not for you to concern yourself with at present." Dreadson seemed, finally, to be about to wrap things up for the time being.

"Yes, sir," Scott replied with hope.

"Good, my boy. Good." Another swift slap on the back. "Okay, so that's the twofold beast. The beast to be feared which is the liberal agenda. And the compassionate, all powerful beast that is not necessarily to be feared, but rather respected and looked at in awe? Well, that beast is us, Dreadson and Associates. We are the megalodon that is chock full of giant sea turtle and not out to harm, per say, but to be a beacon of respect. All the while we still harness fear and guide it toward the areas we want to guide it toward."

Dreadson, presently appeased, smacked his hand down on the desk. "Boom! Done! Put it in the books. Now then, on to the next topic. This new kid we got. This, McCannon. He's going to be the new face of Marmot News. Real crackerjack of a young man, too. Full of piss and vinegar, he is. This guy doesn't fuck around, my boy. I need you to go meet with him, work some of your magic over there, like you been doing so well already. You old chip off the old block, you. Offer some advice on how he can get his message out more effectively to our audience. You up for that?"

"Yes, sir." Grant exhaustedly wondered what kind of hours this would add to his already bloated schedule, and for a moment was upset and ashamed of himself for not standing up to Dreadson and telling him that he did not have the time for this, or for several other of his recently added duties. He thought for a moment of a movie he had enjoyed not long ago where the boss caught his poor sap of an employee and told him he needed him to work on Saturday, then started to walk away before coming back and adding, by the way, that he would need him to come in on Sunday, too. And the poor sap just sat there and took it. Just like he was right now. And what other choice did he really have? Just like the poor sonnuva bitch in the movie.

"Good! Good boy!" Dreadson effused in one of his tones that always seemed to presuppose a treat would follow. "Of course, there will be a tidy bonus for you. Aw shit, son. Here's a bonus right now. Merry Christmas, Happy Chanukah and all that shit."

Dreadson slid open one of his desk drawers and pulled out a cinder block sized stack of hundred-dollar bills, sealed with tightly wrapped plastic. Held it up for a moment like a trophy, did a couple of bicep curls with it, then threw it, willy nilly, at Grant. Grant, whose mind had drifted off momentarily into a hypnagogic state, was caught off-guard by a brick of cash hitting him hard in the tummy tums, which momentarily took the wind out of him and initiated yet another round of guttural wheezing for the night.

"Watch yourself, my boy," advised Dreadson, full of the sage wisdom of an armchair quarterback.

"Thank you sir (cough)," added Grant, while thinking about the irony of receiving yet more money that he currently had neither the time nor energy to enjoy using in any way, shape, or form.

"No problem, my boy. There's another fat stack in it if you get this McCannon guy to hit our ratings goals. Fat stack of cheddar. You want some cheddar, my boy!" Dreadson leaned forward and slapped his hands on his thighs.

"Yes, sir."

"You want a fat stack a cheddar?" Dreadson continued slapping his thights.

"Yes, sir. I would like the fat stack of cheddar, sir."

"Go get me my ratings, boy!"

"Yes, sir."

"Get me my ratings!"

"Yes, sir!"

"Alright! Heh, fat stack of cheddar. I like that one. You know, those negroes really can come up with some doozies from time to time."

"I guess so, sir (wheeze)."

"Well, hop to it, my boy. Time's a wastin'," and with that, Dreadson shooed Grant, dismissively, from of his penthouse office.

Grant stood up and pivoted around, to leave briskly, carrying his fat stack of cheddar cradled between his right arm and upper abdomen like a rugby ball. He instinctively flinched as he approached Betty; looked toward his feet to avoid the sight of the beast. The initial trauma had not yet worn off, it appeared.

Grant noted, as he approached the familiar door, a hint of discomfort in his core. It took him a moment to realize what it was, but after this moment he could identify it. It was a feeling of doubt as to what he was doing and why. He had heretofor viewed his work simply as an exercise in mathematics and probabilities, strictly as applied to the social sciences and the influence of politics. Now, he began to wonder about the wider repercussions of it. At least, momentarily he did. He made his way back to his own comparatively plebeian office dwelling and the thought was put away for the time being. Now, replaced with putting together plans for his upcoming work with this McCannon fellow over at Marmot News.

Chapter X

McCannon

Grant started his Monday morning commute just the other side of the wee hours. He started the drive to Marmot News headquarters, in Mid City, at approximately 4:45 in the AM. His drive would be practically unhindered by traffic; a rare and much cherished experience for the greater L.A. resident. Grant was sipping (if not, so much, enjoying) Kopi Luwak coffee that his Ginny had lovingly prepared. She set the coffee maker the night before; this morning scheduled for a predawn 4:00AM. Bold setting today. It was shit coffee, made even shittier on this day. Interestingly, whenever anybody at worked asked him how his coffee was, he would tell them it *was* shit, and felt that should suffice as a response. "Well, if you really want to know, it's shit." He would usually be met by empathetic chuckles, and phrases like, "oh well, what are you gonna do," yet none of his coworkers understood the literality of the statement. Kopi Luwak was coffee harvested from the excrement of some strange cat- shaped, rodent-faced critter somewhere out in Indonesia or some such, similarly geographically situated, locale. This was an ambiguous little beastie that ate coffee berries and shit out the beans in jagged little brown loaves that looked remarkably similar to so many chocolate-covered nut rolls.

Ginny bought the coffee in bulk at six hundred dollars a pound and stubbornly attested to its quality, though personally Grant felt it tasted like stale, instant crystals. The type of coffee you might find in an old survival cabin out in the Yukon somewhere on a desperate, two dog night, looking for just about anything to warm the gut against a fifty below wind chill. Oh well, it got the job done and he wasn't about to ask her to buy anything different. It had come to pass, some time ago, that she was the authority on all things culinary, home décor, and fashion related in the family. Dreadson had once told him, "happy wife, happy life, my boy," and he had found this, through actual lived experience, to be a most logical creed.

Presently, Grant pulled up to Dreadson's reserved spot, as Dreadson had informed him he could on this particular day. The sunrise had started to illuminate a sleek, though purposely nondescript building; a structure impressive in stature, though most sterile. It boasted translucent black tint windows, like smoky quartz, adorning a polished steel shell of a vaguely aquatic hue. The building looked so nondescript as to, almost, seem to be hiding within the background of already uninspired and glaringly utilitarian office structures. And it did succeed. A similarly uninspired gray carpeting met his stride as he entered the open lobby through sliding doors that opened with a gentle exhaling sound.

He observed, along his stroll toward the receptionist's desk, a few coffee guzzling suits on their cell phones. Up at the asscrack of dawn- like him- and already yacking away with much immediacy about things that were personally important in their assorted ways- yet sounded like so much unnecessarily loud, arrogant blather, to passersby. Suits hunched forward on those little black couches with two-inch wide arms and short backs, maybe twelve inches high with stiff pillows. Couches sitting low; so low that you had to fall into them. Couches that conveyed the idea, "don't get too comfy, there's work to do, Spencer."

Grant made his way to the secretary; an overly tanned specimen with straight, bleached blonde hair. She was a little overweight and wearing, just, way the hell too much make-up. She was not particularly attractive, though she seemed to be trying her God damnedest to look like the universally agreed upon (and lowest common denominator) version of what female attractiveness was considered to be. Tanned. Straight blonde hair.

Perky tits- in defiance of any age beyond the late teens- that were probably fake; and who cares anyway. Perpetual, vaguely flirty presentation. She flashed him a well-rehearsed smile that fooled no one in terms of genuine feeling being reflected within it and commenced the days greeting. Her nametag read *Skylair*.

"Good morning, Mr. Scott, pleased to see you this morning." She put her hand out for wimpy, foppy man in a turtleneck, handshake. Grant took the hand and shook it with the vigor of a stressed man who drank too much coffee. "Mr. Dreadson called and informed us that you would be gracing us with your presence." She gestured with a number two pencil down the hallway, behind her and to the left. "Mr. McCannon is in suite one ten and I've been informed by him, personally, that you may see him at your leisure." She shook the number two pen playfully at Grant. "By the way, can I get you anything, sir? *Ooh*!" The smile shifted to something more genuine and animated. "We have blackberry, thyme and sage infused, vapor distilled spring water. Would you like to try some?"

"Blackberry, thyme and sage?" Grant queried.

"Blackberry, *sage*, and thyme," came the clarification.

"Blackberry, *sage*, and thyme." Came Scott's growingly sarcastic reply. "Why did the order matter?"

"Mmm hmm, yes, that's correct. And...vapor distilled!"

"Yes. And vaper distilled."

"Yes sir, it's delightful."

"Do you have a parsley, sage, rosemary, and thyme?" Scott quipped.

"Oh no, sir, that would be far too herby. See, you need to have a fruity element in there." She placed the pencil on her lower lip in thought. "See, it's to balance out the herbiness."

"Are you going to Scarborough Fair?"

"I don't think so. When is it coming to town?"

"Never mind." Clearly the reference had passed over her bleached blonde head by a good twenty yards. Scott shook his head and rubbed his puffy orbitals. "I don't think I would like any. I didn't know all those things went together. I'm going to be honest with you."

"You can be honest with me, Mr. Scott."

"Well, I'm going to."

"Well, you should!"

"Well, I'll tell you this, then, ma'am." Scott took a moment to organize his thoughts and verbalize just how he felt. Skylair looked at him with her head cocked, tapping her pencil on the desk. "It sounds like…well…it sounds like a bunch of mismatched ingredients to the world's shittiest turkey stuffing. That's what it sounds like to *me*! And I, well, I will just not hear otherwise about it!"

"*Hah*! Oh *you*, Mr. Scott." A flirty flick of the wrist wafted the air in front of his face. "It is not like that. It's really quite nice. See, we have various alternating *infusions* in our water that are quite delicious. They alternate daily, the *infusions* that is. Yesterday, we had a carrot, orange, and turmeric infusion. We had a lot of fans. Believe me, mister."

"I don't need an *infusion*." Scott mocked the emphasis Skylair had put on the word. Clearly she and others seemed to feel adding this pandering and obnoxious description would elevate the status of throwing some random produce into H20.

"Have you ever tried an *infusion*, sir?" Skylair cocked her head to the side, with a semi genuine affectation of curiosity.

"I don't think I would like an *infusion*." Grant replied, flustered.

"Pardon me, sir. I don't mean to speak out of place and pardon me if I'm sounding a bit bold here, but I think you might *like* an *infusion*…sir."

"I don't think I *want* an *infusion*."

"Are you sure about that? You see, it's *infused* into the water. The blackberry, the thyme and the sage, that is. They *infuse* it."

"I *know* that! I *know* what's *infused* into it! I don't want anything *infused* into my water, Goddamnit! I want Goddamn H2O infused into my water, with couple of ice cube infusions, maybe. You got it!" Scott was uncharacteristically upset now.

"Okay, sir, no infusion." The secretary appeared genuinely hurt by this little exchange.

"No infusion!"

"No infusion, sir." She appeared as though denied the opportunity to have given something significant and heartfelt to another human being.

"Okay. I'm glad we straightened that out." Grant noticed that the young woman was flustered and looking downward and away now. She seemed like a shamed puppy, to him.

Grant eased off a little, instantly sorry for how heated the exchange had gotten. He was a generally caring man, so did not like to hurt people's feelings.

"I'm sorry I got a little upset there, I've been working long hours. Sorry I took out my frustrations on you. That, er, that wasn't fair. I genuinely apologize" Grant looked at the secretary's nametag, again, to refresh his memory. "Sky Layer. That's a cool name by the way. Sounds like something out of a sci-fi movie. I've been stressed from the long hours, *Sky Layer*, and I am genuinely apologetic for my getting upset at you."

"It's pronounced Skylar Mr. Scott, it's just spelled differently than usual, you know, like the black people do with their names." Skylair perked up again, now and continued jubilantly. "Hah! Like they do. You know how they always say that. 'You know how *they* do.' I love how those black people talk."

"Okay."

"You do you. That's another one. Hah!" She clapped her hands together, then gave a sassy hand wave. "You do you, girlfriend!" Then Skylair put both hands on her hips and started to shake her head side to side, comically, and shimmy her shoulders before continuing, "Shit, girl. You do you do!"

"I know that one. And I *do* do me. I do. I do myself every day. Every day, girlfriend." Scott was trying his best to be playful.

"Actually, that sounds kind of weird when you say it like that, sir," replied Skylair, her features growing more serious. "I think that could be misinterpreted by people." As often proved to be the case, in face to face conversation, Skylair was much more aware of the seemingly ridiculous things done by others, than the seemingly ridiculous things done by herself.

"I'm sorry, Skylair. I'm just…very busy." Scott was seeking to cut this nonsense short, appeased now that he had brought the exchange at least back to civil terms. "Could you please direct me to Mr. McCannon's office?"

"Sure, Mr. Scott. It's the last door down the hall on your right side, just before you get to the studio doors."

"Thank you, Skylair. Pleasure to meet you." Grant held his hand out and shook hers lightly and respectfully.

"Pleasure to meet you, sir. Have a good one."

"Have a good one, friend." Scott replied, thinking, "God that sounded fucking awkward."

Grant recommenced with a brisk walk down the long corridor. He heard Skylair's voice in the distance behind him say, "you do *you*, Mr. Scott!" and winced. He traversed a corridor overlit by otherworldly tube structures of fluorescent lighting with their familiar, steady buzzing noise and occasional, lethargic strobe light flickering. An element of it reminded him of something like those neon blue lamps that people hung on their porches that zapped bugs. He half expected to hear a quick 'zzt' from time to time. A moth that came too close.

Grant reached McCannon's door and knocked in a loud staccato. By the second knock he already heard a stereotypical, cocky youthful whiteboy voice tell him to come in. The exact words used were, "Get your ass in here, homeslice!"

Grant pushed open the door and was pulled off his feet with the force of a rib-crushing bear hug, followed directly with a couple hearty back slaps by a young Irishman who looked fresh out of college. So, this was McCannon. He wore a pair of black, pleated polyester pants with a gray sweatshirt that had "U of I" printed on it, in black letters. It was snugly draped over the striped, starched collar of a dress shirt lying underneath. He had an overtly athletic build; the type that conveyed a maintenance regimen of daily two to three-hour workouts and around a half gallon a day, parceled out every few hours, of those shitty tasting protein shakes. He stood about six foot four, with the type of full build you might see in a college linebacker. He had rosacea on his cheeks and whisky on his breath. His nose was well-formed, but bulbous. It was 5:30 AM, and Scott wondered if this man had just started (or had not yet stopped) drinking, since the night prior. He would soon guess it was more likely the latter.

"Have a seat, you fuckin' *cock gobbler*! Good to see you, man!" McCannon guided him with a firm hand on his rear shoulder over to his desk. He half guided, half pushed him into it.

Grant huffed, indignant, straightened his tie and shifted uncomfortably in the padded armchair. He felt the need to set a few initial boundaries and said, "This is the first time we are meeting, Mr. McCannon. Please do have the courtesy to refrain from calling me a cock gobbler. I do *not* gobble cocks. I have *never* gobbled cocks in the past, nor do I have any intention to gobble cocks in the future. Some may do so in their free time. That's their business. I don't. Therefore, ipso facto, I hope I have sufficiently supported my claim to you, sir, that I am not a cock gobbler. Do you see?"

McCannon, still standing next to the seated Scott and momentarily wordless, scanned him with his half-glazed, though still intense, eyes, before easing back to a more carefree expression and saying, "Fucking shit, broham. You're a funny guy. You know that? Scott's the name. Scott…Scott…Scottie… Scotch. Scotch Tape! Yeah…I'm gonna call you Scotch Tape, mother fucker! Have a seat, Scotch Tape. By the way, you can call me Motor Boat. That's what all my boys call me. My fuckin' *boys*!" McCannon leaned in close, to add. "Woo!" Then he leaned back again and elaborated. "They call me that on account of I'm one motor boating sumbitch. Shit! You know what motor boating is? Shit! Man, of course you do. It means I likes it when bitches smack me across the face with them titties. You like that, Scotch Tape?" McCannon propelled himself back forward and prodded a finger into Scott's sternum, as he said this, and then repeated, "Huh? You like that (poke)? You like that (poke, poke)?"

"Umm, getting smacked across the face with them titties? …By bitches?"

"Yes, sir. Yeah. *Shit* yeah!" McCannon shot back, with an aura of presumed comradery. He took a sip of his whiskey and said, to no one in particular, "this guy gets it." He recommenced poking Scott in the sternum several more times. "*This* guy gets it." He continued:

"Me? What I like to do is, I like to hit up the strip club with my *boys*. My fuckin' *home* boys. Gentlemen's club, son." Needlessly, he leaned in right close again, and added, "*Woo!* Shit, and every time I get a lap dance, which is *every* time. You know how it is. You get what I'm saying. See, I tell them bitches to slap the shit out my face with them titties." McCannon's mood turned momentarily serious as he added, behind a slowly waving finger, "They've got to be natural, though. I tried that one time with this middle aged, burnt out hooker type with fake tits. You know what happened, Scotch Tape? Them shits knocked a couple fillings out my teeth, I swear to God, man. I swear to *Gawd*!"

"That's what them shits did?" Scott replied in a sarcastic tone falling on deaf ears.

"Yes, sir. Take that as a warning next time your out with you own boys, homeslice."

"McCannon, can we…"

"Motor Boat! Come on, now. What did I just say to call me, Bro Montana? We gonna be boys or what?" McCannon grasped Scott, his arm around his back, clasping his opposite shoulder and shaking him vigorously.

"Errr, Motor Boat, can we just get down to business?" A wobbling Scott asked.

"Scotch Tape, let me ask you a question." Scott pointed his left finger several inches away from Scott's left eyeball. "Dead serious, now. Can you imagine how emasculating that is to ask a female to stop smacking you in the face with her titties? To stop smacking you in the face with her fucking' jugs because your teeth started to hurt. Shit, I was so drunk at the time I could barely even feel my face…or so I thought. Oh ho! Senorita bonita!"

"Motor Boat!"

"Yeah, Scotch Tape!"

"God damn it, Motor Boat! We're here to do work that I, frankly, don't have very much time to commit to, and would like to finish up with, in a timely manner! Can we stop this dog dicking around and get on with it, man?"

"God damn, Scotch Tape!" McCannon effused, before mocking Grant's contrastingly serious expression and tone. "Let's get to business. Oh, oh, let's get serious. Hrumph. You need to relax, my compadre. You want something to drink, by the way?" McCannon took a stroll behind his desk and gestured toward a mini fridge behind it.

"No, I'm not thirsty, Mr. McCannon, er, Motor Boat. See, I've already been offered a blackberry, *sage*, and thyme infusion by Skylair over there. That was followed by a lengthy, and needless in existing, conversation about the practice of infusing water with, what appear, to be completely random fruits and herbs that have no business comingling. No business at all! I will stand firm in my assessment of that, sir."

"Those infusions?" McCannon's face lit up. "Oh, them shits are fuckin' *good* Bromaste," McCannon said, "but no, I mean a *real* drink, Scotch Tape. Can I offer you a cola, infused with whisky? That's what I'm drinking, my broham. My Brohamster. Brohammy ham sandwich with muenster, red onion, and a little dijonaisse." Scott pointed to the tumbler in his right hand. "This is what they like to call a fuckin', umm, a fuckin'...*whiskey* cola infusion!" McCannon held his glass up in cheers.

"No, sir. I will not." Scott pointed out the shaded window behind Motor Boat. "The sun barely rises in the sky, as we speak. It is *not* the time for libations!"

"Oh, no sir. No, no. Oh, no, I just *can't,* sir," McCannon mimicked in an obnoxiously whiny, nasally sounding voice. His voice grew deeper. "And *fuck* sir, by the way. It's not *sir*. You don't have to call me *sir*. I already done told you, you can call me Motor Boat, like my fuckin' *boys* do. My *boys*!' He lurched over his desk to get his mouth right close, once more, and added, "Woooo!" The "woo" went almost directly into Scott's left ear, which, beginning several minutes later, would ring unceasingly for the rest of the day.

"Have you considered that certain others." Scott was rubbing his ear, "especially, *female* certain others, might not feel comfortable referring to you by the name Motor Boat."

"Ah, fuck that PC shit. Don't tell me you buy into that garbage, Scotch Tape. Now come on. If you're going to work with me, let's nip that PC nonsense in the bud, my man. Fuck all that nonsense right up the cornhole, my man." McCannon kicked his feat up and over his desk and scooted on his rump toward Scott. He was sitting on top of his desk now, resting his arms on his hamstrings. He took a swig of the potion just inches from Scott's face and clasped him again by the shoulder.

"You know what, I'm not going to get into it." Scott pushed the hand away, then swatted at it like a mosquito when it came back to try and grasp his shoulder once more. "No. No! You stop that! I am here for business. Let's get down to *business*, Motor Boat. I'm here to offer you my advice on how to boost your ratings. That's it and that's all. Though, I've been forewarned that you're a difficult person. A loose cannon, if you will. No pun intended. That you like to do things your own way, and that apparently, I guess, you are considered by some to be the future of Marmot News." Scott couldn't help but grimace a little as these last few words exited his oral cavity.

"Oh, I *am* the future, Scotch Tape." McCannon protruded his index finger out from the tumbler toward Scott. "I'm the present too. And if you want to know about my past, shit, ask my bros back at U of I about that. Fuckin' legendary shit, sonny son. *Woo*! Now, let me tell you a little about myself…"

"Okay, so that's how it is going to go, *you're* going to tell *me*, right? Because you're the boss by what accord? Sheer force of personality?" Grant was surprising himself by how uncharacteristically blunt he was being this morning.

"That's right, cock gobbler." McCannon's demeanor grew darker for a moment, with the burgeoning sense of being challenged. He was silent, for a rare moment, before he continued:

"I know why you're here, Scott. I do. And I get it. The problem is, that there are things about me, and what I know, that you don't get. Now let me educate you, so you can learn about some things that I can bring to the table that, just maybe, you haven't considered, Ilyanovich Brohamsky. Perhaps I might be the expert on a thing or two myself."

"Fine." Grant started to rub his temples, "and fuck it, pour me a whiskey infused cola. Give me a double infusion of whiskey while you're at it."

"Good man!" McCannon exclaimed, his mood immediately more relaxed, happily appeased in the knowledge that a man who indulged in strong mixed drinks- before his morning coffee had even worn off- could not be such a bad guy after all. McCannon commenced to pour Grant about three shots worth of whiskey in a twelve-ounce tumbler with a blue, stained-glass marlin on the side. He popped in one large spherical ice cube from a hard rubber cast, taken from his mini fridge behind his desk. He finished it all with a splash of cola, for color, more or less; gave it to Scott before continuing with his spiel.

"You see, I'm of the, what you would call, millennial persuasion. Graduated college three years back and kicking ass like a rock star over here at Marmot News already. U of mother*fuckin' I*, baby! Represent! Woooo! Hey, why did you cover your ears at the end, there?"

"U of I?" Scott asked, immediately after downing about half his beverage in one glug.

"Yeah, *baby*! U of fucking *I*!"

"And?"

"And…*woooo*!"

"U of I?

"Yup, yup. Sir."

"U of I? What in shit's sake does that mean? Idaho? Illinois? Iowa? Fucking Indochina?"

"Don't worry about it, Scotch Tape. Now looky her. Here's what you need to understand." McCannon plopped himself back down in his posh leather office chair. "I am simply appealing to the rather vast and growing multitudes of trolls that now exist within the context of what I like to call a 'post truth' society (McCannon leaned forward and made quotation marks with his index and middle fingers while saying "post truth,"). Okay? The internet trolls, especially the millennials. That's my job and I do it well. Now, see, within this 'post truth society'…"

"Could you please stop making those quotation marks with your fingers, Motor Boat?" Scott asked, before downing most of what was left of his drink.

"No problem, Scotch Tape. Sorry, thanks for checking me on that. Good looking out. Okay, so like I was saying, in this (McCannon made a noticeable effort, now, *not* to add the air quotation marks) *post* truth society we live in, I can say whatever I want. That's real freedom there, baby. There's always going to be some sketchy news sight, internet article, magazine, or the like, somewhat out there, that backs up what I say. If not outright validates it, then at least ambiguously validates it, and that's good enough for me…also, good enough for my fans, who want to accept what I have to say, anyhow. Why not tell the truth as I know it, you might ask? Well, people don't *want* the truth, Scotch Tape. It's as easy as that. People just want to have their wants validated."

"What do you mean by that, specifically, Motor Boat?" It was already sounding to Scott like this McCannon guy was coming to similar conclusions as Dreadson about what people wanted from their news. It was no wonder Dreadson was so over the moon about this loutish tool that sat before him; reeking of booze and pole dancer perfume.

"There's a new movement out there, Scotch Tape, called the ARP. The Alternative Republican Party. See, those are my brethren. My people. And I am especially in touch with the younger generation who feel shafted. You see, we are the current result of everybody kicking the can on down the road to the next generation. You haven't really done shit for us. You've all just taken what you could from this world for yourselves, maybe a good deed here and there at various times, but mostly you've just all been cashing in the best you could, passing on the worsening social problems to the next generation. While the job market changed all around us. While the old jobs left. While the racial demographics changed. The mainstream culture changed."

"That happened with my generation too, Motor Boat," Scott clarified. "All of that."

"Sure thing, Scotch Tape." McCannon nonchalantly acknowledged, clearly not caring too much. "Props to you for that, but shits gotten even worse and you know it. Climate change worsening. Career politicians that are only in the game to appeal to their corporate interests and collect their kickbacks for doing it. Nepotism based on special interests running amok. Education not going as far. Jobs being outsourced and sure as shit not coming back, no matter what fucking David P. Betty has to say about it. Automation taking over and companies not really giving a shit about taking jobs away as long as the higher ups can pump out more product quicker and, hence, collect more money. You think all this doesn't have a falling out?"

"Of course, it has a falling out. Nobody argues that, but…" Grant interrupted, before catching himself. He knew that whenever he interrupted someone, it tended to be his emotions getting in the way. He considered this ineffective policy and a sign of a personal failing of sorts. He was finding himself now having the urge to air grievances with Motor Boat's line of thinking. A mood already irritable, fed by lack of sleep, a long and gratuitous discussion about infusions, and now a conversation he did not want to be having, with a man-child whose modus operandi was to get shitfaced, go on paid rants, and chase pussy with his boys nightly, screaming "woo," frequently and unnecessarily along the way. Often, and for reasons unknown, far too close to someone else's inner auditory canal.

Grant took a deep breath, held it, and exhaled slowly, repeating the process three more times. Five second inhale. Five second hold. Five second exhale. Motor Boat cocked his head and gave him a funny look. He seemed to want to say something, before taking a big swig of his mixed drink; thinking better of it. Scott, in his own right, could see it was the unmistakable swig of an alcoholic; the act of drinking hard liquor as facile as if it were water. Grown minimally affected by the stuff anymore.

Grant thought, for a brief moment, about this man's hyperbole. He found his mind starting to drift in the direction of what this all was about. Why it was being done? Wasn't this supposed to be just news? Wasn't it supposed to reporting, as opposed to trying to direct and control the thoughts of others? What was this all for? He had started to have these feelings of late, but he knew, once having them, in the end he was here for a purpose. This was his job. He was here to do a job. He resumed:

"I'm here to do my job, Motor Boat. I'm not here to discuss your political beliefs, your real or presumed generational woes, your personal goals with whom you cater to on your show, or what you hope to accomplish with your dialogue. I am here, specifically, to boost your ratings to reach a wider audience, so that your network can thrive and that I can remain in the lifestyle that myself, and, especially, my wife and kids, have grown accustomed to." Grant took pause for a moment, realizing that his last sentence was exactly the reason he put up with so much shit from Dreadson, including having to deal with this here pretentious ass now sitting in front of him.

McCannon grinned smugly back at Grant. He took a long, drawn out sip of his whiskey and coke before pouring another finger of whiskey back in with the remaining ice. He looked at the drink through the side of the tumbler to assess its color. A shade just slightly darker than straight whiskey would be. He seemed pleased and noted as much.

"That's just right. Last one was weak sauce."

McCannon took another sip and gave Grant a piercing look, again indicative of seeing him as, just maybe, a challenger of some sort. A usurper. His gaze, though, softened after a moment, appeased in some way by what Grant had just stated. The dull concreteness of it, which seemed to leave little room for a personal element that the man might find displeasing. A flat personality, this Grant Scott had. Like beige. It neither added to, nor detracted from anything around it.

"Alright, Scotch Tape. You're all business I see. That's good. I respect that. But you need to understand *me*. Okay? If you want to do business with *me*, then you need to understand *me*. Who I am. And who *am* I? I'm the voice of a budding element, my friend. An element that has, certain…*connotations* to it. An element that has been told they can't talk about race if they're white. An element who has been silenced. An element whose voices have been suppressed because their problems weren't deemed worthwhile compared to those of the immigrants and the minorities. An element of angry white people, often times working minimum wage. Killing themselves on drugs. Heroin…Fentanyl. Internalizing everything because they've been taught nobody wants to hear their bitching, though people are certainly willing to hear *other* people's bitching well enough. Including Mexicans who've been here in this country a fucking week."

"Where is this going, Motor Boat?" Scott said while exhaling exhaustedly. He was so very tired.

McCannon seemed pleased with this question, smiling back at Grant, with a hint of malice in his features.

"Simple, Scotch Tape. I've identified the *issue*. The issue is that these working white people are angry. Angry because they aren't heard. Angry because the only chance at advancing that they perceive of is a master's degree or higher, when their parents and grandparents were doing fine...*just fine*...with a high school diploma, or less, even. As long as they had a desire to work hard; back when that's all it took. Now, then. Now that I've defined this element, I cater to their wants. What do they want, you might ask?" McCannon began to count off on his fingers. "They want their anger validated. They want a clear and simple solution spoon fed to them. They want their lifestyle validated. That's an important one. They want racism, in all its forms, exposed as a crock of shit because we all get a fair shake if we work hard. That never changes and no exceptions! They want to feel that those who disagree with them are pampered, over-educated, disconnected, and unconcerned about them, because then they don't have to listen to the opposing viewpoint. That's what they want, Scotch Tape, and that's what I give them. Sure, some of them are maybe in the Klan. Sure, some are, probably, of the so-called neo-Nazi persuasion. That's okay. They're my viewers, and when I cater to them, they make my paycheck fatter. And if you want to increase my audience to make that stack of cheddar pile up even higher, you go right ahead. There is abso-tooting-lutely no limit to what I'll spend on booze and pussy, believe me, broham. I keeps it real! But I warn you, Scotch Tape. Don't alienate my people. You got me."

"Motor Boat. I don't get into politics. I've survived just fine not doing so, and I make a fat stack of *cheddar*, as you say, myself. My wife spends it all on coffee beans that come out of a rodent's asshole, from halfway around the world."

"Well, whatever floats your boat, Scotch Tape. I mean, believe me, I've heard of, and *experienced*, much crazier shit than that. Here's a good example. Have you ever heard of a Cleveland steamer? See, this one escort I've been using for years. Real classy broad, goes by the name Cocoa Bay. I was so fucking shit-faced this one night. Oh Lord, bro. She had to use the bathroom, and my toilet was plugged. So I says to her, I says…"

"Goddamnit! Enough of this nonsense. I am not interested in your adventures with Cocoa Bay! I'm trying to make a point!"

"Alright, Scotch Tape, all right." McCannon gestured Scott to relax. "Go ahead, hit me with your data and your recommendations and all that shit. I'll warn you I'm just going to do what I'm going to do anyhoo."

"Please at least consider the information that I give you."

"Okay, whatever."

With that, Grant commenced to educate McCannon in his typical manner. He provided him with data regarding the effects of presentation, vernacular, and various intangibles made tangible in relation to garnering higher ratings and a wider audience. Country music playing on intros and outros, conveying shared interests with the audience and selecting songs specifically seeming to validate a certain lifestyle and belief system. Cleavage statistics to use for his female field reporters. Ways to most effectively dominate time of conversation with liberal guests. Ways to present information of contradictory viewpoints in a manner that seemed just validating enough of the opposing liberal viewpoint to allow the Marmot News viewer to feel that liberal viewpoint was given a fair shake. Then, ravaging it, in a prescribed manner focusing on its weak points, predominantly, and ignoring context; creating a feeling of ambiguity in the merit of said opposing viewpoint and juxtaposing it to presumed tried and true conservative values. McCannon seemed unexpectedly interested at various times, which was a pleasant surprise to Grant. Grant capped off his presentation to

McCannon with a handshake, and with the knowledge that he would be available semi-regularly to collaborate.

They parted ways civilly, in the end, and McCannon seemed to show a level of respect for Grant, though Grant left feeling unclean in some way; questioning more so, the nature of his work, though trusting that, at the end of the day people had the power to make their own decisions no matter what was presented to them. After all, it was their responsibility to do so. He simply worked in the area of information presentation, with focus on entertainment elements to bolster audience support. That was all. Thoughts beyond this were unwelcome and made Grant uneasy in a visceral sense, which always lead, as it did now, to his mind simply moving on to other matters. He felt he sufficiently stood up to McCannon and it made him feel emboldened. And with this thought he decided, once and for all, that he was no longer going to drink anymore of that Kopi Luwak shit his wife always made for him every morning. He'd tell Ginny "no more," and dramatically pour his cup down the drain. Squirt some lemon-scented, kitchen counter sanitizer to clear the haze of excrement in the air. And that would be that, madame. Problem solved.

Chapter XI

With David Betty

The boy cried in anguish as he looked down, in burgeoning horror, at the raw, freshly scuffed knee. A deep red patch, showing inner layers of dermis surrounding an initial trickle of blood that was starting to flow down his right shin, presented itself to the boy's wide-eyed horror. Little pieces of soft spring grass, adorned with a grayish tinged medley of assorted colors and sizes; little rocks and pebbles picked up from the crag of the New England coast just beyond the sloping, rocky precipice of the north Atlantic coast.

It was the front yard of his family's summertime estate in Saco, Maine; early June 1958. His older brother had, less than a minute ago, pushed him, callously out of the way to catch a deep pass while playing football with a group of their friends. The eight-year-old boy had fallen hard on his knee as his brother made the winning catch, trotting nonplussed to the agreed upon touchdown territory- the pebbled section surrounding the fire pit and beach chairs, overlooking the ocean. His brother had celebrated triumphantly for a moment, with his small handful of teammates patting his back and giving quick hugs; before a dawning realization of what he had done. A faint gesture of empathy was directed toward the boy in this moment, though the moment proved fleeting, based on what they had both learned. A faint moment of remorse and sympathy shown on the older brother's face, though it abruptly hardened just as the younger boy could start to make it out. And his brother ran, followed by his jubilant team, to the padded Adirondack chairs on the three-season porch of the Tudor mansion. That was where he would tell his parents that the younger boy had fallen by accident, when they could see he was not with the others.

The younger boy continued to cry, inconsolably now, and made worse by a moment of kindness taken away; this on top of the physical pain and the added sting of indifference his brother had shown. A few moments later, his father exited the home's porch; strode out to him. The boy tried to regain his composure that he was so ashamed, in this moment, for having lost. He worked to catch his breath, first. Then, he gritted his teeth and made a tough, bitter face, as though taking a spoon of castor oil but getting through it alright. He knew his father's usual response to his crying was not a welcome one.

He didn't know quite when it had started, exactly. Didn't know quite when the crying had become unacceptable, but he knew two things now. One was that this used to be okay and father was almost always kind. The other was that this was no longer okay and that moments of kindness were, almost, gone. He thought, however, that a few tears during times of extreme pain such as this might still be forgiven. And maybe he could go back, for a moment, to that place of compassion he used to occupy in his father's eyes.

Father arrived. His figure, tall and fit, now partially blotting out the soft Spring warmth of the sun, looked at him with a gesture that may have conveyed empathy and understanding at some faint level, but these aspects superseded by a set of principles that were far more important than that. These were principals of not showing weakness and, somehow, being able to avoid having pain caused to one, in any way.

His father's face played at the boy's fears and insecurities. A severe face with an intensity of feature. Lines etched deep in his forehead and the underside of his lips. Lines associated with an intense, always slighting frowning look. It was as though the man were, always, mildly irritated and bothered by the various everyday things that occurred all around him. This expression could turn to outward disgust and anger, and quickly. The boy knew this, already; knew that he was always in imminent danger of arousing a look of shame and disgust on father's face. He tried so hard to avoid that.

The boy was at a particular age in which he could not verbalize these feelings of internal and questionably warranted fear. But he had some level of understanding of his father's principals when it came to these types of things. The boy just didn't know, yet, how to realistically instill this form of...discipline. Discipline was it? Within himself.

The father looked at his child for a moment from a short distance; internally admiring his attempts to suppress the pain, to stop crying, and to not be noticeably weak, even in a moment like this. "That's a good boy. An admirable boy," thought the father, as he looked on. And he was learning quickly. A boy with potential, this certainly was. The right kind of potential, too. Precocious, but not so much so as to be awkward with it. Able to get along with the other children, even the older ones. Also, a good-looking boy. That helped; especially for girls, but for boys quite a lot too, as they knew he would be an asset and a conduit, one day, when they'd start to like girls in other ways.

The boy had chestnut brown hair with soul piercing, greyish blue eyes that conveyed confidence, and that looked into the eyes of others naturally, and without hesitation, in conversation. The eyes of one who leads and knows well that he is in the position to do so. The father knew this and worked to foster the traits that would allow this special one to lead from an early age; taking full advantage of the privileges he had been allotted in life in order to secure his place in the upper ranks. And why shouldn't he? He would need each privilege he had to attain the eventual lofty heights his potential deserved. Didn't all of us?

The father's feelings were masked by the culture and aesthetics of living amongst the elite. The culture superseded personal feelings and demanded a response in line with what it taught. Weakness in any form certainly was not taught to one's offspring. It was like blood in the water. And with this firmly in mind, the father would never let his fondness be known -that is-beyond fleeting moments of talk, behind closed doors, with the boy's doting mother. The boy would have to seek out the affections of his father; which were rarely doled out; were dangled in front of him, but almost always ungraspable. Like a carrot jiggling from a stick before the eyes of a donkey, to keep it moving steadily forward. It worked just as well for people, this little trick. The rewards and the terms changed, simply to what was required for people, but that was all. There would be no affectionate understanding now, as that was tantamount to giving him the proverbial carrot outright and impeding his will to progress in the way he needed to. So never this giving; this appeasement. Not years later, when he came of age. Not ever, in fact. And father would indeed end up dead of sudden cardiac arrest (ashes scattered soon after into the Atlantic, from off a 19th century schooner) before he could ever tell the son why he played it as he did.

All that there could be now were just allusions to why he was this way. Allusions that were like a puzzle to be figured out and pondered over. He knew that explaining why he did as he did would weaken the child and he felt secure in the knowledge his boy would come to understand this someday. To understand why he had to treat him as he did. If he didn't, that would be a shame. It might be long after he left this earth. A shame as well. However, the boy's knowledge of the reasons for the fathering he had was not the main point of it all. His coming to understand would simply be a luxury, in the end. The main point was quite simple. He was hard on the boy because he had to be. Because the boy's circumstances and future aspirations would require it. These people would not forgive, or even understand, an outward expression of vulnerability. He would not give it to them in the form of his most cherished son. His face softened, ever so slightly and outside of his awareness, as he broke his silence.

"My son, what happened here?"

"I'm sorry, father," the boy sniffed, trying his best to compose himself, though the pain remained intense and all-consuming.

"Calvin pushed me, and I hurt my knee. It hurt so bad, I started to cry. I'm sorry father. It just hurts so much, and then I saw the blood, and all the rocks stuck in it and it scared me. I'm sorry, father. I'm sorry."

"My boy, you said your brother *pushed* you. Are you sure that's what happened?" His father gave him a look that conveyed it would do the boy well to be thoughtful about this one. It was a hint.

The child reflected for a moment about whether he should have said this. He didn't want to tattle, so he altered his story a little. "Yes, he pushed me out of the way, so he could catch the ball. But, but I don't think he meant it. Maybe he just didn't see me, so it wasn't really a push, then. Don't tell him I said that he pushed me, father. I don't want him to think I tattled."

"I understand, my son." The father's lips curled upward into some faint semblance of a smile. "We don't want tattlers in this family. After all, we all fall short of the glory sometimes, don't we, boy? So then, what did you learn?" His father was, internally, growing more pleased, though his expression remained unchanged.

The boy looked back at the father, perplexed. He did not know just how to respond. Or, maybe he did, but couldn't yet wrap his budding mind around why something that seemed like a hazy type of lie could be the right answer. He didn't think this sought-after response was the point at all, and the resulting confusion stunned him for a moment. He thought the point was, simply, that he was in pain and should be consoled by his father. Yet this always remained a hope. He knew this was not what to expect. But maybe this time? Always, it was, *maybe* this time. Because it simply seemed like that's what should happen during an instant like this and he could not get away from that feeling. Not yet. He looked up toward his father's tall, thin, yet sturdy and athletic frame. The soft warm glow of the early June sun made him have to squint his eyes hard to put the familiar face of little affect and expression into focus. He stared at his father with his mouth open, not knowing what to tell him. Stymied by always having to offer a response and verbalize a lesson that seemed, somehow, *off* in a way he, for the life of him, could not quite describe.

Father's face gave away very little. Very few hints of what he might expect the other person to say. Nothing betrayed the uncanny steadfastess, and the hard dullness within his eyes. But the boy usually knew, already, how to read what little was given him. And right now, he knew one thing, at least; that saying the play should have been done fairly was the wrong response. That one thing, he knew, was not what he was supposed to have thought about this; certainly not what he should have learned about it. The voice came back louder, startling the boy, making his spine shake.

"Are you confused? Answer my question, boy. Don't stall! Don't be an indecisive little pipsqueak. Speak your mind, boy! What do you do?" His tone was urgent, and he was clearly growing upset. He was upset because he was unsure, at the moment, if the boy knew; and the thought upset his father in a very immediate type of way. But the boy would show he knew the answer his father was seeking with his next response.

"Win or die, father." The boy said it softly and in fear; trying to keep his lips from quivering in this, just moments after he had cried. And now, hearing something and having to agree with it. A something that did not match his feelings, wants, or needs. He knew what winning was supposed to involve. A win was supposed to involve fairplay, otherwise it wasn't a win at all. Was it? He couldn't shake this feeling, just yet, even though he had been told it was wrong. He didn't like how his brother's victory looked today and he still wouldn't want to be the one to do it like that. He did not want to hurt his brother, or make that same look of cold indifference toward another, when he knew he had hurt them. But, then again, he had seen how his father had looked at Calvin from inside the porch; had even given him a hearty pat on the back and a genuine smile, before it went away when he walked outside.

His father's lips curled upward into something close to a smile now. The boy had chosen the right words. "*Win*, my son.

Win no matter what. Win or die. If you know your brother is coming to push you, then you push *him* first. You trip him, if you have to. *You* knock his arm down with your curled fist, so he can't catch the ball. Do it on the side opposite of where others are standing and observing you. You pull him down with you if he pushes you. Wrap your arm around him from behind so they cannot see what you did. Do you understand, boy?"

"Yes," the boy replied. "Win, father. Win no matter what."

"Win or die, son. This is what we do in this family. You will not be a victim."

The boy, surprising himself, formulated what could be considered a challenge to the man. Afterwards he felt sorry for doing so and apologized profusely. But what he said now, holding his head down, was:

"I only wanted a fair game."

The father's semblance of a smile erased itself in an instant. His favored son just had to go and ruin this moment. Just as he was starting to really *get* it.

"Do you think you win by being fair? Answer me this instant! Look at me when I'm speaking to you!" His voice was menacing; instilling fear and respect.

"No, father." The boy looked up and made his best imitation of his father's stone face. "You win by doing what it takes." The boy looked back down again and tried to suppress the tears welling back into his eyes through it all.

His father grew pleased once again, though more cautiously this time around. A flicker of weakness, yes, but it had faded quickly. Weakness didn't extinguish so easily, but clearly it was on the way out. He now felt the matter settled and turned to walk back toward the porch, though after a moment turned back around, slowly and with great purpose, to face the child. He observed the boy once more, and knew he was trying his best not to cry. He took a slow sip of his gin and club soda. He seemed, to the boy, to be thinking briefly. His father nodded his head, just slightly, his eyes squinting just a little, in thought, as though something had just come to him; something significant that now seemed the appropriate time to share with the lad.

"Don't *ever* let me see you in this position again." He said. "No son of mine allows himself to be a victim. You know now what you should do. Yes? You have the answer, and therefore, you have no excuse that you can tell me in the future. Do you understand what I mean by that? You will not burden me with something like this ever again."

"Yes, father." The boy suddenly had a seering urge to bawl, which came welling back up in full force and which, unbeknownst to his father, he was having an even harder time suppressing than before. It was because he sensed the weight of this moment. He knew that this was, definitively, the end. The end of the time in his childhood where he would have any compassion from his father; any bend in the lessons father was teaching. In this moment, the child knew it.

"Wipe that mess off and come meet us for lunch." His father talked more softly with what followed; aware that the other boys might still be in ear shot on the porch. "When you come into the sun room, you will congratulate your brother on his victory. Shake his hand with vigor. Let him know it won't be so easily won next time. Maybe give him a little wink to let the point set in, yes?" His face perused the boy blankly.

"Yes, father. I understand. I'll make you proud."

"You have some work to do." A rare moment of praise followed, though his father's face and words hardened again directly after saying it. "But I know you will be able to do what needs to be done to win." The boy forced a slight smile and nodded before the father added, louder and sterner than he had been before, "Well, don't just sit there like a little pantywaist. Get inside and wipe those tears! You won't want your brother to see them and I don't want your mother to see them, either. She won't want to think she's raised a little Nancy boy, now will she."

"Mr. Betty?"

"Father?"

"Mr. Betty?"

"I'm no Nancy boy, father. I'm no Nancy boy. I'm not! You'll see, father! I'll show you!"

"Mr. Betty. Time to wake up, sir."

David P. Betty opened his eyes, sucked in the small pool of spittle that had collected on his lips and chin, and looked around momentarily; trying to orient himself and coming to realize he had dozed off on the couch. He was nestled within the private waiting room. It was just prior to his radio interview with Bud Harbaugh. His assistant, Dennis, was sitting next to him on a bar stool, leaning forward and presenting David with a large cup of Earl Grey tea, three sugar lumps, a generous pour of half and half, two tea bags steeped long and kept in the mug. Just the way he liked it. He would take the tea bags out when in public forums. Tell people it was Kona bean coffee from Hawaii because he only bought Murican. Foppy-assed tea from Indonesia would never do with quite a large swath of his constituency.

David Betty worked now on getting his barings. Big interview coming and time to play the role. He adjusted his trucker hat. It read, "Bring it Back." Betty, as it were, had never so much as had a brief conversation with a trucker in the entirety of his life thus far. He had swiftly shaken hands with more than a few, in the mostly rural areas that he hit hard; giving the same speech, sometimes half a dozen times a day, in upwards of three states. Smaller urban areas in mostly rural states. He worked his way into a sitting position. He tried to appear livelier, more energetic than he actually felt at the moment.

"Sorry to wake you, boss," came the calming, reassuring voice of his most noble servant. "I know you were napping, but I've been told Bud is expecting you in about five minutes. Up and at 'em, sir. And I just wanted to add, for the record, nobody thinks you're a Nancy boy around these parts."

"Nancy boy?" Betty questioned, picking off an errant, crusty eye goober. "Nancy boy?" He repeated, more to himself than anyone else, perplexed. "Oh yes, yes, I remember now. Hah! Dreaming, that's all." Betty pulled himself off the couch, gave himself a quick stretch and went to check on his presentation in a tall mirror, adjacent the couch. "Don't worry about that, good man," Betty said as he checked on himself. "Old stuff from way way back, it was. Past experiences that come back in my dreams, from time to time. Not particularly pleasant, but, then again, the most important learning experiences usually aren't, are they?" Betty gave Dennis a paternal pat on the back and took a healthy swig from his cup.

"I guess not, sir," Dennis answered reflectively, as it brought back to mind, for a moment, some hard knocks from the past he had gone through at the hands of his own, often drunk, autocratic father.

"Thank you for waking me up, Dennis, and thank you for making the tea just right, once again," David said, as he grabbed the mug and began to down it quickly; stockpiling the caffeine. He rubbed his temples for a moment and yawned once before taking another long sip. The sixteen-ounce cup was half drained already. Perfect brew. Not too hot. He didn't have time to deal with, among other things, a beverage that was too hot. Dennis was one in ten million for a plethora of reasons; among them, knowing just how long to wait before the tea reached its ideal level of warmth. A hefty cup drinkable, at once, upon being handed over to the boss. This guy could've worked with Sinatra and never once gotten an earful from old blue eyes himself.

"Been a long campaign, season," the ever-present, always dependable voice continued. "Will be nice to wrap this up in a couple months. They're saying we can't win."

"Do you believe that, Dennis?" Betty asked him, as he readjusted his tie.

"Hell no," retorted Dennis enthusiastically. Dennis meant it, too. He was a man with absolute faith in his leader.

"*Hell* no! That is quite right, my friend," bellowed Mr. Betty, shooting his right fist high in a gesture of conquering triumph. He continued, as he messed with the crooked tie that gave him fuss, "it's all warped statistics and fake news." He waved it off with the flop of a hand. "We both know that. The media don't want the people to know we stand much more than just a chance. They're figuring our supporters won't come out to the polls if they can get them to thinking its hopeless. Well, we know better, don't we friend." Betty turned to Dennis, flashing a million-dollar smile.

"Yes sir." Dennis wasn't sure he fully believed Betty was right about this, but he sure wanted to. He knew the man was quick to delve into conspiracy theories from the minor, all the way to the absurdly vast and improbably orchestrated. He also knew that Betty tended to dismiss news he disagreed with, or simply didn't like, by exclaiming it *fake* and moving on. His constituents were just as quick to follow suit. Still, he wholeheartedly believed this man would be standing on that podium, addressing the nation, in redemptive glory, very soon. Bringing hope back to the people; bringing- among other things- the coal mining jobs back to his own, now destitute and drug-addled, West Virginia small town. This had been an early promise. Maybe his first big promise of the campaign.

David Betty, more assured now of proper presentation, plopped back into the couch and took in his surroundings; admiring the private waiting room for a moment. Bud's love for mahogany was evident, as it made up the frames of the couch and various chairs. The walls themselves were also mahogany, complete with Louis XIV panel designs framed in sleek, polished bronze. Golden crown moldings and various golden framed oil paintings of past Republican presidents dotted them. Madison, McKinley, and Eisenhower among others. Of course, Reagan. Betty looked around at the paintings in a detached sort of manner, not with the reverence that his various assistants seemed to peruse them with. David Betty was not a man interested in seeing other men's faces hanging on walls. When looking upon them he felt an odd sort of contempt in the pit of his being. Not a contempt for the men he observed. No, never that. It was more contempt for the fact that he should be made to respect men who did not matter much to his present life with its own wants and needs. These were men whom he saw no practical, current, use for. Like so many decorative grand pianos that no one ever played.

The makeup woman, Trish, came in to do some final touch ups to Betty's face. He was a striking man. Even well into his sixties. He'd aged like Paul Newman. His eyes were imposing, looking directly back into the eyes of those whom he talked with; probing and without hesitation. Eyes without a trace of apprehension or fear detectable at any time. Often, people would look down from his gaze; intimidated by it as they would become. They felt, a man looking at them so directly and without hesitation, or discomfort of any sort, well this man must (for reasons they could not readily explain) be one to concede to. From their frame of reference, they would likely believe that this man must have no shame; nothing to hide. He must have some knowledge that they didn't, to conjure such calm and assurance. Some claim to authority they didn't own. Betty's eyes, facial expression, nonverbal presentation, and booming, never hesitating voice, projected this superiority so definitively. The thought that he either denied, or hid, his shame, and the skeletons in his closet, more adeptly than they did, rarely occurred to most. Most people would have a much harder time presenting as such out of their honesty, not out of their weakness, as a man like Betty would see it.

Betty's trained presentation took the focus off of him by its very nature, and his verbal deflection skills only enhanced his adept defenses. He could deflect focus to those around him. Feed off of their various insecurities, which they could not hide, or deny, nearly as well as he could. Deny wasn't even the word. Betty had the capacity to shape shift words, experiences, and actions in his own mind to something that suited what he *wanted* to see. Often not what was. He was a clinical narcissist of a most destructive kind, though he did not see himself this way by account of his own pathology and its denial that he could possibly have a mental illness to begin with. Betty knew many media commentators, and, improbably, numerous, suddenly interjecting clinicians (who should've damned well minded their own business, seeing as he was no client of theirs), had voiced their concerns publicly and en masse, feeling he had this psychobabble issue going on. He was content in the knowledge that (A) They were wrong, and that (B) Most of his constituents either flat-out rejected this or felt that narcissism simply meant someone to be a little arrogant; a blowhard maybe. Well, in and of itself, that wasn't so bad, then. He'd come across plenty of salesmen who were that way and they managed to get the job done. Could even manage to be endearing in a way. So, what was the problem? Leave it at that and wipe your hands clean of it.

"Statistics, my friend," Betty recommenced, as Trish put the final touches on.

"Sir?" inquired Dennis.

"It's a numbers game, Dennis. That's it and that's all. I've been working closely with the high ups at Marmot. Dreadson, of course, for one. He's the company president, as you know. Nice guy! A real man's man of an ilk rarely seen these days, Dennis. Often accompanied by that shut-in, eggheaded Grant Scott. I've been informed, by them personally, that I'm guaranteed forty-five percent of the popular vote by saying five different things. How bout that? Five different things! Can you believe it? A trained ape could do it, in sign language, it's so easy. You know what they are?"

"No, sir." Dennis felt suddenly uneasy in the thought that he and millions of others could comprise such a diehard constituency based on just five things. He shook the thought out of his head, along with its associated, difficult to accept connotations.

Betty continued emphatically, beginning to present almost as though putting on a show. Performing, it almost seemed. He threw his hand in the air, in an overblown and kind of silly way; like a cheerful drunk king proclaiming to the court that the hour had arrived to make merry. He began to jut out his various fingers to count off his proclamations. Up came the first.

"*No abortion*! Sixteen percent of the vote right there, friend. Mostly Evangelicals with that one, of course. No big surprise there. You and I know damn well they're not going to overturn Roe V Wade; but fuck it. It doesn't matter. Just say it to let them know you're on the same page is all they really want. Same team here, guys. We're both wearing the red potato sacks. You know? Hah!"

The second finger came up as Betty continued:

"*Less government*! Nine percent, mostly disgruntled laborers and paranoid, jaded, independent types." The third finger rose. "*Traditional Values*! Whatever in hell *that* means. Traditionally, in the fifties, you could run over a kid when you were drunk and they'd call it an unfortunate accident. Whoopsy doodle, Mr. Officer! That's eight percent of the vote, my friend, mostly elderly men who liked it better when their wives stayed their asses in the kitchen and the blacks and Hispanics knew their God Damn place." The fourth finger:

"*Bring jobs Home!* That's good for another six percent. Mostly unemployed former factory and mill workers, there, who actually think I'm going to bring back their nineteen sixties era jobs. That's the dumb fuck vote. Instead of training for, and seeking out, different work, which they *should* have done a long-assed time ago, they're holding out hope for dated and obsolete jobs to magically resurface. Like the automatons don't do most it nowadays, anyhow! Well hell, it's easier to just hope things will go back to where they were than to get off your keister and change with the times. Can't blame 'em, right? And finally, Dennis, wait for it…wait for it, now. The last six percent? They want to hear this." Up went the thumb to complete the hand.

"*Restore Law and Order*! And that implies, of course, mostly stricter policing of the inner cities. Those people? Scared rural white folks who think the minorities are coming to get them. You know, trampling through the corn fields into rural Indiana with their gats." Betty made play guns with both thumbs and index fingers, shooting them at Dennis and going, "Bang, bang,

bang," and laughing heartily. Dennis was a little uncomfortable with the gesture.

"They're coming to get whitey, Dennis!" David proclaimed, looking manic and shooting some spittle. "Coming to get that old cracker and pork his wife and daughter, while they're at it. Turn his girl into a booty shaking ho with corn rows, twerking it in one of them rap videos. There you go, my friend. Count it up and do that math. Forty five percent. Of course, there is overlap among the five, but everyone has their own particular favorite that really secures that vote. I say all of these things over and over and over again. At every speech. Hell, you've heard it. I do it repeatedly, like a radio commercial jingle that gets stuck in your head. Like a TV commercial that repeats their phone number eighteen times in a fucking row in a sing song type of way. Like the God damn *Feliz Navidad* song at Christmas Time. Like that *You'll Save Big Money* song. Shit, the rest is just details. If I get another measly two percent beyond that I'll probably win, the way the electorate is set up right now. You know how I get that?

"I bet you know a way, boss. I have no doubt." Dennis really did have no doubt, and his confidence with Betty was growing by the day as his friends and family back home continued feeling ever more optimistic that he would bring their jobs back. However, for a moment, he felt, somehow, that he and they might be thought of as less than, in some way, based on how Betty just broke down his constituents. He repressed the feeling instantly. He was good at this, mostly unbeknownst to himself. He was good at giving Betty concessions, despite those pesky instincts that screamed at him, from time to time, that this was all just a charade. It was a testament to the power of wanting to believe in something, and someone, despite so much evidence to the contrary. Presently, to maintain his ever-present good faith, he assumed Betty's jibe about dated jobs wouldn't include his beloved coal industry. The man would certainly not make promises he didn't intend to keep. Betty cared deeply about his constituency's wants. He knew that for a fact. Yes, sir. Certainly, there was no doubt about it.

"Oh ye of much faith, Dennis," Betty continued exuberantly. "That's why I like ya. I certainly do." He grew more emboldened as he observed Dennis' almost childlike reverence for him.

"You see, my good buddy, the problem is that the liberal media overestimates the *intelligence* of the average voter. Well, not the intellectual *capacity* so much, just the actual willingness of my potential voters for more prolonged, critical thought about the issues at play. You see, I don't. I'm a realist and it has served me well, friend. See, the average American voter simply wants to be appeased and placated. That's it. I'm sorry, but really, what they want is to be tucked into bed at night by daddy, and I'm daddy. Daddy dearest, see? Why, that's me. I tuck them in and I wrap up their little footsy wootsies, too; with simple answers to complex issues, spoken with authority and certainty. Like saying the boogey man can't come out of the closet if you keep a night light next to it. Problem solved, my child. That's always been the way to get it done and it will continue to be so until the end of time, my friend."

"Yes, sir." Dennis was starting to wish for this conversation to end. He did not like the tone. He did not like when Betty strayed from his campaign speeches and got into this *otherness* about what he really felt and believed about it all, though Betty was not a man who liked to placate those he considered on the *inside* of things; people like Dennis.

"Dennis, I am making them believe that they should be angry with how society is progressing and that they are entitled to more. Adapt to a changing society, you ask? *Hell* no! You know what kind of insecurity and toil goes with that! Nobody wants to hear that shit. Society has failed *you*, and we're going to make life easier by bringing back a society that *did* work for you. Of course, you either weren't there, or probably glamorized it, but hell. It worked back then, right? So?

"So?"

"So bring it back!"

"Hell yes, sir!"

Betty was getting jacked now, pacing the room and making little bunny hops from time to time, in his caffeinated state. He was pumping himself up for one of the biggest interviews of his campaign thus far.

"You see the strategy here, is simple. Imply that it already existed, even though it never did. If they were around in the fifties and still alive, most idealize it from a child's perspective cuz they were kids back then anyway, so you don't have to worry about those folks. If they weren't around back them? Then they want to believe it was as a man like me *says* it was. So many people out there want to believe that life used to be a cake walk. Take a few steps, pay a buck or two, and somebody gives you a big tray of cupcakes and says, 'have at it.' Millenials, especially, want to believe that. There's a lot of fear to be exploited there, Dennis, my friend."

"Uh huh," Dennis had grown less enthusiastic and simply wished for Betty to start his interview.

"Dennis, my man. My dawg. Even though I'm a late middle-aged man from a different era that they probably think they can't relate to, I only have to bring in a few of those youngsters. I use social media and talk in sound bites for the, let's call them, attention span challenged. I speak their language. It will be enough to turn them, and you'll see. Turn enough of them, anyway. I only need a few to tip the scales fully in my direction. Bring in a few minorities by saying, what the hell. What do you have to lose? That's all it takes. Bring in a few undecideds. The longer they stay undecided, the more it behooves me. Believe you me, that's true, friend. Because even with all of these, quote unquote 'controversial ideas' I have. If even *that* doesn't sway them to the opposing side early on in the game? You know what I think? They'll end up voting for me. You wait, my friend." Betty shook a finger at Dennis. "Mark my words, good buddy. A lot of people out there are playing their hands close. Not showing their cards. But in the end, when they flash what they had all along, you'll see a picture of me under the ace of spades, boy. Hoo wee!" Betty slapped his hands together and did a few jumping jacks, like an athlete about to run out of the tunnel before the big game.

"I sure hope it's you, Mr. Betty," Dennis replied. He was flustered and upset with some of the things he had just heard. So as not to deal with this, he decided to deflect those feelings onto the opposing side. "To hell with this libtard agenda. I'm sick of it!" Dennis wasn't fully aware of what he meant when he said that latter part. When he tried to conjure what this meant, from time to time, he felt this *agenda*, that people like Betty talked about, had something to do with turning the nation communist in a style that roughly matched 1950s Russia. This then brought back a visceral fear, from his vulnerable childhood, when he would hear adults talk about the Soviet Union. How they were going to nuke the U.S. and start WWIII at any moment. When that fear was put back in him, he wanted it to go away.

Betty gave Dennis a pat on the back before taking a last look in the mirror to do some final checking of his wardrobe and to make sure there were no issues with the makeup. Usually a guest wouldn't have to concern themselves with appearances on a radio program, but there was a small TV crew on hand today, from Marmot. As Betty was perusing himself, good old Ted walked into the room and put out his hand. The man was itching for a hearty shake and a little, good'ol fashioned, bullshittery.

"Our next president. Sir, it is truly an honor to be meeting with you once more. Bring it back! It can be again!" Ted mimicked the fist pumping gesture that Betty used, over and over again, at rallies across the nation.

"Hah! Good ol' Ted! How bout that? How are ya, my old friend?" said David as he gave him a vigorous handshake and a manly hug.

"Doin' well. And I can't say it enough. It's a pleasure having you here, sir. Been a few years now, hasn't it, friend? They still calling you Captain Pussy Crusher behind closed doors."

"Ha ha! Now Ted," Betty shook a naughty finger at the man, "Now look here, sir, I'm running for president. Let's we show a little class, okay? Those days are (ahem) mostly behind me now."

"Yeah, well, I guess I'll have to get used to you getting back into the political game. Tone it down a bit for the sake of efficacy."

"Well, I stayed out of it for a while, buddy. Until this president we have went too far at that charity dinner and roast party. Tried to point me out. Tried to make fun of me! Making fun of *me*? Motherfucker, you don't do that! You wait and see what happens! And all because I was on *Dancing with One-Time Celebrities*. Yeah, maybe that was a bad career choice, but I'm about to show everyone I'm much more than a washed-up, eighties playboy. That *fucker*! That mother *fucker*! Thinks he can poke fun at me? Well not him and not *anybody* else on this earth, friend. I'm coming after his job now. See what he thinks of that. Anybody can be president with (A) the right amount of money, and (B) the ability to know his constituency. And I'm going to add (C) who will inspire and take the vote of anybody he can get a vote from.

"A vote is a vote, friend."

"Damn right, Ted. I know *you* get it. And, shit, if I get it from the wrong crowd? Well, I'll just wait til the voting is over and denounce them, retroactively. Won't need them anymore at that point, no how." Betty, understanding he had grown heated, forced a quick chuckle and decided to get away from the emotional element of things, and back to his underlying philosophies. "Know your audience, my friend. Know how to work the apparatus. That's show biz in a nutshell." Betty slicked back his hair and straightened his tie, one last time, before the interview.

"Damn, right. They've never given you enough credit for your accomplishments," Ted added, observing the man proudly. "A worldwide investor worth twenty billion. Shit, you damn sure *must* know what you're doing. I thought only computer nerds made that kind of money these days, shit. And with a loan of just two million from your father."

"Twenty-five million, but who's counting. Hah! You 'ol sumbitch, bring it back in." David gave Ted another hearty hug and another backslap. "Good Ol Ted. Hey, where's Walt at?"

"In there waitin' for ya. You ready to do this?"

"Always ready."

"Let's go, friend."

Ted wrapped his arm around Betty's back to lead him on in. They brushed past Dennis, without acknowledgment. He watched them with a hopeful smile as they vanished behind the florid mahogany door and into the radio booth. Ted waved Betty over to the sectional leather couch, hugging the north corner of the room. Bud's desk in front of it, separated by a 1500s era, wooden chest, serving as a coffee table between Bud's desk and the couch. The chest was a gift from Dreadson, who stated that it belonged to Philip II, of Spanish royalty, and that it once sat full to the brim with Spanish Galleon used specifically to buy niceties for his substantial harem; based in large part, por supuesto, on their respective performances.

Bud, extra sweaty today in his tense anticipation, gazed upon David with a sincere look of pride, interrupted by just a moment's flicker of a glare, like a facial tic; a barely perceived show of resentment for the rare man he knew held more social sway than he did. The jealousy was there, certainly, but expertly repressed. He shook hands, hastily, and offered Betty a seat on the couch. His chair was turned around from its usual position, and his desk sat just behind him now. There would be nothing between him and Betty but the coffee table, which would make it appear all the more intimate. Walt and Ted, farther back, sat on their desks for a better view, hugging their east and west sides of the room. They all looked upon David Betty with pride. Microphones hung from the walls and sat on the chest, along with another cup of warm tea that Dennis had placed there, just minutes before. A few of Betty's aides and inner circle members shuffled quietly into the room and found standing space for the radio event of the year.

"Mr. David Peeeeeeee Betty," Bud stated, drawingly, enthusiastically, reverentially, and deliberately. His pudgy features shifted into a beam. "Our fearless leader. It is an honor, sir. A true honor. Make yourself comfortable, my longtime friend. We are going to get started right away, in about ten seconds, cuz I know you're a busy man these days with things to do. So we going to get right to it. Damn, how long has it been, by and by?"

"About four years, Bud, but as you know and already pointed out, I've been busy lately, running this campaign and all," David said, while eyeing Bud and noticing how disgustingly fat this man had become. He was hoping this disgust didn't show, in the moment. Bud must've been thirty pounds heavier than the last time, and he damned sure was already fat as hell the last time. Betty, typically, hated fatties, and substantially more so if they were young women. What a fucking waste. They were most of them lazy, had the sugar foot, and drained the country's medical resources and long-term disabilities funds. However, he supposed Bud, the fat, doped-up, alky fuck, could do as he pleased- considering he had enough money to buy a couple small countries and a large private island in the Caribbean, to boot. All from talking shit all day long. A professional bull shitter of the highest ilk. A fatty or not, that was a man to be respected. A true salesman.

"Four years, well ya look great buddy," came the blubbery voice again, from a mouth that sounded partially filled with cotton. "And, uh, and you out there tearin' up the pea patch these days. Yes, sah! Now you *know* we been watchin' ya ova heeya. Alright, let's get started. We goin' on the air in three…two…one…" Bud grabbed one of the hanging microphones and pulled it close to his thin, purple lips. "True Murican radio, her. Now, fellow patriots, the time…has…come…at last. I am here, with, uh, with the, uh, despite what the liberal elite media might tell you, *the* next president of our great nation; of these *Divided* States of America which he will once again reunite. The esteemed investor. The reality TV star. The King of Manhattan. One of the greatest investors and businessmen of our time. Hell. Of *any* time. Mr. David Peeeeeeeee *Betty!* Thank you for being here and supporting us, my friend."

"I'm happy to have your support, old friend," Betty replied in a thoroughly convincing, mock humility.

"Oh you got it, nah, you sure do," Bud wiped a few beads of sweat off his brow with a kerchief, in a gesture that came to him as automatically as blinking. "You got our respect cuz you, uh, you up in her every damned day tellin' it like it is. Givin' us the troot! And we needs that troot up in heeya, sah. We *needs* it!"

"Truth!" Walt mimicked, in a somewhat more moderated capacity than typically shown; a sign of respect for the republican nominee. He hadn't even snorted coke just prior the broadcast- not even one line- which was quite a rare sacrifice to make in Walt's case.

"Needs it," chimed in Ted.

"Now ain't that right?" Added Bud. "Ain't that just right, friends? That's what we need. The truth. Needs the truth, friends. And we ain't gettin' nuff of it these hah dais. Let me continue by letting our viewers know what the troot is, if'n you don't mind, soon to be president David Betty."

"Be my guest, old friend." Betty was happy to let Bud take control of the mic in any situation. It was an incredibly rare instance of him being able to acknowledge someone else having the ability to do something (maybe just a little) better than he could.

"Alright den, nah her's the truth in one paragraph. Cuz that's all you need for the whole truth, don't you know."

"All you *need*," blurted Walt, losing, already, a touch of his initially more moderated tone.

"It's simple," added Ted.

"Now it really is, nah isn't it?" Bud shifted, to look back at Ted with a proud grin. "Good ol' Ted knows it, folks." Bud pivoted back in his chair toward Betty. "My true patriots, true Muricans know it. Mr. David P. Betty knows it, too. Nah, nah, we've had discussions about the troot before."

"Muricans!" Exclaimed Walt.

"True Muricans," added Ted.

"Dat rot, Ted," Bud affirmed, "And dat rot, Walt. *True* Muricans. *True* Muricans, nah. Nah, them new age liberals we got these days...see...they ain't true Muricans (a pause to let the message sink in). You see what I'm saying? I'm sorry to say it, but they ain't. Don't fit the requirements, ya know. Don't make the passing grade. Don't make the cutoff point and all. Not at the minimum height to get on the ride. Hehe *heee*.

"Hehehe."

"He he *heeee*."

"Dat rot. Now, where was I at? Where was I? Where is I be? Oh yeah, what is the truth? *Here's* the truth, my friends. The liberal agenda is taking away *your* jobs." Bud paused for emphasis, here. "Taking them away! Okay? Nah, nah, if they up'n, uh, comin' in taking 'em away, nah, well den who they givin' em to? Hmm? They takin' em away, right? Well den, so uh, stands to reason, they must be givin' em to someone else, right? So den, who they up and givin' em to? (strategic pause for emphasis)...well I'm fixin' to tell you.

"You fixin' to tell em?"

"I'm fixin' to tell em, Ted. They is, uh, they is givin' em to the Mexicans! Givin' em all to the Mexicans. *Your* jobs, folks!"

"Mex-ee-cans!" Walt shouted, slurring somewhat as he had just taken an absurdly large pinch of snuff (a more moderated than typical substance for the occasion, he felt) the juice of which now dribbled down onto his desk as he made his exclamation.

"Can't even Hablo the English," added Ted.

"That's right, Ted! Yo no hablo the Eeenglish. Can't even speak the damn language. Hmm? How bout dat?

"How bout dat?"

"How bout dat, but yet they still takin' *your* jobs... Muricans. *Your* jobs." Bud jutted a finger into the invisible airwaves. "Now that's duh troot. That's what you done come here for. And here's another troot. Is you ready? Hmm? Is you be ready? They drainin' all this country's resources. Not paying taxes. And the blacks. Hmm? The blacks. They're sitting around collecting welfare and promoting thug culture with the rap music. Taking drugs, dumbing everybody down with their ebonics, 8th grade education before dropping out a school having butts. Eight kids with eight different baby momma havin' butts. Not being a father to any of 'em, neither. Women so used to it, they don't even *expect* them to be father figures to they kids. Libtards not letting you talk about *any* of this, telling you it makes ya racist. Well, what? *Truth* makes ya racist? That don't make no sense, true Muricans."

"Don't make no sense," said Ted.

"Muricans!" Added Walt, needlessly.

"Nah, nah…nah, and dat rot, by the way, but uh," Bud dabbed at his brow again, "nah, nah, uh, nah…nah, what kind of a *libtard* world do we live in where you can't even speak the truth? Truth is, minorities are taking over our jobs *and* our culture. And they be dumbing it down, to be sure. White folks now being made to feel all guilty about what they have and the history of slavery and Jim Crow, so's they don't feel like they can speak up about nothin'.

"Nothin'!" Slurred Walt as a second stream of chaw juice dribbled out down his chin; staining his top left collar.

"Freeloadin' whiners trying to get government entitlements without ever working in they lives. Sittin' on they ass watchin' '*Who's the Father?*' You ever see that show, fellas?" Bud looked back toward Ted and Walt who both shook their heads in affirmation, with knowing smiles (*Who's the Father?* was one of the most masterful shows in history at affirming negative stereotypes, mainly for blacks and so-called white trash). "You know what I'm talkin' bout. Some fat ho bag sittin' der next to the show's host, Larry Ponderosa. They bring in six possible baby daddies. And guess what? Ain't none of them turn out to be the father. Then, after they announce it, then, uh, the guys, each one of 'em, get up, start hoppin' around and flappin' they arms and talkin' trash. And, uh, and that happenin' all the time, all over the place, nah. You bess buh-leev!"

"Ho bags!" screamed Walt.

"Dat rot, Walt! I hates tuh say it, but they is. And den...den...nah, I ain't finished nah. Den, they get the same ho bag. She come on the show three months later. Hmm? She back up on the show, sept, uh, now she with six *other* guys altogether. And guess what? Ain't none a *them* the father neithers! And den day get up, nah, flappin' they arms around, hoppin' around on stage, flappin' they arms and shakin' they heads."

"Ho bags! Ho bags!" Walt jumped up and down in front of his desk, dripping globs of brown spittle all over his shoes and the floor.

"Ok, Walt. Ya done made your point nah. Settle it on down. They's ho bags. We know. Nah, nah...nah, what else? Well, I tell you what else. See, we got these white, new age, libtard hipsters. Nah these some dickless young men you can't even tell apart from they girlfriends, sept by a quarter inch long, impeccably groomed beard. Dat about it. Day is wearing dem skinny jeans and a man bun. Men becoming feminized. Men becoming weak. What else, nah? Debt ballooning out of control cuz people spending money they don't have. Entitling people to government programs that we can't afford. Want to take our guns away, too. No doubt about dat. And did I mention they takin' our jobs!"

"*Took* mah job! They done *took* it!" Walt screamed, slapping his hands hard and randomly, like a chimpanzee run amok in the zoo.

"The Chinese doing it, too," added Ted.

"Dat rot. Dat *rot*, Ted! The Chain-*neeeees*. But we'll get to that another time, friend. I gots ta say. Now Walt. Walt?

"Took mah job! Took mah job!"

"Walt, now you simma! Nobody done took your job. Okay? Now think about it, nah. You still workin' right chair in dat dare chair a yers, buddy, rot over her at True Murican radio. Nah settle down now, okay amigo. I'm gonna have to ask you to tone it down a little earlier than usual on account a our esteemed guest ova her." Bud acknowledged Betty, for the first time in the past ten minutes, on account of his current tirade. "Hmm, nah, where was I? Oh yea, okay, first of all, they didn't take *your* job, okay Walt. My friend. You know you always got you a place rot chair, like I was sayin'. Now settle yo self down, nah." Bud covered the mike, briefly. "Maybe take you a little swig of this here good bourbon, friend."

Bud waddled his way toward Walt and poured him a generous two and half fingers into one of his crystal tumblers. "There you go friend, nah simma on down. I know this is upsettin' to ya, now. Believe me, I know. This can get upsettin' (Bud's calming talk was all audible to his listeners as mics were hooked up from the ceiling all around the room as well)." Bud moseyed his way back to his desk, squeaking out a low-pitched fart along the way that, he thought, would be silent, though which was also audible over the airwaves on account of the much higher than typical mic count. "These puffy chairs and they silly noises," he improvised. "Nah, nah, where was I again?" Oh yea, David P. Betty." Bud beamed once again as he took his seat. "Nah, you know these the truths. You *know* these the truths. But also, uh, you know your Bud needs somebody *else* speaking the troot. Okay?

"Right there with you, Bud," Betty appeased.

"And thank the good lord in Heaven. Somebody else tuh speak the troot, nah, cuz I can't dooze it all by myself. Hmm? Okay? Ah cain't dooze it! Ah cain't."

"He can't dooze it," confirmed Ted.

"He cain't!" Added Walt.

"Dat rot! Though, that hot, blonde, cutesy patootsey, Terri Mehran has been helping me out, as of late, on that new show she's hosting. Fine young woman takin' the reigns for the next generation (Bud was beginning to generate a half chub in his pants thinking about the new twenty something conservative queen with her cute, sassy ass). Nah, where was I again? Yes, yes, I been speakin' that truth for decades, nah, and I'm starting to get a little worn out if I do say so myself."

"I don't hold anything back," said David, matter of factly. He had been quite content in his silence to this point; just sitting back and watching the master entertainer at work for a spell. "That's why the DNC and some of the, let's say, *weaker* members of our own party- holding on to growingly obsolete ideals- can't stand me."

"Tell em what you gon do, David. Tell em what you gon do, nah!" Bud wobbled around in his chair in excitement, like an overgrown fat kid with a piece of chocolate cake held out in front of him. Betty briefly grimaced at the sight of this.

"Well, for starters. Build that fence I've been talking about."

"Build you a fence, nah!"

"An electric fence," clarified Betty.

"Build you one! Hoo wee!" A serious of knee slaps audible to all.

"High voltage," Betty further clarified.

"Got ta have that high voltage. Nah, you got to, nah," Bud replied in more serious reflection.

"Build a high voltage, electrical fence to keep out all the Mexicans. Right along the El Rio Grandy River."

"Right along that El Ree-o Grandy!"

"Murican!" Belted Walt.

"Dat rot. Dat rot, Walt!" Bud pivoted in his chair to talk to Walt. "I got to say, Walt, you gettin' loud again. You sip you some of that fine libation, nah, and you settle down. Settle down nah, you interjectin' inappropriately nah, son. This her the next POTUS, mind you." Bud spun back around to face Betty. "I apologize, Mr. Betty. You been on the show before. You know how Walt gets. We try not to fault him for it. Ted's trying to calm him down over there. Good ol' Ted. Okay, please continue, sir. Okay? Nah, uh, whatcha gon do? Whatcha gon' do when the Mex-ee-cans come for you? Cuz they got some bad boys, bad boys'. Watcha gon do?

"We're going to build a high voltage fence."

"Yes, sah!"

"Three layers to this fence, Bud." Betty held up three fingers. "We're going to do three, count 'em, *three* layers." Betty gestured a span with his hands. "Five feet apart each. It's going to be great. All electrified, each layer, very high voltage. I mean, *very* high. Fantastically high voltage stuff, here. High in terms of height, too, come to think of it. Twenty feet high, ten feet below ground, too. Going to rest in dug out concrete trenches along a steep pit that we'll tunnel out on our side of the river, so as they can't even *get* to the fence easily. Hopefully that alone will stop a lot from trying. That's really our hope. Call it more of a preventative approach, if you will."

"Stop the lazy freeloaders, anyway," said Bud.

"Los perezosos," said Ted.

"Dat rot," replied Bud, not knowing, exactly, what he was saying "dat rot" about.

"Yes, and if anybody can get past those three electric fences. Hell, you know what?" Betty waved both hands high in the air, in a floppy manner. The gesture of giving up. "If they can get past *those* fences, they can just go ahead and have a green card. We'll just go ahead and give it to them. I wouldn't even be mad, I'd just be plum impressed." Betty formed a fist with this thumb poking out between his index and middle fingers, and shook it slowly, with purpose. "See, those would be the type of Mexicans we'd want in this country. Hard working and resourceful 'n all."

"Fair dinkum, ah guess," conceded Bud, though the fact that these people would still be brown irked him, on the inside.

"Separate the Mex-ee-*cans* from the Mex-ee-*cant's*," added Ted.

"Hah! Good one, Ted. I see you chucklin' over there, too, David. Now don't let them snowflakes see that. Hehe. See, they'll go getting all offended. Call that politically incorrect and racist, stead of what it is, that being, uh, nah, that being, uh, that it be's a necessary precaution to secure our borders. Now speakin' uh that, some people are sayin', and you know what I mean by *some* people."

"Libtards," clarified Ted

"Snowflakes! Pussies! Cucks!" added Walt.

"Walt, now dammit it all to hell! Stop usin' inappropriate language!"

"Sorry, Bud." Specks of white were now visible along the slimy chaw dribble on Walt's chin. Bud shook his head in frustration and pointed a stern warning finger toward Walt. Here we go again, for the umpteenth time. He recommenced the moment's tirade:

"Nah, these snowflakes talkin' bout the fence bein', well, they sayin' it's, uh…what's the word they usin'? In-hoo-mane, is, uh, is the word they be usin'. Now, to be clear, we're talkin' about *securing* our borders here. Okay? Let me clarify that to my loyal audience. We…are…talkin'…bout…*securing*…our…borders. *Securing* 'em. Now I ask you, what's wrong with that? Hmmm? And, uh, and how we gonna secure them sept by somethin' like this? Hmmm?" Bud threw his hands up in the air in frustrated resignation, as though there truly was no other solution. "Nah, nah you think we gonna secure em by puttin' up some police tape? Hmmm? Sayin' 'now please just stay back. Stay over in your country, los muchachos. You think that's gon' work? Hmm? Hell, the snowflakes probably do, but you all True Muricans…"

"Muricans!" Screamed Walt.

"*True* Muricans," clarified Ted.

"Dat rot!" Affirmed Bud.

"Amen!" Added Betty.

"Da rot! Now, as I was sayin', ya'll *true* Muricans know that ain't gon' work. This the type of thing you have to do to keep them borders secure. Now you know that's a fact (pausing again). Now you *know*…that's…a fact. A *fact*! This is what we need to do to secure…our…border. Of course, unfortunately, this will, prolly, lead to some deaths. People and animals both. That's unfortunate. But you know what? People should know better for one. And two, that fence is gonna take care of a lot of critters. Possums, Armadillos, coons and what have you. And by coons I mean raccoons, before the liberal elite media tries ta say I done meant something' else."

"Better cover your keister, friend," warned Ted.

"Don't you know it, buddy boy. And by the way, let's not forget this *added* benefit of all them electrified critters, gonna be poppin' up all over the place. You know, you can eat some a them. How about that? Have you a nice barbecue…on your proper side 'o the fence, of course."

"You too bougie to eat a fresh roasted possum?" Asked Walt, in words sloppily strung together.

"Ah ain't, is you?"

"May I interject, friend," came the pleasing to hear, well collected voice of Betty.

"Why, ah, certainly, Mr. soon-to-be President of the United States."

"POTUS!" slurred Walt. His slurring all the more audible after combining a discreet line of coke and taking half a twelve-ounce tumbler like a shot glass." Bud shot him a stink eye, but Walt didn't notice, as he was now properly drunk and high.

"Now, I just want to add something here, Bud. We are aware that there will be numerous animal casualties, as well. And by the way, not a bad idea about making lemons out of lemonade with some of them roasted critters."

"Damn skippy."

"But, as, unfortunately, as you already said, the occasional human being, er, uh, I mean *illegal alien...*"

"Yes, sir, let's us use the proper terminology."

"...tragedy will be occurring. Now, I just want to add, that I will be creating approximately three thousand new jobs. Government positions mind you, with full benefits, for the position of Federal Electrified Corpse Removal Agent. FECRAs, if you will. Now, basically, what this means, is that these FECRAs, and what have you, will be walking along, in between the electrified fences, from various entry points on our side of the border. And, basically, each FECRA agent will traverse along approximately a two-mile strip, end to end, on standard eight-hour shifts. Three separate shifts in total, so that's twenty-four hours a day surveillance. We're even gonna give them little scooters to ride around on, as that's a long time to be walking around for anyone. Okay, so one thousand agents will be scooting around, at all times, three shifts per day. Three times one thousand. Boom! That's three thousand new jobs right there for you good folks. You're welcome. There's more jobs to come, too, believe me. Going to be fantastic!"

"Boom! That's what I'm talking about, sir. You her that, True Muricans? Get you yer resume ready. Three thousand new jobs planned out, rot dare. And we just getting' started. See, this man ain't even in office yet. But he will be. We speakin' to a man who's gonna be the winner come November."

"Winner, winner, chicken dinner," said Ted.

"Dat rot! You heard it here, my friends."

"Now, Bud," Betty continued. "I know this here, well, this particular *type* of work won't be pretty. But, it'll be a fifty k per year occupation. And now, that's also with some of the best benefits you could possibly have. Unfortunately, some of our good friends from Mexico might end up electrified. But…electrified due to making a bad decision. Well, actions *do* have consequences.

"Dat rot!" A desk rattling slam of the fist. "Tell that tuh them libtards, kind sir. They appear to think otherwise."

"But, rest assured, friend," Betty's voice came in a little more upbeat. "We will be humanely collecting the corpses and storing them in designated cooling areas. You know, much like your typical morgue. And our country will be paying the rather hefty electrical bills for all of that AC, by the way. And that's going to be for the families. How about that? To help keep them persevered for identification. And we will certainly try our very best to identify them, if possible. And I also believe, strongly, in a good and proper Christian burial, all said and done. So, of course, the preserved body will be offered back to the Mexican government to do just that. Sent with the sincerest of apologies from the U.S. government too, for the family's loss. We will have cards made, in Spanish, offering condolences, of course."

"Como, lo siento, muchacho," advised Walt.

"Now Walt, you really need to brush up on your Espanol," chided Bud. "Because in a case like this, I think you would be saying 'Lo siento dee el *famiglia* de los muchacho.' Got it? Bud focused his attention back to Mr. David Betty. "Pardon that interjection, sir. Nah, nah, what else we gonna be expectin' from you, Mr. Betty? POTUS!" Bud reached over and playfully wiggled one of Betty's thighs just past the knee.

"Well, Bud, I'm getting plans together regarding the terrorism problem. I don't know about you, but I'm quite ready to be done with all of this."

"Yes, sah. Why is we be draggin' this out to kingdom come?"

"Preeching to the choir, friend. So what we're going to do is, we're going to terminate all the Islamic terrorists in a swift, large-scale military operation. Gonna call it BOOM SHAKA POW!"

"What all that stand for?" Bud asked.

"Oh, well it doesn't really stand for anything, friend. It's not an acronym. I just got kind of liked the sound of it. Catchy, isn't it?"

"Hah! Fair enough. And you damn right, it's catchy. You damn right!"

"Um, now there may be some civilian casualties, of course, but such is the cost of war. And make no mistake, we are in an ongoing state of war with this."

"Damn right, Mr. soon-to-be leader of the free world. War ain't never purdy," Bud replied, in a voice made to sound knowing.

"No sir, my friend. But I am looking to get this terrorist nonsense good and done for ASAP. All these liberals acting like we somehow can't do that. Well, that's how we're going to do things when I am the victor come November. ASAP, my friend. That's what the American people deserve. Instant results. And I'm the man to give to the them."

"Damn right."

"Murica!"

"Walt! Not now!"

"BOOM SHAKA POW! BOOM SHAKA POW!"

"Walt! What I done said? Huh? What I jist done said? Put your shirt back down from ova yo head. Lookin' like Cornholio over there!"

"Friend?"

"Yes sah, Mr. Betty."

"Might I go on to my next point?"

"Proceed, sah."

"Well that is this. I'm going to bring back factory work over here, en masse. Bring in, uh, industry, too. Ease up on a few, really, and really these are, just *unnecessary* environmental restrictions that have been keeping that from happening for years. We're going to have a lot of work coming back, my friend, but we've to got to ease up on some of these factory regulations. And no more of this current set up. This liberal agenda, making college the only way to succeed, and crapping, just dropping trow and crapping all over the common man who just wants work to provide for his family."

"Damn right, sir! Sir, you are, if I may say so, a ray of luminous sunshine casting a double rainbow over calm waters."

"Murican water."

"Dat rot, Ted! And, uh, and dis after eight long years of rain with this whack job, Tahitian, Muslim nut-case we got in office right now."

"A shot of good medicine for this liberal sickness," added Ted.

"A crock pot full of sausage gravy for a plate of warm biscuits," Walt chimed in.

"Mmm-mmm, that sounds *hella good,* my friend. Let's get us some a that for breakfast tomorrow morning, friends. Over there at Esperanza's Café. How bout dat? On me, too. Now, Mr. Betty, we unfortunately running short on time now so, what else we gonna be expectin' from ya?"

"Well, with this whole Muslim problem we're having, we obviously need to do something' about that. Now listen up, constituents. What I'm proposing is this. I'm going to make anyone in this country who is Muslim wear a chip implanted behind their sternum that can track their movements, at all times. In addition, anyone who is Muslim will have their homes bugged by the CIA."

"Yeah!" Bud slapped Betty hard on the same thigh.

"As well as all Muslim-owned businesses. Bugged by the CIA," Betty added, wincing from the force of the slap.

"Hell, yeah! Bug it good!"

"Bug it *real* good. Bug it like the shores of Lake Okeechobee in July," added Walt.

"Also, anyone of the Christian moral majority. The Christian *moral* majority, who is a non-Muslim business owner who notices they have customers, or workers, who look like Muslims."

"What den? What you gon' do? What you don gon' do? Hoo wee!"

"They can have the CIA come and bug the store, free of charge."

"Hell yeah, mother trucker! How bout dat! How bout dat! Nah where they gon' go run and hide now? Where you gon' run to, boy! Hoo wee!"

"Nowhere, my friend, is the answer to that."

Nowhere. Dat right! Because what's going to happen?"

 "Bugged!"

 "Bugged by who, nah?"

"Bugged by the CIA," enthused Betty.

"Bugged by the CIA, hoo *weeeee*, my friend! I'm lovin' it, Mr. Betty, just lovin' it. Nah, nah, what else you gon' do?"

"Well, Bud, I'm glad you asked. Now, we have a problem in our inner cities, as you well know. I'm just going to come out and say it, mostly with the blacks and the Hispanics."

"You go ahead and say it, Mr. Betty, you on *True Murican Radio*. You speak dat troot rot her."

"You know what we're going to do about that?" Betty playfully asked, trying to stir up the excitement.

"What you gon' do?" Bud bit hard. "What you don fixin' ta do? Hoo wee! You tell me, nah! You run telldat!" Bud was flopping up and down in his chair, flapping his arms like a penguin whose trainer was holding up a dead fish.

"Fine sirs. Listen up. We are going to divert a large portion of our military to policing the inner cities. We're not at war, right? Well, except for the terrorists. But they'll all be reduced to ashes within the first few months of *my* presidency. But then, we still have all these hundreds of thousands of soldiers on the mainland that could be put to use, here and now. They're here, right?"

"Dat right."

"Yes, sir, right here in America."

"Dat rot, Ted."

"Murica!"

"Dat rot, Walt."

"Well, why not use them?" Betty asked, looking around at all three of the broadcasters with his hands up as though the answer was obvious. "We'll have them policing designated inner-city areas and declare martial law. Let them do what they need to do until the problem is solved. We are here to solve problems, my friend, not pussy foot around."

"Dat rot! Nobody want ta just come out and say it. These here are war zones, need ta be treated as sich, and that's exactly what you fixin' ta do, good sir." Bud readied himself to slap Betty's knee again, though Betty had knowingly retracted it, eliciting a brief look of childlike disappointment from the pasty folds of Bud's pudgy features.

"(Ahem) I'm fixing to, Bud. Now I know it's a bit *extreme,* and all, but think about it. Aren't the situations in some of these neighborhoods a bit extreme? Wouldn't you say that as well?"

"I would, sir. I would."

"Chicago, now that's a war zone. Let's start right there. Heck, I can't believe anybody would even visit that city the way things are. But I'll be there. Rest assured. Two weeks from today, speaking some harsh truths, but truths just like this that need to be heard."

"You right, David. And you know what it is? The libtards have taken over that city, what with their gun policies and all that nonsense. And lookee what happens. All the thugs have the guns, but yet, none of the proper citizenry do. They should just let everybody have guns over there. Everybody go get you a gun. Guns for free! Ages twelve and up, of course, now don't get me wrong. No little kids. But, yeah, everybody go get you a gun and you'll find out these thugs won't be so trigger happy no more. No sir! These thugs get up in yo grill wit dat gat, you tell em I be packin' heat too! Foo! Now you go run tell *dat*!"

"Well, Bud, you know I certainly agree with you on that. See, these thugs are *emboldened*, and that's the problem. We certainly need reduced restrictions on guns, as opposed to more, so our lawful citizens can defend themselves. Well *duh*, of course! You know, I'm sure some people will have problems, at first, with getting used to carrying a firearm. But, you know, after a few weeks, a few months. You know, a few sessions at the local firing range? Well, they'll come to enjoy having a firearm of their own. Enjoy it! And enjoy the protections it will provide them as well. At the very least we need to start by giving our educators firearms training. Ideally, starting when they're in college."

"You just keep hittin' the nail on the head, my friend. Right on the head. *Bam*!" Bud clapped his hands together, hard.

"Well, I'm hoping to keep doing that for you and my constituency, kind friend."

"*Bam*! *Bam*! Two knocks a that hammer and that nail don gone all the way in ta duh two bah four already."

"*Bam*, my friend," replied Betty, throwing up a fist and mimicking the enthusiasm, despite having no idea what the prior sentence had meant.

"Well, my good man, unfortunately that is all the time we have her for today. We could go on all night, I do believe, and I hope you will take me up on my offer to come join me and my lovely wife, Esperanza, for some cocktails over at our place so as we can discuss further. You and your whole crew. Come put your feet up for the night. You welcome anytime, my friend."

"Well, if Esperanza is going to be there, I just might show up indeed."

"Hah! You old S.O.B! I bet you're hoping I'll be turning in early, too."

"No comment," Betty chuckled while putting some serious thought into the idea of making a pass at this fat fuck's woman. God, how could her womanly needs possibly be getting met with this guy.

"Hah! You old carpet bagger, you!" Bud carried on. "Nah, I want to mention to you, once again, my friend, uh, that, uh, we will be covering your campaign right to the very end. Nah, you got that big rally in Chick-ah-gee coming up. Things pretty rough over there in Chicagee. One week away, nah. We'll be covering it, live. You show them libtards over there what you made of, good sir...you fine gentleman and good sir. You ain't gonna be gettin' much respect, even though all you tryin' to do is clean that mess up for 'em, since they can't do it they selves. God bless you, friend, and God bless your supporters that, I'm sure, will be showing up in droves. Finally, God bless you, my True Muricans. Until tomorrow afternoon my friends. Hot damn! What a fine afternoon its been. This is Your Bud, signin' off."

Chapter XII

Not My Bud

Part One: Kenilworth's Plan

Bob Q Stubbs stood tall and he stood proud; his two hands planted, contentedly, on each respective hip. He was admiring the expanse of early autumn fields of wheat extending to, then well beyond, the distant horizon of the plain. The middle initial, Q, stood for Quincy, which was his paternal grandfather's name. A stoic, hardworking man was grandpa. Grandpa started the farm, from the ground up, sixty years prior. Built the farmhouse and the barn, by hand, and the help of a few simple tools, his devoted young family, and the occasional friend as their time allowed in their own busy schedules. He'd cleared out the fields, pulled the pesky weeds, fertilized the ground. Over the years, it had been added on to, but the beginnings were humble and well-suited to Quincy, a man who lived humbly and honestly; as was the good Lord's will and the honest man's grateful place in life, come what may.

Bob, the third-generation proprietor of his grandpa's land, was a big man who commanded much respect around Perkins county, South Dakota. Six foot three inches and a stocky, but fit, two hundred and sixty pounds. He looked like an offensive lineman in one of those old, black and white football pictures. The players wearing their leather helmets; pre-steroid days. His good wife, Tilly, was partially to blame for that stockiness, on account of her fine, homemade fruit pies. A peach and butterscotch pie, made from fresh, in-season peaches plucked from fruit trees out backside of the house, was cooling on the window sill presently. Apples would be ready in a month and Bob certainly looked forward to this. Dutch apple pie was his favorite, yes sir, and also, one the few "foreign" sounding dishes he indulged. Most everything he ate, whether at home or going out, was of the Americanized variety, anyways, whether beknownst to him or not (the local Mexican restaurant, *El Grande Casa de Tacos y Burritos*, and the local Italian Restaurant, *Aye Mama Mia!*, included).

A generous slice of pie after lunch awaited him, every day, and a generous slice again after dinner, with ice cream. That was what the Dr ordered around Bob's old farmhouse. The butter and lard crust didn't help his cholesterol too much, to be sure, but he'd be damned if he were to give up his third of a pie ration each and every God granted day. And if his lot might be to die on a hot summer day of a massive coronary out in the fields? Well, then so be it. The fields were as much his home as anything else and the good Lord was more than welcome to take him there. He would transition peacefully within the fading glow of the gently swaying wheat. Walk into the light and meet his maker a proud man. A man with nothing to hide from back here on his earthly pilgrimage. Bob felt he was, and indeed was seen by all those in his community who knew him, a good man.

Bob Q, or B.B.Q, pronounced Bah Bah Kee-oo, as his friends called him (the abbreviation for "Big" Bob Quincy, and a reference to his love of the particular cuisine. He could put down beef brisket with a thick tomato and molasses-based, K.C. style sauce, by the pound) ran his leathery, work-calloused fingers across the organized lines of mature, South Dakota durum wheat grown ready for reaping. His hands were those of a farmer. Those of a man who engaged in "real work," as they called it around these parts. None of that pussy footing around in the cubicles variety that the college educated insisted on calling "work." Hells bells, the fact that they even had the audacity to a call that God damn shit a job- or worse yet- the even more pretentious sounding, "career." Work was what mattered for any man who reserved the right to truly call himself one. "Work," was getting up at five AM to start a sixteen-hour day out in the fields. "Work," was sowing, reaping, and tending to the thousand and one little things that could go wrong, at any given time, during the day to day operations of a large farm. A man like B.B.Q. got up with the roosters, ate fresh, steaming biscuits with good sausage gravy, worked the equivalent of nearly two full shifts, six days each week, then ate a hearty casserole or some good 'ol meat and potatoes, for dinner. Fresh pie for dessert, always. An hour to wind down, then a good, proper romp with the missus every evening before bed (well, maybe every *other* evening, these days, but that was still pretty damned good for a fifty-eight-year-old sumbitch out of Perkins county, or "butt fuck nowhere" to most of the civilized world).

Bob observed this year's crop. It certainly was a doozy. When they reaped this year, and this would be very soon now, he might finally be able to afford, with the profits, that hot tub that his wife Tilly had been pestering him about for ages now. Kept on steady saying it would do their old bones good. Tarnation, maybe she was right, the old biddy. And lord knows she didn't ask for much. But Bob would be Gott-damned if he'd engage in using a hot tub if there was any chance of it making him soft. Turn him all effete. Too many comforts in life enslaved men to those same comforts, he well knew. Too many comforts in life were of the devil and if you didn't watch out, Buckaroo, they just might put you in the Devil's keep, all said and done.

Bob Q. Bobba Q with a side of cornbread (as his friend, Dale, called him) was preparing to go inside for his only break of the workday; a half hour break, mid-afternoon. The one break he allowed himself each weekday even when he knew there was workin' to be done and never enough cotton pickin' time to do it in. But he made time each day, at four PM sharp, to get the "straight dope" on things. Bob's smile was plumb etched on his face as he made his slow retreat down the fields of wheat; wheat that would soon be reaped, harvested, and sold as Giovetti's spaghetti, linguine, fettucine, or lasagna sheets. $1.59 per sixteen-ounce box at the regional *Hefty Pig* grocery store.

The fruits of Bob's hard work were being enjoyed at family dinners, each night, all over the Great Plains region- and at an affordable price to boot. He was right proud of that, to be sure. So proud, he was, that he and his wife, Tilly, out of respect, initially, (but now out of the enjoyment and the routine of it) would make Giovetti's pasta most every Saturday night. Complete it with some rich meat sauce, a house salad, and a modest glass of red wine. He was a man of routine. Tilly, well she was a woman of routine. He respected this about himself and her too. A routine helped to keep one on the straight and narrow dirt road to the promised land abutting (which he knew from the good Pastor Dave over at Our Lord and Shephard Mega Church) the ten-lane freeway of sinners going straight to Beelzebub. Bob kept a moseying through the fields. Tilly was coming into sight now, beckoning from the weather worn, powder blue siding with white trim, farmhouse. The hanging shrubs were starting to wither toward the ends, he noticed as he ascended the unfinished, worn oak, of the porch steps. The nights were getting colder now as the nip of fall was coming in, along with the early October nights. Getting colder fast; as locals well knew it tended to, round these parts. The wind was crisper during the daytime, too. Sure signs, the both, of the coming, reliably brutal, northern plains winter.

Tilly greeted Bob presently with a short, but heartfelt and meaningful peck on the cheek, and a staccato squeeze of his worn hand. She handed him a cool Arnold Palmer on ice with the fresh home brewed tea and fresh squeezed lemon juice- just a touch of sugar- that he enjoyed so. Bob accepted the drink with a contented and humble smile and gave Tilly a little, good natured, pat on the behind. Maybe they'd get frisky a little early tonight, Bob thought. He walked now toward his spot in the family room, a worn Chubby Boy brand reclining easy chair that everyone damned sure knew was Bob's and Bob's alone (Okay, maybe sometimes their old flea-bitten hound dog, Roscoe P. Tibbs would have a lie down on it, but damn sure only when Bob was out in the fields).

The radio dial was tuned in to the AM station. It hadn't moved the afternoon prior, nor the afternoon prior, nor many afternoons prior that one. Tilly walked over and simply pressed the power button. Bob released the foot rest with a "ker-thunk," and leaned back in his chair with the freshly fluffed pillow that Tilly had placed behind his neck, preparing for some straight talk the way a good 'ol, Gott fearin', South Dakota boy knew it to be. Bob sipped his drink. Perfect as usual. The sight was of a simple man enjoying a couple of life's simple pleasures. A right fine, alcohol free drink. Some good, straight shooting conversation. Bob settled in for a spell. He was, as anyone who knew him would say, and without so much as a moment's hesitation, a good man.

At around the time that Tilly and Bob were tuning in to True American Radio, Dr. John was wrapping up a session with Kenilworth, in the Chicago Lawn neighborhood, Southside Chicago. During a silent period, Dr. John gazed out of his cracked office window- beyond which lay a poorly tended lawn, overgrown with a multitude of weeds, growing unchecked, amid the distant, aggressive and unrelenting barking of pit bulls kept in another, nearby home. He was reflecting on this week's session; his hands folded, leaning back in his faux leather executive chair with the torn backing and foam gash across the middle of the seat (mostly covered by duct tape) all nestled within the humble six by ten office space.

The young man was looking back at him with that face. That face of perpetual curiosity, minimally appeased amongst the question marks and infinite confusions and contradictions of the life he was living and had come to know as reality. It had, and continued to be, bound to get him into trouble, as his register for personal danger amidst this perpetual ambiguity was so woefully ill-equipped. Of course, who was John to encourage withholding of experience involving oneself for opportunities toward supposed growth? He supposed now, restriction should be suggested when the intellectual curiosity and or/endeavor included the eminent possibility for harm.

"Why are you seeming to disapprove, Doctor? Aren't you supposed to be supportive? Isn't that what you had promised to be from the beginning? Isn't that what you always say? You are here to support me, correct." Kenilworth looked at him with an ongoing, stymied expression. He held this sense of righteous indignation over the source of their current disagreement, which had been going back and forth now for the last twenty or so minutes.

"In general, yes, though there are, at times, situational factors to consider, is what I'm trying to say."

"This being?"

"The strong potential for eminent harm," Dr. John retorted, then, sighed. "Harm to you."

"Why would eminent harm occur to me at a political rally? Is this not the sphere for debate on policy? Policy that is meant to shape social structures toward improvement. How can this be an environment that would produce harmful conditions outside of a war or a breakdown of what this system is intended to be?"

"Your judgment is sound, in theory. But only in theory, I have to remind you of that," Dr. John added, bothered by how often he had repeated lines similar to this only to have the point slip away, seemingly each and every time.

Kenilworth could plainly see that Dr. John was not budging. His face began to tighten, and he looked almost as though in physical pain trying to process a profoundly confusing insight. Dr. John, of course by now, knew the face well.

"I don't understand," the young man continued, "I simply am wishing to engage in an event for the express purpose of furthering my knowledge into an important and relevant realm; the realm of politics. The science of bringing our nation closer to its creed, of instilling greater justice within society, of working toward bolstering individual opportunity, so as to, in turn, bolster the opportunities within the collective, as an inevitable byproduct of that."

"Again, this is all in theory," Dr John repeated with growing emphasis.

Dr John sighed audibly, again, out of a frustration that was growing increasingly difficult to contain. His point was not sinking in, as per the usual; the point that Kenilworth's wants and needs were being identified by the young man in a strictly theoretical fashion, as though his life itself existed in a sterile laboratory setting, in which various factors could be controlled readily and progress toward a goal could invariably proceed in a logical and stepwise sequence-by a hand that operated with educated reasoning.

Kenilworth's mind continued to fall woefully short in its ability to grasp various real-world dynamics. He feared for the young man who seemed to be almost infinitely capable, though also infinitely curious even in situations that put himself in harm's way. He tried to explain once again, his eyes affixed on this familiar, awkward man-child, in his pilled polos and poorly fitting khakis. The dynamics of this particular client were simply, he often feared, beyond his realm of capabilities. He figured most therapists were readily familiar with this feeling; something akin to hunting a Kodiak bear, equipped only with a B.B. gun.

"I don't know if I can explain this to you." Dr. John took a moment, knowing full well that what he would follow up with would not be readily understood, or well-received. "I don't think they *want* you there. They represent, largely, a segment of society that doesn't necessarily include you."

"Why wouldn't they? My goal is to aid them and our society as a whole. I wish to find cures to diseases that may affect them and their families. I wish to prolong their life and health. We may, one day, be quite directly connected, so how could someone like me *not* be included?"

"You are talking, Washington, about a bigger picture idea that I just don't think will be fully considered there. I don't think he will be making points about less direct connections. This man goes right into people's homes in a very insular type of way that doesn't make room for what you are talking about. I don't think this is about logical discourse on social issues and how we are connected by them."

"So then, what do you think it is," asked a confused and irritated Kenilworth.

"What do I think it is?" John thought about it for a moment, before adding, "I think this is a blatant appeal to fear. I think that's what it is. Fear of becoming less relevant as a culture and a way of life, for many people. Fear of, eventually, becoming obsolete. Fear and then appeal. An appeal to a perceived past which has been idealized, and that appeal being woven into current fears. Woven into those current fears so completely that it is viewed as an end all, be all, to them."

"I don't fully understand, Doctor," replied Kenilworth, trying noticeably harder to contain his exasperation (wasn't he making perfect sense in what he was saying to Dr. John?). Kenilworth continued:

"If one fears becoming obsolete, doesn't a person work to adapt toward ways to *not* become so, assuming there are options? And if there exists a supposed solution that has been idealized, doesn't that mean one should research what a more actual reality solution would be?"

"Washington, not everyone wants to do their research," John replied, shaking his head sadly. "A lot of people want, simply, their thoughts and opinions appealed to and will selectively look to have that done as their main, and often, *only* priority on the matter. This, coming at the expense of seeking more objective truths. It's simply easier that way, which is the constant danger in terms of how people fall victim to it; that and the fact that it allows a lot of people a sense of comfort in a world that they find increasingly complex and scary."

"That doesn't make sense." Kenilworth's body was beginning to tremble, slightly, in anger and frustration at how his clear and solid logic was not swaying this argument, seemingly one iota. "Surely, they must know their line of thought is faulty and their end results skewed. These results being their points of view on issues have not been objectively researched, as well as the fact they are being placated based on faulty information portrayed as truth, and how knowledge of that alone should lead to a need to further examine said views."

John decided, at this point, they had spent enough time going in circles for the day. "Unfortunately, that's all the time we have today, Washington," he conceded for now. "This will require quite a bit of time to continue to process. Suffice it to say, I really don't think going to David Betty's rally this weekend would be a wise move. I don't think you will find what you are hoping to find, there. I suggest you make use of your time in other ways."

Kenilworth continued to look, perplexedly, back at Dr. John, and John knew this look all too well from recent weeks. He had not succeeded in convincing him. He also well knew why he had not. The point that he was making to Kenilworth was not particularly logical, taken at face value. Despite this, it did reflect the reality of a situation that was, in and of itself, not necessarily logical. He was hindered simply by the information at hand that even he, personally, could neither fully understand, nor explain in a way that entirely made sense. Beyond this, Kenilworth, simply, did not look the part, talk the part, or act the part of the majority of Betty's supporters; though Dr. John planned to try his best to do so at the rally in five days' time, himself. Of course, John did not mention this to Kenilworth. It would only further confuse things.

Dr. John said goodbye to Kenilworth for the week, doing so with an uneasiness in the very pit of his being. He knew, of course, that Kenilworth would go. He had the incessant drive to follow his thoughts through to their conclusion, and he wondered how the young man had survived to the point he had; this being the case.

After Kenilworth departed hastily, John began to pack up for the day in a state of mental fog; intellectually exhausted from the session and frustrated with how it always seemed to illuminate that his goals for clients had to exist in relation to a larger picture that was often times neither logical, nor fair, nor necessarily set up to reward the best qualities in people. Dr. John was growing lost in these thoughts as he walked out the back entrance to his car. He began the hour-long drive to the near north suburbs, taking his focus off his ruminations and onto the rules of the road and its demand for hypervigilance around here. Keep ten feet back from cars in front while stopped at a red light, to have room to maneuver in case of a carjacker (now that he drove a nicer car than he used to, the odds of this had multiplied several times over). Two, sometimes three cars could turn left at a red light. Unless there was ice on the road, you speed up at a yellow light and go through it. Don't be in the passing lane unless going five to ten mph over the speed limit, whatever it is. Fifteen mph if it's the freeway. All of these were unspoken rules on Chicago roads. Those that didn't abide would usually just be honked at or chewed out; though, tragicomic and darkly absurdist episodes of road rage were known to occur over a violation of any one of these rules and several others.

The day had been a stressful one. Readjusting to the hyperawareness and constant effortful repression of fears involved in working in the inner city had been predictively exhausting. John was growing painfully aware that this had been easier for him a decade prior, when he was a younger man. Back then he was broke, hungry to garner more experience, and could more effectively repress his anxieties. It was because he had no real roots in the area, no money (worse, was in considerable and ever-growing debt), no significant other, and, really, nothing much to lose at the time.

But times had changed. He felt now that something had altered, in a subtle attrition type of way. What was it? I seemed, maybe, to be his ability to navigate situations that made him uncomfortable. He feared part of this was that he was becoming a slave to his comforts and that this made anything that went against this that much harder to deal with. For all the one hundred dollar per person ten course meals. All the eleven ingredient cocktails "crafted" by mixologists. All the high end, shiny tchotchkes (he had recently bought a cross section of a meteorite for an embarrassing amount of cash). All the five-dollar cardamom and honey infused cappuccinos with swan profiles woven into the foam. He had grown more fearful of going back to a time where these things hadn't become part of an urban yuppie identity that he feared he, and others around him, defined themselves with.

Things that once seemed bizarrely extravagant and gratuitous (which they were) had somehow become a part of his ongoing experience. Worse, in doing so, they had illuminated his past as one of somehow not-having when, at the time, it rarely felt that way. He had been content then with what he had. But now, if he went back, he felt certain he could no longer be. This was part of the trappings of earning more money. How it precluded a person to adding extravagances that they didn't need, and how these, in turn lead to defining them. How this, in turn, lead to the need to maintain an identity interwoven with certain luxuries. The more money that was added to the picture, the greater the extravagances added that one then became accustomed to, and then, desperate to keep up and hold onto. He was sure that this only magnified itself for those far wealthier than him; lead, eventually, to a goal of finding some sort of paradise on earth, which could, of course, never fully exist. And the result of all this was always a question. How much was enough? The answer to this question was always the same. Just a little bit more. And then still another question often loomed in his mind only slightly beyond this one. What did some people do for more?

Wanting to relax and to simply shut his mind off for a spell, Dr. John turned on AM radio in search of, ideally, some jazz improv. In fiddling with the dial, he stumbled by accident upon a voice that he recognized. It was the same voice that the prematurely aged woman in the Iron Mistress shirt had been listening to, weeks prior. An almost comically angry voice that, one felt, probably regularly muttered phrases like, "you know what really grinds my gears?" A voice that seemed to vacillate, incomprehensibly, from a down home Texan, to a quasi, deep-bayou Cajun, at random intervals. A voice that sounded tailor made and refined, over time, to instill anger and resentment. The voice having the familiar affectations of an entertainer, though which seemed to be in the overtly dangerous position of meaning itself to be taken stone cold serious by the listener. Certain words stuck out. Words that he had been hearing more so, recently, and that were, somehow, becoming part of an ever more common vernacular associated with the growing Alternative Republican Party in towns like his own hometown. "Snowflake," and "ARP," and phrases like "True Muricans" versus "Tree Huggers" and "Muslim Sympathizers," which inevitably seemed to fuel an "us versus them," mentality aimed at divisiveness. It had dawned on him, recently, that this was beginning to succeed to an alarming extent.

As Dr. John, despite his better instincts, began to listen to the broadcast, he had a growingly potent desire to talk to, and hopefully, *with*, this man, though he presumed that contentious participants on the show were rarely talked *with*, but almost always *to*, in the case of a person like this. He knew what this man had the power of doing. An immense power on a psychological level, based on what he said, how he phrased it, and how he pandered to the presumed wants of his listeners. He knew, almost instantly, and at an instinctive level, that this was all showbiz. He thought of an old movie from the seventies about TV anchors. Particularly of one who had an emotional breakdown, though was kept on air for a sort of bizarre, exploitational entertainment. How he instructed his audience one episode to say, "I'm mad as hell, and I'm not going to take it anymore!" How the audience and even those at home began shouting this out, over and over, so readily and with no context to speak of. The power that even unfounded, undirected ridiculous utterances had when spoken with enough conviction.

John's honed sense of intuition was that this man on the radio was doing this for self-gain, and he questioned, based on the level of intelligence the man seemed to possess, how the man could not possibly know exactly what he was doing; how he could not know that this was simply hyperbole. A puff piece. And dangerous, in the worst kind of way. Dangerous in its pandering to ignorance. Dangerous in its implications that those who thought too much or got too educated- whatever that meant- had lost their ways and become soft, brainwashed, and somehow robbed of common sense. Dangerous in its allusions to minorities as ignorant and freeloading, portrayed as such to people who had very few daily interactions with minorities, or even people of different religions or viewpoints to their own. He pictured a graying, out of shape troll who had found a way to line his pockets by spewing bombastic and damaging rhetoric. Human casualties be damned. Sadly, of course, this was a man that he could not talk with. A man he could not try to expose in any way for what it seemed so clearly that he was doing. Until, that is, he heard of an

opportunity, ten thousand to one, of being able to do just that.
Here and now.

Part II: Hello, Snowflake!

"Okay, True Muricans. Now I'm fixin' tuh…nah…Ima gonna bring you somethin' new ta dis her program. Dis her progrim gonna trah branchin' out little bit, nah. Yah her?" Bud chuckled for a moment as though what were to follow was absurd in some way. "Ya'll…nah, is ya'll ready foe dis, nah? A new segment we up'n gonna staht. Her we go. Gonna staht dis nah, bahs en gurls. Nah, nah…nah, we gon' be talking to a libtard today on dis her segment. Wetchoo tinka bout dat?"

"Talkin' to a libtard!"

"Dat rot, Walt! Dat rot," confirmed Bud.

Bud was trying to push the realms of *down home* a little, on this particular broadcast. Scott and Dreadson were working to establish, what they liked to call, the "outer boundaries," in the area of vernacular. To see at what point ratings might dip, or possibly increase, based on how outlandishly "down home" Bud's voice could go in a *testing the waters* sort of broadcast. His vocalizations and word choice were going deep Texas back woods, with an absurdly bayou Cajun flair. An exaggeration of his usual style. His voice seemed to mimic one who lived in the remote swamp country near Gulf of Mexico Texas, who may, or may not, have ever ventured more than ten miles from his property in the course of his life thus far. Whose accent and word choice might not, necessarily, be regularly understood by a significant part of the population. His voice, this week, was bordering on the need for closed captioning, like a British band with thick Cockney accents might. Of course, closed captions were not feasible over the airwaves. Bud continued in this experimental manner.

"Dat rot, nah, mah fren! Dat rot, nah! Good ol' boy, dat Walt. Nah yessum. Yessum nah! We callin' dis section *Hello Snowflake!* How bout dat? Here we go, nah. *Yessum!* Let it do what it gon do, nah. Squeaky wheel gonna git dat greasin' tuh day, nah, bah. Hoo *weee!* Nah, here we go, nah. Who dis?"

"Who dis? *Dis* John Gavilan out of Chicago.

"Dis her a snowflake?"

"What do you even mean by that? Where did that word come from? The ARP"

"Da ARP, bah. Dat rot! Hoo-wee! *Yessum!*"

"Dat, rot, bah! You lock dat, bah! You lock dat? *Yessum!*" An audible, drawn out sniffing noise over the airwaves followed. Bud had not been looking in Walt's direction at the time, to catch him doing a line. Bud cocked his head back for the routine, affecation of a gentle scold.

"Now, Walt! Walt. You simma! Simma down, nah!....Hoo wee, ya best simma down cuz you lock a...uh...lock a..., uh, potta gumbo sittin' out on da stove to that, uh, that bout ta overcook dem shrimp. *Simma!* Okay, friend? Cuz, looka her, we don' want nunna dem chewy-assed shrimp, nah. Bustin' out fillins 'n what not. No sah. I say *no* sah!"

"Who are you talking to?"

"Dat Walt, nah, snowflake. Don't worry yo self nun bout it."

"Datwalt? His name is Datwalt?"

"No! Walt! Snowflake. Dat *Walt!*"

"Are you aware that millions of people are going to you for their information on politics, every day?

"Yes sah. *Yessum!* Rot prodda dat. Nah, who you is? Who is you be?"

"Well, I gues I'd say I is be a Psychologist. I is be working in the suburbs and inner city of Chicago. Chicago. You know, your poster child for a failed PC liberal state."

"Dat who you is be?"

"Dat is who I is be. Or, more specifically, what I is be doing. I is be more than just what I is be doing for work, sah."

"All rot, snowflake, here we go, nah. You ready? And you rot bout Chicagee, bah and bah. Damned shame wet's hap'nin in Chicagee." Bud was gearing to hit this Gavilan guy upside the head with some real talk.

"Ready for what? And what do you even know about Chicago? I heard you live in L.A. And I'm guessing you probably hardly ever leave your gated compound there which, by and by, I'm sure in no way resembles the *down home* bayou shack community you're making it sound like you live in and relate to."

"Don't start, bah! What you know uh bout dat? Huh? What you know uh bout dat? Cuz I know all about dat!"

"You sound like you're quoting rap lyrics from the dirty south."

"Wet?"

"Huh?"

"Wet you say!"

"You sound like you need closed captioning, complete with one of those little bubbles that bounces across the bottom of the screen on each syllable. Except, I think, in your case, maybe instead of a bubble, it should be a cornbread muffin."

"Wet! Wet you say! Bah, don't *staht!*" A smack of Bud's desk came in audible through over the airwaves. "Wet's a matter, you gotta act all high n' mighty like all these liberal elitists her."

"Wet I'm saying is people are smarter than you make them out to be. They don't need to be talked *down* to with some silly parody of what you think regular folks talk like and want. And you shouldn't set the bar so low with what you talk about and how you choose to talk about it. It insults everyone, yourself included."

"Bah, dis nothin' but a distraction her, wet you talkin' bout. Stop playin' round, nah bah. Nah, nah...nah bah, we gon' get rot to it, nah. Okay hee, bah! Lessuh, lessuh get tuh it, sah, nah, stop pussafootin' around up in hee-aw."

"What in the name of sweet baby Jesus are you saying? People actually take this seriously? Does anything even matter anymore? Are you serious?"

"Serious as a heart attack, nah, bah."

"You sound like a ten-month-old baby trying to form their first words. You know that?

"Nah, bah! Bah? *Whah*! Wet? Wet you tryin' ta say, nah? Dis mah show." Bud stuffed a chubby thumb into his chest. "*Mah* show, and we gon' git to it, nah. Git ta steppin if'n ya ain't down wit dat. Nah, is you down wit it?"

"You really do sound like you're quoting rap lyrics, which is bizarre considering you seem to disregard the actual lives of black people, almost completely."

Bud, with a burgeoning fear that his voice was, indeed, delving headfirst into the realms of the absurd, even to a large portion of his loyal audience, stepped back from the contrived presentation a bit. Fuck Scott and Dreadson. They could test the ratings on this persona the next time around. This caricature who, if it had a name, would probably be something like Country Don Q. Bosco Molasses. He wasn't about to give these uppity liberals any more advantages than they already had with their biased media outlets (none of whom, of course, leaned as far to the left as Marmot News did, proportionately, to the right- though "Your Bud," would never hear of this). Bud changed tack and went back to his usual, somewhat less contrived, down-home voice. His bread and butter; tried and true for the past thirty some years.

"Alright, nah, folks. Let's try ta talk a little more proper, as this libtard seems to want to do it that way. Ya know, they don't tend to know too much about us down home folks. We gonna need to ease it on back to protect this man's delicate, how do ya say, cons-tit- ooshin. Isn't that rot, nah, cuck?"

"How about you just use the entire word, cuckold. Even though if anyone's wife around here isn't satisfied, and looking elsewhere, I'm guessing it's yours."

"Leave the wives out of this. And I do just fine by the way."

"You brought up the wives using a word like that, but fine with me. And just so you know, as long as you insist on creating an "us versus them" country versus city division of the people, I actually grew up in a small working-class town in northern Michigan. Spent my first twenty years there and go back regularly. Went to public school all the way, community college for a year, too. All with mostly "down home" people, like you talk about and presume to know. How about you? I heard you grew up with the upper crust of New York."

"Don't you worry about it, son." Bud was quick to get off this fact. "I know the people," he insisted. He was getting agitated quickly, rarely being used to a challenge over the air with a liberal minded person, aside from the occasional trolls whom he would cut off quick whenever they found a way onto his show, before taking pot shots at them for a couple minutes afterward. "Control the vernacular, Bud. Control the vernacular," his mind repeated to itself. Dreadson would talk about that almost daily. That's all it was about. That really was everything. Bud continued, after a pre-emptive sip of good bourbon to calm his nerves and placate one of his addictions.

"Back to the question. The *question*, son. Stop tryin' to get off topic. The *question*….mmmkay? Nah haw is you gonna feel when our good David *Peeeee* Betty is the next president of the U-nigh-teed States."

"I thought you always told your viewers that they were the *divided* states."

"Answer the question, snowflake. Stop tryin' ta avoid it. You can't even answer the *question* can you?" Motherfucker. He would keep him on the proper line of questioning to suit the arguments he was looking to make. Sip of bourbon with an audible smack at the end.

"Liberals try to avoid a lot of things," added Ted.

"Dat's *rot*, Ted!" Bud emphatically agreed. "They dun do that, don't they? Yes, sah! So, uh, what do you have to say about it, John Gavilan? What you know bout that?"

"Ok, and let's get back to that whole avoidance thing later. I've got a few thoughts on that."

"Answer the question, nah. The *question*, nah, bah!"

"What do I think? I think if David Peeeeeeeeee Betty…"

"Watch yuh self."

"Check yo self for you wreck yourself!" Chimed Walt

"…if David Betty wins, it will be an indication that this country is a lot more willfully ignorant than I'd like to believe." John searched his mind for a visual to attach to his thoughts on the matter. "I'll put it this way. Somebody can present you with a piece of crap, put garnish around it, serve it on a silver platter. However, it's up to you, the customer, so to speak, to distinguish that it's still a piece of crap, nonetheless. See, that's on you."

"How dare you! How *dare* you, sir!" Bud smacked his desk two times, hard. "You have offended the honor of a good man by insinuating he is a piece of fecal matter. Dat will not stand! This man is made out of patriotism and, uh, and sinew! And, uh…and bone matter with the tendons attached to it. This insult will not stand on mah show! It will not stand it, sir!"

"You sound like it's the seventeen hundreds and you're trying to start a duel."

"Oh believe me, if it were the seventeen hundreds, I would do just that and you would lose, son." Bud jutted a finger forcefully into the nothingness of the airwaves. "Make no bones about it (a short pause for another sip of bourbon). So you think David Betty is a piece of crap, huh? A steaming turd? Dat what you think bout duh man who gonna be your president?"

Dr. John took a moment to park his car now on the street out front of his condo, as he had just arrived back home in Evanston. For a moment, all he wanted to do was go in and hug his wife. Hold his dog, Toby, and let him lick his face. He wanted to brew a pot of decaf and sit on the couch for a little while, sipping it. But, he had to hold off on these simple life pleasures to talk with this fat fucker. To try to make some sort of impression on his audience; if this was at all possible. Like many things in life, he felt a certain fear in matters like this. It was the fear that he was, simply, wasting his time. The fear of energy sapping efforts leading to, ultimately, absolutely nothing to speak of, in the end. He took a deep breath to compose himself, sensing that this was going to get ugly, and soon. He knew, from years of watching and listening to, this type of perverted shtick, that he was being baited. He didn't bite now, on this whole *piece of crap*, bit. It would be turned around on him to make him seem unreasonable, hopelessly partisan, and emotionally unstable if he did, even though, in John's mind, whether or not David Betty was a piece of crap could be debated. This "Your Bud" guy was much worse than that, though. *This* was a man who was actively pushing Betty into power via distortions, half-truths, and appeals to fear and a baser human nature. A moment to reflect, then Dr. John followed up.

"I *don't* think David Betty is a piece of crap. I think he's a rich, privileged man; not unlike yourself. A rich, privileged man whose wants in life exist along a smooth path that is continually paved for him. A man who has found a way to appeal to voters that have painfully little in common with him, his upbringing, his lifestyle, or his values, though they are led to believe, through skillful manipulation, that they do. They are led to do so, in large part, through the efforts of people like yourself."

"So he's a fraud, hmm? That's what you think?"

"No, I didn't say that," John clarified. "I think he's a low-grade, C list celebrity entertainer with an above average IQ, and, more importantly, a well above average business acumen. He knows how to sell himself and he knows how to get votes. On top of that, I think he's a man who has minimal to no shame in terms of *how* he gets votes or *who* he gets them from. A vote is a vote, just like a sale is a sale. Or maybe they're just one in the same thing, in the end. I think he has a massive support system of right wing analysts, strategists, and industrial/organizational psychologists, who are feeding him information on ways to gather support, continuously, and that they are exploiting good, but somewhat simple, people, while retaining a wealthy support system looking to maintain their own interests despite the consequences; whether it's manipulating or straight up screwing over the working classes, the global alliance, the environment, or all three. And when I say simple, by the way, I don't mean simple in an *inferior* way, before you put those words into my mouth."

"Wasn't gonna," Bud lied, let down by having the opportunity taken away, just then.

"Uh huh," John replied, sarcastically, before continuing, "well what I mean by simple is, simple in terms of people who want a plain, minimally complicated life, in their home town preferably, surrounded by family, living quietly and trying their best to do good; not wanting to get too involved in the larger world around them. Which, that is all fine, if that's what they want, and that's what they feel their place is. What's *not* fine, though, is people like you trying to appeal to them and exploit their vote simply for your own interests and to maintain a power structure that has little use for them. That has little concern for them, their job opportunities, their local environment, their families, their communities, their general security."

"Wow." Bud pffted in a showy, mock exasperation. "You hear that, True Muricans? What is this guy even trying to say?" A drawn out, faintly audible sip in the background followed. A planned avoidance of this part of the topic that Bud didn't want to explore and, more importantly, indulge his viewers in exploring. He continued selectively.

"Speck-oo-lation, snowflake! Nothin' but speck-oo-lashe-eon. This man is a man a duh people. A true Murican! You think yer candidate, yer Kenton Dilman is a man a da people?" Bud sat back and folded his arms. He'd trump the motherfucker on this one. The liberal candidate, Kenton Dilman, was a career politician with, though mostly a solid past of calculated political strategizing, had also shown some nearly inevitable lapses in judgment made over a thirty plus year political career. Lapses that were quickly exploited by news outlets like this, and worse, placed out of context and speculated on to inflate a negative portrayal already being relentlessly pushed. A portrayal that was succeeding. There was an additional disadvantage, as well, which was that his lapses in political judgment could not be compared with David Betty because David Betty had absolutely no political career for which to exploit (and this was being turned into something that the people should want within an assumedly corrupt system). The idea that he might not know what he was doing? This was, quite willfully, never brought up by Bud's show, or by Marmot News and its various affiliates.

Dr. John responded, "I think Kenton Dilman is a man of the people, insomuch as he's trying to push for realistic ways for people to get jobs as well as push for conservation of this, the only planet they have to live on. Though he doesn't run on a platform of exploiting being 'of the people' like David Betty, who's only interactions with common people his entire life have been with the help."

"Bah! Wet! Bah! *Falsuds.* Ya speakin' falsuds, bah!"

"What?"

"Simma down, nah, bah. How bow dah!" Added Walt.

"Git ta steppin, nah bah," contributed Ted. "How bow dah?"

"What? Who are you people? How are you somehow appealing to the political beliefs of nearly half the voting power of this country?"

"Nuff questions, bah. We speak *truth* her. How bow dah, friend? Wet you speak? Hmm?" Queried Bud.

"Wet I speak is *realism*. And I don't presume to tell people I know the truth in terms of highly complex and ever-evolving issues that simply don't have easy answers, despite how much we all *wish* they did. I respect others who do the same. All you people do is to take complex issues and to try to pervert them into something simplistic. That's because you know that's the easiest way to subdue people's fears. You give them simple answers and make them believe those simple answers are the *actual* way to deal with things. It's like a pill that makes the bad stuff go away, instantly. You have a built-in advantage by doing that, too; the advantage of not having to make people think, too much, about difficult things. People who are tired from a long day at work. People who want to just relax in their free time and not worry about all these inconvenient truths of the modern world. We liberals don't presume to offer them made up solace and easy solutions that, by the way, don't exist. And we have paid for it, to an extent. Maybe we're paying for it even more as the world grows more complex. The price we've paid has been worsened by people like you, who say things like 'Oh, we have terrorists over in the Middle East. How are we going to handle this? Well, let's bomb the *crap* out of the entire region, like, yesterday. *That's* the solution!'"

"Boom!" agreed Bud, making an explosion gesture with both hands from behind his desk.

"Boom shaka laka!" screamed Walt.

"Boom shaka pow!" Added Bud, before reflecting, silently, that those words did consistent of Betty's actual plan of action on the matter.

"No. *No* boom!" Dr. John interjected.

"Boom!" Repeated Bud, smacking a fat, pasty hand onto the desk for emphasis this time. "Boom boom! Shake the *room!*"

"Ok, now I am just positive those are rap lyrics. And *no* boom! Okay? *No* boom. All that's going to do is make the problem worse by perpetuating people's anger with us, generation after generation, in the confines of a shrinking world in which it's ever easier for them to, in turn, attack us. If we alienate even a small fraction of law-abiding Muslims, that creates thousands of possible additional violent terrorists. Diplomacy is the only answer, but that takes time, patience, and doesn't offer people a false sense of being easily protected. Okay, but never mind. How about something else that directly relates to. How about diversity? Different races and religions. Different cultures. It's a little scary, sometimes, to not necessarily have your thoughts and beliefs reflected back to you in another person the way you'd want them to be. It's a little scary living around people that don't always look just like you, or always speak the same language. So, what's your solution? Instead of valuing diversity, you run from it. Flee the city. Go to homogenous suburbs. Live in more rural areas even when you don't farm and never venture into the cities, especially ones like Chicago, that have been vilified by media outlets like yours; turned into after school special horror stories where there is nothing but rampant murder, rape, burglary and grand theft auto. Convince yourselves and your audience that minorities are a bunch of thugs and freeloaders. Except for Asians, they can stick around cuz you don't see them as a threat, and you look your Chinese take out."

"Have you looked at the statistics in some of these black and Hispanic neighborhoods?" Bud cut him off. "Hmm? Let me ask you that, bah. You say that there *aren't* problems, or that they're exaggerated. What about statistics. What about the actual numbers? Math-eee-matics."

"Whah nah, bah?" (sniff, snort)

"Walt, simma down. Member what I said about you bein' like a pot a gumbo been on high heat on the stove too long? Memba that? How nobody like a mess a gummy shrimp. Memba that? Now simma. Go ahead, continue, sah."

"Ok, fine. I never said there aren't problems, by the way. In answer to your question. Yes, there is a lot of crime, but most of it is gang related, and in a small handful of neighborhoods.

Gang members killing other gang members and doing so because they don't really care about their own lives and don't see a way out of their circumstances. And by *acknowledging* that, I'm not *excusing* it. I am not excusing it, but I am offering a reason for it. People like you like to exploit that type of thing all the time. And the statistics? They are almost identical to similarly poor white neighborhoods, with some variations based on types of crime, but the overall crime rate is more or less the same, and this even with higher rates for minorities of being profiled by police and other entities. Also, when you take poverty out of the equation, get people to a less desperate standard of living, there are no significant differences in crime by race. How about you look up that statistic and then talk about it? And here's another on: Across any race, you are much more likely to be victimized by your *own* race than another. Do you know that, or ever tell people that? Let that sink in when you directly, or indirectly, push for homogenous and self-segregated communities, or even allude to the possibility of ethno-states."

"This guy is talkin' nonsense," Bud projected onto his audience in a booming voice portraying complete confidence in his views. "I can't even follow this guy. I think he's just tryin' to confuse you listeners out there. You see, these libtards like to do that. Try ta confuse your beliefs so's that they can come in and push theirs on to you. And the hypocrisy here. You talk about the right moving out of the cities and into the burbs. There's plenty of you liberals out there, too, mah friend."

"There are. There is a level of hypocrisy among liberals which I don't deny. But that shouldn't be perverted by people like you into trying to nullify the entirety of our viewpoints. You've done a really good job exploiting that one, too. But anyway, we're much more likely to live in diverse areas, or, at the very least, work in them."

"Okay, good for you. Do what you want in them cities. Most of my audience is straight up country folks, anyway. Good, simple, God fearing, community minded folks. Me too. And unlike you, yuh big city fancy pants."

"Good, simple people, yes…who you exploit…from your radio booth in downtown L.A."

"Bah, don't test me nah, bah!"

"You sound like a sheep."

"Bah! Don't you worry what I sound like." Two more loud smacks on the desk were audible again.

"Why don't you just go ahead and get a gavel? Say things like, 'case closed,' after you think you've made a point."

"Don't interrupt me, son! Mah audience knows one of their kind when they hears it and you damned sure ain't one uh dem. You soundin' like a damned professor, over here. You sound like you talkin' *down* to the people."

"Talking down from your high horse," added Ted.

"Dat rot, Ted! Gavilan, what do you know bout true Muricans? Huh? Not much."

"Not much, son!" Screamed Walt.

"Not much…cuz you is out of touch, libtard." Bud poured himself two more fingers. His hands were starting to shake in anger and indignation.

"I'm not talking *down* to anybody," Dr. John replied. "*You're* talking down to people by portraying a made-up persona of what you think it is that they want. A persona that clearly shows how little you think of them. And out of touch? You never *were* in touch. Neither is your candidate. He's a Manhattan socialite posing as one of the people. He puts on a trucker hat and campaigns in the plains states and thinks that is going to convince people he's one of them."

"Those people are smarter than you give them credit for, snowflake. See, *ah* know that. *Ah* know the people. They see a good, honest man who achieved the American dream and not some career politician who is be, uh, is just in the business, uh, just to line they own pockets."

"Yes, achieved the American dream with the help of a bountiful trust fund from a cutthroat patriarch who probably screwed over hundreds, if not thousands, of hardworking Americans to build his fortune."

"Speck-ooo-lashe-on!" Bud pounded his desk with a clenched fist so hard, that his standing desk mic shifted several inches.

"Need that gavel? Is the case closed?"

"Shut it, bah!"

"Fine. Go ahead and call it speculation. My point is this. He's exploiting good, hardworking, largely rural and suburban Americans by acting like he's both *one* of them and working *for* them. And let me address your whole 'man of the people' thing you talk about it. If you really were a man of the people, why not offer them open discourse? You keep trying to minimize my points instead of being objective and letting your audience actually hear what people like me have to say and make what *they* want out of it. That's what the media is supposed to do. At one time, maybe it actually did do that, as opposed to exploiting minor divisions in people and trying to turn those into more major divisions. And why do you do that? Maybe your viewers should be asking themselves that. My guess is, more than anything, to create drama and boost ratings off it. That, and to keep the people squabbling amongst themselves while your corporate sponsors get progressively wealthier by exploiting loopholes, paying employees less, and blaming it on the liberals for making it "more difficult" for them to do business here in this country. Well if it is so difficult to do business here, how come CEOs in this nation make an average of three hundred times what their workers earn, when in the 1950s, they only made about thirty times the average worker salary. And wasn't that plenty enough back then? Three hundred times? Who even *needs* that kind of money? And administration higher-up salaries are getting ever more bloated too, while worker salaries are going down. The top one percent now control twice as much of our country's money, proportionately, than they did in the fifties, through multiple methods they didn't use to have access to in our supposed heyday…heyday according to you and your candidate, anyway."

"Getting off topic again, nah, son. There's a lot of other things to consider when you talk about pay related issues."

"Yes, there are, but nothing that justifies that kind of gross inflation *or* that kind of financial control by a select few. There is absolutely no way to justify that, beyond rampant greed."

"Bah, just get back to the topic. The people. The people are listenin' to mah show cuz I gives it to 'em straight." Bud took a swig, straight from his bottle of bourbon, this time. "And they goin' for David Betty cuz he does the same. Unlike you. And he's gonna win. How you like dem apples? A good, honest man uh the people gon' be our president eee-lekt, come Novembah."

"He gon' win, bah!" Slurred a growingly congested sounding Walt.

"Dat rot, Walt!"

"A man of the people," added Ted, in a calm and measured tone as usual.

"Dat rot, too, Ted!"

"David Betty a good, honest man?" Dr. John questioned with a clear tone of irony. "I'll say he's a smart man. I will say that. Smarter than he comes across and smarter than people give him credit for. He understands that a lot of people out there are scared. They're scared of changes like globalization, terrorism; a more multiracial and developed world. Scared of having jobs that may be growing obsolete and being replaced by computers, or machines. Scared and looking for answers. *Looking* for answers. Then a man like him comes in and just creates ready-made, simplistic and placating, *supposed* answers, and feeds them to the people. Like I said, that's what you guys do. You know they're scared and you exploit it through offering them answers that really aren't answers. Then you discourage the act of thought by insisting the answers are always simple. Like the whole terrorists in the Middle East problem. What's the answer? Blow 'em up."

"Damn right!"

"Now you're talking sense," added Ted.

"Sure, yeah, whether you believe that or not you have to *sell* it, right? Damn right! Sure! As though blowing stuff up over there in the past hasn't directly tied into what we have right now and for the foreseeable future."

"I'm not *selling* anything here, friend."

"Multiculturalism. What's the answer?" Dr. John continued. "Everyone go out and adapt traditional Christian values. That will eliminate crime. Good ol' Christian values."

"Damned straight. Down *home* Christian values. Now you're finally making a little sense, bah."

"Speaking a little truth. Who'd a thought?" Said Ted.

"Well I'll be sorry to burst your bubble then, because among the more secular nations of the world, you'll find the lowest crime rates as well as the highest rates of life satisfaction. Japan, Australia, Iceland, Norway. They're all among the most secular nations in the world. They have not only some of the lowest rates of crime, but some of the highest rates of life satisfaction."

"Sure, because they get to do whatever they want with no accountability," clarified Bud. "You know, I've really heard it all from these libtards. Now they saying to drop down home Christian values and *that* will actually help to make the world a better place."

"I'm not saying anything about *dropping* traditional Christian values. You *insinuate* that to your audience when people even bring up other value systems or lifestyles. It isn't a one or the other thing. All I am doing is acknowledging you can be a good, law abiding citizen and have differing views that should be accepted based on the fact that you are helping, not harming society. You and your media corporation love to imply this thing about liberals, that we don't have a solid foundation like religion. That they aren't religious and don't care about religious values, and that's not true and it's not what I'm saying at all. What I'm saying is *allow* people the choice of what their religious values will be and don't push a certain one onto them, or not accept them if they don't share your faith or even if they *don't* have faith. People who don't have faith at all can and *do* create a lot of good for this world because they tend to value it highly. They aren't simply living for the next life, like so many hardline religious people are. So, the end result is, they highly value their life and their planet. They value the here and now. And they, usually, in turn try to make it better for themselves, their children, and others. But you would describe them as potentially hell bound and evil. The gays too. Despite any good they have done for this world."

"Don't put words in my mouth, snowflake. Ah never done said that atheists or other religions are hell bound. I just say that traditional Christian values are what made this country and are a big part of what makes America great."

"I agree. Just don't exclude people who don't fit that criteria or try to make their thoughts and views less valid, in your mind and in your listeners minds, if they don't share your religion."

"Okay, so what if yer a Muslim? Should that be okay? Being taught that all others outside your religion are infidels and that you can kill them? Cut them off by the head? What you got ta say about that, libtard?"

"Libtard mother trucker! *Hooo*!" (Sniff sniff)

"Walt, I dun warned you, nah!" Bud swung around in his chair toward the beady eyed, powder covered monstrosity that was late broadcast Walt. "That's yer last warnin' nah."

"Bud, why don't you help you viewers understand that being a Muslim doesn't mean you're a terrorist or a terrorist sympathizer?"

"Never said that, friend."

"Maybe not, but you imply it by *only* talking about Muslims in relation to terrorist events. Just like you imply blacks and Hispanics are a bunch of criminals when you almost *only* talk about them in context of crimes, or as being lazy freeloaders."

"I don't say that, friend. You're trying to portray me as a racist and I will not have that. Git that liberal fascism nonsense on outta her."

"Right on outta here," chided Ted.

"You might not be racist in a blatant way, from what I know, but racism isn't limited to openly attacking people of other races. Racism also exists in context of not caring about other races that share your country, and in creating an image of other races as inferior through only focusing on their worst elements. Their worst moments. You might not say explicitly racist things outright, but you don't even have to. Which is ingenious in a really messed up sort of way. You don't make conclusions for people, you just lead people to the conclusions *you* want them to be led to. That's even more dangerous than just offering your own conclusions because when you prime people to think a certain way, *they* start to think that that's how they really think *themselves*, not that that's simply how they've been lead to think about things, over months and years of listening to, and watching, people like yourself. In all of these things you lead them to believe, you're exploiting their desperation for answers in a world that doesn't offer enough of them. You selectively report on crimes committed by minorities. You selectively focus on the negatives of the bigger cities and not the positives. You selectively report on Muslims only when it involves violent or terrorist actions. You repeat the mantra of Christian family values so often that it prescribes this as a way of life that should be led by all. You talk about the poor only when they commit welfare fraud, or arson fires, or things of that nature to make them look like lazy, undeserving cheats looking for a hand out."

"Well ain't they, friend."

"Yes. *Some* of them. Not *all* of them. But you only report on the some and lead people to believe that that's the *all*, or at least much more of a *some* than it actually is. Do you ever report on whites who are on welfare? Yes. I'll stop you right there. I know that *proportionately* there are more of some minorities than whites on welfare, yet there are still a *massive* amount of whites on welfare who you never talk about. It's like you're trying to lead people to believe they don't exist. It couldn't possibly be *us*, could it?"

"So what do you believe, friend? Hmm? You think I simplify things? First of all, maybe the answers are simpler than you think. Maybe you complicate things with your degrees, and yer over educated yuppie nonsense. Maybe that's why you don't speak for the people lock I do."

"Yuppie sumbitch!" Interjected Walt at high volume. This came at an appropriate time, as Bud was searching for an interlude away from this conversation. One that had been more difficult for him than he would have initially thought. He was hoping a fresh out of college liberal arts major, maybe. A far left, idealistic yet out of touch hippie type, who was the archetype of a modern liberal on his show. This gave him a good idea for the future. Screen for the type of liberal whose views he could exploit more readily. That was the key to making this little segment work in the days to come. He would run that thought by Dreadson and Grant, stat. For now, he seized the opportunity to direct focus onto Walt, who's right nostril, caked in white, was starting to bleed profusely. Sumbitch was snorting too much of that damned white powder again.

"Walt, damn it! Wet I tell you bout cursin' on the radio. Yah gone, my friend. Yah *gone*! Git to steppin' on outta here. Up on outta here, nah! We'll see you next time round. Okay, now what was I saying? Alright nah, here's wet I'm sayin'. You liberals always do this, by and by. Yuh overcomplicate things. The answers really is simple. And sometimes the answers is ugly, but you gotta be willing to do some ugly things from time to time to make the world a better place. That's what wars are about. Just like our current war on terror. Our good veterans know that. God bless 'em. For God and country, mah friends."

Dr. John took a moment to compose himself. The old God and Country routine. Whether or not this man believed in God or gave a rat's ass about his country, beyond the luxuries it provided him (through his exploitations of it), was debatable. John knew that he had to tread lightly in this area.

"Hmm? You stallin' for time liberal?" Bud said smugly now, sensing an opportunity to convey Dr. John as possibly stymied in this area.

"No, I'm not. I just sometimes like to think about what I'm going to say, first."

"If'n it's truth, it should come to ya right away, friend."

"You think you can speak of truth so quickly when it comes to war? Let me tell you something about war from a man who actually lived it. Dwight Eisenhower."

"Great man."

"Yes, he was. He said he hated war. Said that he hated war in a way that only a soldier could hate war. One of his main concerns, for much of his later life, was the arms race. How much it would tax our resources over time. What would be its result? Could it ever end? People like you talk about our soldiers with such seeming reverence for their sacrifices. But, if you really cared about them, you wouldn't be so quick to send them into harm's way because that's the only way you know of to try to resolve international conflicts. And you're all the quicker to go that route when it involves other religions."

"Sure, because the terrorists want us dead."

"Yes they do. But the other billion plus Muslims don't, and you lump them all together as evil because their values aren't…you guessed it…good old fashioned traditional Christian ones. I made air quotation marks when I said that, by the way.

"Don't sass me!"

"Also, I want to add that their values are pretty much the same, but since they aren't defined the same *way*, you discount them. And, by the same way, I mean 'Good Ol Traditional Christian Values.' I made the air quotations again."

"Don't test me nah, bah!"

"Pardon me. That's my bad. Anyway, you disenchant them on a major scale because you don't differentiate among them at all. Do you think Timothy McVeigh should be lumped in with the Christian religion? Or Robert Lewis Dear?"

"They don't represent us, friend."

"Neither does Abu Bakr Al-Baghdadi represent Islam."

"But you're talkin' bout a couple of examples of Christian terrorism in the face of tens of thousands of Islamic terrorists."

"Yes, it's on a larger scale and it is much more of a problem in that religion right now. I'm not disagreeing with you and I'm not afraid to say that it's a problem because of some false narrative you have about liberals somehow not being able to acknowledge that. Don't you see that not just going along with an overly simplified rhetoric of Muslims as terrorists doesn't mean that I don't understand that, unfortunately, a pretty significant number are? Yes, of course it's a problem that we have to continue addressing. But we have to try to work with people in Muslim countries. Would you want to affiliate with somebody who didn't have respect for your religion? Of course not. Show them and their religion some respect if we want to get anywhere with them. Even if we disagree with parts of it. Even if we're directly threatened by some fringe elements of it. You know how important religion is to people, and how important it is to respect it. Religion is so important in this country that we can hardly imagine having an atheist, or even an agnostic president elected. Even though at the end of day, they're there to do a job, not prescribe a lifestyle."

"So what are you proposin'? Hmmm? You pretty good at tellin' the good people at True Murican radio wet you think's wrong with 'em. What should we be tellin' the people?" Bud folded his arms behind his head and sat back. This should be rich, he thought.

"I'm proposing you tell people what will actually help them get through their lives with less pain, less frustration, and less fear.

Not stoke pain, frustration and fear. That just serves to make their lives more miserable and their minds more susceptible to wanting answers to their fears from people like you. Answers that end up being simplified and false most of the time."

"Ah am workin' for the people every day, my friend. I'll have you know that."

"Not in a way that benefits them. Telling people that Mexicans are stealing their jobs doesn't benefit them. However, telling them that computer technologies and robots are taking their old jobs and that they need to try to work with changing circumstances does. Telling people that building a giant electrified fence on our border will make them safe will not help them. Telling people that having inclusive communities and providing opportunities to others, both inside and outside of our nation, so that they are not so desperate, does. Telling people that lack of jobs is the liberals' fault will not help them. Telling people that the job market is evolving, becoming more global, and will require specialized skills and training that might differ from past skills and training will. Telling people that they need to preserve a traditional white Christian culture will not help them adapt to growing diversity. Telling people that lives are almost always enriched by other cultures, when they give other cultures a fair shake, does help them. Telling people that a bygone era of the 1950s was the peak of our nation and that we need to get back to it will not help them. Telling them that the 1950s had plenty of its own problems such as open racism, sexism, the cold war, and rampant alcoholism does help. It keeps people from idealizing the *Great Never Was* and helps them to see their present isn't as bad as they make it out to be when they're comparing it to a more realistic portrayal of the past."

John paused to catch his breath and collect himself, fearing, for a moment, that he might be rambling, though not caring too much if he was. He had tried providing a glimpse into a perspective that was both vast, and rarely given an opportunity to be heard, in outlets like this; nd he only had minutes to distill so much of this down into a relatively short conversation. He wondered, for a moment, if Bud would now have anything to interject. Seeing that he did not, he continued trying to fill -as best he could- whatever time he had left. He took a deep breath and added:

"Just don't lie to people and don't have them focus so much on blaming others outside of themselves. If they're having trouble finding jobs in coal mining? Talk about developing green energies. If they're having trouble finding work in a factory position? Let's develop some skilled labor jobs, of which there are over two million potential openings, last I checked. Let's work to develop green energies, too. Even more potential openings in that area and less concern about creating pollution that we simply have to be more vigilant about; and there's no way around that. The point is that even though the job market is changing and becoming more globalized, there are ways to adapt. So help them *adapt* instead of encouraging them to sit back and just rant about the conditions; find someone to blame so they don't have to look at themselves- goaded on by people like you, all the while. Having trouble relating to people with different political views? Talk to them with mutual respect instead of trying to vilify them. More importantly than any of this, promote *thinking* about issues, not just trying to come to quick, simple conclusions when the answer is hardly ever quick and simple, and you know it. And stop trying to divide the people. I might be a libtard in your book, but I'm more in touch with small town America than you ever were or could be. That's where I'm from and my community still supports me. You'd love it if they cut people like me off, though. Labeled me as an out of touch urban elitist instead of someone from the same stock as them who worked hard and did well for themselves, and who, for the most part, they're proud of and still connected to."

"You sure know how to talk, Gavilan." Bud made a long, drawn out sigh. "I can tell you're well acquainted with prescribed PC communication. You sound like one of the sheeple. Just sayin' wet you think you're supposed to say. Classify people with different views as racists, sexists. Act like strugglin' people have all these other choices in life. Well, you can talk til your blue in the face for all I care, son. We gettin' to be low on time. I'm gonna let you go back to yer mochaccino and your marathon of some urban TV show complete with loose sexual mores, a gay best friend, and all that nonsense. Buh bye, nah."

"Buh bye!" Chimed in Ted, sarcastically; sounding like a burned-out air stewardess addressing passengers after a long, turbulent haul across the Pacific.

And with that, the conversation ended, quite abruptly. Dr. John sunk back into his car seat and groaned, wondering what the last fifteen minutes accomplished. He told himself what he often did, during times like this. You can only try. That is all. He was getting to an age where he was growing more comfortable with certain harsh truths just like that one. He gathered his bag and trudged back to his home to unwind. He hoped that he had made some sort of difference in at least providing an alternative viewpoint to Bud's listeners.

One of the growing issues of the time, John realized as he walked, was how easy it was for people to simply attend to the information they wanted to attend to; then, to disregard information they just did not want to process. It was one of the effects of the internet that had not been fully anticipated. Easy access to a myriad of information also meant that one could, selectively, choose what information to take in. And worse, with the problem of so much information going largely unchecked, it was growing increasingly difficult to differentiate the accuracy of that information. This, now and in the years to come, he knew, would be one of the pressing priorities of the people to maintain a functioning society. Accuracy of, and openness to (at least the more honest and objective parts of), this growingly vast amount of readily accessible information.

Back in the radio booth Bud was, for his part, uneasy. He was a feeling a bit dizzy from the blood pressure spike this conversation brought on. He asked Ted to fill some time by talking about the upcoming rally in Chicago, just days away now, while he collected himself and bided his time to gather his summarizing thoughts. Bud would, of course, be reporting on that rally. McCannon's show would be covering it live and Bud was recently honored by being selected to his panel as a special guest; to broadcast on Marmot News, live, as the events unfolded. Bud finished the last of his bourbon. A moment later, he gestured to Ted that he would take over again. He folded his hands together and pushed them outward, cracking his knuckles. He hunched forward, put his elbows on his desk, and leaned slowly into the mic.

"True Muricans. Let's talk about what just happened today with Mr. Snowflake."

What ensued, in the closing five minutes of that afternoon's show, was a skillfully crafted rebuttal of Dr. John Gavilan's views, to which John (who was now enjoying some decaf on the couch with his wife, Nora and his dog, Toby) could not respond. By the time these five minutes came to a close, his multitude of viewers would scarcely recall the points Dr. John had made, aside from, maybe, a small handful that had nonetheless lost much of their initial punch. The rest, directed by Bud's closing comments on the matter, would come to see this John Gavilan as just another of so many urban elite liberals. "Out of touch," was the wording Bud would use to describe him over half a dozen times in the ensuing three hundred seconds. Out of touch with their plight. Out of touch with their wants and their lifestyle. This absurdly wealthy man from a gated compound in L.A. made sure of pushing that point in his uncontested closing remarks. This man who made more money in two days than Dr. Gavilan earned in a year. Good old Ted's well-timed affirmations, along the way, sealed the deal on his various points.

As the program ended, one of Bud's most loyal and steady listeners slowly got up from his easy chair. Appeased, he told his wife, Tilly, who was sitting peacefully across the room, doing her knitting, "what an exceptional broadcast. He sure handled *that* snowflake." Tilly did not seem to appreciate the last word, wincing slightly upon hearing it, though reacting no more beyond this. She simply went back to her knitting: a thick scarf. The cold would be here before they would know it, even with all the prep work and all the years of experience, trying to keep ahead of it.

Bob made his way up off the weathered chair. His body creaked audibly, especially from the knees. A brief, pained wince, came with a little pop in his lower back. There was work to be done in the fields yet and he had to be moseying on out. He blew Tilly a loving kiss and made his exit to the front door. Just before he left, Tilly reminded him, gently, to be back by six thirty for supper. It was Spaghetti night. "Big" Bob Q. told Tilly that he loved her and he wouldn't miss it for the world. He turned around and walked into the dimming afternoon light.

Chapter XIII

The Rally

Part I: Crowds Gathering

October always was a capricious month in Chicago. The temperature might fluctuate thirty degrees in a day- and even something like this could be dismissed in conversations with the words, "oh, you know how it is around here," or, "if you don't like it, wait ten minutes," maybe followed with, "now let's go git a hyot dawg and watch da Bears, Bob." The temperature was capable of fluctuating forty degrees between one day and the next. October could be "difficult," and it was well suited for an event that was also sure to be such. It surely was the last time. By all accounts, it would probably be even more so, this time around; as both sides- and everyone in between- left the last fiasco feeling slighted, unsatisfied, beaten up emotionally and, sometimes, physically.

The setting sun faded quickly; as it tended to these days. The dull orange-cicle glow hung on, feebly and impudently; doing little to warm the crowds gathering on the intersection of Racine Avenue and Congress Parkway. This day-October the 12th- had started out as what might well be expected; in the mid fifties and partly to mostly cloudy. These were nice conditions for, maybe a late season kayak on Lake Michigan. Perhaps, a last barbecue at one of the various lakefront parks. Around midafternoon the conditions began their shift. The first of several imminent cold fronts of the autumn was taking place as predicted. The temperature was expected to drop to near freezing by late evening.

A diverse crowd was gathering amid these conditions. Hundreds, and, soon-to be, thousands, of well-prepared Chicagoans in down jackets pulled out of previously hibernating winter wardrobe hampers from out the backs of so many closets. Nothing more than a flannel or fleece had been required between the previous April and now. The crowds were growing rapidly in number. Roads would soon be cordoned off. Detour signs to be put in place. Law enforcement personnel stood in formation, with guns, tear gas, and batons at ready.

A young man; a most curious fellow, was making his way off the el. The Roosevelt stop on the red line, that wound its way up from the southside. The wind hit him like a cold cock as the double doors of the train receded with their familiar, robotic ding; a sound like you might hear if you were a pigeon in a lab somewhere who pushed the correct button and was about to receive a treat for the effort: A frizzy, gray-haired psychology professor looking on. Kenilworth's reward was the instant blast of a cruel and bitter Chicago wind; severe and unrelenting by nature. It was made even more so when tunneling through open entryways, or skyscrapers; seizing opportunity to gather momentum.

Kenilworth began the trek in his raggedy tennies. He had a couple miles to go from here. This distance would be straight west, into the wind head-on, to see a man who's following was growing. Thi man whose supporters were coming out of the woodwork in droves; emerging from the depths of myriad apartment buildings, mostly alone, or in small groups- all walking alongside him to the same destination. They were a constituency who, up until now, was largely unknown and unheard of (as many had rarely voted or made themselves heard before). But now that they had someone who was finally seeming to speak their particular brand of language, here they were. Kenilworth was going to see their champion who, in less than one month's time, could become the president-elect.

Several miles north, Dr. Gavilan was driving southbound. The cutting wind was shifting his car on the axles every time he passed a major East-West road along Sheridan Avenue. He was hitting the bottleneck where Sheridan turned onto Lake Shore at Hollywood Ave. This had started at least a dozen blocks premature of where it usually would this time of day; even in the worst of afternoon rush hour.

It was 5:30PM on a Saturday. John had told Nora that he was working late today, heading back to the southside for an impromptu, emergency after-school conference. He was dressed in a worn flannel that he'd owned since his teens in the U.P. A flannel that had been around since Dr. John was jamming out to Nirvana and Soundgarden (though not fully sure how to feel or respond to the depressing and detached grunge movement he was compelled to go along with, at the time). He wore a canvas, three season jacket from the same era. It was pilled, patched, and faded. A sweat-soaked, non-descript baseball cap, with wobbly lines of salt stains. One reserved general admission ticket was tucked away in his flannel's left chest pocket. His face practiced in the vanity. He was affecting an only semi-repressed frustration, and anger. Trying to convey a premature bitterness- though through it all, a level of stubborn hope yet clinging, like a spider on the resting window wiper of a speeding car.

John had seen the look he was practicing often enough in his youth, so it was not so hard to affect now. There was less of it where he lived now, though it still came back surprisingly natural to him, even these days. Years ago, he had worn it, from time to time (and often subconsciously, looking back on it in the rearview) to blend in with others who wore that same face from their teen years up. Their futures, they had prematurely decided, were predetermined to be rough going. Destined to be dealing with a bunch of ongoing bullshit there was little they could do to impede the coming onslaught thereof. This affect summed up how they felt about their continued existence. And now, against his better judgment, his radio was tuned into what helped feed that look and the mindset that helped to form and maintain it. The now familiar, superficially crafted, "down home" accent that he knew would be reigning over tonight's debacle was about to go on proud display.

Dr. John had heard rumors of what these rallies often times involved. He aimed to find out, tonight, just how much truth might lie behind these claims. News coverage could always cherry pick what they wanted to show, he well knew. Not necessarily the best representation of what happens, overall. And even if they did try to be objective in what they were showing, it was too bad so many others weren't, because the differences would cast a shadown and create the possibility of calling *everyone* into doubt.

He was expecting a minor spectacle. Probably not as bad as what he'd heard secondhand. He could live with a tempered, as opposed to full blown, shitshow. He was, also, hoping to find Kenilworth in the crowd and felt, if so, he could help him in some way. That is, if the young man was really going through with what he'd been threatening, in sessions.

John's thoughts were redirected in an instant, as a familiar voice came on the radio, giving its standard greeting; a greeting that never changed, and in so doing, comforted the audience on some small level each day. This, they would think, at least stays the same. Other things change, but this; this stays around, decade after decade, like great grandma's hand-sewn quilt. Dr. John was a little surprised to hear the voice joined by a specially assembled Marmot News panel; broadcasting over the airwaves and on prime-time TV, simultaneously. This panel apparently included a man who went by the title of Edward "Boom Pow!" McCannon. Off the airwaves and off the cameras, seen by neither viewers nor listeners, stood Dreadson and Scott, ready to come out from behind the side curtains to dispense advice as needed, during scheduled commercial breaks (during one upcoming break, a new show was going to be advertised for the first time. A show that would combine the two most prominent panel members, Bud Harbaugh and Edward McCannon, for their very own prime time spot. It was tentatively titled *Boom Pow, My Good Bud!* The old wily dog and the young buck come to carry on the torch. The past, present and future of Marmot News). The familiar voice was the first he heard from the panel, just as his car came to a long idle near the head of the bottleneck.

"True Muricans!" It boomed. "...The time has come, mah friends. Dis her da moment a truth. In T minus fifty-six minutes, our next POTUS will commence his victorious return to dis her lost liberal city. A *lost*...liberal city. And dis her, lost liberal controlled city bout ta get a dose a dat der no spin-zone troot!"

"Boom *pow,* mother trucker!" Shot McCannon.

"Dat rot, son! Hoo-wee, I like dis young man." Bud gave the thumb point to him over his shoulder and a jovial wink. "You got even more moxy than mah good 'ol amigo, Walt, back der on True Murican Radio!"

"Boom!" A right fist cut a jab at the camera

Dat Rot.

"*Pow!*" The left fist came in with an upper cut

"Dat rot too, son! Yes, sah! Nah, nah...folks...nah I don't think ah even have ta mention, nah, nah, haw things, uh, who they got, *last* time, uh, up in her. Over her in *thug* capital U.S.A, that is... more commonly known as Chicago."

"Like a kegger gone too far," explained McCannon.

"Actually," added a meek, infrequently heard voice from the panel, "it was, for the most part, peaceful protests, though turning violent after some of David Betty's supporters started pockets of fist fighting."

"Wet you talkin' bout, Flowers! 'Patty Cake' Flowers, how bout you go on back to sippin' on yer lavender and agave flavored cap-oo-ccino and let those of us who know the troot a tings git back ta some real talk."

"But...I mean, listen...what I'm trying to say is, um..."

"Shut it, Flowers, ya pencil neck!" Added McCannon, putting his fist up toward the man, shaking it in an almost comically menacing sort of way, which prompted Pat 'Patty Cake'

Flowers to put his head down and sip from whatever was in his cup (and, probably, to reflect on whether or not the paycheck he was getting from Marmot News to portray this meek, overtly PC liberal stereotype, was worth it).

"Nah, nah. We was sayin', uh, that is, before we was so *rudely* interrupted, that bein' the case. Uh, where was we? Oh yes, that things went too far and, unlike Flowers, we ain't lookin' ta make no excuses for deez her liberal protesters."

"Like it done turned into a jungle out there! Liberal protesters straight chimping out!" Blurted McCannon, which lead to Flowers briefly putting his head up and raising a half-elevated finger, as though wanting to ask the teacher if he could make a comment. After a moment he dropped the hand back down, thinking better of it.

"Hold on, nah, son." Bud put a calming, fatherly, hand on McCannon's shoulder- playing out a visual of his relationship with Walt from on his own show. "Ya don't know how dat dere liberal media *elite* gonna interpret dat, friend. Gonna call it racist, even though you didn't bring race into it, and what not."

"I don't give a rat's A, MFer. Wooo! *Wooo!*" McCannon had pivoted in his chair, from his initial spot looking onto the camer, and the second *woo* was screamed directly into Bud's left ear.

"Hoo *wee!*" Bud quipped, trying his best not to look explicitly upset and annoyed. "Dat'll wake ya up in the mornin.' Ah am likin' dis energy, son," Bud lied, convincingly. "Lock a famlee reunion kickin' off ahn da bayou over a big crock uh jambalah. Hoo *wee!* But just wash yourself, nah. Have a little restraint, nah."

"*Future* right here, baby! Wooo!" McCannon pointed both of his thumbs inward toward his chest.

"Nah, nah. We ain't gonna have tuh worry dis her time bout things gettin' *too* outta hand. Not lock last time around, no sah. We gots dubble tha police this time yer. Outta have triple the police in dis her city, come ta think of it. Ought to, anyways…case dare any snowflakes gettin' their feelings hurt and start actin' out."

"That's right, take care of business, mother trucker. Now let me take it from here, 'ol Buddy Boy." The camera panned now to McCannon, leaning forward for what suddenly became a serious one on one with his audience/fans. He began:

"Good folks, this night will be David Betty's moment of triumph. And, mind you, one moment of *many* to come. Now, to all the *young* voters out there. And also, to all my disenchanted ARP friends. Listen good to this man. Your party has let you down, and the DNC has been even worse. Shipping your jobs overseas. We are gonna be hearing about the way *forward*, tonight. Not some PC, liberal bunk about how we should all join hands with the minorities and the foreigners and sing campfire songs. Listen hear and listen good. *Pow!* McCannon slammed a fist onto the marble table in front of him. *Pow pow!* He repeated, throwing his fists forward at the camera like he was doing karate, then aiming a fist toward poor Flowers and waving it intimidatingly, inches from his face (causing Flowers to choke on a sip of coffee, which began to gush down his chin and send him into a violent coughing fit on air). Oh, for the love a…Flowers. Oh, for God's sake. Buddy? (cough, hack!) Buddy? Dang, sir, I was just joking (a swift smack on Flowers back sent him lurching forward and coughing even harder). There, does that help, little precious? Watch yourself now.

"I'm fine." (Cough, blurp, hack!)

"Take some deep breathes, just joshing ya. We'll go out, get a beer and laugh about it later. Alrighty, Patty boy?" A short affirmative nod from a still convulsively coughing Flowers followed.

"Ah don know bout what you just did there, son," interjected Bud in a disapproving tone. "Ah got to say, I don't tink dat der was, uh, was entarly necessary."

McCannon pivoted back toward Bud and made a staccato finger point toward him. "Don't worry about it, Bud. Now let me finish. Anyway, just trying to toughen up Flowers, a little bit is all, anyways. Seems his daddy never bothered to. Lot of these other liberals could use use some toughening up too, you ask me." McCannon panned back toward the main camera. "Now what I am saying is this, people. We are *not* all going to get along. Betty is going to address that fact, and it is a *fact*, my friends. We are *different*. We are *not* all the same. We are *not* better with diversity. We were at our best without it, as a white *Christian* nation. That's what made it great before. That's the only way it's going to be made great again and deep down you all know it. Most people are afraid to say it. I'm not. I'm here to come out and say it now. And there, I said it. *Pow!*"

"Strong words, friend," Bud added, a little shocked to say much more than this, at present, and wondering if he shouldn't have researched this McCannon guy a little further before appearing on air with him.

"Sure they are. Sure they are, friend, but strong words that need to be heard. *Boom*!" A right jab toward the camera.

"Nah, wait a minute, nah."

"*Pow*!" A left jab toward the camera.

"Son…just, now let's…"

McCannon was beginning to look openly irritated at the older man now. He put a hand on Bud's shoulder; gripped him tight with it. "Look, I love ya, Bud, but you're getting a little soft. Time to let 'ol McCannon take the reigns for a spell. These young voters have been duped. You understand? *Duped*!" McCannon looked back into the camera again, pointing directly towards it now, with his other hand still on Bud's shoulder.

"You've been *duped*, friends, into thinking diversity is the answer. They duped you into thinking global alliances were the answer. They duped you into thinking college was the answer. They duped you into thinking PC was the answer. Well, let me ask you a question, America." An aggressive pointer finger shaking at the camera- like stock footage of cocky terrorists in the nineties. The camera panned closer to the figure of McCannon at this

336

moment before he added another question. The expression on his face was stone cold.

"How's that working for ya?"

A long pause, with the addition of an upturned, querying left eyebrow followed. "Think about that for the next time you hear some liberal B.S. nonsense. Our good David P. Betty knows what the real answers are. A strong National *not* International identity. Saying what you mean without filtering yourself just for some snowflake's gentle persuasion, warped by neo-hippie professors living in academic bubbles. Good, *hard* work. *Real* work, not sitting around growing an office butt, doing some nonsense cubicle nonsense in a corporate building. Bringing back jobs! *Jobs*, my friends! And helping our women to be proud too. David Betty knows a good, strong female knows how to care for her kids and keep a home, as opposed to these young liberal women, can't even sew a damn button. That good 'ol fashion kind of woman, that's what he'll make society respect. A woman just like his good wife Katarina. And as far as a diverse society? Well, not one that accepts destructive religions, thug culture, or a never-ending flow of freeloaders- enabled by their first of the month government aid checks. That's what you'll be hearing about tonight, amigos."

A meek voice interjected; trying to be more audible than usual in the docile message that followed, and which would not be challenged by anyone in the room, by its very nature. "And with that, Marmot viewers, we'll be back after a quick message from our sponsors. This is Pat C. Flowers for Marmot News. We'll see you back soon, friends."

McCannon leaned back in his chair, folded his hands behind his neck and smacked Bud heartily on the back. His face held a confident and smuggley conveyed grin, though it morphed into a cautious perusing as he scanned the zaftig old man that was looking back at him, less than pleased.

"How you like that, ol' Buddy boy?" McCannon asked/stated, knowing the response would not be pleasant, but caring minimally.

Bud, growing flustered by this young man- this apparent stuck in the frathouse douchebag given a power position- answered him, "I don' know, mah friend. Sounds a lot to me like you pushin' pretty hard for the ARP crowd up in her. Nah don' get me wrong, they got a few points and we'll be needing their vote come Novembah…but outright support lock dis? I don' know bout that, son. They not exactly our *finest* element."

"The ARP is the future, old man," McCannon sharply scolded. His confidence only grew at the assertion. He wasn't willing to concede an inch- not to this fossil- about what his views should be. Yet he felt sorry for him, growing less relevant, by the day, as it were.

McCannon opined, "You know, I got some pretty big shoes to fill, old man. I respect you for making it to the level you did, over the airwaves and all. I sure do. But, see, the problem is, you're the old guard." McCannon gave Bud a little pat on the back, of condolence. "See, you're sugar coating things too much. I've got to take the framework you've made, and I've gotta one up it. Bam! Pow! That's the only way to keep the viewers interested, you see. They've heard everything you've had to say. So, I can't just repeat it, can I? I've got to step up my game a notch." McCannon shook his head, slowly and affirmatively, at Bud, seeming to want him to simply follow suit with an affirmative nod in response. It only served to further rile Bud Harbaugh. This youngin' trying to play the role of sage teacher. A fuckin' frat boy guru.

"It ain't about one uppin', son." Bud argued, growing now simultaneously upset and nauseous around this man. A rare feeling. He had come across despicable men in his time, to be sure (and despicable men, by Bud's standards, were despicable indeed). But Bud now did what he always would in such situations. He bit his tongue knowing full well that this simply came with the turf. He knew that most of those men had relatively little influence overall, which was what helped Bud get through the interviews with the overtly racist, sexist, culturally and religiously isolationist, and militant fear mongers. He was all of these, to a certain extent, himself, though in a somewhat milder form which went well under the radar within his own conscience. Like many of his supporters, if he possessed these ignorant and shameful qualities to a degree that wasn't outright blatant, he presumed they did not exist at a level warranting much concern.

"Oh, don't be naïve, gramps!" McCannon blathered on, "that's the only way I'm going be able to pave my own path. You one upped *your* predecessors, didn't you? That's just how it goes. Hell, they called you 'shock radio' back in the day. That's what got *you* on the map. Well guess what. I'll be shocking the people from here on out. And guess what else, old Buddy old pal." McCannon put his hand on Bud's shoulder and grasped it more firmly than necessary. "Takes a hell of a lot more to shock 'em these days than it did back in your heyday. And you sure are partially to blame for it. Just how it goes. But hey, whatever. I'm up to the task, mother fucker. Now let's get back to it, commercial break's almost over."

McCannon reached under his desk, pulled out a fifth of whiskey, poured a double shot and downed it like so much lukewarm water. He swiveled his chair toward Bud, stuck both index fingers inches from the man's face and screamed, "*woo!* Woo!*" Then, McCannon swirled his chair to the other side, toward Pat Flowers, stuck both fingers inches from Pat's eyes, and repeated, "*woo!*" He turned his chair back to the middle, facing the cameras, primed to start, and slapped each man on their respective shoulder closest to him; smacked them so hard that both their shoulders dipped noticeaebly forward from the force. McCannon, loaded with alcohol and quasi-steroid cocktails from his afternoon workout, kicked it up a notch.

"Mother *fuckers*!" He manically eyeballed them both. "When we're done with this broadcast, I hope we can talk more about this over some beers. Some fuckin' *beers* with me and my boys. You know I'm gonna have my boys with me. My fuckin' *boys*! *Woo*!" McCannon toned it down momentarily when he turned to Pat and added gently, as though taking to a little girl, "and I hope you'll come too, Mr. Pat C. Flowers. Even if you don't drink, you widdle biddy guy." McCannon pinched Pat's cheek. "Are you even able to finish a beer, by the way? Huh?" A round of elbow nudges into Pat's nine-and-a-half-inch diameter upper arm. "Or maybe you drink that spiked lemonade shit?" Another series of elbow nudges. "Huh? Huh? Oh God damn, Flowers, lighten your ass up. You know I'm just fuckin' with ya."

McCannon, growing less merciful by the second, now grasped Pat Flowers by his shoulders and pulled him down hard to give him a noogie. He was still doing so, for an unknowing moment, when the cameras started to roll: Pat Flowers, flailing his stick-like arms, pleading pathetically for him to stop. Bud was looking on in noticeable exasperation during the brief, outlandish event. For the first time in a long while he found himself beginning to reflect on the messages that Marmot News was putting out to the public. This, of course, was no easy feat. Maybe it was a burgeoning sense that he was, finally, begrudgingly, accepting he might not be around all that much longer. And when that time came, he would have no control over the vernacular carried on. None at all. Oh, the all-encompassing vernacular. This was not exactly where he thought it might go. This level of rhetoric was growing more reckless and unsubstantiated. He repressed the bothersome thoughts and feelings that went with them as he saw the frantic cameramen reminding them all that they were, indeed, back on the air. Bud's good old boy façade painted its way back on his face -stern, though with a soft, caring and fatherly element to it- before many viewers could have noticed his moment of on-air disgust with McCannon.

And poor 'ol Flowers. Flowers was, at present time, quite disheartened about this particular night's broadcast. It wasn't a horrible showing for him. No, he'd had worse. It was, however, a below average night in a realm where he could barely live with himself on an above average night. The show, of course, would eventually, and mercifully, end. And when the show ended tonight, Dreadson would hug poor Flowers backstage with a paternal type of understanding. Empathizing, though also conveying throughout that this was how the life he chose could get; cruel. Dreadson would also, on this night, slip ten thousand in cash in Pat's inner suit pocket to show him that, though this job of his may get nasty, it was certainly not to be mistaken as indifferent to his plight. Appeased enough, at least, to go on doing this a little while longer, Pat even went out for those beers later that evening. He would be near bullet proof to an unrelenting spree of douchebaggary with McCannon and his "fuckin' boys," well into the wee hours. He would even buy a couple rounds.

At this moment, less than a mile away, Kenilworth and Dr. John Gavilan arrived, though unbeknownst to each other, just outside of their respective entry points at the UIC Pavilion. Dr. John had parked his car in an open lot several blocks away, in anticipation that getting out of the near area might be difficult later. He walked hastily now along Racine Avenue toward the southwest entry to the complex. He scanned the crowd emerging in ever greater numbers- coming out of buses, cabs, and nearby residences. He was hoping for an off chance that he would see the young man, though the emerging chaos of the protesters having shouting matches with the rally participants made just walking in a straight path toward the destination, unscathed and hopefully without engaging others, highly burdensome. As he approached the northwest side of the pavilion, vitriol could be heard on both sides. Chants broke out from a pack of counter protesters.

"Ray...cist...*fucks*!...Ray...cist...*fucks*!" Met by chants from ARP members of, "Snow...flake...*tards*! ...Snow...flake...*tards*!"

Errant nazi salutes flashed by young men with shaved heads and black combat boots; a relatively small, but vocal, minority. Their stone faces conveyed certainty of their views along with little patience for those who would not tolerate their version of a supposed truth. A few dozen of them stood in random patches within the crowd of thousands. Standing in groups to make their numbers more intimidating. Packs of half a dozen, up to maybe twenty or more. Ready and eager, all of them, to fight together at any moment in time. Some were holding the salutes defiantly in position; their smug and seemingly knowing smiles projected at minorities and presumed left wingers.

There were ubiquitous signs with caricatures of David Betty. Hundreds of people on both sides making physical threats in a great, foul cacophony. Things were getting physical already, pre-rally, with quick underhanded and aggressive pushing back and forth between opposing viewpoints. People being pushed and bouncing off others like so many oversized, clumsy pinballs. The ones they were pushed into usually pushed them right back, and the crowd pulsated with them.

People held up fists and shook them as though weapons. A make-believe mace appendage. Chests puffed out. Others thumped with open hands like gorillas. Like a collective of miniature King Kongs, each living with a Napoleon complex. Like juicy nature show fights for territory displays. People on both sides were using the moment as an opportunity to unleash pent up aggression and many used the moment for little more than this alone. Both sides feeling entirely justified in how they were letting their views show in this way. A deeper level and more ambiguous anger was therefore ignored.

One side viewed the other as hateful, closed off, and willfully ignorant. The other side viewed those who opposed them as lost sheep who didn't speak their minds. Further, they thought, with utmost confidence that, if they did, they would surely be coming to the same conclusions. Even the neo-nazis felt this. A diverse crowd of protesters versus a much more homogenous crowd of rally participants. A level of homogeneity for the latter that, ironically, far from represented the demographics of their modern nation. The homogenous one was unknowing or simply unaccepting of the ignorance that, inevitably, must come from having little contact with races and cultures outside their own. A fact that, in an ideal world, should have bred openness and humility in the knowing of this. Both sides had actively chosen their way of living and relating to others, usually from early childhood on up. One side showed a lack of fear due to exposure. The other side; fear due to a lack of exposure. And this fear was so easy to fuel.

In the short, block and a half walk from the parking lot, Dr. John navigated three separate shoving matches, sidestepping each to keep from getting brought in. During one instance of this, a voice shouted aggressively from behind him while he passed. A voice that brought to life a fear he had back home in the aura in some of those around him whose anger had overcome them young. The voice stated outright:

"Who's side are you on?" Huh? Who's side are you on, *fucker*? Stand your ground against these fuckin' commies if you aren't one of them!"

A protester passed him by, bumping his right shoulder, hard, though oblivious to it. John could see he was oblivious due to a more pressing concern. The man sported a red, swollen left cheek and ocular cavity. He had a cold, bottled water pushed up against it, to cool it. A grimace, leaking blood from a split lip, which dripped down and past his shirt, forming a trail on the pavement behind him that went on for another half a block abutting John's path. Scowling and ugly faces were all around him. Scowls as though resting face. Scowling as the result of anger that was fed into them and magnified in their, often already painfully frustrating, day to day lives. Fingers pointing at each other. Jutting into chests, too, like dull knives trying to break flesh. As though maybe if they jutted enough times, and with enough force, they could cut through to another's core. Back and forth verbal tirades and random, hateful words picked up during what amounted to just a four-minute walk to the entry line.

These past four minutes John would come to remember almost verbatim, along with most of what was to come this night, for the rest of his time on this earth. Trauma had the power to do this, he well knew, from his work at nursing homes. Ninety-year-old women, riddled with end stage dementia, who wandered the halls screaming at a visual delusion of their drug addicted son. Kicking them out of the house, screaming just as they did forty years ago, word for word. Crying in anger and despair. Reliving it over and over, the moment frozen in time to be replayed until the end.

"Racist!"

"Snowflake!"

"Redneck!"

"Libtard!"

"Fuckin' hillbilly! Go back to your God damned *swamp*!"

"Race traitors! Apologists! Go marry a sand nigger, mother *fucker*!"

As words escalated, what lie beneath unleashed itself and took shape. Two sides opposing eath other despite their vast commonalities. One side, driven by a fear of a changing world and mainstream culture that they seemed to be, and maybe sometimes *wanted* to be, less and less a part of. The other, driven by an unrelenting anxiety as they watched a large part of their fellow humanity now breaking off from them, uncontrollably. Worse, seeming to do so quite abruptly and with so little prompting; in large part just from the words of men like David P. Betty and Bud Harbaugh.

A fear from the protesters, too, of an inability to maintain respect, from the other side, for their viewpoints that they had thought to be both progressive and good-natured. How could these views be growing less accepted? And so readily so? It seemed very recently that their views were growing more accepted. And why wouldn't they be? Weren't their views informed, and weren't their policies making things better? Weren't people beginning to come together and address statistics-based, as opposed to emotionally, and largely fear-based, issues?

Dr. John finally reached the line with a relieved exhale and was greeted warmly upon arrival. A random hand gripped his right shoulder, which made him tense up, into a fight or flight reaction. His fears were quickly allayed as the other hand extended, not to cause harm, but to reach in for a handshake. Dr. John took the hand and shook it brusquely. He heard a a country accent in an older man's voice:

"How are you, friend? What's yer name?" The words emitted in a warm manner, and one that meant no apparent harm.

"John," he responded after a moment.

"Good to meet you, John. My name's Bob, but friends call me Bobba Q, so you go ahead and call me that, friend. Came all the way here from Perkins County, South Dakota, praying to God my old Chevy wouldn't break down along the way. Say, I detect a hint of...what is that? A Minnesota accent? Jah der, eh? You from Minnie-*so*-tah?"

"The U.P."

"Ah! A Yooper!" This seemed to please him even more so. "You guys are like an endangered species, huh? Don't see too many of you. Like seeing an albino or something. You know, I been over there a couple times. Over to a place called, uh, what is it? Colored Rocks?" A loud shattering noise erupted, and both men ducked in instinct. An errant glass bottle had shattered against the brick façade of the complex; just in front of the two of them."

"Umm, Pictured Rocks," John clarified, as he collected himself. "It's called Pictured Rocks. Over by Munising." John's voice was inadvertently growing shaky though trying to focus on the conversation.

"*Pictured* Rocks. That's right. Beautiful country up there. God's country. Well, welcome fellow *True* Murican."

"Thank you, Bobba Q."

Bob perused John for a moment, and nodding his head lightly, seemed to acknowledge a sort of comradery. Bob added, "you know, you seem like a good guy. No surprise, though. Good stock up there in that part of the country."

The line was starting to move at a steady pace now, to John's immediate sense of relief. It could not move fast enough, though, and he doubted that things would be much better inside. He had no false hopes of this. After a moment's hesitation, John thought to respond, his voice still trying to repress edginess and fear that his body and mind urgently kept reminding him were now constantly warranted:

"Thanks, Bobba Q. You seem like a good man, too."

Dr. John realized instantly, after saying this as a matter of course, that Bobba Q really did strike him as a good, friendly and caring man. His first impression was that this seemed like the kind of guy you could spend a whole afternoon out fishing with, and he would have stories to tell you the entire time and you would enjoy it all the while whether you ended up just "fishing" or actually "catching." A type of man, also, you instinctively felt would not knowingly cause harm to another.

The line continued to shuffle forward at a moderate pace amid the shouting that only grew in volume, aided by the voices coming out of the arena that were contained and magnified by the shell around them; rather than lost in the wind and air. Growing in anger. Palpably louder. Becoming more unsteady and uncomfortable, seemingly by the minute. He repressed a sudden urge to flee. Volume increasing. Voices becoming shriller and conveying loss of patience. Pushing boundaries more so with their growing impatience.

As Dr. John neared the ticket takers he glanced toward his right, where in a separate entry line, appeared to be a group of skin heads. The leader was a short, taut, and muscular man with a look of unshakable pride as he held a nazi salute toward a group of black protesters looking back at him, in sadness and learned resignation, several yards away.

Police were there by the scores. Nearby they were pacing, trying to stay between so many arguing groups to keep something more severe from erupting. John knew, somehow in his gut, they would eventually fail to do so. It was just a matter of when and where this would all break down completely, but it was going to. All the signs were there.

The last time David Betty made an appearance in this town it was a sweltering mid-July evening. The night would prove itself to show no relief from the muggy, low nineties weather conditions. Multiple protests had grown violent then, and so quickly that the event had to be scrapped altogether before it even got underway. Three people wound up in the hospital, one listed in critical condition with severe bleeding caused from a knife wound to the upper abdomen. One woman suffered a concussion from being hit on the head with a fat, rutted wooden cane that an able-bodied ARP member had faked needing to help walk with. He used it for a long while drubbing random protesters, mostly women, with an entertained smile; like a kid playing a game of whack a mole.

John made his way to the ticket collector and held out his stub. What he saw in front of him was a weary, bitterly disappointed looking, middle-aged black woman; her body was thin and sinewy, her voice raspy, dispassionately droning on, "Tickets…tickets…tickets…" He felt momentarily ashamed but this feeling was cut off as he heard pained screams some way behind him. Quickly formed, shockingly pained screams he thought could only come from some sudden, blunt and traumatic force. A police baton, maybe? A previously concealed baseball bat? He saw the ticket holder's eyes looking both through and past him, widening in disdain as she tore his stub. What could have caused this reaction within a face so distant and unattached a moment before, John wondered. Before he could find out, the crowd was already pushing him into the dark gullet of the stadium. An orange flash emerged in the distance behind him and lit up the shadowy figures within for a moment.

John was now inside. Pushed forward, hastily, into the innnards. As his eyes adjusted to the dimmed outer hallways, he thought he saw a familiar form some ways in front of him and he wanted to shout it down. But it was too far away from his voice grown impotent by the aggressive symphony of verbal tirades surrounding him on all sides. The crowd too obnoxiously loud.

Bobba Q's face reappeared directly in front of John's view, startling him just as he was trying to make out the vague, shaded features of the form-which were now suddenly cut off altogether. Bob gave John a quick pat on the shoulder, before shaking his hand with the other, and shouting into his ear, "I'm going around to the other side, John. I'm over in the one hundred section on the east side. Where are you going?"

"General Admission. Floor. Standing room," John replied without much thought, in a detached and distant tone.

347

"Well then, I guess I won't be seeing you again, friend. You take care of yourself with all these protesters here. Okay? All right? Bring it back! Bring it *back*, my friend!" Bob threw up his right fist in triumph.

"Umm, yes, yeah…bring it back. You take care, Bobba Q." He said after a moment.

And with that, the hulking South Dakotan, in his britches and worn flannel, gave a tight-lipped, quick nod, a last handshake, and then, almost instantaneously, was absorbed into the abyss of the crowd; his form engulfed by a bizarre medley of people. The people seemed to be either what were often called rednecks or, conversely, and more rarely, well-off corporate elites. They were mostly white, though interspersed were more minorities than a person might expect. Their faces were charged with excitement and anticipation. The ones looking more hard-up combined this excitement with a baseline face showing weariness and anger. The ones in polos and designer clothes, with an added look of pride and redemption. More than a few smug looking smiles passed by, looking as though they had won some sort of unknown game that they took much pride in. Everyone shared this look of pride, in some form, amongst the other emotions on display. Where did this come from? A validation of underlying wants and beliefs that previously had been suppressed, he supposed. But now, he awkwardly shuffled on at a varied, ramshackle pace within a chain of humans pushing itself along like a drunk, stumbling millipede. Pushed forward past the overpriced stands selling watered-down beer that only served to further stoke the fiasco. The stale nacho and soggy bun hot dog stands. The smell of yeast, highly refined carbohydrates and low-grade, processed meats abounding.

On to the main floor. The feel all around him now was one of angry, righteous indignation that would not be checked or tempered, but rather, prove validated in the night's proceedings. More emotions and presentations passed John by. Tense men with chests puffed out and arms separated from their sides, ready to be used for whatever the fuck might come up. Thousands of jacked up, angry men just waiting; just waiting for someone to talk shit to them or their friends; or anything they could justify as disrespectful in some way. Men and their, nearly as aggressive, women, down for whatever, if and when something sufficed to bring out their rage. And the random shouting of racially toned diatribes that never ended remained ever present in the background- had started soon after he left his car and would not end this night. Spurred on and continuing indefinitely as they were randomly validated by the passersby.

"Wetbacks bout to head back across the river. *Woo!*"

"No more welfare checks for lazy assed niggers!"

"Fuck *yeah*! And fuck them sand nigger terrorists, too!

"Bout to turn these sand niggers to dust! Woo!"

"Boom! *Pow*! Mother trucker."

John could not even make sense of that last one. What did it mean and why were grown men saying it? It sounded like a kid playing with action figures. Another shout behind and above Dr. John. "The fuck you doing here?" It made him wonder who it was directed toward. Whoever that person was, it was clear they didn't fit in. Not among eyes scanning for anything that conveyed something other than a full embrace of their collective viewpoint and, to only a somewhat lesser extent, their race and physical appearance.

Kenilworth looked at the young man quizzically now, just twenty yards from where Dr. John was passing by. Kenilworth gathered the details in his mind's eye. What he saw was a trucker hat, worn bomber jacket, oil-stained and non-descript, and a faded olive-green shirt with deep blue canvas worker jeans, all of them adorning a displeased young man. This young man who asked the question (more of statement, really; it seemed quite rhetorical to Washington) was flanked by peers dressed in similar fashion.

"Seriously, man. The *fuck* are you doin' here? You get lost on the way over to Alabama Fried Chicken Shack?" This last remark was met by requisite laughter. The type of laughter that scared, insecure friends of bullies were so adept at making. A coping skill to inflate the ego of the bully who protected them and to, in turn, reduce the chances this person would harm them; but would carry on taking things out on others, instead.

Kenilworth replied in a cautious, even tone, "I want to hear what David Betty has to say. Nothing more than this."

"Oh really? What the hell would he have to say that you'd wanna hear?" The young man turned toward his friends; their cue to chuckle at what he'd said. Kenilworth could make out the young man's face as it turned back to him- contorting itself sharply and becoming ugly when he formed words.

"I'm here to find that out." Kenilworth continued in the same tone that he had come to associate with the least amount of risk to cause him possible physical harm from someone like this. Confident and non-threatening, but clearly not trying to challenge the other. This was what bullies responded to best, it seemed. *Best* meaning that hopefully they would just leave him alone and not harm him physically. Verbal insults would continue as an unavoidable given, of course.

This response from Kenilworth elicited a prolonged and profoundly confused look in the young man staring back at him. A look which Kenilworth did not fully understand- seeing that he felt he'd made a concise and logical statement.

"*Pfft*! Whatever, man, it's a free country." He eased off a little. "But you ain't gonna like this very much. I'll tell you that right now, *mah nigga*." The last two words were affected in parody thug fashion, eliciting a fresh round of laughter from his clingers on. "He's definitely gonna talk about taking away your welfare check, just so you know. Bet you won't like hearing that, none too much."

"I'm not on welfare," Kenilworth retorted. "I live with grandmother. Grandmother receives S.S.I. That is true, but she worked a full career, first as a maid, then as a secretary."

"What about your mom?" The man was looking for a ghetto stereotype here, clearly.

Kenilworth paused for a moment and looked toward his shoes. His eight-dollar, consignment store Keds. With the sheepishness he'd come to associate with discussing her, he replied, "She's mentally ill. She is now living out what I've observed to be the fate of the terminally untreated mentally ill."

"Which is what?"

"Isolation. That is what seems to await nearly all of them, sooner or later."

The young man's expression eased just slightly. Kenilworth could tell by the physical signs, more than anything. The reduced tension in his facial muscles, his arms falling more toward his sides, his thumbs finding a spot in his front belt loops. Presently, Kenilworth felt he might have struck a chord with him. Maybe the bully could relate to what he had said on some level. Perhaps he had a close family member with similar circumstances? Maybe he simply felt bad for this mom. Maybe he was relieved by the honest and straightforward manner Kenilworth knew of how he conducted himself to be -based, of course, on what people told him. It made sense. So many people didn't seem to just say what they felt was true about a situation. Seemed to try to cover it up when it didn't suit them to make it known. It was one of the many games that people seemed so often to want to play. What a price, though. Storing inside so many elements of a person's thoughts and experiences; rarely or never to be expressed due to the presumed expense of another's possibly harsh, mocking, or pulling away reaction.

After a moment the young man with the trucker hat spoke again. Still terse, but seeming to convey now that no eminent harm would be coming.

"Just have a seat and don't make any trouble. Don't go chimping out, son. There's bound to be enough trouble already tonight. And just remember this. Even though this man doesn't seem to be for your people; he is. He's going to hold all the lazy freeloaders accountable and that goes for any race. All them lazy assed niggers that's giving your people a bad name? He's gonna make people like them go out'n get a fuckin' job; stop bein' lazy

351

freeloaders suckin' on the government's tit. Your people gonna git pissed. Gonna fight against it, cuz they don't wanna work. Might get violent. It might. That's okay. Gotta break a few eggs ta make an omelet, you know. Gettin' ridda these immigrants and fuckin' up these camel jockeys gonna be part of it, but it's all a part a what's gonna make us great again. Part of what's gonna bring it back. Listen up, tonight. You'll see." The bully gestured Kenilworth to his open chair nearby with an uncharacteristic display of graciousness.

Kenilworth looked back at this man-child. Looked at him and wondered if this young man -about his age- actually believed that these were the answers to his own, his friends', and the country's issues. Or did he just want to believe this because it suited him? Believe it because it simplified macro issues? Believe it because it allowed him an outlet for his angers and frustrations? Believe it because it sounded so temptingly simple to accomplish?

Kenilworth wanted desperately to have a discourse on these thoughts. He decided, though- based on the fact that the man and his friends were barely tolerating him to begin with- that he should just go ahead and sit down. This is what Kenilworth did just as bright lights illuminated the stage and the ones above the audience began their slow and steady dim.

Part II: Our Good David P. Betty

Dr. John was about forty yards northwest of Kenilworth; standing, tensely, one level below. His ass cheeks were clenched as though trying to smuggle out a ruby. He had a tangible, uncomfortable and hard feeling in his stomach, as though it held a weighty, jagged stone; one that was not looking to go anywhere anytime soon. He watched the figure that had emerged and for whom the stage lights were illuminated. A late middle-aged man. White- *very* white. Fish belly white would be the best description. The type of white associated with goth acts. The type of white that seemed to indicate going outside was a rare and largely unwelcomde endeavor. His forehead glistened with sweat below his slicked back hair; salt and pepper gray and balding down the middle. Typical male pattern balding. He wore a charcoal gray suit. This was a non-descript, gray suit, unbuttoned and with a portion of an undulating U.S. flag on his necktie. He was a chubby man, though not appearing too much out of shape, as he maintained at least some level of musculature in his physique.

John though this was the type of non-impressive looking man that existed around you at various moments in your life, though whom you would rarely notice. The type of man who would introduce himself at a party and who's name most people would instantly forget. Whose name they would probably not even bother to store in their memory banks due to the presumption he was not someone they would go out of their way to talk with, would probably not have anything interesting to say, and would most likely prefer just hang out by the chips and dip for a couple of hours before turning in to bed, early. The type of man who was, maybe, a regular at some plain, no bones about it, local greasy spoon diner whose décor hadn't changed much since the mid-seventies. A man who ordered the breakfast special with a cup or two of shitty, watered down, instant black coffee, every Monday through Friday. Sometimes Saturday, but never Sunday. A man who sat alone in a booth, early in the morning, and was known by his first name among a handful of local regulars: who had an innocent, vaguely paternal type crush on a thirty-something, prematurely cynical and weathered waitress who still held a hint of youth and hope. Name of Shirley, perhaps. A man who, maybe, felt a little less alone when both around her and passing the hours, nestled, in these familiar confines.

This was the image of the man who took the podium now. He cleared his throat, the dislodging of phlegm clearly audible to all, and began in an unexpectedly confident voice, though a voice that maintained a level of humility learned from the traditional values he now espoused in this public forum. He began:

"Friends! Welcome! My what a crowd of *True* Americans we have here tonight." He held his small, pudgy hands out to the audience in a gesture of warmth and appreciation.

Applause ensued at a moderate level as the amassing crowd continued to get situated. Salmon-like streams of people finding their way toward their respective seats in the scant light. Thousands were still shuffling in, having been delayed by the traffic and the bio-mass of protesters surrounding nearly two square miles of the stadium.

"My name is Robert Herbert Smith, but you can call me Bob, folks. You just might know me as the head of the National Gun Alliance. The NGA!" The same small, pudgy hand, with fingers that seemed cut short by one knuckle each, shot toward the heavens and made a triumphant shaking fist.

A louder, more palpable applause with a few chants of:

"N...G...A!...N...G...A!"

A more validating applause indicating that this non-descript, slightly chubby, five-foot five man had touched on something near and dear to them. He continued, picking up more exuberance. Egged on by the clear support of the growing masses and showing a little more chutzpah now.

"I am here on behalf of the people of the United States of America. I am here, *especially*, for the proud gun owners who will *not!* I repeat. Will *not*...stand for the liberal agenda looking to take their guns away from them. An *agenda*. I repeat. An *agenda* to take away your God given right to bear arms." He panned his hand out, sweeping across the audience.

"God, this sounds a lot like what I'm hearing on the radio," thought Dr. John as a louder applause rose, sounding simultaneously more excited and more hostile. Supporters were becoming situated and the volume made their numbers known.

"The NGA pledges its full support to our good candidate, Mister David P. Betty!"

And with that, Bob H. Smith threw his small, pasty and pudgy fist into the air above as the crowd roared once again.

"My friends! Without further adieu. I am proud to introduce to you our next president, the good...the *honorable*... Mister David *P.* Betty!"

A surging roar. The lights quickly dimmed the rest of the way and the moment extended itself to take in the enthusiasm. Building up what was to follow as though this were a long-beloved rock band about to come out and play the hits after a long hiatus. As the roar reached its zenith, an unseen soundman cranked up the speakers which belted out a song well known among Betty's constituents. A country rock song that would cover all the bases in its lyrics. God. Country. Beer. Fine Women. Simple folk. And, most importantly, and crucially, simple living.

Smoke gathered on the front and sides of the stage, compliments of strategically placed, fan blown, dry ice. The smoke developed quickly into a surreal, grayish white fog, two feet high along the stage. Red and blue beams began to cut through it, flashing in various directions and reflecting off the fog; creating a red, white, and blue haze that spread wide past the stage, into the audience and rose higher into the air. A projector screen, previously black and blending in with the background of the stage, lit up to show a soaring bald eagle, the blue-sky background slowly morphing into a gently undulating American flag. An eagle's screech blared through the speakers, though the eagle's beak remained shut as it coasted through the sky. Lights all around now, flashed their beams into the audience as the people roared manically. Deep hues of blue, purple, scarlet red, green and yellow. The full spectrum of colors danced across the audience in speckled bursts. The hue of the lights blended seamlessly into the foggy mass onstage in a dreamlike sequence.

The curtain parted abruptly just behind the podium and with it, a gaudily bright spotlight shown on one David P. Betty striding toward the crowd. He circumnavigated the podium, holding both arms spread in triumph above his shoulders. As he walked to the front of the stage to shake hands and give high fives, the speakers hit the chorus of the catchy country rock anthem.

"I'm a true American!...Bein' the best man I can beeee!...A cold beer in mah hand, I'm gonna take a stand fer my *right*...to be freeee!....I got my girl by me, and you best believe, that that's all I'll ever neeeeed....(a catchy guitar riff). And when the day comes when the lord takes me, he gonna ask me about my creeeed...I'll look him straight in the eye and give him mah reply (a pause for five bass drum kicks)...that I'm a true American!"

David Betty jogged across the front of the stage with his right hand held out as though someone might pass him a baton. He lowered it down toward the audience and slapped hands with the front row for a spell, before running back to the podium doing a round of fist pumps into the air. The crowd began to chant along with the pumps:

"Beh...*Tee*!...Beh...*Tee*!. Beh...*Tee*!"

The whole scene seemed rehearsed with an aim to prove youthfulness and virility despite the late middle-aged body of the man before them. The song cut out and he stood behind the podium- jutted both index fingers out in front of him toward the

356

crowd just as red, white, and blue pyrotechnics spewed ten-foot-high plumes of sparks.

"Yes! Now chant it with me, my friends! Ima…trua…mer-i-*kin*!

The crowd instantly followed suit:

"Ima…trua…mer-i-k*in*!...Ima…trua…mer-i-*kin*!"

David Betty clapped his hands in unison with the chat. Clap-a! Clap-a! Clap..clap..clap! Following this he leaned forward, bringing his right hand up to his right ear with a flourish.

"Ima…trua…mer-i-*kin*!...Ima…trua…mer-i-*kin*!"

"What? I can't hear you! I can't *hear* you! *Louder*, my friends!"

"Ima…trua…mer-i-*kin*!....Ima…trua…mer-i-*kin*!" Clap-a! Clap-a! Clap..clap…clap! Betty and the crowd both clapping in unison to the chant now.

"What's that, my friends?"

"Ima…trua…mer-i-*kin*!"

"One more time!"

"Ima…trua…mer-i-*kin*!"

"Yes!" A jumping fist pump into the air from in front of the podium, in unison to a second burst of red, white, and blue pillars of sparks. The image of David Betty's jump conjured a late middle-aged Rocky after reaching the top of the stairs of the Philadelphia Museum of Art. As though Betty were training for a near geriatric exhibition match with Clubber Lang.

"Yes! Yes, my friends! I believe I only have *True* Americans with me here tonight. Am I right about that? (Audience roaring in approval). I *see* you! I see you and I *hear* you, friends! We are going to bring this country *back* to when it was great. *Back* to when we stood proud on the world stage. *Back* to when the culture of this great nation was its rightful culture.

Our culture!" An eruption from the crowd. They new exactly what he was implying with that last line. Feet stomped now in addition to the wild clapping, shouting, and chanting. The crowd started belting out:

"Bring…it…back!...Bring…it…back!" The stadium physically shook.

Betty crisscrossed his arms and took in the scene unfolding to his delight. He had them in the palm of his hand already. After a moment to savor it, he put his cupped hand up to his right ear and asked, "What's that? What are we gonna do?"

"Bring…it…*back*!...Bring…it…*back*!"

"Huh? What's that again?"

"Bring…it…*back*!...Bring…it…*back*!"

"*Yes*, my friends! *Yes*, my true Americans! We are going to bring it *back*!" He began pacing around the podium. Walking a circle around it like a dog marking its territory.

"Bring it *back,* friends. Back to when nobody in their right minds would ever even *think* about messing with us. Bring it *back* to when a good, hard working man could provide for his woman. His *woman*! And his kids, on one salary. What are we gonna do? We're going to bring it *back*, my friends!" Betty began to pull something imaginary and roundish in toward him with his hands, as though it were all a large, tangible thing, about the size of a beach ball. The crowd roared ecstatically.

"Bring…it..*back*!...Bring…it…*back*! Bring…it…*back*!"

"Yes, my friends! Yes! Let's get to it!" Both open hands smacking the podium hard.

"Bring…it…back!...Bring…it…back!"

"Yes! Go get it! Let's get to it!" Both hands smacked the podium again, harder. David Betty went back to pace the stage with his chest puffed out- each arm held a foot plus away from his torso. After a few more paces, he held the microphone up toward the chanting crowd while they continued their bellows. He resembled a veteran comedian who knew, full well, when he had complete command of his crowd. Indeed, knowing that the support of his audience had long since been established. He turned suddenly from his left to right side pacing, contorted his form downward to the crowd and poked his head into the microphone.

"Immigration!" A scan across the audience from left to right. He repeated it with more emphasis and authority, belting out, "Im...eee...*gration*!" A pause to let the roar of the audience surge to its highest decibel yet. Satisfied with this reaction, he continued:

"We've got to restrict it. *Restrict*...it. *Got* to! We've got millions of illegal aliens. Illegal *aliens*!...taking over this country right now as we speak. Taking it over! Coming in, practically unchecked, too. Now let me ask you something. Hmm? How does that happen? Hmm? Coming in *unchecked* and taking advantage of our social services. Committing *crimes*!

"Boooo!"

"That's right! Committing all sorts of *heinous* crimes right in front of our eyes!"

"Boooo!"

"That's right, friends. Knowing all the while they won't get prosecuted ninety percent of the time cuz, heck, they're not even in the system!" A strategic pause and a gesture mimicking thoughtfulness before continuing, "Now, don't get me wrong. *Some* of 'em good. Sure enough. But does that *some* mean we've got to let *all* of them in? Hmm? Think about it! And they can't even speak our language! *English*!" David repeated the line again, now screaming as though he were the late Sam Kinnison. "*English*! *ENGLISH*!

"Ing...*lish*!...Ing...*lish*!

"*English! ENGLISH*!!!" Resembling, now, Sam Kinnison amidst a crack binge. Spittle had sprayed the mic and some of the first-row audience members upon his last utterance.

"Ing…*lish*!...Ing…*lish*! The crowd chanted anew.

"What?"

"Ing…*lish*!...Ing…*lish*!"

"Huh?"

"Ing…*lish*!...Ing…*lish*!"

"Now that's the language *I* speak!"

"Ing…*lish*!...Ing…*lish*!"

"Now that's the language *we* speak! Id'nt it?"

"Ing…*lish*!...Ing…*lish*!"

David Betty continued to pace the stage as the chanting went on. As he did, dark figures could be seen gathering on the left side of the stage, facing the audience. Two men arranging some structure in front of another, shorter figure, who was approaching in the background between them. All of this was visible through a partially translucent, vaguely rectangular shape. David Betty continued exuberantly pacing across the stage-near frolicking, really- just as a bright light projected onto a brown-skinned man donning tattered clothes and a small plaid sack, attached to the end of a stick. He looked like a dated hobo stereotype. At this moment two separate spotlights shone. One on the brown man and one on Betty.

"You know what I say?"

"What…do you…*say*?" Chanted the audience in well-timed unison, knowing the lines they had developed on their own over what had been months of rallies now. Like wrestling fans playing along with their favorite character's schtick; many knew, and carried on traditions developed on the live stage over time.

"You know what I have to say about it?"

"What...do you...say?"

"I say *build...that...fence!*"

Manic applause ensued as the spotlight cut from Betty and the only light on the stage now shone on the brown-skinned, hobo-caricature of a man who began to struggle on cue from behind the prop electric fence. After several seconds doing this, the prop fence lit up with various, brilliantly flashing lights. The man jumped back as this happened, landing flat on his rump- his hobo stick flying through the air. He got up, shaking, and blew on his two hands that had touched the fence. Smoke was wafting around off of them from some prop installed under his long sleeves. The second spotlight re-illuminated David Betty as he walked up to the man at left stage.

"And what do you have to say, Paco?" Betty pointed the mic toward the man.

The man pathetically crept toward the microphone, like a beat dog, and responded, startled and humbled, "Aye chihuaha! Dios *Mio*, senior!"

"Dios mio?" Betty inflected into the mic. "Well, Paco, I'm sorry but there's too many immigrants from trash heap countries here already. All I can say to you is, 'Lo siento, senor.'"

Deafening applause erupted spontaneously as the lights now faded from "Paco" and the dark figures reconvened to move the prop electrical fence off the stage. The crowd began with another chant.

"Lo..siento..*senor*!...Lo...siento...*senor*!"

David Betty paced the stage, shaking his head in a sort of "I'm sorry but there's nothing I can do about it" fashion- trying his best to convey that he had some level of empathy for Paco. The chant continued, growing louder and livelier as though in celebration. Betty did not encourage this particular chant, but he did not discourage it either- much the same as he would for various other chants throughout this and his other rallies. He allowed the audience to do or say what it wanted, whenever it wanted, with no apparent limits-that is, except (and it was only a strong maybe even in those cases) during certain times when things got violent.

Things did get violent at this particular moment (though David Betty was unaware of it) when a large man with an IQ of seventy-six, and arms resembling tree limbs, full-force cold-cocked a slightly brownish man in front of and adjacent to him; sending the poor man sprawling to the floor in a fraction of a second. In a state of immense and immediate pain and stunned confusion, the brownish man, woozily, got up. Swaying and slurring a bit, he slurred, "What the *fuck*? I'm *Sicilian* and my family's been here over a hundred years! Seriously, what the *fuck* are you hitting *me* for?" The large man looked back at him, perplexed, before a woman behind the large man tapped him on the shoulder and said, "that means he's Italian, hun. You've got to say, umm. What is it you say? Oh yeah, it's, *me scuzzi*." The large man nodded toward the woman, then turned back to pat the brownish man on top of the head. He looked at him, sincerely apologetic and said:

"Me scuzzi."

The fifth generation Sicilian looked back at the large man with wide, confused eyes. He had a bloody nose and a growing shiner on his right eye, which made the large man's form rather blurry and out of focus. Pudding headed, he replied.

"Me scuzzi? What the *fuck* does that mean? I thought we spoke English here!" He looked around from side to side to the other people standing next to him. "What the fuck does *me scuzzi* mean?"

Meanwhile, David Betty continued, ushering in the next topic, with his preferred, one word header.

"Thuggery!"

"Boooo!" Jeering and foot stomping.

"*Thuggery!*"

"*Boooo!*" More jeering. More foot stomping.

"*Thuggery,* my friends! That's right. Now, just, how in tarnation did we let this happen! Hmm? Young black men running around with their guns blazin' and their pants done fell off. Done fell *off*! Rat-a-tat-tatting their Tech Nines and killin' kids." Betty started gesturing his fingers like a five-year old making play guns. "And they're killing everybody around them! Killing them willy nilly! Killin' little kids even! Got no education. Can't even speak proper English. What up with that, son? You know what we're gonna do?"

"Whatter we...gonna...*do*?"

"You know what we're gonna do?" His hand came up with a flourish to his right ear as he bent down toward the crowd.

"Whatter we...gonna....*do*?"

"Ah *tell* you what we're gonna do!"

"Whatter we...gonna...*do*!"

"Ah *tell* you what we're gonna do! We're gonna go into these *thug* communities to establish martial law!"

The crowd erupted just as the lights blared again, back to the familiar left side of the stage. This time they shone upon a group of young black men. All of them wore wife beaters. All had their pants sagged so low you could see the entirety of their boxers. One, his pants had simply fallen down onto the floor, laying in a crumpled heap around his tan, suede boots. All held semi-automatic weapons; one in each hand. The middle one began clacking his two guns together, pointing them out toward the audience, shouting "papuh pap pap! Papuh pap-pap-pap!" Fear was, of course, viscerally being instilled in them at this moment.

Kenilworth observed this scene disgustedly. These were clearly caricatures of even the worst elements of black society, yet, here this audience was-taking this in as an unquestioned interpretation of what young black men were. He turned to the bully and said, "What is this?"

"Shut the *fuck* up, bitch!" Came a curt reply.

As Kenilworth looked back on the scene, he observed a group of men dressed in military fatigues walk toward the pack of young black men. They pointed their own, much larger, futuristic looking guns, back at them before one came up and took the now impotent looking guns of the young black men away. A winning situation was being conveyed as, simply, bringing bigger guns than the other guys. The roar of the crowd boomed as the young black men then shrugged and put their hands up as if to say, "Oh well, what are you gonna do?"

"But don't worry," interjected Betty, placing himself in between the two groups like Michael Jackson trying to keep rival gang members at bay in his video for *Beat It*. "Don't worry there, Tyresius. We got your back, son! What what! Huh? What what, son."

And with that, one of the military men pulled a book out from his satchel and gave it to the young man in the middle. Betty continued, on cue.

"We're gonna help you get an education, Tyresius. Get you an education so you can go get a job and stop freeloadin'! Freeloadin' and gang bangin'! Those days are over, son." The crowd erupted and a new chant began.

"Stop...free...*loading*!...Stop...free...*loading*!..."

David Betty gestured toward the military men. "Hey guys, don't forget about the two friends. Okay? Give one to DeHavashaw. Yeah. Yeah, okay, and give one to Ronquarius, too. Uh-huh. Ok? Ronquarius, we good? Give him a book, now. Okay? Ronquarius, you got it now? Alright, G. We good."

Tyresius, Ronquarius, and DeHavashaw looked down at their books, then back toward each other. They seemed to be thinking about it for a moment. Then Tyresius formed a beaming smile showing off a platinum grill, pulled up his pants, and gave a double thumbs up toward the audience. Both friends followed suit. Flashing grills. Pull up the pants. Double thumbs up. The crowd continued their chant anew.

"Stop...free...*loading*!...Stop...free...*loading*!..."

David Betty paced back across the stage smacking both hands together in a brisk rubbing fashion-as though he had just completed some overtly tangible task; like cutting two by fours on a circular saw to make a display for his son's 4th grade science project. His face was starting to glisten, and a shock of his slick, auburn hair had come out of place- the wet gelled strands pinned close together down the middle of his forehead and giving him a fifties-style greaser look. The crowd continued their chant.

"Stop…free…*loading*!....Stop…free…*loading*!"

More than a few younger members of the crowd had never seen a black man except on television, and even then, often on a Marmot News crime report-almost always involving violence. The crowd continued to chant their three-word interpretation of the problem regarding young black men and Betty let them go for the better part of a minute or so. Betty was craftily fostering a certain level of tension in his verbal ceasefire for the moment, stirring up the crowd for what was to come next when he did decide to speak into the microphone. He paced confidently, chest puffed out, arms splaying out to his side like he was about to go up to another man and say, "What's up, brah? You got a problem, brah? We can do this right here, right now, if you want to, brah. Don't start with me, brah!" He added random staccato finger pointing into the blackness in front of him, as a gesture of seeing the audience members one by one, though they were, to him, only indistinguishable phantasms beyond the blinding bright lights. He lifted the mic and uttered, again, just one word.

"Terrorism"

"Boooo!"

"*Terrorism*!"

"*Booooo*! Hiss! Boooo!"

"What you think bout terrorism, huh?" Mic pointed back to the audience.

"Booooo!"

"I said, I said, uh, what you think 'bout terrorism?" Mic point.

"Booooo!" A few isolated slurs peppered in; from various pockets of the audience. "Camel Jockeys! Sand Niggers! Towel heads! *Terrorizers*!"

David Betty took it all in with his arms folded in front of his puffed-out chest. He followed up with a question, once more.

"What er we gon' do? Hmm?"

"Whatter we…gonna…*do*!" The crowd boomed.

"Whatter we gon' do? *Hmmmm*?" Betty held both hands up high. Looked side to side.

"Whatter we…gonna…*do*?"

"Well, I'll tell you what we gon' do!" David Betty continued to pace the stage and let the crowd roar, before elaborating.

"Whatter we…*gon'*…do?" The crowd continued chanting as he paced.

"Ah tell ya what I'm gon' do!" Another pause, the mic dropped low before he brought it back up to rightly scream out, "Blow 'em sky high!" As Betty said this, he dropped low, almost down to one knee, and pumped his fist back and forth like a tennis player who'd just saved match point in the fifth set final.

Blow 'em…sky…*high*!...Blow 'em….sky…*high*!" The crowd carried on.

"What?"

"Blow 'em…sky…*high*!...Blow 'em…sky…*high*!"

"What's that, again?"

"Blow 'em…sky…*high*!...Blow 'em…sky…*high*!"

"Blow 'em up *real* good, my friends! Real *real* good! That's what we gonna do! Huh? Excuse me. What's that,

Mubakka Ala-Habibi?" Betty had formed his thumb and pinkey as though speaking into a phone, as he strode the stage. "Oh, you wanna mess with Merica? Hmm? That's what you want? You wanna mess with Merica? Hmm? What you think is gonna happen to you?"

"Blow…you…*up!*"

"What's that?" Betty looked to the crowd again.

"Blow…you…*up!*"

"Huh?" Betty pointed the make-believe phone toward the audience.

"Blow…you…*up!*"

"What gonna happen to ya!"

"Blow…you…*up!*"

"Dat right."

"Blow…you…*up!*"

"You hear that, Ala-Habibi?"

"Blow...you…*up!*"

"Dat right!"

"Blow…you…*up!*"

"Dat *right*! Now fix thine eyes on the projector screen and watch what happens to Mr. Mohammed Burka Lurka Durka! And with that, Betty's form went black as the spotlight cut and the soaring eagle on the twenty-foot-high projector screen morphed into a cartoon Muslim man wearing a turban and a gallabiyah. At first, only his face and turban were visible; cartoon beads of sweat on his brow, his teeth bared- biting his writhing, curled lips in highly focused concentration. Looney Tunes era sound effects and musical accompaniment complimented the image. His eyes blinked to comedic sounds as he made absurd, grunting noises, tinkering away at some, as of yet unknown, task. "Ak burka la la!" He exclaimed. The cartoon started to pan out. Slowly, it became apparent that Mr. Mohammed Burka Lurka Durka was sitting, Indian style, on the ground of a cave, working on a suicide vest. A large pile of them surrounded him in the background, along with about a dozen terrorists standing by, waiting for the completion of this apparent last and final vest of the bunch. Mohammed Burka Lurka Durka was spouting gibberish as he worked. "Murk Burka Lurka Abadinana Mamadinanajad! *Ack*! Lurka burka Mohammed hala mana la-la-la!"

David Betty's audience stood captivated, quietly observing the 1940s style cartoon. Their silence broken occasionally by errant, aggressive racial slurs, a few anti-Muslim innuendos and condescending chuckles. Dr. John's jaw was agape in the blackness that, thankfully, surrounded the audience and largely concealed his reaction. It was abundantly clear to him how David Betty was connecting with this audience. Portraying his idea, aided by dozens of professional advisors, of what his constituency's fears were. Blacks were thugs. Muslims were terrorists. Mexicans were robbers of jobs, etc. Then validating all of those fears by taking whole races and cultures, simplifying the entirety of them into their worst elements- even parodies of their worst elements. The whole thing struck Dr. John as a grandiose and well-presented piece of shit. But wasn't it the responsibility of the people to see it as such? Weren't they able to? Or, were they simply not willing to in the face of these absurdly simplistic supposed solutions to- what were presented as- the most pressing problems of the country?

Meanwhile, onscreen, the adventures of one Mohammed Burka Lurka Durka continued to unfold. A sausage-fingered, cartoon hand flipped a switch on the completed vest and a button lit up; a blinking, fire truck red. With this, Mohammed and his fellow terrorists threw up their hands and started to cheer in various tones of gibberish. "Ak makka dinanajad! Ak mahala a-la-la-la-*laaa*! Zabiha! Zabiha *Halal*! *Zabiha halal*! Zabiha halal mamadinnanajad!" Mohammed and his associates began dancing, kicking their feet up, as a Snake charmer played flute music in the background; a cobra gyrating in a basket in front of him.

Just as the terrorist cheering and dancing display reached its zenith, a large cartoon bomb dropped down into the center of the cave. Crumbled rocks scattered in its wake, in the "ker-plump!" sound effect of its landing. Mohammed and his friends looked through the hole, created by the bunker busting bomb, to see a U.S. warplane hovering above in the sky. The camera zoomed onto the pilot, who gave a thumbs up and a wink along to its accompanying sound effect. The camera panned back to where it all began; a closeup of Mohammed Burka Lurka Durka, sweating more profusely, shaking and eyes bulging. "Ak ma dinnanijad bobba loosa murka durka, la-la-la-*laaaa*!" And at that moment, stock footage of a nuclear explosion in the desert lit up the screen.

The crowd was worked into a frenzy now as the spotlight re-merged onto David P. Betty, making a majestic explosion gesture with both hands splaying upward and out to mimic the mushroom cloud. He brought the mic back to his face and shouted into it, projecting spittle, and displacing more shocks of gelled hair onto his forehead.

"Turned him to *glass*, my friends!"

The crowd exploded. Cheering on par with a climactic moment at a bible belt mega church now. Completely enthralled and enraptured. Enthusiastically all-consumed by the messages of the presenter, in whatever form they were given; whatever their motives were. The parroting cheer began.

"Turn…them…to *glass*!...Turn…them…to *glass*!"

"What?" A flourish of the hand to the ear.

"Turn…them…to *glass*!"

"Huh?"

"Turn…them…to *glass*!"

"Heh?"

"Turn…them…to *glass*!"

David Betty paced aggressively across the stage, chest puffed out, arms becoming near comically outstretched from his sides (what you wanna do brah? Let's go right now, brah!). David stopped abruptly and continued:

"And what do you think they're all going to say about it? The media. Hmmm? Blowing up terrorists who wanted to nuke us all along? Their underlings and the kids they're brainwashing who are coming up as the next generation?" What are they gonna say about it? Hmm?

A light focused beyond David Betty as he looked over toward the right side of the stage. The light beamed down on a chubby, red-headed twenty-something. The boylike young man sported a vintage, stained and faded, black Star Wars shirt. Atop his head a small, red, white-boy afro. A pasty, chubby stomach protruded out the bottom of the shirt- a happy trail of curly red hairs illuminated as he sat slouched in his office chair with a desk, a laptop, and various empty junk food wrappers strewn all about. He was in the habit of pushing his bandaged glasses upwards on his face every several seconds as he talked aloud to himself, tapping away at his PC.

"Hmmm, yes," he began in a comically dweeby voice: nasal and irritating in that classical, elitist nerd tone of casual, unchallenged smugness. "This is another column brought to you by Leon Quincy Schmeckelberger the Third, Esquire, writing for CBNN. It appears that our president…"

Leon's voice was drowned out for several seconds as the crowd booed and hissed. This parody of a nerdy, young, liberal millennial looked back at the crowd in shocked indignation while they booed, before shooing them off with a flop of his hand and turning back to his desk; munching on a few cheese puffs, continuing his talking aloud to the screen.

"Hmm, now where was I before I was so *rudely* interrupted?" Leon looked toward the audience as he said this, initiating a fresh round of boos and hisses. "Oh yes, our president, David Betty (another roar of the crowd upon hearing this). Umm, excuse me, people! Will you hush up, please, while I continue my work. It is of the utmost importance." The crowd booed again to Leon's continued dismay, until he eventually recommenced talking to himself. "Our president, David Betty, just ordered a military strike in Pakistan that may have killed a top terrorist. But, I ask you. At what cost? It appears he wiped out scores of civilians in the process and forgot the golden rule. Start with diplomacy, my friends. We don't need to resort to violence like this. Why can't we all just hold hands and talk this out?" A pause while Leon munched on a few more cheese poofs and started to rub the detritus of neon orange cheese powder from off his vintage store shirt. He paused to crack his knuckles and, just before resuming his work, a booming voice of authority stopped him dead in his tracks, making his glasses fall off his face and his voice squeal in fear, like a little girl.

"Leon Q. Schmeckleberger, you *putz*! I'm sick of your liberal, P.C. bull corn!"

"Oh, my goodness, folks. It's our president, David Betty (cheers from the crowd)." Schmeckleberger waved off the crowd's reaction and continued with growing confidence, "Well, I'll tell you what, mister. *I* certainly didn't vote for you. And, furthermore (picking up his glasses speckled with cheese product and putting them back on his face) I intend to tell the people what you're really doing, sir. They deserve to know the truth!"

"The truth? Son, the only truth they need to find is on the good 'ol Marmot News network (a pause now as the crowd erupted into an aggressive applause)...certainly not your PC, weak-handed CBNN network. You know what CBNN is, by the way people? Hmm?" Betty looked to the crowd for their sought-after response.

"Fake...News!...Fake...News!"

"Heh?"

"Fake...News!...Fake...News!"

"Heh? Well what's *real* news then?"

"Mar...Mot...News!"

"What's that?"

"Mar...Mot...News!"

"You got it."

"Mar...Mot...News!"

"You got it, folks! The only *real* news network out there amidst all this detached, liberal media elite nonsense!"

Leon Quincy Shmeckleberger had resumed his aghast expression, with undertones of shocked disappointment that his message was somehow being rebuked.

"Leon Schmeckleberger!" Betty's voice boomed louder and with more authority than ever.

"Yes, sir." Nervous hand wringing, and noticeably high and shaky voice worked their way into the Schmeckleberger persona.

"Come, over here, my boy. Come, on, it's okay, boy." Betty sounded as though he were talking to a recently disciplined dog, as Leon Q. lifted himself up off his chair and slowly waddled, head down, to the exact spot on stage that Betty was gesturing to.

"Why do you want me to stand here, sir?" He looked up, meekly.

"Now don't you go giving me any *lip*, son! I'm your president nowadays whether you like it or not! And you better get used to that fact, right quick. You hear me?"

"Yes, sir." The crowd began to cheer louder, as Schmeckleberger stood humbled.

"Leon! I'm not a big fan of your fake news. You know, you're causing a lot of harm getting people to question and doubt the decisions of your good leader with all these *hateful* lies of yours. Just hateful and mean-spirited. You know what we do with people like you? People who peddle fake news." The crowd surged, with a few, continued errant chants of, "fake news...fake news."

"No, sir. Please, sir. I'm sorry. I won't do it again. Can't I just go back to my parents' basement now? There's a *Whitney the Vampire Killer* marathon on TV as we speak."

"*No!* Boy! I'm not having that! You know what's gonna happen now? (The crowd noise grew and started to drown out the conversation)."

"No, sir."

"You get the *boot,* son!"

"Huh?"

"The *boot!"*

Betty sidestepped away as Leon Quincy Schmeckleberger the Third, Esquire stood cocking his head in confusion. From where Betty previously stood, a giant, muddy, camouflage foam boot -eight feet tall and twelve feet long- came swooping down from the top of the stage toward Leon, ending in a half arc that stopped several inches from the young man (and indeed appeared to the crowd as though it had hit him). Just as it did, a springboard from underneath shot Schmeckleberger twenty feet high and back toward the side stage where the boy (in actuality a chubby professional stunt man) landed on a large inflatable away from the crowd's watchful eye.

"Ah-eeeeeee!" Whined Schmeckleberger as he flew through the air- arms flapping, errant, partially chewed cheese puff remnants cascading from his shirt, like otherworldly rain drops, along the way. As soon as he was out of eyesight, red, white, and blue confetti shot from a set of half a dozen Revolutionary War looking cannons, fixed in front of the stage. The crowd howled with glee. Shouting and laughter coexisting.

"That's what you get, boy! The *boot*! I'm bootin' your ass up on outta here!" Betty shooed him off aggressively, with the flick of his hand, as he shouted into the mic. Betty now paced back toward center stage, before abruptly pivoting on his hip toward the audience, bending down and saying with authority into the mic, "What is it we gonna do with fake news peddlers like Leon?"

"Give…them…the *boot*!"

"What?"

"Give…them…the *boot*!"

"Heh?"

"Give…them…the *boot*!"

And what do we watch?"

"Mar…Mot…*News*!"

"What?"

"Mar….Mot…*News*!"

"And what do we listen to?"

"True…Merican…*Radio*!"

"What?"

"True…Merican…*Radio*!"

"What?"

David Betty continued on in this manner for what would be over two, solid hours. The crowd devoured his every word; primed by the show of it all and converting it into the excrement of mindless chants. The spectacle resembled a pro wrestling entertainment match. Talk of good guys and bad guys, with no in-betweens regarding the matter. Problems inevitably solved with tough words often followed with aggression. There was Smoke. There was confetti. There were the layered colors of stage lights. Prop cannons booming. A cartoon that looked tailor made for eleven-year-olds. All of it capped off at the end of the night by a massive, prop eagle, ten feet tall, that came down from a pulley system toward center stage; flapping its wings in place, as David P. Betty dropped the microphone to the stage and walked out to the same familiar pop country song -strutting off like the wrestling protagonist who took the shit talking, cocky villain out of commission- just like he promised he would, in front of a primetime audience in the tens of millions. A screeching noise blared from the PA system just as red, white, and blue confetti shot out into the audience in multiple bursts from the mouth of the giant eagle that looked as though yanked off the set of a 1980s glam heavy metal band.

By the time David P. Betty was through for the night, he had told his audience that his liberal competitors were a bunch of hippies; brainwashed by out of touch professors and not possessing the street smarts to know what was *really* going on in the world. Told them what the intentions of the masses outside of their country really were. Told them that a liberal government would take away their guns. Would take away their rights. Would take away their free speech. Told them that tax cuts for the rich and less regulations on big business would make the wealth trickle down to the good common folk of his constituency. Told them that higher taxes would only go into politicians' pockets and nowhere else. He told them all that a prerogative toward global involvement was only meant to short change Americans now and forever. He told them that an education might well brainwash them and turn them soft; this being aimed at the menfolk especially, *soft* being a subtle equating to impotent, or homosexual, in the minds of those who listened.

Betty implied, as well. He implied, on this night- as in so many other nights of the past year and a half of campaigning- that a simple life was the life of the true American patriot; always was and always would be. Implied that white culture and identity were the features most strongly associated with the best of times for the country. Implied that the 1950s and early 60s were the ideal era while ignoring any issues, whatsoever, that those times had. Ignored all context, like a WWII devastated and rebuilding Europe and Japan unable to compete; like kind, but spiritually deprived women diverting back to their traditional roles -for a time- to comfort and appease their shell-shocked men. Implied that minorities were inferior and, for the most part, deserved their various levels of social oppression and their worst stereotypes.

Betty Implied that hard work would *always* get a person ahead. No question about it. No matter what. Implied that rich and powerful men almost invariably came by their wealth honestly, were therefore entitled to it, and would invariably dole out a good chunk of it -on their own accord, thank you very much- to help the less fortunate. So long as they weren't forced to. Implied, as well, that wealth itself was the result of hard work, and that lack thereof was the result of laziness. Implied that those without Christian values were lost and dangerous in some, intangible, way that did not require further explanation. But they were certainly not to be associated with and not to be trusted. Implied that Christian values in one's upbringing inevitably lead to upright and upstanding moral citizenship. Implied that religious principles were far more important for society to focus on than scientific facts. Implied that scientists were not actually in agreement about many issues in which they, in fact, were in- almost universally.

The lights finally illuminated the crowd once again, amidst the fog of disturbing messages that had enveloped Dr. John's mind. It shocked and appalled him that, at times, he found himself almost compelled to just go along with the spectacle. From somewhere deep within the lizard brain, he was compelled. From some place that primitively removed, nearly altogether, the burden of critical thought or the idea that it was needed. It would be so easy to go along with this. It was so cathartic, albeit, in the most misguided and overtly harmful of ways. At no point had Betty given tangible plans about what he would do, directly for the people, in their day to day lives. Nothing about *how* he would be developing new jobs for them. Nothing about the promising future of green energy. Nothing about ways to individually adapt to changing job markets and diversity, beyond trying to revive the former in a way it never could be, and to minimize and hold back the latter. And none of that, somehow, seemed to matter to the audience as he focused, instead, on embellished *outside* entities; why they should be immentently feared, and the people's need for protection from them.

Dr. John looked around him without capacity to organize this thoughts or emotions. He felt he might fall at any time. He perceived his body now beginning to shake with anger in the aftermath of this; most of all, over the fact that this spectacle was clearly working. It was *clearly* working. He was struck suddenly with the feeling that he lived in a bubble. Practically everyone he knew and met where he lived viewed this person as something of a sick joke, though lately, with a growing realization that he was not so to more people than they could have possibly imagined. This man did have myriad followers despite the clear falsehood of his message; which John knew many of his supporters must have, at least, sensed on some level.

It hit him now, and a feeling of nausea accompanied his shaking body. This man could win. This realization came to him at a velocity he could not cope with. A Multitude of emotions were co-occurring so strongly that he could not act. He could not so much as formulate any actions to move from where he stood. His breathing became stressed. He was growing lightheaded and unable to focus, as though witnessing a trauma that overwhelmed and enveloped him and, worse yet, he knew he could do absolutely nothing about.

Dr. John's mind took him back to the only time and place that he could compare this experience with. It took him back to September 11th, 2001 and watching the twin towers toppling; as viewed from helicopter footage above. Desperate, suffocating people on rooftops disappeared into plumes of flame and rubble. He was a senior in college, in the early fall semester. Just before seeing the images, he realized, bizarrely, that he was alone at the computer lab in a nearly abandoned library- everyone initially with him having shuffled out, at various times, outside of his purview while his eyes were glued to the screen- his hands typing desperately in attempt to finish his first essay for Poli-Sci, which was due in less than an hour. When he could hear nothing but the clacking of his own two hands on the keyboard, he realized how odd this was in a very immediate sort of way. He got up and walked around the library that looked as though it were somehow closed in the late morning of a weekday, in the heart of the semester.

The sun cast dust particles in slanted rectangles through the window panes; floating lazily and undisturbed by non-existent passersby. The whirling of the air conditioning system that was never heard so audibly, due to being obscured by the activity of people walking, clacking keyboards, and conversing in hushed tones. He realized, by seeing an occasional student jogging (jogging in a library?) from time to time, that everyone was congregating in the same room. It was the main conference room. He joined the sporadic procession and came upon dozens of young faces staring- jaws agape, watery eyes with white visible on tops and bottoms of the irises- at replays of the recent tragedy flickering in front of them from a large projector screen. An unkempt Psychology professor that he'd had once had (and instinctively disliked) looked about the room at the students taking it all in; finding it more important to study their reactions, as an observer, as opposed to subjecting herself to sharing in the trauma alongside them; a trauma that would be a defining moment of his generation, with lasting social, political, and personal consequences for his country and much of the world.

In a mind state that could only be compared to where he was at in that particular moment in time, Dr. John effortfully forced himself to shuffle back toward the exits. His shocked body was soon inundated anew. Splashed back into the shouting and the slurs. Into the palpable, cathartic anger being regurgitated. As he came to the outer corridor there were sounds of things breaking. Glass hitting walls and the splashing of its pieces as they sprawled outward like clusters of scrambling, crystalline arachnids across pavement. All of it seemed muffled for a moment until a glass bottle shattered just to his side- inches away- right as he exited the building.

Before this moment, John's mind had temporarily lost its ability to take in any additional stimuli. It had wrapped him up in a blanket of self-protective, mental fog. But now, with the renewed chaos surrounding him, his senses sharpened as adrenaline hit. The sudden smack of the below freezing wind chill, combined with the bizarrely wavelike sounds of the shattering glass (like holding a conch to his ear) brought him even more so to his senses. Finally, the image of a client just several yards in front of him succeeded in bringing Dr. John fully back and ready to do whatever it took to get both himself, and this young man, away from the mayhem.

Part III: The Aftermath

It was Kenilworth, clear as day, no less than ten yards in front of him, walking stiffly with his head down; winding through the departing crowd. The familiar, pilled polo shirt was visible above his jacket's zipper.

"Washington!" John screamed, breaking the rule of never verbally engaging with a client in public without having their express permission first.

Kenilworth looked over his shoulder, fixated his eyes on John, and greeted him, "Dr. John?" His face began to contort in shock and disbelief before questioning, "You're a David Betty supporter?"

Dr. John nudged his way through the jacked-up crowd and grabbed Kenilworth with a surprising amount of force. He replied in a more subdued and hushed tone, "of course not. I'm just here on research. I'm guessing you're doing the same?"

"Yes, I am trying to understand," Kenilworth responded. His facial features looked fearful in an unexpected way, as though they had tried, but could not possibly make sense of, how this type of event could elicit this sort of emotional response in which he was now embedded. Dr. John could relate, though his own response was mitigated by the fact that he knew how people could behave illogically; knew, as well, how outside messages could spur this on and magnify it. John responded in shared understanding of the feeling.

"I don't fully get it either, Kenilworth, and I've studied and practiced psychology for over fifteen years. But we'll talk about it later. Let's get you out of here."

Dr. John guided Kenilworth toward an area north of where they met, which seemed at present to be the least chaotic in their vicinity (though this wasn't saying much). Both walked briskly and tried to keep their heads low. Suddenly, Dr. John felt Kenilworth lurch into his side, before falling in a jumbled heap of failed limbs to the pavement. An errant fist had landed unexpectedly into Kenilworth's right temple. He rubbed it from the ground.

"Get up, Washington!" John shouted as he propped the woozy young man up and forced him on; grasping his arm around his back and pressing his body to his own side for support. "Keep walking!"

John pushed through what ever miniscule space was available on the sidewalk; Kenilworth in tow as he bumped and side-stepped through the masses. They passed through, sluggishly, like two red blood cells pushing, single file, through the thinnest of capillaries. He saw pockets of police men beating back protesters with batons. Some were beating them, almost rythymically. Like pounding out a beat on a drum. Many of the protesters seemed to be of no significant threat; just trying to get out of the way while holding both hands above their skulls to protect their brain. He heard the pop in the distance of what sounded like projectiles shooting out of a plastic tube. Tear gas? No, something else, but he didn't know what. A flash of deep orange on the brick wall of the UIC pavilion illuminated angry faces attached to wildly flailing arms and feet, trying to make contact with any person who seemed on the opposing side.

Fire rained down on the concrete behind them. It was a Molotov cocktail. Dr. John felt myriad, fleeting tinges of pain from limbs hitting the various parts of his body, whether accidental or on purpose. He moved through the crowds, gripping the side of Kenilworth, whose body movements timed with his, albeit in a weak, limb dragging limp. That was as fast as they could push through, anyway. John's senses, alert beyond what they may have ever been, picked up on everything. Pockets of growing, acrid smelling fumes. Ambulances and fire truck lights flashing on all sides. Writhing, aggressive body movements. Fighting, and the ever present, contorted hateful faces yelling.

"Fuck you nigger! Fuck these Muslims! White power!"

"Motherfucking bigots! Ima fuck you up!"

"Fuckin' libtards! Go back to your yuppie assed, hippie assed, condos!"

"Fuckin' rednecks! Get the fuck outta my city! Go back to your trailer park off the highway!"

Dr. John made his way to a small clearing and spotted a cab driver slowing down on this, the first open road he saw, just north of the Pavilion. He pushed the limp form of Kenilworth into the backseat, threw three twenty-dollar bills at the cabbie and shouted, "Take him to Englewood! He'll tell you where from there."

"Fuck that, I ain't takin' him to Englewood."

Dr. John threw two more twenties at the cabbie. "How about now?"

The cabbie gave a curt, appeased nod. Dr. John slammed the door shut and the cabbie sped off as soon as he heard the familiar clack. John, now alone, without Kenilworth to look after, felt an abrupt re-emerging fear for his own body, though as soon as the thought hit him, a menacing group of men came upon him.

"You motherfucking racist, bigot!" The leader shouted.

"I'm not! That's not who I am!" Dr. John implored.

"Fuck you, you scared ass mother fucker. You just afraid to admit it like all those other mother fuckers in there. Closeted racist mother fucker!"

"I'm not! I work on the south side! That's not who I am." He pleaded.

Just as the group's leader, a large black man, grabbed him by the collar of his flannel, another group came upon them.

"What are you spicks, niggers, and self-hating whites doing to this good man?"

"Mother fucker! What'd you call us?"

Dr. John was pushed away as the two groups quickly came to blows. He wasn't sure why they had helped him, but soon remembered it was obvious he looked the part of a Betty supporter. John supposed, if Betty won, he would for some time to come; have awkward moments with any number of minorities who would be right to question if he was, indeed, a closeted racist, or at least a tribalist, which was not much better, but simply sounded better to those who used the word. This, among a number of other undesirable traits he'd seen in many of Betty's supporters, could easily become suspect in him, and the sad fact now hit him now, with its full weight.

John continued shoving his way through the remaining traffic jam of people, until he spied enough of an opening to break into a jog as the crowd cleared just enough to gain some momentum. Bumping, changing direction, nearly tripping several times along the way toward the parking lot; he finally made his way safely to his car, turned on the engine and sped out as quickly as possible down Congress Parkway. He was less than a half a block out of the lot, picking up speed, when a glass bottle smacked into his front windshield-instantly forming a spider's web on the glass along the driver's side. John hunched forward toward the steering wheel and squinted through the visible part just above. He took a sharp turn north and wound his way through neighborhood roads to avoid the sporadic crowds. He found his way to 290 heading toward Lake Shore and sped off back to Evanston. A thirty-foot high billboard with a beaming, confident David P. Betty, adorned with American flag background and a soaring eagle, greeted him as he drove the onramp. Soft lights, glowing white, jutted through his car windows, fleeting and at random, from helicopter spotlights overhead.

Less than a mile from where Dr. John was hauling ass away, the specially assembled Marmot News panel was continuing their coverage from downtown. McCannon looking at the camera in serious composure; at the moment, running play by play of the aftermath. Bud looked on in only slightly suppressed shock while Pat C. Flowers looked meekly in various directions-avoiding direct eye contact with the other two panelists, and the camera. Until moments ago, the panel was reporting along to the events inside of the vast stadium. David Betty's message catered to, all the while, aside from brief periods of Flowers pitifully attempting to offer alternative explanations. The reporting on this dischord as being anything but liberals having run amuck would not be had tonight.

The event was described-in a broadcast that had become progressively more dominated by McCannon- as a resounding success by the network. A strong and able man, far removed from the trappings of the career politicians, had brought his message to the masses, and with authority. His use of effects, actors, and props had skillfully created a most powerful visual medium for his audience. It was entertaining, sure, but it was certainly not a "spectacle" or a "circus," like the liberal media elite were trying to portray it.

This panel, and McCannon especially, preferred to view it as a way to both enrich his audience with his message and entertain them as well. And what was wrong with a little entertainment? As opposed to, let's face it, just having to listen to another late middle-aged, upper-class man drone on all night from behind a podium? With that thought thoroughly in mind all along, and with an almost universal acceptance of his viewpoints (albeit, with some feigned hesitation, at times, to the harsher points of the night), the panelists moved on to the aftermath. McCannon commenced his assessment:

"Well, Bud…Flowers. Look at this spectacle we have here. And I'm not surprised. Once again, our good David Betty comes to a liberal city, bringing his message. His message that makes a whole lot of sense, by the way, for those whose minds haven't been clouded with PC liberal nonsense. And guess what happens.

Pow! Bunch of liberal protesters turn violent at the drop of a hat. Just like last time!"

"Actually," added Pat Flowers in a slightly less meek voice that almost (almost) conveyed some level of confidence in his viewpoints, "from what I saw, many if not *most* of the fights seemed to be brought on by Betty's audience and/or pro-Betty groups."

"Oh, shut up, Flowers! (a fist in the air toward Flowers that made him coil back) What? Yeah, that's right. *Shut* it! How do you even know who's who, anyway, to say what side they were on?"

"Well, signs for one. It's pretty easy to identify pro versus anti-Betty groups from the signs they're holding. Also, the neo-Nazis have a certain wardrobe, and they're almost always in support of Betty."

"Shut up, Flowers! With your nonsense about signs. If you had a sign it would say *Pencil Neck Brain-washed Libtard.* Written in hot pink sharpie!"

"No, I certainly would not. I would…"

"*Boom*!"

"Huh? Umm, I mean, I would..."

"*Pow*!" McCannon's fist came back toward Flowers' head.

"Umm, I would.."

"*Pow*! Pow *pow*!" McCannon was using his index fingers like little pistols now.

"Are you making pistol noises with your hands? Is that what you're doing right now?"

"Shut up, Flowers. Patty Cake Flowers."

"Hey," interjected Bud, who had grown progressively less verbal as the show went on. "Just lay off the guy, McCannon. Yah don' have tah bully him on air. Poor S.O.B. that he is n' all."

"Aw shucks." McCannon toned it down just slightly for the moment. "Settle down, old man. Just havin' some fun with the guy. Don't go getting soft on me, now. Haven't heard much from you tonight either, come to think of it."

McCannon turned back toward the camera, after a brief ensuing moment in which he waited to see if Bud was going to add anything else, before continuing:

"Anyway, like I always tell you, my faithful Marmot News followers. This is what you get when you a have a sound, strong, no-nonsense man come into a hopeless, failed liberal city like Chicago. You get a bunch of entitled welfare kings and queens trying to halt his message cuz they're afraid of losing their government aid. You get a bunch of self-hating liberal whites trying to stick up for freeloaders, Muslims, and thugs because they've been brainwashed to think it was *society* as opposed to *individual choices* that put these people in their current life circumstances. Beyond that, you get a bunch of PC libtards who want to ignore the hard truths in life rather than address them. You get a failed, so-called 'diverse' city up in arms because they know. Deep down, they know, mind you, that their views are flawed, but they're too self-deluded to admit it. *Pow!*" A fist punch toward the camera. "There's a dose of truth for ya'all. Now, this concludes our broadcast of our good David P. Betty's rally here in Chicago tonight. Stay tuned to Marmot News for coverage continuing through the night on this. Next up is the *No Spin Hour* with our veteran newscaster, Scoop O'Mulligan. Stay tuned."

The cameras panned away from the group as old-time country music with patriotic themes played in the background. McCannon could be seen playfully (in his view) pushing Pat Flowers in his chair, several times over, before firmly mussing his hair again. Bud sat looking directly forward as though not wanting to be in the room, which was most definitely the case. Right now, Bud wanted simply to get back on his private jet for L.A. He longed to sit next to his pool and drink a Bourbon milk punch with his Esperanza reading quietly by his side. His mind was reflecting on this simple fantasy of just getting back to day to day life when he felt a moderately hard punch on his left arm. The flabbiness made it sound quite a lot like a baker punching rising bread in a bowl.

"Motherfucker what was *that*!" Unsurprisingly, the voice belonged to Edward McCannon.

"Huh?" Bud was trying to register what had just happened, having previously felt relatively certain that Flowers was the only one who got punched on the show.

"You're Bud Harbaugh, mother fucker." McCannon railed in seeming exasperation at having to remind him. "Did you forget that? Who was that meek guy on the show tonight? Started out strong, sure, but by the end of the night you were pretty much like pencil-neck over there. Sitting around without an opinion and just leaving it all for me to carry your candy ass. The fuck's going on, old man?" McCannon thought about it for a moment before adding, "You know, I think you need a vacation or something, Bud. I mean, seriously. Looks like you got your mind on things, bro. Hey, maybe you should come out tonight with me and my boys."

"Your fuckin' boys," replied Bud with just a hint of sarcasm.

"That's right! My fuckin' *boys*! *Woo*!" replied McCannon with the enthusiasm often seen in the initial stages of a crack high. The sarcasm was clearly lost on him. "Flowers is goin'. How bout that?" He added, pointing his thumb over his shoulder back at Pat C.

"That's alright, son. You have fun. I gotta get home." Bud began the process of removing himself from his chair, trying to make haste, as much as he could, given his significant heft.

"Suits me just fine. But hey, seriously Bud." McCannon guided him back into his chair by pushing down on his shoulder; clearly not consenting to letting Bud leave, yet. "You should take a little break. Heck, come to think of it, maybe you should consider retirement. You been at it a long time, my friend. I mean a long, *long* time. And I got the future covered over here, don't you worry about that." McCannon added a hearty back slap-

generating the familiar sound of a dough punch and sending Bud lurching forward in his chair. Bud, uncharacteristically agitated at a fellow Marmot News associate, shot back at him.

"If you're the future then we're *fucked*, son. You're supposed to show people why they should be supporting our party and making it clear that the liberals are lost and misguided. What you're doing is getting militant about things and willfully associating yourself with our worst elements."

McCannon gave Bud a serious and perusing look for a moment, as though trying to figure out where this little hissy fit came from. After a moment, he decided not to further pursue the conversation, got up from his chair and began to walk away from the table.

"Flowers, you coming?" He said nonchalantly, as he strutted, unaffected, toward backstage.

Flowers walked over to McCannon briskly and with his head held high. His persona had changed from a meek, nerdy and bullied one to a man with some level of composure and self-confidence; the man he was in real life as opposed to his TV facade. Just before the two began to walk away together, out the side entryway to the set, McCannon turned back to Bud and added, with a flat expression and a stone-cold gaze:

"You know, Bud. Whether you like it or not, I *am* the future of Marmot News. You better get used to that fact right now. And you better understand this, too. The only way a person can become a bigger name than you in this business is to one up you. That's what I'm doing and that's what I'll continue to do. I'm suggesting you go along with it or get the hell out of the way. Cuz I just got a five-year deal with a fat bonus check and my ratings are off the Goddamned chart." He jutted his finger toward Bud. "You better watch yourself, old man. I'm telling you right now, you better not get on my bad side. Take some time off and think about it. Then you come back and see me. Alright? We'll have a few drinks and shoot the shit."

Bud looked back at McCannon, met his gaze and said, "Fuck you, you perpetual frat boy fuck."

McCannon held Bud's stern gaze for a moment, before his expression softened and he started to chuckle.

"That's the spirit, old man. Maybe you ain't done for, just yet," and with that he turned and walked out, arm around Flower's back giving him a good-natured shake.

Bud would be fuming the rest of the night. In a state of semi-repressed rage, he boarded the private helicopter from the pad atop Marmot News' Chicago offices, which from there took him directly to his private jet at Chicago Executive Airport for his flight back to L.A. Bud could not bring himself to falling asleep on the flight- no chance- and downed several tumblers half full of fine bourbon liquor well into the wee hours.

In a state of drunkenness that Bud rarely attained these days (due to his absurdly high tolerance for alcohol in combination with his weight and the fact he almost always had food in his stomach) he found himself fantasizing about harming McCannon. Harming him severely, for that matter. It gave him much comfort, doing so. He played out various scenarios in his mind. Him drop kicking McCannon in the kiwis and then sending him flying backwards- like an end of the level bad guy in a video game- with a powerful uppercut. Him catching McCannon with a devastating kidney punch before taking him down with a well-placed kick to the side of the knee, tearing his ACL tendon in the process and making him scream in agony. A greatly pleasing sound to Bud's ear. Him punching McCannon square in the throat then jumping up, Bruce Less style, to present him with a round house kick to the face. Begrudgingly, Bud acknowledged that the last option was certainly not the most realistic."

Bud, distracted by thoughts of abusing McCannon, unmercifully, eventually found himself driven by his private chauffeur, in the morning twilight, toward his compound. He was still unable to rest, still fuming over a display of disrespect that had grown rare for him these days. The familiar palms lining the roads of the greater L.A. area began as dark outlines against the deep, purple-ish blue hues of the early dawn. A growing orb of bright orange beginning to peek just above the horizon. Over the roughly forty-five-minute drive, the palms became progressively more visible. The horizontal lines along the bark. The light, sun kissed green of the high fronds, overlaid by the amber and golden hues of the dying leaves of the inner foliage. The cream white of mansions with their Spanish tiles in Burnt Sienna. By the time they reached the familiar Cahuenga Boulevard, the Hollywood Hills were glowing brilliantly with the sunrise, and it gave Bud something almost akin to comfort as the limo pulled into the compound.

Bud thanked his driver, Alberto, and walked through the custom waterfall mirage door with inlaid aquamarine lining. Bud traversed the compound's interior and soon fixed his eyes upon Esperanza, who appeared to have just recently settled in by the pool. She was sipping her customary morning drink; a cafe au lait. Bud went to sit next to her in his Adirondack chair with attached canvas cushioning.

"Long night?" Came a familiar voice from the opposite side of Esperanza. A small extent of care seemed evident, within its overall passive detachment, in regarding him.

"Yes. Thank you, Paulo." Paulo had presently brought Bud his bourbon milk punch, nearly as quickly as he'd sat down. "Yes indeed, a long night (a drawn-out slurp, then, a contented smack of the lips). Damn, that McCannon guy is a real asshole," Bud fumed, looking straight ahead at nothing in particular. "Fucking openly bigoted, cocky, obnoxious, frat house fuck."

"Sorry, you're describing *who*?" Queried Esperanza, as she put down her magazine.

"Oh, fuck you, woman. I know what you're thinking, you can just stop right there," Bud shot back, before sighing, adding, "look, the difference is, I do what I do for *show*. And this guy, this mother fucker, McCannon. He *believes* his own bullshit. That's his problem." Bud looked toward Esperanza as though he had just made a profound insight in identifying this relatively common occurrence. "He agrees with the worst elements of our constituency. And worst of all. Worst of all, chica, he has no respect for a more level-headed person such as myself."

"Level headed? Really?" Esperanza had gone back to her magazine, talking to him without bothering to look up from it.

"Oh, piss off, missy! Can't you see how upset I am by all of this?" Bud took a long glug of his drink, downing the remaining half of the concoction of simple sugar, hard liquor, heavy cream and recent addition Paulo loogie. He took a look at the finished glass and then chucked it into the infinity pool. A marble-sized floating white chunked eventually dislodged from it and bobbed around nearby in the water.

Esperanza perused him for a moment. She gathered that he was going to be taking things a little more seriously; be a little more sensitive to her responses than usual this morning. Despite her better instincts, she thought she might make some headway with a little constructive criticism. She added:

"He's trying to one up you. What else would you expect? You don't get famous peddling something that people have already been peddling before. Doing it the exact same way. What's the appeal of that? This guy, this McCannon, feels like he has to go beyond what you've done in order to be heard. To get famous and to get rich. I mean, that's all it's about anyway, right? Get rich. Who gives a flying fuck about how you do it or what harm it causes. So, way to go, Bud. There's your legacy." Esperanza put down her magazine and gave him a half-hearted round of applause, before getting serious again and concluding. "This McCannon is a beast of your own creation."

Bud suppressed a look of understanding- as he did understand and agree with everything she had just said- though he had much difficulty, as of yet, in fully admitting this. Bud chose, instead of acknowledging the harsh truth of her words, to simply glare back at Esperanza; bitter toward her for pointing out something he already knew but was hoping she would have a more comforting answer for. Esperanza met Bud's glare for a moment with one of her own behind her dark sunglasses, and eventually sighed in exasperation before responding. "Well this morning is starting out just *great*. I think I'm about ready to go take a coffee shit now. Enjoy wallowing in your self-pity, you fat fucking asshole."

"Fuck off, bitch! I hope there's no toilet paper!"

Esperanza walked away. Bud fumed silently. He observed that Paulo had already, with expert timing and stealth, placed another cocktail in the beverage holder to his left and he downed it in a quick series of glugs. He held the tumbler up and jiggled the ice cubes around, before chucking this glass past the infinity pool, into the brush in the distance beyond. A dog barked aggressively, some ways away.

Bud found himself in a growingly hypnagogic state. The vast amounts of alcohol, combined with the accumulated waking hours, were finally beating out the bursts of adrenaline he'd been having all night long. He lay back to rest his head on the canvas cushion, and gazed toward the Hollywood Reservoir, its slowly undulating waters reflecting the fleeting feathery plumes of white light reflected from the rising sun. He glanced out toward Griffith Park and its lush, deep green hues; compliments of the various conifer trees strewn about within the forest. It was a bright, clear view accompanied by a soothing morning breeze that Bud Harbaugh began to notice and take in as he calmed himself. After a few deep breaths he closed his eyes and felt a welcoming sense of peace coming to him at last. Behind him, audible through the second story, open bathroom window, he heard several obnoxious, juicy farts, followed by what could only be a sloppy flow of excrement. Bud's anger rushed back instantaneously. "Close the fucking window!" He chided, and just then a moment of intense pain intruded, and his body slumped to the side. Soon after, Paulo was upon him, another fresh cocktail in hand.

At first, Paulo thought the fat asshole was just sleeping. He was prone to nodding off like this and it happened not infrequently. As he gave him a gentle nudge on the shoulder, he realized, this was not sleep. The look pasted to his face was one of sloppiness and irritability. He pulled out his cell phone and dialed the numbers slowly. Nine one one, then casually brought the phone to his ear. He very much doubted the man would be coming back from this one. Paulo was connected promptly and did his civic duty. He reported what happened coolly, gave the address, and hung up the phone. He began to sip the cold beverage and to look out over the view that Bud had seen in his last moments. Not a bad way to go, he thought. Certainly, he could have done much worse. An impressively long, muffled trumpet blare of a fart sounded off in the background, serving as Bud's final serenade.

Chapter XIV

A Crafted Beast

"Kitty!...Kitty!" Dreadson spouted, obnoxiously, into the intercom. "Oh, where the hell is she?" He added, to himself, in the small handful of seconds that ensued. "Seriously, I never know what that half useless 'ol biddy is doing over there."

"Yes, Mr. Dreadson. Sorry about that," an exhausted and panting voice came through.

"You're slipping, Kitty," came the scolding reply. "Don't like that one bit, missy. And here I thought we were making improvements in your efficiency."

"Sorry, sir," added Kitty, now trying to muffle the sounds of her chewing with a cupped hand. She had popped a wild cherry stool softener just prior to Dreadson's call.

"Kitty?"

"Yes, sir."

"Damn it!"

"I'm so sorry, sir."

"Oh God damn it. I'm sorry about that," Dreadson relented, to her great surprise. "It's just been such stressful times recently, Kitty. I shouldn't have taken that out on you, especially now. You know what? Take the rest of the day off, sweet heart.

Once you get that fine young man into my office, your work is done for the day. How you like them apples, darlin'?"

"Thank you, sir. I like them apples just fine." Kitty added before patching through to Grant on the other line to inform him of Dreadson's request. Kitty looked at the foot long, three inch diameter, diabetes-inducing candy cane atop her desk. It had arrived a few weeks ago at her home address and she liked to look at it, from to time, as she fantasized about beating Dreadson to death with it, screaming "Ho ho ho, Mr. Dreadson, ho ho, fucking, ho!" over and over. She patted it, lovingly, for a moment before putting it back into her desk. She thought to herself, "another day, Kitty. Get a cocktail at happy hour and enjoy your time off."

Grant was in a state neither fully conscious nor asleep. He sat, reclined in a near stupor, afraid to fully let himself drift to sleep lest Dreadson had some last minute, pressing business that would invariably involve him. In front of Scott; a quart sized, Sasquatch brand thermos of Kopi Luwak shit brew sat reeking. It was not doing the trick in taking him out of his quarter conscious haze. He was still drinking that putrid mud water, day in and day out, damn it all to hell. He simply could not bring himself to say no to his wife's coffee of choice, after all. He'd resigned himself to his fate. Worse, Patty had gotten him this, comically oversized, steel thermos that even a veteran long-haul trucker would probably look at and think was overdoing it, maybe just a tad.

These days, his entire office continued to smell vaguely of washed out excrement, like poopy jeans that had been washed in a sink without soap. Compliments, of course, of the vapor emanating from the Sasquatch brand, rhinoceros stampede-proof (there were online videos to prove this), ultra-thermos. The vapor working its way into the walls, day by day. Strange glances from visitors to his office; who wondered if Scott might have an indisclosed personal issue with anal seepage.

His head would fall into a series of nods, followed by jerking itself back to consciousness. A beeping from his phone intervened, just as he was losing his battle to stay awake. He jerked his head all the way back from where it had rested briefly on the desk. He patched Kitty through.

"Mr. Scott? Are you there, sir?"

"Huh? Uh, yuh. Yuh. Uh huh."

"Mr. Dreadson would like to meet with you. And Mr. Scott, on behalf of me personally, would you please go home and get some rest tonight. I'm worried about you."

"Uh huh, okay. Yuh…yuh huh."

Grant opened the lid of his half gallon size cup of of coffee and impulsively decided to dip his entire left hand in it.

"*Ack*! Hummana hummana, hummana."

He felt confident this might give him another ten minutes, tentatively, of wakefulness. He wiped the coffee off his hand with a few Kleenex and made his way up toward his door, forgetting even to straighten out his tie. He progressed down the hallway, at a speed on par with a 1960s era zombie, toward Dreadson's office. As he came upon the door, he lurched the handle with as much force as he could muster from his latissimus dorsi and began the trudge toward Dreadson's desk. So tired was he, that the momentary shock of the massive, hanging megalodon scarcely made an impression at all. It was late morning, November 3rd.

"Scott! Get your ass over here, boy. Hah hah! Mother fucker we did it! President-Elect David P. Betty. Hot damn!" Dreadson smacked his hands together loudly at the latter two words.

Scott continued to wobbily mosey, suppressing yawns, his head looking down toward the floor; getting a visual of his duty to simply keep putting one foot in front of the other. Eventually, he made it to the familiar, antique nobleman's chairs and plopped down with the enthusiasm of a sexually active teen attending a mandatory lecture on abstinence. Dreadson, clearly excited, though slightly perturbed by Scott's presentation, added:

"Damn, son. You need to perk up. We won, mother fucker! We *won!*" He beamed a smile toward Scott in the hopes that he would get one back.

"Yes, sir."

"Betty is *in!* Against all odds! Thanks, in no small part mind you, to your efforts, my friend. Hoo-*wee*, son!" He leaned the top half of his body over the desk and started jutting his right finger into Scott's sternum repetitively. "And they didn't think he had a chance (poke, poke). We knew better (poke, poke, poke). Didn't we (poke)."

"Yes, sir, Mr. Dreadson. We did."

"Got a fat bonus for you, son." Dreadson went back behind his desk and pulled something from a lower drawer. "Think fast!" And in that moment, Dreadson threw a black duffel bag full of cash at Scott.

"Hoof! Ahh!" Barked Scott, as the bag landed squarely on his solar plexus and sent him, and the chair, leaning back a full thirty degrees for a moment. Fuck it all. How did this keep happening?

"Watch yourself now, son. That's a cool million for ya, for a job well done! Now I'm going to get up and shake your hand, my boy."

"Mr. Dreadson, no! Please, no, that's fine," Scott implored. His look confounded Dreadson for a moment as he seemed...disgusted? Yes, disgusted, for some reason.

"What is it, son? Oh...oh, yeah." He looked downward. "Ah yes, the erection. I'm sorry about that," replied Dreadson, who had gotten up and was standing directly in front of Scott with his fully erect penis looking as though about to burst the flimsy button of his boxer shorts. The old man was not wearing any pants under his desk, apparently, and Scott was made hastily aware of this with a fossilized chubby a foot away from his head.

"You know, son," Dreadson continued, unhindered by the awkwardness that could accompany such a display for most people. "I've had this for the past three hours, at least. Plum forgot I did for a minute, there. And you know what? Didn't even have to take one of those little blue pills neither. How about that? Okay, well maybe just one of 'em. But, still, not too shabby, eh?"

"Sir, please. Could you *please* just put some pants on?"

"Ah hah hah! Why, no! Of course not, son, of course not. But tell you what, I will when I go back out in public, alright. Not quite as rowdy as in my younger days anymore and they're bound to come down harder on you for that type of thing these days, any hows. Now, son, go home and spend that money. You did it, boy!" Dreadson came in for a hug, but saw Scott reeling back. "Oh, yeah, forgot about that, hehehe. Well anyway, son, I have never been prouder of you. Go on and get now, shoosh!" He playfully shook Scott out of his office.

Scott collected himself slowly; strapped the large duffel bag around his shoulder. The weight of it caused his limp body to stoop toward the side, several inches, under the weight. Duffle bag in tow, he now looked like a zombie coming back from the gym. He slowly shuffled out of the office, when, around halfway, he was struck by a sudden thought. A thought that had never occurred to him until this moment, though came to him now, for reasons unknown. He turned back to Dreadson and spoke, with more candor than typically. He was too tired to care what came out when he asked the old man:

"Sir, have you ever considered whether we should be doing what we are doing? From a moral standpoint, I mean. Do you think we should be doing this?"

Dreadson slowly eased his head up from the paperwork he was looking at on his desk and eyeballed the young man for a time. His face was flat, though his eyes intensely focused. He seemed both surprised and irritated by the utterance. Dreadson, holding this look for a time, got up slowly. He began to walk toward the wall of windows and looked out of them to gaze upon the mid-day sun. Scott knew this as his routine for when he wanted to gather his thoughts. Scott remained in waiting for what appeared to be some time as Dreadson held his gaze off into the distance. Scott could also see the boner had receded, a sure sign that this had made him unhappy. Dreadson was not a man who's parade you should rain on; the young man well knew. Folding his hands behind his back, Dreadson continued looking out the window, then he began to shake his head slowly. He replied:

"Scott, your old man asked me that same question not long before he passed," he spoke with a slow exhale. "Asked it a few times, matter of fact, toward the end. That question was what started him on the path to ruin, young man."

Dreadson, turned back toward Scott, and his expression was hard to read. Sadness in it, to be sure, but also frustration, concern, and disappointment.

"I'm sorry, sir." Scott always felt compelled to apologize when he upset Dreadson. "It's just, I'm tired, and, for the first time in months, I've actually had the time to think and reflect about something outside of work."

"Well, *don't*, son," Dreadson shot a cold glance toward him. "Alright? Don't. And if you need to think about something, think about how to spend that money. Or think about getting frisky with your wife. Think about playing with your kids. These thoughts you just brought up? That line of thought will get you nowhere. That line of thinking will cause you needless stress. When you're here, you focus on one thing, which is doing *your* job and getting *our* ratings up. People have a choice to decide what they want to decide, like I said before. If they think there's something wrong with what we're doing, they can click a button to turn to another channel. Turn the knob to another radio program. They can read a book. Shit, they can go start an ant farm, for all I care. You got me? Get those thoughts out of your head, young man. This is a job to you and nothing more. You got me?"

"Yes, sir." Scott was too exhausted to continue, and he wondered what could have gotten into him. He should have just left to go home, to go to bed.

Dreadson relaxed a tad and let out a long sigh. His paternal instincts toward the boy kicked in; always winning out in the end.

"Go home, son. Take the next couple weeks off and then get your ass back here ready to start fresh around the middle of the month. Or the end of the month for that matter. Hell, take off until the week after Thanksgiving. And, son?"

"Yes, Mr. Dreadson."

"Don't go thinking too hard about the bigger picture." Dreadson waved a didactic finger at him for emphasis. "We're all just tiny little cogs in a machine we can neither see nor understand as an entity. Remember that."

"Yes, sir. Thank you for the bonus." And Grant left without another word, not wanting to spoil this neutral ending for the afternoon.

Grant Scott kept his car parked today, not trusting he wouldn't fall asleep on the road. He had the doorman wave a taxi back home. Maybe Ginny could taxi or rideshare back later and get the car for him. He would remember little after getting into the cab and giving his home address. He fell asleep instantly in the backseat, and seemingly moments after he did so, the cabbie was stopped in front of his driveway, asking Scott to please pay his fare. Scott pulled a hundred-dollar bill out of one of the bundles of hundreds lying within the overstuffed duffle bag and gave it to him. The cabbie took it quickly and gave him a meek, sheepish and overly thankful look; the type of look you give a man not to be fucked with. Perhaps the driver was a little perturbed by thoughts of what a passenger with a large bag of money like that might do for a living.

Scott pulled himself out of the car and tottered a path toward the house. Ginny greeted him as he entered. He kissed her, dropped the bag on the kitchen floor with a resounding thud, went over and fell onto the living room couch. Ginny implored her hubby to take a nap for the next couple of hours and assured him she would just be busy cooking anyway. She had recently popped a PG-13 movie in for the kids down in the basement (one of those, slightly toned-down, blockbuster action movies that cut back on the nudity and swearing just enough to keep it below R) which she felt would probably keep their attention; semi-taboo nature of it and all. Scott pointed at the bag from his supine position on the couch and slurred something along the lines of, "buy yuh self sumpa noss." Scott wanted her to buy anything she wanted. Utterly spent as he was, it gave him a moment of pride knowing how few men ever even had the opportunity to say something like this to their significant other. The priviledge wasn't lost on him. Within a minute, he was out.

Scott found himself swimming alone in a vast ocean. Land was visible far ahead of him, though the coast must have been at least a mile off, enveloped in a hazy mist reflecting an intense tropical sun. The water was warm. Undulating heat waves blanketed the horizon. Rather bizarrely he was submerged in the deep, navy blue of a much more northerly ocean. Like something off the coast of Greenland. Water almost black in color and seeming, to the eye, unforgivingly frigid. Able to kill a man in minutes flat. The setting sun illuminated cascades of shimmering crystal atop the briskly rolling, white capped waves. He looked steadily forward, toward land, as his arms and legs pumped vigorously; churning the water as he made his way forward. He had the vigor of his teenage self; his body doing what he wanted it to do efficiently. Better than it ever could, even. He saw within the mist, the angular trunks of lazily swaying trees and small rolling hills beyond a large swath of marshland with high reeds. The trees were of bizarre shapes and sizes. Some seemed squashed down, somehow, like those trees you always saw on African safari programs. Others resembled trees from a Dr. Seuss novel. Strange, wispy, otherworldly pines. These trees and this landscape, he realized, were of a different time. He saw creatures roaming about, their forms becoming more recognizable as his eyes began to focus and scrutinize the topography. There were large cats with tusks. Big, gray, lumbering creatures that looked as though a cross between a hippopotamus and a rhino. It all seemed prehistoric. A time millions of years before humans. A time that humankind, indeed, had never known, though might yearn to travel back to, to see firsthand.

He looked over his right shoulder as he pushed forward through the troughs of the rolling sea. He saw Dreadson, coming into focus maybe twenty yards away- swimming toward land. He was parallel with him and some thirty yards away. Dreadson looked at Scott with hopeful exuberance. He appeared young and virile. His youthful face glowed. He seemed to enjoy the brisk exercise. The vigorous nature of it. He hollered vivaciously across the short expanse between them:

"How are you, boy?"

"I swim." He tried to make the words that were in his head come out of his mouth, though struggled with them. Struggled as though a toddler with an impressive vocabulary. "Animals on the shore. Are we in Cenozoic? I swim in the Cenozoic?"

"Yes you do, boy. Animals on the shore to where we go. We go now. Come, boy!" Dreadson waved him toward the horizon and shore.

"What water? Safe water?"

"Water *not* safe, boy." His look grew foreboding. "Watch yourself for the black!"

"The black? What the black?"

"Watch yourself, boy." Dreadson's expression was stern with warning. "If you see the black, swim away. Understand, boy? Swim we now. Swim we to shore!"

Scott jerked his head back toward the land he was swimming to and his body began stiffening its muscles. He began to feel them straining more urgently. His movements flowing less naturally now and his legs more desperately jerking with this ambiguous fear now instilled in him. His eyes squinted once more, though it was at something new. He noticed the deep blue shade beginning to go black all around him. The black rapidly grew to surround him on all sides and already there seemed no way to escape it. Like he was in the middle of an oil spill that was sluggishly spreading out all around him. He began to scream, unable to comprehend what was happening now, though feeling, instinctively, that he must be in the black that Dreadson had warned him of. He screamed in fear and looked back toward Dreadson- who was looking at him with his eyes wide open- so wide open they appeared to be protruding out his head. Yes, that is what they were doing. His eyes were protruding out like two ping pong ball halves on either side of his nose. The sickening, impossible sight caused Scott's heart to pump so hard that each beat started to physically pain him.

"Leave the black, son! Get out! Do not swim in the black! You *die* in the black!" Dreadson's eyes began to leek blood as they pushed themselves out of his ocular cavities and hung from the ocular nerve, looking back at him from fleshy strands.

"I no move! I no, but want..." Grant whined as he looked away. His horror only worsened by the sight of Dreadson's fear. He continued to struggle making the words. He could not make the words to match the thoughts in his head. He felt the helplessness of an infant unable to convey what he wanted; unable to understand what was happening to him and why. Looking for help from someone who knew what to do. "The black all around me now? What I do? I die? Do I die in black? What I? What is I do?"

"You *die*! Don't be the victim!" Dreadson's eyes were floating from the optic nerve. Levitating above his head.

"What I do? What I..."

Scott cut himself off now. He ducked his head under the water to try to see the black. To try to get some idea of what it was and how it would harm him. What could a color do? He looked into the black, comforted briefly by the peace of being underwater. Something was beginning to take shape. A growing, grayish white patch in the middle of the darkness around it, with a tarnished pink area at its center. Like pink peppered in the charcoal gray of the dark, murky water surrounding it. The pink shape was like an old, early twentieth century football-somewhere between a circle and an oval. It was moving toward him like a giant, rising football turned on its side. Not spinning, just slowly floating toward him from beneath. As less and less water separated him from the pink, its color became clearer and be began to see details. He saw what looked like mottled red spots and lines like large cuts. It dawned on him what this was. It matched the beast that hung from Dreadson's office ceiling. The beast named Betty. A muffled voice could be heard underwater now.

"The beast, boy! The beast! Do not be the victim of a crafted beast! Do you hear me boy? Swim you now. Swim you now *away*!"

Grant tried to speak, though lost his breath in this instant as rows of large, jagged triangles emerged within the pink. No, not triangles. Teeth! Massive teeth of myriad colors. Copper, bronze, ebony, slate, sandstone, and chalky matte white. Within these teeth he could see a pale pink beginning to form, with ribs in it. A moment's hope that his fears might be unwarranted died in a flash. This was the megalodon named Betty, coming out of the depths, toward him. Two pitch black eyes, somehow darker than the blackness of its massive frame, on either side of it and the jet-black water. Its mouth was held wide open and coming at Scott too fast for him to do anything about it but to watch it all unfold. Scott tried to scream, though when he did, water began to pour into his mouth causing his chest to convulse trying to push it out. Choking out his voice; unable to do anything but produce pathetic little bubbles that floated up and away. The mouth emerging toward him surrounded him on all sides. It was big enough to swallow him as easily as a prize fish eating a minnow as an aperitif. Its cold and dead obsidian eyes were upon him and showed no emotional involvement. No life of their own. Not a hint of feeling with regards to taking this little life of his. Within an instant, the jaws came down on Scott and tore him apart. Red haze clouded his vision. His blood in the water. Scott tried to fight. Reached his right arm out to punch one of the eyes, but his punch was met by solid, black glass that cracked the bones in his hand. He could feel entire body parts ripped off his frame as the massive jaw opened and shut on him. He tried to punch the eye again but could not. Then he saw that same arm floating away with strips of torn flesh, bobbing and waving, from its end. Somehow, after a moment of intense pain, his body went numb. He tried to scream, though could not make a sound beyond a small, sad whimper at his death that came so sudden. His death that was so heartless. A sack of flesh and bone devoured without emotion. He heard Dreadson's muffled voice as he saw the man's form kicking furiously away from the creature, spewing a trail of white foam and bubbles like carbonation, as the last visions of his life faded to black. All darkness now. There was nothing left but a voice. Detached and dreamlike.

"You are a victim now, son. You are a victim of a crafted beast! Do you hear me, boy? A victim of a crafted beast!"

Scott screamed with primal dread. He curled his hands into fists and wailed into them. He screamed over and over in state of fear beyond what he could have ever before fathomed. His body shook without mercy and his chest emitted sharp, jutting pains. Somehow, there was no blood. He felt the warmth of another presence and shuddered at its touch. Not the shark again. But it was dry and warm. He soon realized what it was. It was Ginny who was now upon him, holding him tight and swaying his body gently side to side.

"You're okay, my love. Shhh, you're safe. Shhh." She was looking at him with equal parts fear and compassion showing on her face.

Scott grabbed her tightly and began to cry. Tears flowing like they hadn't in decades. Tears like a child in shock and debilitating injury; fallen off a bike into gravel at full speed. The kids were running up from the basement stairs and Ginny sternly commanded them to go outside right away and sit at the patio table until she came out. Scott continued to cry for a long spell. As he did, slowly, the intervals between his bodily shakes grew longer. He began to reorient and realize where he was. The pain of his heartbeat eventually subsided and slid back to somewhere in the vicinity of its normal resting pace. He tried to compose himself, and broke his silence to tell his wife:

"I'm sorry, Ginny. I didn't mean to scare you or the kids."

"Don't worry about that," she replied, her hair damp now from his tears, and some of hers. "Are you okay, now?"

"Yes, yes I think I am." Scott sniffled and rubbed his face. "I'm going to go to the bathroom for a minute to put myself together, then I'll come meet you all on the patio."

"Okay," said Ginny, tentatively, worried somehow in her shock that something bad might happen even here in this moment. She rubbed his upper back gently. "Take your time, I just set the table and put out dinner." Her look conveyed empathy, concern, and genuine love for him. It was in the rare moments like this- when he was feeling vulnerable- that he could see just how much this woman meant to him. Moments in which he could appreciate just how rare this kind of simple and innocent comfort could be, in life.

"Okay, I'll be back in a minute." And with that Scott walked, cautiously and shaken, toward the main level bathroom. He steadied himself on the sink and splashed cold water on his face. He looked in the mirror and repeated to himself over and over. "Just a dream, Grant. Just a dream."

Scott rubbed his face dry and walked slowly, still in a half daze, out toward the patio. As he pulled the sliding door open, he took a deep breath and greeted his family assembled outside; trying his damnedest to look composed.

"Hey guys, sorry about all that. Just a nightmare. Everything's fine."

Grant looked upon his wife smiling, hopeful and concerned, back at him. His eyes went to his young son, Jackson. Then, his daughter, Lily. They both looked relieved in this moment. Their dad must have looked at okay enough to at least warrant this. The smells of Ginny's cooking wafted toward Grant and calmed him in the unique way that familiar, welcoming smells tied a person to history. To a series of pleasant memories that went with it. A combination of rich, savory chicken and puff pastry. The unmistakable and pleasing scents of a homemade chicken pot pie that his family enjoyed time and again, going back to when he used to pick little strings of chicken sinews to give to Jackson when he was a baby. How he would gum them and smile at his daddy with little smudges of gravy in disarray on his pudgy face.

Now there was also the sharp, tart smell of a freshly tossed spring greens, goat cheese, strawberry and pecan salad with balsamic vinagrette. A raspberry pie for dessert and a pint of cream cheese ice cream- softening in a bucket of ice- to go with it. Grant took it in and was growing content again in his home. In this warm repose surrounded by those who loved and cared about him, beyond any others in this world. The backdrop of a beautiful, late afternoon sky. Lush, rolling hills and safe upper middle-class homes of Burbank enveloping it like a seemingly impenetrable cocoon. Grant felt, and it was surprising even to himself, the fear of his nightmare beginning to fade away already. Soon he would come to forget, nearly altogether, the encounter with the crafted beast.

Kenilworth

Kenilworth was again on the bus this morning. In his seat up front, sandwiched between an overstuffed, nineties-era backpack and a scuffed, canvas duffle bag. He was admiring the view out his window -as it had been, what was often referred to, an Indian summer. In the low fifties with clear, pleasant skies. The colors of the trees were in full bloom. Maybe not trees necessarily (quite a bit of the vegetation around here was weeds) but what was around him had changed colors to reflect an array of vibrant autumn hues.

Kenilworth had gotten to the bus relatively early today; around 8:30AM. It would be among the last days for a while, he observed, where he would be able to have daylight and warmth at this hour. Fall daylight savings time would be here shortly, and to Chicago, being just the wrong side of the Eastern time zone as it was, daylight savings hit people hard. Starting in late November it wouldn't be uncommon for a person to find themselves in darkness before getting to work as well as when finishing up with work each day of the week. Sleep in on the weekends and awake to a sun that was beginning, already, its descent. This darkness would last until late January. At its worst, around late December, by four PM, there was darkness. Trips to psychologists for seasonal depression would be skyrocketing in just a few days (as Dr. John well knew).

Kenilworth was beaming noticeably from his seat, kitty corner to Mr. Landry. Mr. Landry drove cautiously and steadily, as always, toward his destination of Washington Park. He drove ready to navigate what may come, with tempered reaction and the ever-present mindfulness of what he could, and could not, do from within the confines of a twenty ton, fourty foot leviathon. Nothing surprised him on these roads anymore. His vigilance was informed by decades of the craziest shit you could ever expect to see from automobiles and the occasional drunk or drug-addled pedestrians walking right out into traffic. Just the other day, an older model, faded-yellow Camry, had cut him off to make a right turn onto 55th. Before Mr. Landry was even finished blasting his horn at the car, it had already attempted a quick left down the next alley, a full twenty feet too early, and wrapped itself around a fire hydrant. An old lady on a walker took it in from five feet behind the hydrant that had just saved her from being pinned between a speeding car and a brick wall. She shook her head and nonchalantly kept a trudging on. Mr. Landry was glad to have reason, this morning, to reflect on happier things. He observed Kenilworth's jubilant expression through the mirror and couldn't help but crack a smile himself. He'd heard the news.

"Starting at the University of Chicago, huh?"

"Yes, sir, how did you know," replied Kenilworth, unaware of how much his steady, proud grin gave away.

"I heard about it from your grandmother yesterday morning. Congratulations, young man. I'm proud of you, Washington." Mr. Landry reached out a meaty hand for a fist bump, which Kenilworth gave, somewhat awkwardly as per usual; this particular time managing to connect on two of four knuckles.

"Thank you, Mr. Landry. I'm very excited to be going," he replied. And he was indeed excited. His body was alive in a way that it had rarely been in his life, aside from those moments when he knew he was in imminent danger of being harmed. That type of excitement had never been the welcome kind. It was nice to, finally, have the sensation for the reason he would want it.

"You're going to make us all proud, son," Mr. Landry went on. "I know it. I've been rooting for you a long time, young buck. Wasn't sure you'd make it this far, sometimes. That's for damn sure. But, here you are. Glad to say I was wrong about that." Mr. Landry sure was, with the ongoing history of lost potential he saw unfold on this bus over the years. Youngsters who threw away their potentials to gangs, to drugs, or simply over time to the grinding hopelessness, in this war of attrition, with life in the so-called ghettos.

"Here I am," replied Kenilworth, as he looked back out the window at the colors.

"Take care of yourself." Mr. Landry warned him with the natural, wisened authority that he held. "Understand you just as bright as anybody else at that campus. Don't ever think otherwise." He turned around from the stop at a red light to look him in the eyes. "You deserve to be there, son."

"Thank you, Mr. Landry."

"Washington, one thing I'm asking you, though."

"Yes, sir."

Mr. Landry took a sip from his quart size coffed mug and looked at him through the rearview as the bus chugged forward again. He wore an expression of immediacy. "Stay in your lane, alright?" He held the gaze to make sure Kenilworth was hearing him.

"Yes, sir."

"You understand what I mean by that? That means don't go looking for answers in places you're not going to find them. Go looking for answers in the places you will."

"I think I know what you mean, sir." And Kenilworth was content in the moment to know he wasn't simply playing lip service. His recent trip to Betty's political rally had seemed to finally nail that lesson home.

"Good, that's all for now. I'm sure we'll have plenty more chances to talk to each other when you're visiting your grandma. And that better be at least once a week, you got me? I drive this bus five, sometime six days a week. I better see you on here regularly. And in the morning time, alright?"

"You will, sir."

Mr. Landry nodded and his expression brightened a little in the hopes that what he had said would sink in. He pulled the bus toward a stop on Garfield Boulevard and Michigan Avenue. Here he started a conversation with Ms. Dawson, a regular who took three buses to get to U of C, for her job in the cafeteria. Two stops later, it was Kenilworth's turn. He traversed the aisle, gave Mr. Landry a quick nod, and began the walk through Washington Park's crimson, amber, and golden foliage. It was as much on the ground as on the trees recently, but the color was still vibrant and welcoming against the usual cold, gray skies of November. He was on the trek toward the growingly familiar Department of Organismal Biology.

Soon, the form of Dr. Williams was visible outside the south entryway, sitting on the front steps, waiting. He was munching casually from a bag of honey roasted peanuts. Dr. Williams spotted Kenilworth from a distance and got up to stroll toward the young man. He gave him a hug and a pat on the back. He poured some peanuts into Kenilworth's hand, without asking him if he wanted any.

"Breakfast," he clarified.

"Umm, yes, sir."

"Looks like we've got you for good now," he said between munches. "That Dr. Gavilan guy and McCarver outpatient were on our admissions department like white on rice trying to get something worked out for your early admission. We'll start you first thing in January, as planned. In the meantime, we'll find some ways to keep you busy. Let me show you to your new dorm."

"Thank you, sir. I'm happy to have the opportunity," Kenilworth replied, holding his peanuts out in front of him like an offering to squirrels.

With that, Dr. Williams lead Washington on a brief walk over to the Max Palevsky Residential Commons. As the building came into focus, Kenilworth was struck by how well kept up that both it, and the surrounding area, were. No cracks in the concrete with weeds growing through them. No litter to speak of. And, of course, dozens of students nearby hanging out in the open air with no fears to speak of; complimenting it all. No one but him, he realized, seemed surprised in the moment by any of this.

He continued the traverse inside, through a bustling hallway with students plodding past him on the way to class. Their various paces from leisurely strolls to harried run-walks, depending on how far they had to go. They came up to a second-floor room. Dr. Williams opened the door for him, which swung open to reveal the single occupant room. It held a lumpy, twin-sized bed atop a humble wooden frame, a wooden desk with cloth cushioned chair, a small bookshelf, a mini-fridge, and a utilitarian closet.

"Welcome to your humble abode." Dr. Williams observed without a hint irony. The expression was quite appropriate. "What do you think?"

"I think this suits my needs well, Dr. Williams. I'm very happy with this. Thank you." Kenilworth was smiling again, even more brightly than on the bus ride over.

Dr. Williams looked back at Kenilworth, initially a bit perplexed by his reaction to this sub-Raskolnikovian dwelling, though also pleasantly surprised at his level of excitement over the two hundred square foot room. Most of the privileged students who came upon rooms like this, as far as Dr Williams could tell, probably started to play the song *Like a Rolling Stone* in their head, upon seeing it. How does it feel? To be on your own. Dr. Williams crinkled up the, now empty, bag of peanuts and stuffed it in his front pocket.

"I'm looking forward to seeing you around campus and in class, Washington. Stop by my office anytime you want to chat. Here are some contacts in the department and in student affairs." He handed Kenilworth a memento pad with a fridge magnet attachment on the back. "You can put that on your mini fridge. We will be seeing a lot of each other." Dr. Williams pulled out another bag of peanuts from his other front pocket and popped a few more in his mouth. He saw Kenilworth looking at him with amusement.

"Second breakfast."

"Like a hobbit?" Kenilworth smiled.

"Yes, like a hobbit," Dr. Williams returned a sly grin at the nerdy reference and laughed. He gestured toward the room. "We'll get you set up here today. Then, we'll get you into work study as per the terms of your coming here a little early."

"Thank you, Dr. Williams. I appreciate it."

"We appreciate having you here. I'll let you get set up now. Goodbye, Washington." Dr. Williams gave him another quick pat on the shoulder, pivoted, and strolled away down the hallway.

And with that Kenilworth was alone in his new room. This room that would be his home for the next several years. He dropped his burden; the hefty backpack and duffle bag and he looked out onto mid campus, from the single bay window. His sense of pride intermingled with something relatively unfamiliar. He could feel his body becoming, just slightly, less tense. He could feel his mind relaxing just a little- no longer feeling the need to scan everything around him so acutely. For once there did not seem to be a need to. A few moments later, he felt his breathing flowing a little more freely; more slowly, more leisurely.

All of these things Kenilworth felt that now came upon him. They were each rather miniscule, though, with the impact of them all in combination, Kenilworth became acutely aware of a change of sensation. His mind seemed, somehow, just faintly sharper with all of this- able to place more focus outside of survival and able to look at, and dedicate, more time and effort into things outside of merely maintaining his existence on this earth. He would be prepared, in the coming months, in a way that he never before would have been. In a way that he, indeed, never before felt he could have been.

Dr John

Dr. John was at about the halfway point of an exceptionally long walk with Nora and their dog, Toby. Nora was depressed, as was John. Both had been the entire day and all-night prior. Nora had gone to bed early when it became clear that Betty would be president the following day when she woke up. Betty, a businessman of questionable practices and a B-list entertainer (and in all honesty, probably better at the latter than the former) would be leading the free world for, at least, the next four years. Her mind simply could not wrap itself around this fact. She could not put herself inside the mind of those who thought this could be either a logical or a moral decision to make; let alone both. John felt that he could, maybe, understand this, though his ability to do so took him to a pretty dark and hopeless place.

"How? I just don't get it," she said with her head held low. This broke the silence of the past fifteen minutes. A silence followed for another spell as they strolled slowly along the lake front trail. Toby was off leash nearby, sniffing piles of leaves, running from one to another in search of some unknown treasure. Like a stick, or a dead squirrel.

John thought about it for a moment, before suggesting, "should we go sit on the rocks?"

"Sure, you grab Toby." She called him over.

John, Nora, and Toby walked off the narrow dirt trail of Elliot Park and made the short climb onto the wall of large, craggy rocks that served as breakers for the, often times, ocean-like waters of Lake Michigan. The waters were brisk, relentlessly crashing into the rocks. The crashing of the waves against the rocks sent a light, chill mist onto their coats and jeans. For a time, John and Nora looked out toward the Chicago skyline, sitting to their immediate south, in the twilight of the day. The varied hues of color reflected from the skyscrapers illuminated the night with a pinkish glow. Two distinct lines of commercial air planes dotted the dark skies beyond, with their flashing red and white lights. A dozen or so planes hovering, like slow moving satellites, over the lake. One swath of them going off to O'Hare. The other going to Midway. The outline of Chicago was cut off abruptly to its left by the comparatively strange and dark nothingness of the water stretching to and past the horizon. Twilight crept into night. The mist of the water stung their faces with cold. Dr. John finally found words, for the first time that night, as he tried to make sense of what happened.

"He offered them easy answers. Worse yet, they believed it. I guess, this is what people want." He thought about it for another moment before adding, "He offered them a philosophy that requires them not to think. I guess they also want this. He served up an outlet for the people's anger. He painted a fantasy of a past life that can happen again, but nobody questioned that it was a fantasy to begin with, and surely would be a fantasy again. But they want to believe it all. Even against their better judgment. It's just, that they so desperately want to *believe* this."

"People know this isn't true, though John." Nora responded immediately, having thought about the events for some time as well. "They know the 1950s weren't this ideal time. They know that the answers to globalization aren't simple, and certainly aren't to fight against or deny it. They know the old jobs aren't coming back and they have to deal with the changes of the future. They know that most people of different religions or races aren't against them or trying to harm them. I truly can't believe that they don't, deep down, know all of these things." Nora was showing the frustration of this all in a way that Dr. John couldn't yet allow himself to feel. He was afraid to.

Dr. John sighed and felt the hopelessness of a growing depression sinking in. He had had this feeling on rare occasions in his life and it was moments like these that seemed to pave the way. From what he could gather, the experience of depression happened when you wrapped your mind around something that you desperately wanted to fix; felt you desperately *needed* to fix. Yet, for all your thoughts on it and for all the mental gymnastics you went through, you could not come up with a viable solution to the problem. This left you with having to accept something that was impossible to amend, which left you with the internal black hole that was depression. And it lead to an actual feeling of hollowness inside and knowing, in that moment, that there was no way to remove this feeling because the reason it was there was synonymous with its answer; Not having a solution. That was the desperation inherent within depression. That was why the final escape from hopeless depression was considered the ultimate act of desperation. This was a place that a person tried fiercely not to go, even if the solution was denial, repression and distraction. At times, those were the best decisions to make to preserve yourself. John looked out into the void of the black, crashing waters and mentioned something that had been on his mind for some time. Something that was only an idea until the idea became a sickening reality.

"You know what I think? I think he won because deep down, this is what a lot of people out there want. Not so much that they've been duped by the spectacle of it all; though that is a part of it. I don't think that's the main reason, though. I think that they actually *want* to be told what to think. Like children who yearn for a parent figure to guide their thoughts and actions. Beyond that, they want that information they are getting to be simplified for them. They want to feel that things are not that complicated, so they can feel a semblance of control in this world. Betty gave that to them. It's an advantage he had over Kenton Dilman, who didn't sugar coat things. Didn't presume to know and put himself in a position to tell people what the definitive answers to problems were or that those answers would come as easily as picking a fucking booger. *He* trusted that the people could accept this level of ambiguity but work toward making improvements while knowing and accepting that. But Betty, he *did* presume to tell people what the definitive answers to their problems were. He incorporated fear, racism, black and white thinking, ignoring context, into that all along the way. And when anybody challenged him on it, he just doubled down and his supporters loved him for it. But, in the end, he did offer direct and immediate solutions to problems. I think people know a lot of it is unrealistic and misguided. I mean, they must, but their need for answers and solutions to happen more immediately trumped all of that."

Dr. John sighed, rubbed driplets of lake mist off his cheeks and continued: "What scares me the most is this. If people are willing to put their stock in someone who is giving them simplified, unrealistic, and fear and ignorance-based answers to problems. If that's really what they're willing to do? Well, then this man can win again. Then a man or woman like him can win after that using the same formula. And at the end of the day, this is how the people are choosing their leader and representative to the world. Their champion. If anyone beats him, they might well have to do the same thing coming from another viewpoint. It sets a precedent. A more realistic approach will *not* work because eventually it won't be wanted by the people on either side. They'll want someone who tells them what they want to hear as opposed to telling them a more realistic truth that is never as simple or appealing to hear. Never will be, either. It *never* will be. What does that say about us? Who respects a nation that directs itself based on fear and willful ignorance? Whose wants are, basically, to be lied to because they can't accept the complexities of hard truths. Whose insecurities are worn on their sleeve by the decisions that they make. Decisions like electing someone who is placating their deepest fears and insecurities by telling pretty little lies of simple black and white solutions. Who is also willing to confirm their fears to be real, simply if those fears play into his own political aspirations. Who is dividing people like opposing sports teams locked in bitter rivalry. Will this be the requirements of a leader from now on?"

Dr. John looked downward and rubbed his forehead and temples. He felt tired and spent, even though he hadn't done much physically on this day aside from the long walk. He knew this feeling of a worn body was related to depression sinking in. Somatization, they called it. He hoped that he would be able to shake this one off but had a feeling that it would be months in the making before he would fully be able to; and *if* then. He knew that the news networks, people in the neighborhood, TV, the internet, would all be blowing up daily about his election. It would be difficult to escape the information glut and he would have to filter out what he could to preserve himself. Filtering out all the excessive stimuli of the information age. All that unrelenting, agenda-pushing bullshit. It was a burden that had been placed on his and the following generations in a way never before seen and it was driving some of them crazy, often destructively so.

Was this seeming regression in the voting body related to people not having the will, the effort, or the time to sort through it to come to their own conclusions about things? Were they resorting to wanting to be spoon fed clearly simplified answers as a hasty solution to the overload of their information age? Well, if everything aside from Marmot News was being touted as fake news by people sporting stone cold serious expressions as they said that, he presumed a lot of people could now justify doing just that. If they let themselves; not bothering with the task of researching their own conclusions based on multiple, hopefully at least semi-objective sources. Or maybe, since there weren't too many clearly objective sources, people began to willfully gravitate toward the sources that told them what they *wanted* to hear. Then call everything else fake. Not biased. Not, partially informed. Fake. Then leave it at that and walk away. Simplifying a complex modern world even when the stakes of doing so could well be to the downfall of everyone. Climate, religious and racial tolerance, gender roles (and rights), all wrapped up into a neat little box of dismissive, tribally informed viewpoints. An overwhelming desire to have these views echoed back to them by people who wanted to appease each other over anything else.

Dr. John and Nora looked out on the turbulent waters for a spell. They seemed symbolic of what might lie ahead. A dark and aggressive time. A growing coldness in everything around them that they could feel soaking into the cores of their being. A coldness that somehow seemed necessary to cope with it all, though with an underlying destructive power. Dr. John, wanting to change focus for a moment, added:

"I got a letter at my office yesterday. It was from a local radio network. They mentioned hearing me talk on True American Radio. They must have found out who I was through my contacts at McCarver. Anyway, they invited me to come meet with them about a possible radio show opportunity. Something where people could just talk about modern issues and how to cope with them. Political elements of course, but mostly just people trying to air out their concerns about national and world issues. Having a psychologist and a panel with him to talk about these things on air. I'm thinking about it."

Nora, with her gaze still on the waves, replied, "I think you should meet with them. Hear what they have to say. Might be a nice opportunity for you."

"Thanks, LMB. I think I'll set up a meeting. Might be a nice change for me."

"Speaking of radio broadcasters, isn't that guy from *True American Radio* in the hospital right now? I thought I heard something about that earlier today."

"I heard about it, too. I think they said he's in a medically induced coma. Cardiac arrest. Said its miraculous that he's still alive at all." John shrugged his shoulders and added, "I'm not surprised. That asshole probably had a private helicopter take him to the ER right after it happened. World class surgeon on standby for him."

"I wonder if he'll make it," Nora added after a pause; showing a level of concern despite knowing what kind of man Bud Harbaugh was. It was one of the many things that attracted Dr. John to her. Unlike many people, most people even, she could show at least a level of empathy and concern for just about anyone. She was strong enough as a person not to shut herself off from this, conscious decision, of allowing herself to feel even for people others might dismiss simply as enemies, lost, stupid, or some other connotation that would allow them to simply pass the buck and move on, without another thought on the matter.

"Knowing him, he'll probably recover and be back on the radio in a few weeks," Dr. John added, with a sense of bitter irony regarding the fact that a man like this could be given so many additional chances in life, only to cause continued harm and destruction after given them. "I don't think he'd want to miss the opportunity to relish over Betty's victory."

"Probably not," Nora laughed.

John and Nora climbed back down the rocks, John holding their spoiled mutt in place as he navigated down and back toward the trail. They continued to look out on the waves as they walked. The cold mists accumulating in small pools of mud along the dirt trail. The rhythmic crashing noise of the water. They carried on mostly in silence, holding hands. Their walks would be long in the coming days and they found them helpful to a certain extent. Keep moving together was part of what the walks meant to them both. That was just what they needed to do.

Bobba Q.

It was late in the evening of November 3rd and the wee hours found Bob set down on his porch, observing the recently cleared durum wheat fields. It always struck him, around this time of year, how desolate the landscape could appear. Just a few weeks back he could look out over an expanse of gently swaying, life giving flaxen grain at its peak in the mild warmth of the mid-October sun. At twilight, the wheat would resemble a gently rolling sea of amber, which faded into the horizon of deep purple speckled with silver stars and otherworldly, golden green dots cast by lightning bugs. This was a beauty few could fathom. A heavenly display few could even know about, to begin with, in this fly over state that most seemed to have neither the time, nor the want, to visit.

Watching it all in a calming sway from his great grandmother's rocking chair, passed down through the generations. A cold one in tow, setting here on this porch, was a greater reward after a hard day's work than any money, fame, or title could offer. Bob hoped to fade from this world, one day, in time with the setting sun atop the lush wheat. What better way could there ever be to meet his maker on that fast approaching and most blessed day?

Now, in contrast with the height of its full, near dusk beauty; it always struck him so suddenly, thinking about the fields of plenty now lying reaped and desolate. It was always a loss in a way, coinciding as it did with the darker days ahead; moving toward the winter solstice. The winter would be moving in quick. Sometimes it was even here by this time of year. Everyone-people who had lived in the Dakotas all their lives not excluded-had some trouble adjusting to just how quick the weather could transition from balmy, to temperate, to near unimaginably frigid. Often, it was only a handful of weeks from one extreme to the next.

It never failed that Bob would struggle for a time with how the desolation coincided with the growing dark. How the stripped fields ushered in a time in which he would have months away from doing his work, while he holed himself in for the season. And there was getting the farmhouse winter ready, too. Putting in the storm windows. Hauling in plenty of wood for the fireplace. Tying ropes from the home to the barn and from the barn to the shed. Ropes to the garage and any other place he needed to go. Ropes so that, when the blinding winter squalls came, he would not be among those poor bastards who froze solid, often no more than a hundred feet from their dwelling place, in a white out.

Stocking food was a must, as well. Several weeks supply available at all times. Emergency supplies, in addition, for his truck. Water and trail mix, blankets, extra wool socks, heavy mitts, and flashlights. People could die being stranded in their cars on the lonely highways. Victims of errant, several feet high, snow drifts leaving them no place to turn to. People who didn't prepare could meet the harshest of circumstances, then suffer the harshest of consequences. He thought, for a spell, about death and all the ways it could come to a man these here parts. The thoughts distracted him, if just for a time, from his mood which had a tinge of foulness to it that he just couldn't seem to shake.

"Bob?" Came Tilly's voice in a warm, though tired and distressed tone from the sitting room.

"Yes, hon," Bob replied, trying to sound calm despite his presently heightened nerves.

"How are you?" She continued, her voice sounding a little closer. She was hoping to get him to talk a little more; about earlier.

Bob was silent; trying to buy a little time. He could sense what she wanted to talk about. He knew she'd get find a way to get it out of him, so's he figured he might as well bring it up himself. "I'm alright. Just upset about 'ol Doug." There. Cat out of the box.

Tilly's petite form emerged from out the front door and onto the porch. She wrapped her knit shawl tight around her shoulders as the cold hit her. She greeted her husband with a calm and patient nod. It was slower than usual, which lead Bob to feel she was concerned. He was guessing it was concern more for what he had done than how he was feeling, though Bob was nonplussed. He damned well knew, already, that it had gotten heated. Bob exhaled in a prolonged sigh. These womenfolk always seemed so intent on talking these damned things out. Until they beat it into the ground. He looked at her and tried his best to not appear upset in having to go over it.

"I know things got a little out of hand, okay? I regret that, I do. I didn't want it to happen that way. It's just (sigh). Tilly, it's just." Bob averted her gaze, and looked back onto the bare fields before adding, "I was having a *great* day. Just a perfect, effing day. Betty wins. Does it against *everybody's* expectations. And now we, finally, got a true man of the people who's going to bring us back to the best of times. Then comes our weekly poker night and Doug has to come and shit all over everything." His look was growing irritated despite himself. "This time of year is hard enough for me, as you well know. Then Doug comes over and talks all this nonsense about Betty being a sham. A Manhattan elitist, with no real plans in place, that duped us all. Duped us, huh? Well, no ma'am, I am not having that!" Bob smacked the arm of his rocking chair, causing it's one hundred place year-old frame to creek and wobble.

"Things got more than a little heated, honey," Tilly clarified, wrapping her shawl still tighter. "Things got really ugly there. You know, he brought up some good points that deserve a listen, too. I mean, you have to admit, Betty never gets too specific on just *how* he's going to make things better for people like us. It's only right to question things now and then, and about people promising you things even more than anything else. And honey, it's *okay* to disagree with your friends. It's only politics that you guys differ about anyways. You agree on almost everything else in life. You do the same type of work, have the same friends. You go to the same church."

"Are you going to give me shit about it, too!" Bob scowled back at Tilly. His volume had gone higher than he almost ever talked to her. This caught her off guard. This harsh and ugly expression and tone; and how *quickly* it came on. It was something that, almost all their life had very rarely occurred, though lately…lately, something was different. It had grown more frequent, this look. And the anger, that accompanied it, more severe.

Bob had not noticed what Tilly had, but yet it was there. The anger. And it was taking root. When it started, Tilly was not exactly sure- but now, she began to wonder if the root had already grown too deep to pluck out of the earth. Earlier tonight, it had culminated in Bob threatening to grab his shotgun if his longtime friend, Doug, didn't get the hell out of his house and never come back. Over an argument about politics that had lasted all of five minutes.

"I'm sorry," Tilly begrudgingly relented. She knew that they needed to talk about this growing problem, but she knew her husband well enough that now was not the time. She had grown wise through the necessary traits of hardship combined with experience. She knew the importance of time, place, and mood all congregating just such, so as to be able to make headway in matters like these.

"Let's talk about it some other time," she added with a deep nod that Bob would know as conveying the matter had been given enough attention for now. She gave him a little out, adding:

"You're getting tired, Bob. I know your tired mood. Let's go to bed now, dear. I do so *hope* you can hash things out with Doug. You don't want to throw away decades because of five minutes. Maybe we can have him and Kate over for dinner this weekend. Apologize to each other and let them know there's no hard feelings about it?"

Tilly knew the odds were against this and it sickened her to feel it now. In the not too distant past, this wouldn't have been the case. But something had changed and by the time she realized it fully, it had already unpacked its bags settled itself in, and now she felt a growing sense of helplessness in her ability to do much of anything about it. That, and shame for not having done something earlier. For not having corrected Bob more sternly and for not having argued with him over points of contention on some of his views that she knew were coming directly from that radio program. That radio program that she was beginning to see as unhealthy and unhelpful, though knew would only sink its teeth further into her husband in the coming years.

"I don't think so," Bob shot back after a pause wherein he'd taken a drawn out sigh and a long sip of ice-cold beer. He was drinking more, too, and drinking when the anger came. "I don't want to put up with that shit from him no more. I'm gettin' too old for it. He just doesn't get it. He's never going to. He's a damned libtard."

"A what?" Tilly was caught off guard for a second time tonight by this comment. "You know, Bob, I've never heard you use that word before. And you know what? I really don't *like* it. You want to describe Doug? How about describing him as a decades long friend whose been with you through countless ups and downs in your life. Helped you out of more than a few pickles, too."

"I've got plenty of friends, Tilly," Bob shot back, his rage only seeming to grow as his words started to slur just slightly. "Friends who I don't have to put up with shit like this from. And why in Gott-damned hell should I?"

The couple shared an uncomfortable silence for a spell. Tilly, at length, decided to change the subject. Decided to put focus back on what they mutually cared about and were invested in. She sighed, walked out onto the porch and over to its railing. She took in the sight of the vast, reaped fields.

"Quite a harvest this year, Bob. We are blessed, you know."

"Yes, ma'am," a long swig and nod in affirmation. Bob was clearly put at ease by the change of focus.

"Bob?" Her tone was gentle. Gentle and a bit sad.

"Yes, Tilly."

She turned back around and touched his shoulder. "I'm going to bed now. Take as much time as you see fit out here."

"Yes ma'am. Sleep well. I'll be up in just a minute." He forced a smile and tried to calm himself, knowing that's what his Tilly wanted for him. "Just need a little more time out here to get my thoughts in order."

"Okay, Bob. I love you."

"Love you too, Tilly my dear."

Tilly leaned in and Bob kissed his wife on the cheek. Smiled lovingly at her. He noticed, offhand, that she looked tired tonight. Worn down, even. He hoped that she would take a long rest and not work too hard around the house for a spell. He'd encourage her to take it easy tomorrow. They could order a pizza for dinner. Maybe she could just focus on her knitting. That red sweater for their baby grandson, Austin, was coming along nicely. His folks would be happy to see it next month when the family would get together for Tilly's sixtieth birthday. He hoped that she wasn't coming down with something. She worked too hard, God bless her. Just like he tended to. They were alike in that way, he supposed. Understood that about each other and caught each other when they were trying to do a little too much. That became more important, with age, he supposed.

The sky was black and the moon just a small, glowing sliver in the distance; offering little of its usual illumination. The dustlike gray of the fields- compliments of the first frost of the year- only added to the dearth of color in the surrounding black mass. Black and ashy gray was all the eye could behold. It held an otherworldly quality. Almost like being on the moon alone. Bob finished his beer with haste and sighed again. He supposed Tilly was right. He was clearly tired, and it was time to pack it on in.

A long winter would come in a matter of days now. The first snowstorm was recently forecast and less than a week away. Bob took a moment to look out on the fields and reflected on the hard work of the season. He felt the familiar pride of a job well done, though also, this year, something different. A tinge of anger within that seemed to have worked its way into him, like an unwanted and ever-present passenger. Anger over the fact that some of the people around town, and around the country at large, didn't have the good sense to know what was right for them. Didn't have the sense to know a man like Betty could bring back those golden days of his youth. A happy and simple youth that the younger people didn't know nothing about and couldn't understand no how. Maybe it was, in part, a growing anger that more and more of the youngsters were going off to college instead of staying on the family farms where God intended. They came back with all these cockamamie ideas about what was best for the people and the country. Talked all this nonsense that had nothing to do with their traditions and their roots. Maybe the anger came from the fact that you couldn't talk sense into these kids no more, neither. Maybe that was it.

Bob decided best not to give these matters any more attention for tonight. Enough was enough and no sense beating a dead horse. It was getting late and he was surely tired. He began the slow and familiar trudge upstairs to his good wife and his bed amidst the peaceful calm of the black country night.

Robert Q. Stubbs. You could call him Bob. Bobba Q if'n you knew him well. A hard-working man. A man involved in his community. A man who loved good, honest work and his good, honest and kind wife, Tilly. A man who, sure, got a little heated of late at town hall meetings. A man who, maybe lost his temper from time to time- especially around the topic of current politics. But in the end, everyone who knew Bob. And by that, meaning all of those in his, maybe, somewhat diminishing in size, group of family and friends. Well, they would all tell you the same thing. With no more than, maybe a moment's hesitation, they would surely tell you this: Bob Q. Stubbs was a good man.

www.ingramcontent.com/pod-product-compliance
Lightning Source LLC
Chambersburg PA
CBHW051311250626
47155CB00007B/2281